PATHWAYS
IN THE
MIND

M. KELLY

To order additional copy of this book, contact:

2708 Armidale Road Baxland's Creek New South Wales Australia
+1 347 878 1961/+612 8006 0204
info@shrubspublishing.com

Contents

Foreword

In her article "*Is it real*" Elise Lebeau PhD Describes an empath, as "The experience where an individual feels the emotions of someone else as their own".

Through this description, I examined the biological processes involved in the empath experience, such as mirror neurones. What I will also discuss is the relationship between the psychological concept of empathy and the empath experience as well as the challenges faced by empath's, such as mental illness, lack of comprehensive information and a fear of being ridiculed upon disclosure of their experience. The reader can view this book as an exploration of the deeper purpose behind the emergence of this ability that strengthens the possibility that the empath experience has transcended fiction to become part of our everyday life. Such as another step in the evolution of man. Thus it has become a serious field of psychological study.

Empathy is on a continuum the same ways many other emotional experiences. If you take numbers from one to ten, where one has no empathy such as a person with severe Autism, and ten is an acutely sensitive empath.

Most people would fit in about three to five. Everyone has had experiences where they know things before being told or the phone rings, and they know who it is.

People report experiencing this in everyday life, often without being aware that a process is taking place in their brain. It is the ability to feed into other people's emotions directly. For example, if someone close to them lies they can feel the confusion that causes in the mind of the liar. The person knows they have bean told a lie. Often without knowing why they know this.

Unfortunately, empaths tend to have no idea what is happening to them. They either assume that everyone feels the way they do or deny their feelings. And since this is not a topic that they're likely to discuss with family and friends, the confusion can carry on for many years. Individuals who talk about feeling the emotions of others are not automatically delusional. They are perfectly aware that this is considered impossible by our society's current standards. They spend an enormous amount of time and energy trying to find a more standard answer to their question before diving into a loaded word like empath. Often, they will report having tried therapy, medication, drugs, or alcohol to alleviate their painful emotional symptoms. However, there comes the point where avoidance feels empty. That seems to be a time when the mind opens itself up to new possibilities.

Symptoms of the empath can be anxiety, nausea, vertigo, or a knot in their stomach even though there is no circumstance in their life that could explain these sensations. These feelings are not connected to their being personally anxious or scared. They just suddenly feel this emotional combination either in a mild form or as with people who are close quite strongly.

Eventually, for the individual, the notion of coincidence, is eliminated. They understand that the relationship between their symptoms and the proximity of someone who is experiencing emotional turmoil what is making them feel uncomfortable. Empaths often report feeling nauseated when they go to areas where so many people are feeling so many emotions. They can describe how deeply anxious they became as a friend was describing their financial struggle.

In the book "*Molecules of Emotions*," Candace Pert describes some fascinating biological processes that are involved in our emotional experiences. When we feel emotions, there's a flurry of physical activity that comes along with them. But it's in the brain that we find the most interesting research on the potential biological basis for the empath experience.

Research on mirror neurones is finally shedding some light on a possible explanation for the way empaths experience the emotions of others.

Mirror neurones are thought to be a neurophysiological mechanism involved in how we understand the actions of others and learn to imitate them (Rizzolatti and

Craighero 169-192). These neurones were first studied in the context of motor skills and were observed to fire up when a monkey was watching someone else perform an action. This lead to the hypothesis that watching others do something triggers an internal response that can help us mimic and imitate what we see. The very act of watching another experiencing something activates neurones in our brain (Bastiaansen, Thioux, and Keysers 2391-2404), even when we are not personally performing the action.

In his groundbreaking book "*Mirroring People*," Marco Lacoboni relates the evolution of this fascinating new field of research. He introduces mirror neurones as the potential physiological basis for empathy and morality since they seem to be involved in how we can perceive and interpret the experiences of other people (Lacoboni 4). In its simplest form, a mirror neurone is triggered by the observation of a physical gesture, in someone else which in turns fires the same physiological neurones in the observer. What is striking about this process is that it happens consistently even though the observer does not move his muscles at all. It's only an internal representation of the action, not a physical imitation of it. There is also a very high level of sophistication in the mirror neurones firing pattern. In fact, the model is specific to the context or meaning of the action being observed, such as raising your hand to grab a ball or raising your hand to ask a question. These two actions involve the same muscle, but not the same intention, and they trigger different mirror neurones pathways. In short, mirror neurones allow us to create a very particular, internal contextual representation of what others are experiencing by firing our brain cells to bring meaning and understanding to the actions of others.

Lacoboni postulates that the firing pattern of mirror neurones is involved enough that it allows us to understand the intention of other people (i.e. "what they are feeling") depending on the context of their action (Lacoboni 30). The presence of this biological process is critical when you consider that being able to understand and relate to other people is essential to our ability to survive in human society.

Empaths are often described to be "sensitive" people, through their self-evaluation and the observation of their family and friends. They might also have a more sympathetic nervous system.

Research shows that some people are naturally more sensitive than others. Even young babies exhibit differences in the way they respond to strange events (Kagan 139-143). In a large study of 462 healthy subjects, Kagan found that about 20% of these children were more reactive and became more distressed when exposed to unfamiliar visual, auditory, and tactile stimulations. These sensitive children might grow up to become emotionally vulnerable adults as well.

Most importantly, Aron in the *"Highly Sensitive Person"*

is adamant that being highly sensitive is a gift, skill, a talent that should be praised and appreciated instead of criticised and ridiculed. She hopes that once highly sensitive people understand why they react the way they do when over stimulated, things will make sense, and can finally understand themselves better accept themselves as they are. Just like some people have better hearing or vision, empaths might have a more acute sensitivity to emotional signals. The biological apparatus is there for everyone, but for empaths the signal is always on, always loud and usually disruptive.

The concepts of mirror neurones and emotional contagion also support the view that humans might be biologically equipped to perceive the emotions of another person, but that the empath simply has a more sensitive receptivity for these signals.

There is an aspect of the empath experience going beyond what has been explored so far by researchers. Empaths report being able to perceive other people's emotions even when they are not in their physical presence, often across vast distances. This idea suggests that the emotional stimuli are not visual (seeing someone's facial expression), auditory (hearing a baby cry) or tactile (feeling the bodily spasms of sobbing). Empaths report being affected by the emotions of their family and friends who live hundreds or thousands of miles away.

However unbelievable, the process involved in such

a feat could be relatively straightforward. If certain emotions trigger very specific neuronal pathways, the magnetic field generated by this electrical activity might be picked up by someone else's mirror neurones, triggering emotional contagion. If we think of person A as being the emitter and person B as being the receiver, both parties possess the biological equipment necessary to "send" and "receive" emotional signals. Person, A is automatically transmitting a magnetic field that reflects the electrical activity associated with their emotional activation, much like the images of an MRI (Magnetic Resonance Imaging) indicates the internal operations of the brain. Meanwhile, person B could receive and interpret this magnetic activity through their mirror neurones, providing them with a personal experience of person A's emotional state.

This mechanism could explain why empaths can feel the emotions of people who are not in their physical presence. Contrary to an electrical current which needs a conductive substance to travel, magnetic waves can go through solids and keep travelling great distances with minimal (or theoretically inexistent) loss. An MRI can digitalize pictures of soft tissue located inside of the skull because of this property. As such, the magnetic field emitted by a person, albeit extremely faint and complex, can travel unaltered indefinitely. Electrosensitivity (i.e. the ability to feel electromagnetic fields) is highly controversial and often deemed inexistent. However, its persistence presence is postulated by some psychologists as theoretical.

What would it take for this process to work? First, person A would have to experience an emotion that is robust and distinct enough to emit a signal that can be read and interpreted by another person. It is highly consistent with the empath experience, where people report being overwhelmed primarily by strong negative emotions such as anger and depression. They also say that the emotions they pick up from others stay with them longer when the feeling is adamant. Second, person B would have to be sensitive enough to be able to perceive this weak magnetic field and isolate it from every other bit of magnetic information that always surrounds us. Empaths report having these emotional experiences without meaning to do so, thus indicating that the process is more likely to be biological instead of cognitive.

Empathy is a concept widely used in psychology to define the ability to imagine what another person is feeling, colloquially known as "walking in someone else's shoes." It plays a crucial role in our social interactions. Feeling empathy towards someone else may alter how we act towards them. For example, empathy might lead us to hug someone who is crying from emotional distress. It's an intricate part of the glue that holds human beings together as a society.

Theodore Lipps is considered the father of the term empathy (Montag, Gallinat and Heinz 1261). He used it to describe how we perceive the mental state of others by process of inner imitation. This internal process involves several areas of the brain, such as the cortex, the autonomic nervous system, the hypothalamic-pituitary-adrenal axis, and endocrine system (J. Decety 92-108).

Most fundamentally, empathy and the empath experience differ in the following way: the trigger to empathy is an external cue, such as a negative facial expression, while the trigger to the empath experience is an internal signal, such as a change in one's emotional state. Empathy involves thinking first, then feeling. The empath experience includes feeling first, then thinking. Unfortunately, many empaths do not know how to process this external emotional experience which can lead to a confusing situation where both types of emotions become entangled and thus tough to differentiate.

No matter how it happens, self-awareness is a complicated process for empaths because we know so little about it. Beyond some basic commonalities, different people experience it differently, making it even harder to pinpoint a good description to help identify empaths. And even when someone is aware that they are an empath, then comes the delicate transition of talking about it. Some empaths relate that an event triggered the awakening of their abilities, such as a car accident, a sudden illness or even pregnancy. Although some of these incidents were traumatic, others were not. But they all seem to be a turning point where the unusual nature of their experience could not be denied anymore: it forced itself to consciousness and demanded the individual to examined their feelings. An extensive phase of denial may accompany the trigger, where they think they know what is happening, and yet they still reject the idea.

But no matter how it revealed itself, empaths usually don't feel they had a choice. On the contrary, whether they had a traumatic awakening or a smooth transition, most them believe that this experience was forced upon them, an inevitable and often undesirable part of their spiritual growth. Empaths don't choose to be this way. It just happens to them. It's not a skill that they tried to develop, like being good at sports. Most of them would probably compare it more to getting a terrible disease. No wonder so many empaths assume that they're either already crazy or on the express lane in that direction.

It is particularly the case in our Western culture where so many social conventions actively discourage people from being authentic. For example, lying about not liking someone "to be polite" or concealing feelings of anger because it's "not feminine". There are a plethora of reasons why people hide their feelings, which has led us to a very emotionally challenging situation where we want to relate to other people but we can't because we don't know how they feel. All society is left with are tenuous social contracts, often based on obligation or self-interest, which push us farther and farther way from each other Given the circumstances, it might not be that surprising that empaths would surface in our society. They bring an invaluable ability to be empathically accurate (Mast, Ickes, and Farrow 408-427), meaning that they can tell what another person is feeling, even when it is not perceivable through verbal or nonverbal cues. They can connect to other people's true feelings. An empath experience is a drastic push in the opposite direction of emotional distinction. It's like blowing up the dam on a mighty river that had been diverted in an unnatural direction. Unfortunately, the empath is explosive.

Some people just keep searching for an answer to their seemingly unexplainable emotional symptoms. The empath reflex to take away the emotional pain of others is not a conscious decision. On the contrary, every fibre of their being wants to run away screaming. But they also get an innate sense that there is a reason for this; that somehow their experience is opening something that has been blocked; and this can be healing; that it can have a purpose. Even when they can't explain it in words, empaths have an inner sense that they are some sort healer of emotions. A balanced empath has figured out, either on their own or with help, how to detangle their personal feelings from the emotions of others, which is a crucial step in the evolution of the empath experience. Novice empaths often reject the ability to turn down or turn off their empath skills. If they are to help others, empaths must learn to control their sensitivity to ensure it does not drain them. Emotional burnout is a clear and present danger for all empaths. By the time, they are overwhelmed by others, empaths become dysfunctional and cannot help anyone at all. As such, the very first step is the healing journey of empaths is often to take a break and learn to modulate their emotional intensity. Bringing peace and quiet to their mind prepare them to become like a blank canvas for the helpful insights that can facilitate emotional healing.

Aron, Elaine N. *The Highly Sensitive Person*. New York: Broadway Books, 1997. Print.

Bastiaansen, J, M Theroux and C Keysers. "Evidence for mirror systems in emotions." *Philosophical Transactions of the Royal Society of London –*

Series B: Biological Sciences 2009: 2391-2404. Print.

Chartrand, Tanya L, and John A Bargh. "The chameleon effect: the perception-behavior link and social interaction." *Journal of Personality and Social Psychology* 76.6 (1999): 893-910. Print.

Decety, J and P L Jackson. "The functional architecture of human empathy." *Behavioural and Cognitive Neuroscience Reviews* 3.2 (2004): 71-100. Print.

Decety, Jean. "Dissecting the Neural Mechanisms Mediating Empathy." *Emotion Review* 2011: 92-108. Print.

Whatis an Empath? 30 April 2009. Web. 19 December 2012.

<http://www.eliselebeau.com/empaths>.

Mast, Marianne Schmid, et al. *Empathy in mental illness*. Cambridge University Press, 2007. Print. Marco Lacoboni, *Mirroring People. Book* Montag, Christiane, Jurgen Gallinat, and Andreas Heinz. "Theodor Lipps and the concept of empathy: 1851-1914." *The American Journal of*

Psychiatry 2008: 1261. Print.

Rizzolatti, Giacomo and Laila Craighero. "The Mirror Neurones System." *Annual Review of Neuroscience*2004: 169-192.

Shamay-Tsoory, Simone G, Judith Aharon-Peretz and Daniella Perry. "Two systems for empathy: a double dissociation." *Brain: A Journal of Neurology* 132.Pt 3 (2009): 617-627.

Chapter 1
WHAT AM I

Riccardo had spent the peaceful day fishing. He enjoyed the time out from his busy schedule to just relax and do nothing. He was thirty-three years old, tall, good-looking without being effeminate, with short dark curly hair and brown eyes with long dark eyelashes. His olive skin was a golden brown from the time spent in the sun. His sleek sixteen-meter boat was named Yolanda, called after a past girlfriend, the nearest he came to getting engaged. It was a perfect day. The crystal-clear water was calm, and the boat skimmed across the Ionian Sea as if it was flying. He was heading into the Port at Pylos, located in the Bay of Navarino where he kept a mooring and a small house for the times he decided not to drive the 224-kilometre home. This was his safe haven; it had a natural harbour enclosed by the Sfaktiria Islet. He did not spend as much time here as he wished because the time spent travelling precluded him from coming here. Pylos is one of the most picturesque fishing towns in the Peloponnese. It is a favourite spot for Greeks but is not on the tourist maps. Its beauty derives from a vast natural harbour, with the town built in such a way that it seems to rise up out of the sea to the hills beyond.

He slowed down a bit to navigate through the entrance of the bay. That is when he noticed something bobbing in the water. He thought it was some kind of fish, but he was curious all the same. As he neared it, it seemed to dive out of the way of the boat. He slowed the boat to idle, and he went to investigate. It was not possible, but it was a person. Pulling out a lifebuoy and checking that the rope was secure, he never imagined he would ever use this thing. He threw it out as far as he could towards the person in the water and waited to see what would happen. Soon an arm came over the life-buoy and grasped on to it. He pulled it in like a fish until he could reach down a hand and pull it out of the water and onto the deck.

It was a young woman, maybe in her early twenties. She had long dark hair that clung to her face; her skin was quite fair. She was small-framed and wearing some sort of black polka dot swimwear. He moved her hair away from her face and was surprised to find she had startling green eyes. She did not look happy. He considered she might be quite attractive, but not really his type. He liked his women to be blond, big-busted, and not too bright. He tried to speak to her but received no response. Feeling a bit annoyed at having his quiet time spoiled, he proceeds to get a blanket from the lower deck and then threw it around her shoulders. She just sat there looking like it was the end of the world. He left her to it and went back to navigating the boat to its anchorage. After a moment, he looked over his shoulder and watched as she leant over the boat and threw up. She sat down again and pulled the blanket tighter around her. Riccardo could not help but muse as to how this person had come to be in the middle of a boat lane and quite far out to sea. He wondered if she had fallen off another boat or had been pushed. He pulled up to the place where he kept his boat moored.

A young man called Pantos, who lived in the outer area of Pylos, waited patiently for the boat to come in. He was olive-skinned and quite dark. He was glad to have a job working for Riccardo as there were few jobs in the town. His job consisted of looking after the red Audi. He washed it and polished it like it was his own. After he had cleaned the car, he would ride it around the town just to show off to his friends. Another part of his job was washing down the boat after the weekend fishing trips, replacing food items that might have been used, and making sure the boat was covered and secured. Riccardo was not really interested in any fish he caught, and thus Pantos could take the fish home as a bonus. He now backed the car up to where the boat was, making it easy for Riccardo to drive it away.

Riccardo again tried to talk to the girl, and she seemed not to hear him or not to understand. His irritation was mixed with curiosity, so he grabbed her blanket and all, took her to the front of the boat, and jumped lightly onto the wharf. Pantos opened the passenger side of the car, and Riccardo dumped her in with little care for how she may feel. He tried to ask her where he should take her, but again, she did not say anything. He noticed she was shaking quite hard, and he felt some responsibility for her. He decided to take her back to his place and see what information if any, he could gather from her.

His house was on the east side of town on the Tsamadou Road. It was a small bungalow-style square place. It had a flat roof like many in the area. On the top was a sort of sun deck that was closed in on three sides so that one could sit up there and view the sea. The building was situated right up to the front path, which meant that he could drive his car right to the front door. The house was painted a sort of pale apricot colour. The inside of the house was snug and functional. It consisted of the main bedroom and bathroom at the back of the home, with the washroom and toilet on the other side. A separate kitchen was on the one hand of the front door, and the dining room and lounge were placed on the other end of the front door. The far end of the room had an electric fire, hardly used, and a large brown settee. In front of the couch was a large coffee table made of a rough cedar wood. The same wood was utilised for the dining table and chairs. A large fluffy rug covered the open floor, adding to the general atmosphere of a place used as drop-in lodgings only. This was not a place where he would bring any of his women.

He dragged her out of the car and brought her into the lounge, sitting her on the settee. He started the fire with the hope he could warm her up. Then he poured two glasses of brandy and took them over to her. He put the glass to her lips and endeavoured to make her drink. At first, she resisted; then she drank it down in one shot. She moved away from the fire to the farthest end of the settee, seeming to be afraid of the fire. The evening glow coming through the windows and the light of the fire added warmth to her skin, and he noticed that she was in fact quite attractive. He went to get another drink, and again, she downed it.

By now, she had stopped shaking, and the blanket had slipped off one shoulder. She did not seem to notice. Riccardo could not resist pulling her hair away from her face and admired the way she held her head. Her neck became irresistible, and he kissed it. 'Don't,' she said. He suddenly realised why she had not previously answered him. He had, for the most part, been educated in England and finished off with a business degree at Cambridge. She may not speak Greek. 'Okay,' he thought, 'at least I know that much about you.' He pulled the strap of her top down and became more affectionate. She pushed him away and said, 'Stop.' In his language, stop meant to go, so he went for it. It ended up with her fighting him; however, it made no difference in the outcome. Somewhere during this engagement, he noticed her go limp and stop fighting. He finished and saw she was out cold. He picked up her naked body and put her into his king-size bed and went back to have another drink. On reflection, he realised that she probably had had a bad day; added with the alcohol, he felt he was not culpable for what happened. With that happy thought, he went off to bed.

The next morning, she woke up. The sun was streaming through the window, and a gentle breeze was blowing. At first, she did not think anything was wrong. She closed her eyes again, willing sleep to come back, but she was awake now. The man beside her stirred, but she was not concerned. He got up and slipped a pair of shorts on and asked her if she would like coffee. She nodded, and he went to put the pot on.

He came back into the room and asked, 'By the way, what is your name?'

She answered, 'My name is.' She started again and said, 'My name is.'

Cold fear coursed through her body. What was her name? She could not remember. In fact, her mind was blank, and she could not remember anything. Her brain seemed to contain no information; it felt just dull. A mind is usually full of history, information, and thoughts about what to do next. It uses preconceived ideas to judge interpersonal relationships. It continues patterns formed from past experiences. But for her, there seemed to be nothing. 'Why am I like this?' she thought. Instinctively, she knew there was another way. She looked at him to gauge what he was feeling. He seemed happy.

'Surely you must know my name?' she asked.

He shook his head. She looked under the sheets and realised she had nothing on. When she looked back at him, he had a grin on his face. She felt mortified. Could she have slept next to a man she did not know? What had happened? He started by introducing himself to her and told her a little bit about how he had saved her life. He did not mention the night before. She looked across at him and said, 'So you found me in the sea and brought me home like a lost puppy?'

Now the smile broadened, and it went to his eyes. Laughter was not far off.

In his mind, he was developing a way to make her stay. This was going to be more fun than he thought. Why not 'have some fun' with this girl? She seemed easy prey. He was always looking for a distraction from the life of responsibility that had been placed on him. He did not choose to take on the family business even though he had trained for it. He had wanted to pursue the life of a playboy for a couple of years yet. But his father had become frail after a bout of the flu and was not up to putting in the long days or being as commanding as he had always been. At first, this came as a shock to Riccardo because he had always been a bit afraid of his father. He could not imagine him being anything different. He had to admit that his father was ageing, and it was his duty to take on the role that he had been prepared for all his life.

'You have amnesia,' he said.

Her eyes filled with tears and they silently slipped down her face. She felt confused and lost. 'Where am I?' she asked. 'What day is it?'

'You are in 'Pylos, Messenia, and the day is Sunday.' This did not really help as she knew instinctively she did not come from here. She sipped the strong hot coffee which tasted bitter and thick and tried to reason back to the last thing she remembered, but there was nothing there. She looked over at Riccardo who was leaning against the doorway drinking his coffee. She could not help noticing his lean and toned body. She thought at least he seemed nice, and to pick her up in his boat, thus saving her life, must mean something.

'I will go out and get something to eat, and while I'm gone, I suggest you have a hot shower, and then you may feel better,' he said. He wanted to give this young lady some time to digest her plight. He hoped she would stop crying as this disconcerted him. He hated the idea of putting up with someone in distress. It was not really his responsibility.

'Where are my clothes?'

'Baby doll, you only came in these.' He picked up the wet clothes and handed them to her. She realised these were underwear, not swimwear. A sick feeling came over her again. He left her and she went into the shower. As she was washing her hair with his shampoo, she noticed how sore her arms were. Then she noticed that she had several quite large bruises. In fact, every part of her body was sore and ached even inside of her. She would be too embarrassed to ask what had happened the night before because he did not say anything happened, but she felt there was more to it than he was saying. Maybe it was because he was a gentleman and did not want to upset her any further. She rinsed out her underwear and got out of the shower. She found a shirt in his cupboard and put it on and tied it at the waist with a cord. She combed back her long hair and pulled a fringe down at the front. She did feel better but did not know how to proceed from here. She stood in the room full of uncertainty, wondering what she should do. Should she wait here or go into another room? She wanted to do the right thing and not to impose by going somewhere she should not. It did not occur to her to consider his motives.

Riccardo came back with a long bread stick, olives, some soft cheese, processed meat, and a bottle of wine, and called to her, together they laid the produce out on the table; and while they ate, they discussed what to do. He told her that amnesia could last a couple of weeks, and then he was sure her memory would come back. Riccardo suggested she may have fallen off another boat and maybe hit her head. Another more sinister scenario he proposed was that she had done something so bad that she had wiped it out of her mind, like killing someone. As she had no papers, the police may be looking for her and arrest her. Sensing her distress, he tried to soften it a bit by saying,

'I'll help you in any way I can.'

He told her he had to leave in the afternoon to go back home, and he asked her where she was going to stay. She had no money or clothes or papers; there had to be something she could do. It was then he made another suggestion.

'You could stay here, nobody comes here, and you would be safe until your memory comes back. Of course, you would have to pay rent.'

She was stunned; he knew she had no money. What did he expect of her? Coming from somewhere inside of her were fear and warnings, telling her if it was too good to be true, maybe it was. She felt trapped because she really believed that the police were after her for a crime she could not remember. It made more sense to her than the notion of a bump on the head.

'How can I pay you if I don't have anything?' she asked.

'Well, you could pay in another way, such as services rendered.'

'What way is that?'

He tried to look thoughtful but did not answer in an unambiguous way but rather he left the question to hang in the air. It seemed like a long time when neither spoke. Then he said, 'Your body for the rent.'

She could not be more surprised. 'You will let me stay here if I have sex with you, is that what you mean? I can't just do it. What if I'm really a killer, and I kill you?'

'I don't think that is likely. Besides, you don't look fit enough to fight me.'

He talked smoothly to her, telling her it was the best and only solution. He promised he would give her money to get some clothes and would find out as much as he could about her. Reluctantly and against her better instincts, she agreed.

Now he had another idea: why not write a contract? 'This way,' he explained, 'there could be no misunderstandings about their new business arrangement.' He went to a drawer of a dresser against the wall in the kitchen and pulled out a pen and paper. He came back to the table and wrote,

The parties to this agreement solemnly agree that the first person will use the house, paying rent with services rendered to the other party.

If either party wishes to end this contract, they will walk away and never speak of it to anyone.

He told her that as she did not know her name, she

would sign it in blood. He pricked his finger and put a print onto the paper and invited her to do the same. He then folded it up as small as he could and tore in half, giving her one-half. 'This is sacred and unique because it is signed in blood. It cannot be broken,' he said. She questioned in her mind, 'Is this the usual way, and why this is necessary?'

Riccardo stood up and stretched; he walked around to her and said, 'Now let me see what I have bought.' She stood still as he undid the buttons of the shirt. He ran his hands over her body, inspecting it as if she were a horse. Her heart was beating fast, and she felt fearful although she could not explain why. He picked her up and carried her to the bed. As his kisses became more demanding, she tensed up, wishing all this would go away. She felt as if this was the first time any man had touched her. She confused real feeling with emotion. She did try not to fight him and remained passive, allowing him to do as he pleased. But it was a bit too much for her to handle and in the end, she was crying. Somehow, she sensed his disaffection but could not do anything about it. She felt perplexed, and could not tell if what she was doing was right or not as she was acting on a primal instinct alone to establish a relationship with a mate.

Later he showered and told her he must leave. He emptied the contents of his wallet onto the bedside table and left without a word.

On the way home, he felt happy that he had found a

new toy. He was also glad of the good road and a fast car. The highway speed was 120 kilometres. His natural speed was 140 kilometres; thus, the miles sped by.

He did not come back for two weeks. In that time, she hovered somewhere between depression and anxiety. Going out of the house filled her with unreasonable fear. She thought about what would happen if she encountered the police. She was isolated for days at a time. She admitted to herself there seemed so many questions and no answers. Her world comprised of those small rooms and even those appeared to hold some darkness and secrets.

A woman came to the door indicating she was the cleaner. She tried to get rid of her, but she would not leave, so she let her in and went out back and waited for her to leave. She was to learn that Melanie came from the town once a week, on Tuesdays. She cleaned the house and washed the sheets and towels and restocked the fridge mostly with alcohol but also with some basics. Every time when Melanie came, she would hide out the back of the house. Melanie was the mothering type and saw her as a child in distress.

Often, she would bake an extra pie or cake to bring with her.

At last, the need for the necessities of life became apparent, and she knew that she would have to make the walk into the town. She put her underwear on and one of his T-shirts, hoping she would look like a tourist.

To her, Pylos was a lovely historic fishing town. She sensed its age, a place of myths and legends. The bay area was full of sailing and fishing boats. From the jetty, she could see the Island of Sfaktiria. The buildings seemed to rise out of the water and blend into the pine tree covered hills at the back of the town. She felt as if she had never seen this place before. The town itself was broad and spacious. The town square located in the centre of the village consisted of a straight memorial to war heroes. It was surrounded by a large number of sycamore trees. Situated around the trees were many groups of tables and chairs, some under umbrellas. This was the place where people gathered to eat or drink coffee and socialise. It seemed to be a happy place. However, she did not feel comfortable. She found a place where one can walk to shops under arches to keep from the heat. She walked along it and admired the elegance of the stores. But it was not for her. An information board showed the population of the area at 2,000; thus, the town is quite small. Away from the main shopping area, there were many smaller shops where the upstairs area was the family home. The buildings were painted in different colours, and many had flower pots hanging from balconies. Her first stop was to acquire some clothes. She did not dare to go to the more upmarket places, rather she chooses to search the second-hand clothes shop where she felt some anonymity. She could get some shorts, tops, and underclothes, and sandals. She also bought two pots to make food in as there seemed little to cook with in the house. She thought he probably did not eat there much. She took it all to the counter and handed them a note. She did not know how the Euro worked. She seemed to get a lot of change.

Next was to get some groceries. She picked the shop nearest to the house where she was staying because she did not want to walk too far with a lot of bags. The lady behind the counter did not speak a word of English; her anxiety caused tears welled up. She tried to mime what she wanted. Maria and her husband came from Italy and had bought the shop there only ten years ago, and understood the difficulty of trying to learn a new language. Maria was a generously sized person who was also kind and gentle and wanted to reassure this woman that she would be able to help. She produced a pencil and paper, indicating for the young lady to draw what she wanted. This worked well, and with each new thing bought, Maria wrote the Greek word for it. At the end of the purchases, she handed the lady payment. Maria looked shocked at the note and indicated for her to stay put as she ran to the next shop for some change. This store did not carry a lot of extra cash because business was very slow at the moment. The country was in the grip of severe depression, and thus people were not spending.

The walk back to the house was tiring because of all the bags she was carrying, and by the time she was home, she was tired. However, she considered her first trip out a success and vowed that this had to be the friendliest town ever. She did not see anyone in a uniform; probably no police around.

On the other hand, her nights were filled with terrible dreams. She would wake up shaking and crying but could not make any sense of them. Fire featured in many of the dreams. The thoughts seemed to be so real that they confused her and sometimes it took a couple of hours for her to realise they were only dreams. They frightened her and so much, so she slept for only a few hours at night. Sleep deprivation caused her to feel sick and dull during the day. She wished there was a way for her to sleep without the dreams. One night, she opened a bottle of wine and drank the whole bottle. She soon realised that she was not used to drinking that much as she became drunk. She threw up and went to bed dizzy. However, she still only slept about four hours. When she got up in the early hours of the morning, she was hung over and very thirsty.

She also spent time staring at the mirror trying to acknowledge that the person staring back at her was, in fact, herself. She could not recognise her mirror self as the person she felt was herself. Who was she? She felt lonely and bored and longed for some diversion to take her mind off things for a while. She would go for walks either very early in the morning or very late at night so to avoid detection. She found an old book on economics at the bottom of the cupboard. She started to read it and found she had no trouble understanding the concepts written in the book. It relaxed her and sometimes she would be able to drift off to sleep for a while.

Riccardo came back early on a Friday evening. She was cooking up some Bolognese sauce to go with pasta. From behind, Riccardo noticed she looked quite sexy in short shorts, a tank top, and her hair tied up in a ponytail. He walked up to her and put his arms around her, his fingers touching her breasts. She jumped, but he pulled her back against him. Kissing her on the neck, he whispered in her ear, 'Time for the rent.'

He was not going to take an excuse or a no for an answer, so he leant over her and turned the stove off.

'By the way, that smells like heaven, it will make great seconds.'

She felt herself stiffen against him. He took no notice and led her into the bedroom. His hot breath smelt like beer, and as he jumped on top of her, his weight felt like it could crush all the wind out of her. He had no doubt that his powers of persuasion would bring her around to his way of thinking. It did not; all she felt was the burden of their contract. She just had to accept she had made a deal with the devil.

During the meal, he brought out a couple of small boxes and gave her one. In it was a golden oval-shaped locket. He then took the little piece of paper they had written two weeks ago, out of his pocket and put it inside the locket and then placed it around his neck. He asked her where her contract was. She went to get it, and then he put the paper in it, walking around the back of her to do up the clasp. 'Now,' he said, 'it is official, although if anytime you want to break it off, you just have to take the locket off.'

It was a pretty and expensive-looking necklace, and she would like wearing it, but she was concerned about how things would turn out. Somehow there seemed to her a darkness radiating from this gift. She felt a deep intuition about the importance the gift would play in her life. She was beginning to realise that her intuition was usually right. She seemed to know about people whom she could trust and whom she did not. Although there were times, she felt she could not work out Riccardo. On the one hand, he seemed kind and on the other, he seemed arrogant and self-centred. She felt there was something dark lurking around him, but nothing he did suggested this. And she thought, 'He did save my life.'

The next morning, Riccardo told her he was going fishing and asked if she would like to come along. Yes, she was jubilant to have a chance to get out of the house. She put on the modest one-piece bathers, a T-shirt, and tied her hair up. She also took a cap out of his cupboard. 'Very cute,' he said.

When they arrived at the wharf, faithful Pantos had everything ready for them to go. She did not remember ever having been on the boat before. The boat glided out into the harbour and then took off. It was another beautiful Mediterranean day, and the water reflected the blue of the sky. The small waves made the boat rock a bit, seeming to invite them to relax and enjoy the motion. On reaching his favourite spot, he lowered the anchor, extracted the fishing gear from the hold, and asked her if she wanted to fish. She declined for today thinking there may be another day when she would feel better. She was just happy to sit back and do nothing but gaze at the water. About an hour passed and she went to get him a bottle of beer and handed it to him. He took a few mouthfuls when he felt a tug on the line; quickly, he gave her the bottle back and concentrated on landing the fish. Meanwhile, she got the net ready to pull it into the boat. It was quite a large fish, and as soon as it came on the deck, she jumped back out of the way. Riccardo expertly took the hook out of its mouth and put it into a large bucket of water. He rebaited his line and sat back in his chair, putting his feet up on the rail. She handed him back his beer and sat back down. Riccardo tilted his cap over his eyes and relaxed. He did not like taking girls on the boat as they chatted all the time. This one was different; she could sit quietly. More importantly, she seemed to anticipate his every need before he even asked her. He did not feel the need to entertain her. He felt the quiet companionship without the intrusion. As the day drifted on and she seemed to be asleep, he noticed her legs were turning pink. He called for her to wake up as she was getting sunburnt. Then he decided to turn back for home. He had only caught one fish, but at least it was a good one.

'I've have had a good day today,' he said.

'And so, have I,' she said. 'Thank you.' He knew she meant it and was not just saying it to please him.

On the way home, they bought some fish and salad at one of the many dining places on the waterfront. The fish was fresh and delicious cooked in olive oil and lemon. Then they drove back home. He asked her if she played chess. She could not remember so he decided to teach her. He carefully explained how each piece moved to a different place. They played a game, which he won. The next game they played to his surprise she won. He thought that maybe she was smarter than she let on.

The next morning, he told her he would have to go early. He asked her if there was anything he could get her.

'I would like to have a good laptop so I can find out what is going on in the world,' she said.

He had up to this point not thought much about what she might need. There was nothing in the house in the way of communication. He wondered what she did to fill her days but did not ask.

'I think you might need a cell phone as well. I don't know if you have any preferences.'

She shook her head. He made a mental note to get his secretary to get these things, put his cell number into the phone, and have them couriered over to her. That way, she would get them the next day.

When they arrived, she opened the laptop box and read how to use it. She was not sure if she could work out how to set it up for her own purposes. When she got onto the Internet, she discovered Google, and then all she had to do was go to any site to find what she was looking for. The rest she found she could learn as some ideas came to her. She was excited to discover she now had no problems in programming or executing different things, such as movies and news of the world in English. It's just like being a baby and learning how to walk. She did not know what she could do or could not do. Everything seemed to be trial and error. She found out that she did not know much about the I-phone. It worked much like the computer but smaller. She noted he had put his cell number in and felt comforted about that because if something went wrong, she could call.

Chapter 2

PASSIONS OF THE SOUL

The next weekend was basically a carbon copy of the last. Riccardo arrived on Friday evening, and after 'paying the rent', they sat down to dinner. He asked her about the laptop and if she knew how to work it. She thanked him for sending it to her and said it was up and running. Again, he felt surprised that she seemed to be quite confident in how to use it. It indicated to him that she must have had some prior experience with computers. He asked if she had had any indication of a returning memory.

'Unfortunately, I have had no flashbacks or any thoughts as to who I am. I have looked it up on Google, and there seem to be many views about recovery. One site I looked at said that retrograde amnesia can last decades. I am still frightened about discovery, and so I tend to keep indoors during the day.'

'That is sad,' he said. 'I have asked thoughtful questions around to see if you're on a missing person list. I cannot understand why nobody has come forward looking for you. Another problem we have is I don't know what to call you, I can't keep calling you 'What's your name.'

She went into the kitchen and got out the pencil and paper and wrote 'what's your name'. Then she tried to abbreviate the words together to make a name and came up with 'Watuna'. He looked at it and thought that a word ending with 'tuna' surely was not a good idea. 'What about Watune or Whatune?'

She agreed to 'Whatune' as a name. She went into the bathroom and looked into the mirror and asked herself if Whatune fitted. It did not seem any more likely than any of the other names she had looked up. 'I guess I'm stuck with it for now,' she thought.

She did not see Riccardo for another couple of weeks. Then she was surprised when the cell phone rang. He called to tell her not to cook anything just lay the table, and he would bring everything. He came earlier than usual with arms full of flowers and food. He told her that a French chef he knew Fixed a five-course meal. It was all still hot, and she wondered where it had come from. She put some in the oven to keep warm and set the rest out with the flowers, and she found a candle in the kitchen and placed it on the table. The wine was good, and he was at his most charming, chatting about an art show he had been to. The food was superb, and she had a little more wine than she was used to. She told him about a website she had been to that gave the news of the world in English and then had documentaries about current affairs. When they had finished eating, he insisted she tries some of the small chocolates to finish with. She was full but did not want to offend him, so she ate one and finished off her wine.

She thought the wine had gone to her head as she started to feel a little dizzy. She got up from the table and nearly fell. He laughed at her and said, 'Steady on there, you had better sit on the settee for a bit.' She felt her legs buckle under her and she would have fallen hard on the rug had he not been there to catch her and lower her down to the floor. Then he kissed her, and it felt as if she had received a small electric shock. His hands raked at her clothes, sending waves of desire through her body. She was aware of what was happening, but somehow at that moment, it seemed just right. The feeling of his naked body against hers filled her with lust, and he did things to her she thought she had probably never experienced before. Her kisses became as demanding as his, and she longed for him to be inside her. The depth of their lovemaking was passionate and demanding. She could feel her heart pounding in her chest, and her breath came out in short gasps. Time stood still, and she felt they could go on like this forever. However, when they were spent she just lay there beside him and fell asleep.

The next morning when she woke up, she felt like she had the biggest hangover ever. At first, it was hard to think, but the events of the night came back to her. She got up and slipped her dress on. And she watched him still in his sleep. He looked so young and innocent.

Suddenly, a deep anger possessed her. She woke him up in a fury.

'You drugged me, didn't you?' she thundered. 'How dare you.'

He sat there grinning at her, and said, 'I knew there was fire in you.'

'I said you could use my body, I said nothing about my soul,' she cried.

She tried to hit out at him, but he just grabbed her wrist and laughed again. Her green eyes blazed at him, and her cheeks were flushed pink. At that moment, he loved her. The fiery passion only made her seem more attractive to him. He had never really had a woman say no to him before. He tried to calm her down by looking contrite and saying sorry even though he was not sorry a bit. He waited to see what would happen next. It was a bit like the cat-and-mouse game. He knew he could beat her down, but he liked the game. He now knew she would struggle against him in their sex life. He did not understand why she would, as he did not have trouble with other women. He also knew he would always win.

'You must promise never to drug me again,' she said. 'I don't care what you do just don't drug me.'

'Do you really mean that? Be careful what you ask for because you might get it.'

'I don't care,' she said.

'You have been warned then.'

He suggested they stay in that day to recover and not go out in the boat. It was probably a good idea as she felt unwell. He spent the day being kind to her, playing chess, and in general being affectionate without any pressure. He told her he lived with his father and sister. His mother had died in a car crash six years ago. He worked hard during the week. He said that his father was getting old and he must take over the family business. She did not enquire what that business was; it just did not matter. It did make her think and wonder if she had parents somewhere or was she an orphan. Right now, she thought she could use a family or even a friend. He was the only person she talked to, and could she trust him?

She felt some relief when he left. There was something she could not explain to him that caused her to fear him. She rationalised that he had saved her life and she should feel grateful instead of this uneasy feeling. The dark foreboding remained with her through the week.

The next time he came down was on a Thursday night. She was not expecting him. From the moment, he walked in the door, she could sense his anger. He grabbed her and took her into the bedroom and threw her face down on the bed. His sex was rough until she was crying for him to stop. He finished and just walked out the room to get a drink. She curled up in a small ball on the bed. She hurt and felt very sorry for herself. At that moment, she hated him and wished she could walk out on him, providing she could walk at all. She berated herself for not seeing it coming. After about an hour, he came to bed and said that she was sulking because she did not get things her way.

'The trouble with you is that you are all fire and ice,' he said.

Why then did she think this was somehow her fault? She thought it was up to him to say sorry instead of her apologising to him, telling him she could not be what he wanted her to be when they were in bed. She could not say why. He left the next morning after kissing her and giving her a hug. He acted as if nothing had happened. She was left to wonder why he was so angry in the first place.

This was the beginning of a cycle of abuse and kindness that was to affect their time at Pyros. It became interwoven with the contract that she had signed in her blood. She felt it was her fault and when he abused her she deserved it.

One Friday morning, he again called on the cell phone. It took her by surprise because she was not expecting it to the phone to ring. She hesitantly asked who it was, He told her to go to town and get a flashy dress as he was going to take her out to meet some of his friends. He told her a car would come to pick her up at 4.00 p.m. He seemed quite decisive about what he expected of her. It was the first time she knew that she would have to brave the better shops in the town. Each week he came, he had placed money on the bedside table. She realised that there was quite a lot of money in there as she really had no use for it. She looked at herself in the mirror and thought she had one day to make herself look better. It was a struggle as she did not care how she looked. She walked into town and bought a simple black dress, high heel shoes, and some makeup. Even getting ready seemed an effort. He was taking her out of the comfort zone she had built for herself. She had been in the house for several months now, and he had never suggested they go anywhere. Now he wanted her to meet some friends. At 4.00 p.m., sharp, a sleek black car arrived, and the driver opened the back door for her. The back of the car was luxuriously appointed: dark leather seats and a small pull-out bar placed for convenience. All this made her feel more nervous than ever. Her mouth felt parched, and she opened the bar and pulled out a lemon soda. Then she sat back and tried to relax. She started dreaming about him. She did not really know much about him as he seldom spoke of himself. She thought about the car and the boat and wondered what he did for a living. Maybe he was a banker or in insurance. He seemed to think that the world owed him a life and everyone should just go along with him. This was not a pleasant thing to think considering all the kindness he had shown to her. The journey took about two hours, and in that time, she was able to observe the scenery along the way. The road wound its way through hills covered with trees and small groups of houses. As they headed towards Athens, the city sprawl came out to meet them. It all seemed quite exotic to her. Had she ever been here before? Here she was, in one of the oldest cities in Europe. Its skyline dominated by Lycabettus Hill and the famous Acropolis. They drove through the centre of town past the Greek Parliament that was once a royal palace. She thought how nice it would be to explore this city.

At last, they came to a modern apartment block where the driver let her out. Riccardo was there to meet her; he looked debonair in a suit. It was the first time she had seen him dressed in a suit and it seemed to fit his personality, maybe better than the beach clothes she was used to. He thought she looked quite startling with her long dark hair that was now sleek and reaching down to her mid-back. On her fair skin, there was minimal makeup and green eye shadow that enhanced her large green eyes. The elegant black dress fitted her nicely. 'Yes,' he thought, 'you'll do.' He guided her to the elevator and pushed the sixth floor. The door opened directly into a reception foyer. It seemed to her that the place was crowded with what she would call 'the beautiful people'. The apartment was mostly decorated with neutral colours and had elegant furniture. The background music was different from any she knew; however, it was pleasant. There were waiters serving champagne and wine and girls serving some different food platters.

Riccardo introduced her to a few people until a beautiful blonde dressed in a dress that could only be described as 'barely there' draped herself around him. She said that she was sorry not to have taken any of his calls as she had been busy. While be seemed to ignore her, she kissed him and sighed as if this was the greatest thing in her life. Whatune wandered over to the other side of the room already feeling bored. She was approached by a man in a blue jacket and light-brown pants.

'Are you anybody?' He asked.

She sensed that he was only interested in people who could further his social status.

'Of course, I'm somebody,' she said.

He told her about his latest collection but failed to mention what that collection was. She was expected to know. After a while, he wandered off, and she had time to observe the crowd. The group as a whole seemed to be sophisticated and superficial. They created a lot of clamour as they seemed to be trying to outdo each other with better and better stories. The noise was starting to bother her and made her feel tense. Together they sounded like a flock of ducks all quacking together. Another person approached her, and she tried to engage him in intelligent conservation. This did not really work either as he said, 'You are a bit of a brain, aren't you?' She had another drink and looked for the person who was least involved. It happened to be a young woman sitting in a corner chair. Whatune asked if she could join her. She made up her mind to find out as much as she could without saying much about herself. Calista said she was the girlfriend of the painter she had seen Whatune with earlier. She stated that she worked at a library three days a week. And on other days, she helped her boyfriend and sometimes posed for him. Whatune found her easy to talk to, and they chatted away for most of the evening.

Riccardo came to talk to them and finally said that they should go as he had quite a drive to take her home. In the car, he asked her what she thought of his friends. She felt wary of saying what she really thought in fear she might offend him. She found it easier to blame herself for not having good social skills. It was the tension in the room that had upset her; there was a feeling of overall anxiety instead of relaxation. Then he asked her she how she felt about the blonde.

She asked, 'Was she your girlfriend?'

He laughed at this and said, 'No, she is just a want-to-be.' He told her he in fact never called her and would not do so in the future. 'Were you jealous'?

'So, was this all about showing me how irresistible you are to women?'

Now he literally laughed aloud. 'What a funny thing you are, I don't think I needed to prove anything. But I have to agree with you about the blonde, she is outrageous.'

The tension was broken, and now they could talk about different people they had spoken to. Riccardo soon realised she had a somewhat black sense of humour and could accurately describe the personalities of the people she met. He told her at least she was not a 'clinging vine' and could circulate the room on her own. He was driving slower than usual because he had more to drink than usual.

'A thought has just occurred to me.' He said. 'Do you drive?'

Again, she did not know, how ludicrous wondering if you could do something or not. She shrugged at this enigmatic man hoping he would understand.

'I'll have to take you out in the car and give you some driving lessons unless it's like the chess and you really know and are just kidding me.'

When they finally arrived home and she 'paid the rent', she settled beside him feeling some contentment that she had not felt in a while. He was nice when he had too much to drink. He was more relaxed and funny.

The next day, he took her out driving. At first, she was quite tentative about the car. But as her confidence is built, she found she was quite a good driver, if maybe a bit reckless. 'You handle corners well. I don't think you will have any trouble with our roads. But you should stay off the tracks as they can be dangerous.

'Strange,' she said. 'To me, it's like starting life anew. I cannot remember any of my past, what teaching my parents may have given me or what I may have learnt at school because I have no history. I can only follow what my instinct and intuition tell me. I think there must be something wrong with my brain.'

She did not express the panic and fear she felt, or how vulnerable that left her. She was now aware that Riccardo was capable of exploiting her, but because she felt depressed a lot of the time, she did not care what happened to her.

He laughed at her, thinking it must be great to start life again. It would be like having an adventure. If only he could change his life, he wondered, what would he choose?

They spent the afternoon exploring a castle behind the town and the Antonopculeion museum. In the Palace of Nestor, there were 105 ground-floor apartments, a large rectangular 'Throne Room' with a circular hearth. The walls were decorated with fine paintings. They also discovered many artefacts taken from around the area. It was strange because she had felt the age of the place the first time she had gone into town Several days later, she had a particularly bad dream. She woke up shaking and choking, feeling like she had just been through a war. It was hard to shake the dream out of her mind; it felt so real. She was standing in a basement when the building started to shake. She looked at the foundations and saw instinctively that the builders had cut some corners when building; using more sand and less concrete, the foundations were not safe. She started to scream, trying to let the people above know that the building was about to fall. Then the earth shook a lot more, and she felt the building collapse, folding in at the centre. Bricks, furniture, and people started to fall in. The dust was such that she began to choke. Suddenly, she was back in bed again, and she was not hurt. She got up to get a glass of water and tried to tell herself that it was just a nightmare. However, she could not go back to bed and went for a walk instead. Several days later, she read of a severe earthquake in Wellington, New Zealand. As she followed the story, she found out that one of the buildings had collapsed, killing several people, and injuring a lot more. The stories that came out in the press described exactly what she had seen. An inquiry later found that the foundations of the building were not built to the correct specifications, and the builders were held responsible. When she checked the time zones, she realised that all these things happened as she dreamed it. She was frightened by this and confused. How could she have known? Why did these dreams disturb her? What did it mean if she could not change anything? More questions she could not answer. Her only thought was to pretend it did not happen or think that it was only a coincidence. She was determined to put it out of her mind.

Riccardo came back on Friday, and she was conscious of trying to please him. She wanted their relationship to be congenial and easy going. She hated it when there was tension between them. It brought back all her fears, and he noticed and seemed to react to it. She 'paid the rent' and they spent longer in bed than usual. He told her that he had a friend coming over to have a holiday nearby and they would be going to see him next week. He said that she should dress in smart casual. He knew she did not like shopping and suggested they go together to find something that she could wear. She felt fortunate because his being there would make her feel safe. They bought a black pair of slacks, a black jacket, and a white silk shirt with rows of pintucks down the front and pearl buttons. She thought that she liked the classic style better than the flashy type of dressing. Before going back to the house, they had coffee and cake in the town square, sitting under the trees. She found that she could drink the coffee if it were "café au lait" rather than dark coffee. Riccardo commented that she was the only girl he had known that did not like shopping and she did not spend much of the money he left for her to use. How could she explain it made her feel like a kept woman?

Ricardo arrived late on the next Friday evening. He was tired, cranky, and quite short-tempered with her, 'paying the rent' was only rough sex, and he had fallen asleep straight after. She hated this, feeling hurting inside as well as coping with the bruises he inflicted. She was left wondering what she had done. There seemed to her some periods when he was remorseful, saying it would never happen again followed by times when he was charming and kind. Somehow, he made it seem as if she was at fault for doing something that displeased him. She seldom complained even when things became terrible.

The next afternoon, they set out for Kalamata. Along the way, Riccardo spoke about their host Brian. He told her that Brian had attended the same college as he had, except he was doing economics, but had switched to music. Riccardo told her Brian had rented a place for holidays and warned her there may be a lot of alcohol and drugs there. He reminded her that she was going to drive home and thus should not drink too much. When they arrived, she discovered a large property that seemed to have several small houses and a large rambling house. At the back of the large dwelling was a pool and entrainment area, and this is where most people had gathered. Brian was of medium build with a shock of long blond hair that looked as if it seldom saw a comb. His blue eyes seemed to be intelligent, and there seemed little he missed. He wore old faded jeans, a white T-shirt and, a black leather jacket. He looked her up and down as if appraising whether he would like her or not.

He turned to Riccardo and said, 'Not your usual type,' with a wink and a nudge.

Ricardo ignored him and went on to introduce her to others standing around. This group was so different from his other friends. They seemed to be 'laid back' and not to care what others thought about them. In turn, this relaxed her, and she did not feel as if she had to be anything different than what she was. It was harder to say no to drink and drugs as the place seemed to be awash with every kind of drug. She laughed and said, 'We have flipped a coin to see who was driving home, and I guess I lost, so I can only have a couple of wines.'

As the evening progressed, she decided it was fun to watch people make fools of themselves while she remained sober. Nobody questioned her or made her feel she had to explain anything. And she felt free to wander the house. In one room off the hallway, there seemed to be a music room. There was also a lot of technological gear. Leaning against the back wall was an acoustic guitar. She felt drawn to it as if it called up something inside her that needed to be satisfied. She picked it up and ran her hand down the strings. It was out of tune, and the strings were too loose. She decided to tune it and see what happened. It was another surprise for her. She realised that she could play some notes. She tried a couple of styles. It seemed to fit with the music she often felt in her head. She started to sing along with tunes long forgotten, old traditional folk songs. The boys came into the room, and Brian asked what she was doing. Suddenly, she felt as if she had intruded into his world. She was embarrassed and said defensively, 'It was out of tune.'

'Well then, go on and play it,' Brian said.

She started again and sang a mysterious and ancient ballad which tells of a '*Silkie*, a superhuman who lives under the sea and begets a child of a human woman. She had a naturally sweet and vigorous voice that carried through the crowd. It was only when she finished that she realised that people were standing at the door and she blushed and handed the guitar back to him.

'Wow! That was good,' he said. 'If I were auditioning now, you would get the job.'

'I don't want a job,' she said and got up to go outside.

He wandered over to the equipment and turned a switch on and came back to her and said, 'Stay here and play all you want. I'll shut the door if you like.' He grabbed Riccardo and dragged him out the door and closed it. He took him to the corner of the bar where he turned on a speaker. They could hear her in the other room. At first, there was only her strumming the guitar. And then she began to sing another song.

'Where did you get her? She is lovely and a good singer too, you lucky old dog.'

Riccardo did not want to go into their relationship, so he just shrugged and smiled. She sang a couple of songs that just came to her, and when she forgot the words, she made up words to fit. After a while, she put the guitar back and came out. Brian quickly turned off the speaker. He smiled at her and said if she liked the guitar she could keep it as he had plenty. She looked at Riccardo to see what he thought, and he nodded at her as if to say it's okay. She was happy and thought she might be able to remember some other tunes.

On the way home, he said, 'You are full of surprises, aren't you? I never would have thought you could sing like that.'

'Neither did I, although I often have music in my head or bits of songs. I think most people do. You know when you hear a catchy tune, and you keep humming it and can't get it out of your head. It is the same for me, but sometimes I remember the whole song. I make music in my head when I feel stressed. I think having the guitar in my hands did something for me.'

'But does it bring back any memories?'

'No, I hear just music'.

He fell asleep in the car, and she continued to ponder on how she could remember something like a song and not know where she had heard it or even maybe learned it. Sadness came over her as she wondered if she would ever be a whole person again. Would music be the trigger that may cause her to remember something? She looked over at him for a moment and noticed the innocence in his face again; he slept like a child with nothing to worry him. Why was it then he could be so cruel and so kind and not notice the difference? She liked to think of his kindness and overlook the other times. She had no wish to change their arrangement as it suited her, but she had the feeling that their lives were about to change anyway.

On Sunday, they went fishing in *Yolanda*. The boat had a calming feeling that washed over both of them. She tried her hand at fishing but hoped she would catch nothing. But as it turned out, she caught five fish to his three. Just enough to keep them occupied without strain. They returned happily, and Pantos was there to meet them. The car sparkled in the late sun, and all seemed well with the world. He left late that night, and she wondered how he was going to get home safely.

Three days later there was a knock on the door. She jumped because nobody came to the house except the cleaner, then she usually hid out the back until she had gone. She peeked out the window and saw it was Brian and a young girl. She opened the door just partly enough to say something, but he just walked past. He stopped in the middle of the room and said, 'This is Christie, my daughter. I came to see how you are getting along with the guitar.'

'I'm doing fine, thank you,' she said. 'Would you like a cup of coffee or tea?'

'Yes, please, tea would be great. I hate the coffee here. I think you are a woman after my own heart, where have you been all my life?' He laughed. 'So you are shacked up with my mate Rick, huh?'

She felt embarrassed, not understanding why. She turned her attention to Christie and asked her about what she liked to do; did she like school? What were her best subjects, and was she enjoying her holiday? Christie said she loved art and math. She did not make music because her mum did not want her to. Brian explained that Christie's mum thought she was on to a good steady thing when they got together. Then he became a 'pop star'; that was the end of their relationship. The only good thing to come out of it was his beautiful daughter. Whatune went to the drawer and pulled out some paper and pencils. 'I am afraid I don't have any coloured pencils,' she said. 'But you can draw a beautiful picture for your dad anyway, for him to keep when you go back home.'

'I'll get to the point,' Brian said. 'I have an appointment this Arvo, and I don't fancy any of the ladies in our group to look after Christie. Even though I don't know much about you, you seem a lovely lady, and I am hoping you can have her for a couple of hours.'

'Of course, I can, and maybe she could make some music with me.'

He looked pleased with himself for finding a pleasant person for his daughter. He did not really respect the women that hung around the group and drank and used whatever drug that was on hand. Christie seemed a bit shy and did not say much. Brian left, promising to be back as soon as he could. They spent some time looking up things on the laptop. Christie found a game to play, and she spent about an hour quietly playing the game.

They had lunch and then she brought out the guitar and sang a song from the *Wizard of Oz*. She got Christie to sing along to the chorus.

Brian came back about 4.30 p.m. He had changed his clothes and combed his hair. He looked more like a business person and less like a 'rock star'. Christie became more animated, showing her father the finished drawing and telling him she had an enjoyable time. They sang the song that they had practised in the afternoon. He told her how happy he was that she could sing nicely. He said, 'Thank you for looking after my daughter,' and they left together, chatting as they went.

Chapter 3

WATERS OF DISCONTENT

Riccardo did not come on the Friday evening as he usually did, arriving early on Saturday morning. He strolled in, looking cool and refreshed. He asked her what she had been doing. She told him about Brian's visit. Suddenly, he became angry, his eyes blazed, and he grabbed her by the shoulders and shook her hard, saying, 'You are never to let anyone in my house without my expressed permission, particularly another man.'

She was stunned and tried to say something, but he would not listen. He slammed her against the wall. Hitting her head on the side. The force knocked the wind out of her. He then punched her in the stomach using the palm of his hand. She crumbled to the floor dry reaching. Riccardo acted as if it was nothing and said.

'Well, let's go fishing.'

Out on the boat, the tension was palatable. Riccardo nursed his anger like an old injury. Usually, he liked to show off his women; his name had been linked with several beautiful women, but this was different. She was vulnerable and naive about men and Brian could easily sway her. He did not want to share her with anybody, not even for a short time. Women liked Brian for some reason, and they had music in common. He did not want her to go anywhere near him.

She felt miserable, wishing she could fix it. The water that was usually calming made her felt seasick. She realised she was getting a migraine but dared not mention it to him. She sat quietly and did all she could to calm him down by getting him drinks and making him lunch, but nothing changed. She realised that she was afraid of him and what he might do to her if he did not calm down.

By the time they got back to the house, her head was pounding, and she could scarcely stand up. His grim face stared back at her, saying, 'What's the matter with you?'

He made like he was ready to grab her and fear took over. Faced with the choice of putting up with him or not, she hesitated for a moment then she pulled off the chain about her neck and ran out the back door saying, 'I can't do this anymore.' She ran and ran, not caring where she was going, just following the instinct of self-preservation. She did not see the headlights in the distance until they were nearly on top of her. She felt a sickening grinding against her body, and everything went black.

She slowly came back to consciousness. At first, she could not open her eyes, just heard sounds as people came and went around her. When she thought there was nobody there, she opened her eyes and looked around. She perceived she was in a hospital. She felt as if she could not move. She tried to wiggle her fingers and move her hands. As soon as she did, this she felt a sharp pain. She tried to turn her head to find what was holding her hand down. She had the worst headache ever, and any movement hurt. She noticed that her arm had a board under it and an IV drip was in it. She tried to move her feet; one seemed to be okay, but the other would not move. The room was small, white, and had the blinds drawn down. Opposite her bed, the wall was clear glass, and outside was a uniformed policeman. She tried to think, but all she could feel was the pain. Something had happened to her, but what?

A nurse came in and noticed she was awake and went to call a doctor. The two of them stood around her bed and mumbled something. She had an idea that she was supposed to respond, but she only moaned. The doctor spoke something to the nurse who wrote things down on some sort of chart. They left for a while, and the nurse came back and did something with the plug on her arm. It took only a few minutes for the pain to ease, and she drifted off to sleep. She woke up again when she felt people moving her around. The doctor was looking at her with some concern. He spoke to her, but she did not understand him. He produced a small torch and looked into her eyes, instantly, the pain in her head re-emerged. He gave further orders and left the room, and the nurse covered her up again. She gave her another shot into the plug in her arm, and she felt the pain diminish.

Some time later, another person came into the room. She spoke to her in what seemed to be a couple of languages. Then she said, 'Do you speak English?' She nodded and the lady seemed pleased. She said something about being a social worker and was here to help. She asked for her name and address. She said she could not remember. The social worker stated that she had been in a car accident and had received some brain damage and some broken bones. She explained that it was necessary to call the family to let them know where she was. All Watune could say was she could not remember. She looked across at the uniformed policeman standing at the door. The social worker followed her gaze and told her that she had been abused before the accident and the police were there to make sure the attacker did not come back. He also needed to ask her some questions when she was up to answering them. The social worker suggested that right now, she should just rest and not try to find answers until she felt better. She was sure all would come back in time. Finally, the social worker left the room, and she felt an absolute peace come over her. She did not want to answer questions or reconstruct what had happened.

Time seemed to merge into day and night; she drifted in and out of sleep. Weird thoughts took over, and there were times when she saw Riccardo's face. She remembered the boat and the house. Swirling through these dreams seemed to be laughter and tears. Everything appeared to be distorted, and she could not follow any pattern. At some point, she was taken for a brain scan. This appeared to concern the doctor. Maybe she was mad or indeed brain damaged. How could she tell? The policeman came into the room with the social worker to translate for him. He asked questions which she could not or would not answer. Her perception of the situation told her not to trust him with any information that she may remember, and thus it was easier just to say she did not know. He took a photo of her and left. She started to cry out of fear and frustration. The social worker tried to soothe her by promising her everything would be all right. But she knew it would not be "all right" again. The bubble she had been living in had burst, and there was nobody who could help her. She asked the social worker how long she had been in the hospital and was told she had been there for three weeks. Had nobody asked about her? Again, she was informed that nobody had been in to ask about her. How was she going to face the future with no name or memory?

A couple of days later, she had a disturbing encounter with a strange man. He came into her room flanked by two men dressed in suits, which she mentally called 'the suits'. He was in a wheelchair, but there was nothing feeble about him. She sensed he was powerful and probably ruthless. He came up to her bed and stared at her. She stared back, wondering who he was. He had brown eyes that seemed to see right through her, a shock of pure white hair, and a beak nose. The suits stood to attention behind him. They had bland faces that gave nothing away, and she thought they looked as if they could tear one apart if they wanted.

'Well, how much will it take to get rid of you?' He asked. He spoke with a heavily accented voice that was low as it was menacing.

She did not answer him as she did not know what to say.

'I can set you up well in anyplace you want to go,' he said.

'Why would you do that, are you mad?' she asked.

'Do you know who I am? I can do you a lot of good or a lot of harm, depending on how you want to play it.'

'Do you know me?' she asked, hoping he could tell her something that would make sense.

'I don't know you, but I know your type, so how much do you want?'

She felt incensed that this person should speak to her as if she was a piece of dirt. 'I don't care who you are, but will you please leave me alone.'

He pulled out a chequebook indicating he would write her any amount she wanted.

'Go to hell,' she said and turned her face away from him.

He left the room, leaving her wondering what kind of harm he intended to do to her.

A few days after the strange encounter, Riccardo appeared at her door. He had a worried look on his face and a big bunch of flowers in his hand. She could not help but feel relieved to see him.

'I'm sorry I could not come to see you before, but I did not know where you were. The police turned up at my home accusing me of abusing you both physically and sexually. They told me that they had traced you to my beach house.'

She turned pale, realising why the police were so interested in her. They must have examined her all over when she had been brought into the hospital. Riccardo looked at her thoughtfully and asked her if she had spoken to the police. She shook her head in the negative. He sighed and said, 'You remember our contract, don't you'? Again she nodded.

Then he asked, 'Why did you bolt?'

She tried to recreate that night. 'It's all a bit hazy, but I think you were going to kill me.'

He looked her with affection in his eyes.

'I like you; I would never kill you, that's a silly idea'.

He told her that his father was furious at him and that they had had a couple of rows over her.

'My father said you told him to go to hell. Nobody tells my father 'to go to hell'. I wish I'd been there, I would have loved to see his face.'

He laughed at the thought of the confrontation she had with him, and the considered that his father came off second best. She looked startled as the story of the old man suddenly made sense.

'That man in a wheelchair was your father?'

'You really don't know who he is, do you? I thought a smart girl like you would have looked my family up.'

'I had no reason to,' she said. 'And anyway, I don't care, the old man was just rude, and there is no excuse for bad manners.'

He told her that his father was the richest man in the country and so was he. The news did not surprise her because, in a way, she knew something was different about him. She thought about the way other people talked to him and acted around him. It did not make any difference to her as she had more pressing things to worry about.

'It's over between us. I cannot go back to the house because something terrible is going to happen that you could regret for the rest of your life, and I don't want to be responsible for causing you any further embarrassment.'

He looked concerned. 'But I care about you, and I don't want to lose you. There must be a way we can stay together. I'm not sure how yet, but if I can find another way, will you stay with me?' He slipped his hand under the sheet and ran it down her body. It was soft and warm, and he felt his excitement grow. 'I need you now,' he said.

She gave him a cynical look. 'If you don't take your hands away, you are not going to be able to walk out of here. I like being with you, but I have never lied to you. I have never pretended to be anything other than what I am. Even when you wanted me to act like I was having great sex with you, I would not. I don't know where our relationship is going. It could end up a disaster, and it has already caused friction in your family. I had a brain scan, and the doctor seemed concerned. The social worker said I have brain damage. I don't know what that means.'

Another idea crossed her mind.

'Does your father know you are here?'

'It's none of his business,' he said.

'Well yes, it is, because if you told the police that you did not know I was staying in the house, they might wonder why you are here. I suggest that you say, when you heard about me you felt sorry for me and tried to help me as a charity case. I will keep your cover.' 'Then we have a plan,' he said.

She smiled up at him, feeling like some kind of mother.

He told her that Brian had asked about her and that he had said she had gone for a break.

'Oh! Now, I remember what our fight was about.' She told him about Brian's daughter and that he had come to the house looking for a babysitter.

He asked, 'Why didn't you tell me?'

'I tried to, but you would not listen. Brian is so memorable to me that I had forgotten all about him. So you see, you had no cause to be jealous."

He asked how long she thought she would remain in the hospital. She did not know but thought it would still be a couple of weeks. Reluctantly, he told her he should go. He said he would stop by the front desk to make sure she had the best treatment and he would be paying the bill.

Things changed for her almost straight away. It seemed as if people looked at her in a different way. She was moved to a better room that was painted in a soft green with big windows and soft print drapes. The flowers he had brought had been arranged in a lovely vase. Even the cuisine was different and set on a tray with silver cutlery. She lay back, thought about it and wondered about the power of money. Did it make her feel any different that he was rich? It did answer some of the questions that had plagued her mind about why he was the way he was. She thought of the 'the old man' who was his father; she could not imagine he would ever accept her and there was the threat that he would harm her. She believed he was capable of carrying out his threat. Maybe she was right to run, but then she thought of Riccardo. Did she really have feelings for him or was he just an easy way out? She thought of the good times they had shared and the closeness she felt to him. She did not love him, she thought, but there was a connection. Was it borne out of the contract she signed with him? Whatever way it was, she wanted to be near him and feel the comfort he brought, particularly when he took command and told her what to do. Safety was a big issue with her because most of the time, she felt unsafe.

The next day, they took off the cast on her leg and sent her for another x-ray. This would mean that she could start to do exercises to walk again. The social worker came to see her again; she had been great acting as an interpreter for her with the doctor. Even she seemed to have a new respect for her. She told her that the physician had been happy with her leg; however, the bone in her foot had not healed, and she would need to have a plate put in. This would require another operation, but she assured her that she would be able to walk again soon. She told her that the hospital had arranged for her to see a psychiatrist the next day. He was English and would help her regain her memory. She felt a surge of hope and was happy to be able to put an end to the confusion.

Chapter 4
MIND GAMES

The next morning, she awoke full of positive thoughts. She felt elated that things may have taken a turn for the better. Breakfast was very nice, and she showered with some help and dressed in fresh clothes, combed her hair, and almost felt human again. A new bunch of flowers had appeared in her room; the card attached just said *R*.

Ten thirty in the morning, someone came to take her down to see the psychiatrist. He had consulting rooms off from the main hospital. He was a small old-wizard kind of person. His clothes had seen better days. He wore glasses perched on the end of his nose, and he looked as if he spent most of his time in his books that were stacked up on the floor. There was a large desk on one side of the room and a couch and a low chair on the other end of the chamber. In all, it had the effect of comfort before style. He spoke with a soft English accent. He guided her wheelchair to the couch and got her to hop on to it. It was important that she feel relaxed. While he was covering her up with a blanket, he told her he would be using deep hypnosis to help her regain her memory. The most important thing was just to relax and go with whatever Suggestion he placed in her mind. He asked her if she was afraid or if she had any questions. She shook her head no.

Everything started off easily; all she had to do was take deep breaths and listen to some soft music. He spoke to her in such a calm way it was easy to forget why she was here, and she let herself drift off to sleep. She was awoken by a sharp slap to her face. She blinked as tears came to her eyes. He started screaming at her, 'Look what you have done'. She stared around the room. Papers that were on the desk were all over the floor, the table lamp was smashed on the floor, and the books from the shelf were scattered across the floor. He looked as if his hair was standing on end and his eyes were wild.

'I could not have done this,' she said. 'I was asleep.'

'This did not happen by itself!' he yelled at her. The place looked like a small tornado had hit it.

'There must have been a window open.' That was the logical answer.

'There are no open windows. You did this. Now get out of my office. I'll refer you to someone who can deal with your kind.'

Although she did not know what had happened, she

was sure she had nothing to do with it; however, better to make a strategic withdrawal, so she wheeled herself out. She was frightened by his accusations. She was alone and friendless. What sort of repercussions would this have on her?

The social worker came to her room after lunch. She had a grim look on her face. She looked down at her hands as if she did not want to look at her.

'Tell me what happened at the psychiatrist's office,' she asked in a soft voice.

'I don't know, I just fell asleep, and then he slapped me across the face. He yelled at me, and then told me to get out. There is no way I could have messed up his room, I can't walk. I don't know why he should lie about me.' She started to cry. She felt angry at herself for displaying this weakness. The social worker told her that Mr Rodregious had spoken to the administration staff and was prepared to pick up the entire bill for her care.

'Who is he?' she asked.

The social worker displayed some mild surprise and said he was the man that visited her the other day.

'I'm sorry I did not know what his name was.'

The social worker went on to tell her that he was not aware her name either. She said this is causing the hospital some concern because the paperwork could not be filled out correctly. They had hoped things would be sorted out by this afternoon.

Whantune wondered was this her fault? She felt shattered; she was lost again. Depression descended upon her like a dark cloud; she could think of no way out. She lay in the bed, not able to say anything, and the social worker sat silently also. After a while, the social worker got up and said she would try to find out what to do next. After such a disastrous day, she was unable to eat anything. The nurse tried to get her to have something as she would be fasting the next day for her operation.

'I don't care,' she said.

The night was filled with terrible dreams again. She was running away from something, her heart was pounding, and she could barely breathe. She tried to wake herself up from the grim scene. She woke up for a while, but when she fell asleep, the dream became even more frightening, and this time she woke up screaming. Someone came in and gave her a shot in the arm. It hurt for a minute and then all was black and still.

She barely remembered the next day because of the anaesthesia but was vaguely aware that somebody was sitting beside her.

When she opened her eyes, she saw Riccardo leaning back in a chair, half awake. As soon as he saw movement, he came straight to the bed. How pleased was she to see him. She told him all about what had been happening to her. She said, 'You have got to get me out of this place.

I think I am going mad and I believe that they feel so too. I am fearful they are going to lock me up in a mental hospital and never let me go'.

He laughed at her and told her things were not as bad as she imagined. Anyway, he could splash some money around and get the staff to cooperate. 'I'll try to get them to let you out for the afternoon tomorrow. Brian is leaving soon, and I want to catch him up before he leaves. I'm sure you would like to see them again.'

Riccardo told her his big news: he had a raging fight with his father. He explained that in his culture, the family was everything. He had never stood up to his father before. He had been a good son and did everything that was expected of him because there was never any reason not to. There was a house rule that they did not bring their love life into the home, and family meals were important. He wanted her to come to his house to live when she got out of the hospital. At first, his father had categorically said no. He had told his father that if he did not agree, he would walk away from the family and business forever. His father had relented, and so they could be together, and she would be safe at the same time. There were always people around the house, and so she would have the protection of the whole household. This astounded her because she perceived that the 'the old man' would not give in easily. They may let her stay, but she thought they would never accept her. When she voiced her doubts to Riccardo, he brushed them aside and instead produced the locket from the inner pocket of his jacket. He had it fixed and he gently placed it around her neck. The symbolism was not lost on her. It renewed their contract; only this time, for a while, she felt some comfort in it.

True to his word, he arranged an outing for the following afternoon. He had dropped off some clothes for her to wear, and the staff had kindly helped her to get ready. They could see her excitement and were caught up in the romance of the story. Gorgeous boy finds out the girl was squatting in his house; she has an accident, and he tries to help her, even taking her out. It was the kind of thing that makes their job interesting. As she still could not walk, they had to instruct him in taking the wheelchair apart to fit into the car. They also reminded him that she needed to be back in time for her 'meds'.

The drive through the winding roads, around tree-covered hills, the impossible houses perched on outcroppings of hills and the mild weather combined was wonderful to lift her spirits. When they arrived at the place where Brian was staying, Riccardo got the wheelchair out of the car but was having trouble putting it together until one of the men standing around offered to help. Then he lifted her slowly into it. Christie came running out of the house, glad to see her new friend. She wanted to take her to her room to show her the artwork she had done. That left Brian and Riccardo to settle down with a beer. Brian was full of questions, which Riccardo tried to evade as best he could. He told Brian that she had had an accident and he was not made aware of it for a couple of weeks. He said that although the injuries were serious, she would probably recover. He told Brian he was going to take her home when she was released from the hospital. Brian laughed at him and said in an accusing tone.

'Rick, me mate, you're smitten. I never thought I'd see the day. Ha-ha! How did you fall in love with the girl? Have you told her you love her?'

'I'm not sure I am. I just know I don't want to lose her.'

'Take it from an Englishman, she's a thoroughbred. If I'd seen her first, you wouldn't have got a look-in. I definitely would give her a job.'

Riccardo looked carefully at him, feeling anger at the pit of his stomach.

Brian just grabbed another bottle and handed it to him.

'Remember when we were in college and I spent a holiday at your house? I was scared shitless of your father. On the other hand, your girlfriend would probably stand up to him. Oh boy, I think you are in for the ride of your life with that one. Sure, you can handle it?'

The girls came out of the house. Christie looked happy and wanted to stay for a while with them.

Brian said, 'Come on, let's jam.'

He went into the house and came out with a couple of

guitars.

Together they fiddled with them, making sure they were in tune, and then just started playing along, making up a song as they went along; the sound was as melodious as it was soft. Riccardo sat back and enjoyed the scene. She sang a couple of old ballads, and the afternoon drifted by, all too soon it was time to take her back to the hospital. This time he had no trouble getting the wheelchair into the car.

Brian insisted he lift her into the car and kissed her on the cheek, saying 'Take care." He shook hands with Riccardo and whispered in his ear, 'Don't forget to invite me to the wedding.'

On the way back to the hospital, Riccardo pulled off the road at a small inlet that acted as a look out over a valley. He leant over her and pressed his lips to hers while pulling a lever that dropped the seat down to nearly flat. She wanted to protest that this was not appropriate and someone might see then. But his kisses would not refrain from their objective. His tongue sought hers hungrily. He fumbled with the buttons of her shirt, and as soon as her nipples were exposed to the light breeze, they became hard, only made more so by his hot mouth. He pulled up her skirt and her pants down, kissing every part of exposed skin. He grabbed her hand to show her his intense maleness, and when she did so, he sighed with contentment. She did not think and just surrendered to the moment. Overwrought emotion gave way to passion. His strength overpowered her, and she felt glad to yield to him. They both felt drained of passion long before one of them was able to speak. He gave a small laugh and said it had been many years since he 'made out' in a car. He detangled himself and helped her to dress; pulling out a comb, he brushed her hair for her. They sat in silence for a while just looking at the valley, a picture in the dying sun. It felt surreal sitting there so close that no words were necessary. They both realised how important it was that they live together soon. She promised to work hard, do her exercises, and walk as quickly as she could.

When they got back, he dropped her off, handing her over to the nurse and walked away as if nothing had happened. She knew they had to keep the cover story they had made to keep him out of trouble. But she could not eat anything and went straight to sleep. She dreamed of their lovemaking, but it turned out to be a fight. In her dream, she felt as if she was fighting for her life; fear seized her, and she wanted to run away. Thankfully she woke up and told herself it was only a dream or was it a warning. She pushed the thought away and focused on the positive. The social worker came to see her and commented that she looked a lot brighter.

'I have been thinking, and I know I am not mad,' she said. 'I have thought it through, and I did not mess up the doctor's office. It is not logical, I cannot walk, and unless I could grow wings, it is not possible. The only answer is that the French doors were left open and a gush of wind came in and gave him a fright. Then later, he did not want to seem silly, so he continued the story. That makes more sense, doesn't it?'

The social worker conceded that it is more likely than any other explanation. He was not particularly liked at the hospital, and it would be easier to accept her explanation than his. Freed of the burden of the accusation of having somehow done something extraordinary, she was able to focus on the work at hand, to dispel the sense of doom and to get better as fast as she could and not think about anything else.

One week later, she was discharged. She walked a bit slowly to the car. Rick (as she now called him when nobody was around) arrived to take her to his house. The hospital staff seemed pleased to see her go and she was equipped with letters to local doctors as well as the name of her new psychiatrist. It seemed to her she just got used to one place and she moved to another. She felt this was the major changing point in her new life. He said he was looking forward to showing her his home. They stopped on the way for a bite to eat and coffee. He seemed calm and in control, and this put her at ease.

Chapter 5

A NEW LIFE

They arrived at the house mid-afternoon. The house was situated in the district of Megara. It was on the west part of Athens. On one side of the road, trees were growing sparsely in a field with some animals. On the other there was a fence and an iron gate that slid open with a press of a button from the inside of the car, to reveal a rather long driveway. At first sight of the house, she saw what one would describe as a mansion built in a classical Greek style and set in immaculate gardens. She would call it merely 'the big house'. They drove up to the front doors. Riccardo helped her out of the car.

The 'old man' himself came to the door. He was back on his feet now, and he looked a fierce as ever. Riccardo introduced them. 'Sarvas Rodregious, this is Whatune.' He extended his hand and said, 'Welcome to my home.' Riccardo smiled as was the custom in his country; his father had extended a warm welcome even though he did not approve. The entrance hall was impressive with a massive chandelier hanging down from the high part of the ceiling. A beautiful staircase curved down towards the foyer. She thought that it was designed for someone to make a grand entrance. Mr Rodregious said goodbye and left them. Standing beside the door was another man who was small, neat, and trim. He was dressed in a dark grey suit, white shirt, and black tie. Riccardo introduced them saying, 'This is Faustus, he is our commissionaire. He makes sure that the house runs smoothly. He can answer all your questions and knows everything we are doing.'

They climbed up the stairs and along a hallway that seemed to extend forever. The second story comprised mainly of sleeping quarters. They reached a door that faced the back part of the house overlooking the sea. He opened it and said, 'This is your room.' The room was not a large room; along the back wall a cupboard partly blocked the windows, a single bed was along one side of the chamber, and a desk was on the other side. She saw her laptop was placed on the desk and beside it was her guitar. Her clothes were put in the cupboard.

'As soon as I heard about you, I took the liberty of removing all your things from the beach house,' he said.

The room looked as if it had been freshly painted in a soft pink with furnishings that complemented the walls.

'This is nice,' she said. He showed her the next room with a big toilet block dominated by a large bath-cum-spa, a shower, and a smaller room that housed a toilet and a bidet.

'Now let me show our room,' he said. He opened another door that had been covered by the already open door to her room. 'That was my nanny's room,' he said. 'For appearance's sake, we will say it is your room, but this is where you will sleep.'

On entering the next room, she saw a large bed in a big room. The big windows looked out onto the back gardens and through to the sea. The room was in intense colours of grape and cream. It too had all the furnishings that matched the décor. Off to the right was a walk through dressing room followed by an ensuite.

He kicked off his shoes and dropped down to the bed, holding his arms out to her. She followed, looking enquiringly at him.

'I have taken the afternoon off to talk to you about what is expected of you now you are here. My home offers quite a different lifestyle from our other house. There we could do as we liked. Here, there are strong rules that my father wants us to maintain. The first is around meals, mostly breakfast and dinner. We are expected to be at breakfast at 7.00 a.m. and be dressed ready for the day. We have tea at six when we get home, it is usually something simple. The evening meal is at 9.30 to 10.00 p.m. We need to be dressed appropriately and be downstairs at nine thirty so we can go have an evening meal together. We have our night meal at this time because it is good for our staff and then we can go out if we want later. Everything starts going quite late here. If we cannot attend, we must let Faustus know in advance. If I am working late, I usually get something to eat out. Most people have a two-hour lunchtime here, so we don't tend too much about lunch, but you can arrange to have something light anytime. We have quite a large staff. My sister, for instance, has her own personal staff for dressing and a secretary. If you need help, let me know, and I will get you, someone. We also have security staff. They live separately in the small house you saw by the front gate. They wander around the house and grounds, keeping us safe. They change around, so don't be surprised if you see a stranger looking around dressed in a suit. The house is big as you can see but some areas are off limits such as the other bedrooms and Father's study. You can go in there when invited and it's best to stay away from that. Does this sound too formal for you?'

'I think I shall be able to handle that. Don't worry about me,' she said.

'You will need more outfits. Maybe my sister can take you out as she knows the best places to shop.'

He then took her all through the house and into the garden. The front rooms were more formal with a large entertainment area that acted as a sitting room. The walls were covered with wallpaper that had a soft golden pattern and some large paintings. There were groups of lounge chairs towards the door end. She could see that the room was large and could easily be changed into a ballroom. The dining room had similar furnishings with a very long table in the centre and a sideboard that travelled along the wall on one side. This led to the kitchen area; however, he did not take her into it. Behind the kitchen was a library with books that covered the wall from top to bottom. In the centre was a desk and a computer was placed at one end. 'I think there are enough books to keep you going for a long time,' he said. They walked towards the back of the house, and there was a partly shaded sunroom with long windows covered with green curtains and chairs of red. At the shaded area, a grand piano stood alone; there were a couple of chairs on the opposite side. It was a pleasant room; it had two doors: one door was off the dining room, and the other opened out into the side of the house. There, the garden was planted with grass that stretched towards a rail that marked the end of the property with a deep drop down to the sea. They walked to the side, and there was a walkway through to a pool area. It was an extensive area. The floor was covered with shimmering light-coloured tiles. There were changing rooms at the far end and a spa at the end of the pool. On the house side was a bar and in front of that was a line of deck chairs. Situated around the pool were pots of every description filled with flowering shrubs. 'Are you impressed?'

'It's a beautiful house,' she said noncommittally. She noticed 'two suits' standing at the side of the house talking, and they looked like the ones she had seen at the hospital. On the other end of the house, there was a large garage, and several cars were parked in there. One was a black limousine like the one that had picked her up previously. The front garden had lines of rose bushes in neat squares. Placed inside these gardens were assorted flowers none of which she could recognise. The long driveway was made of terracotta brick, which added to the ambience of the house. It circled around the back door as well. He explained that most people dropped off their cars or picked them up at the back of his home as this was more convenient for the staff to put them away. He looked pleased with himself as they walked back towards the house. She wondered why she was not really that impressed. A house is a house, she thought. It does not matter what the size but rather how the people who live in it interact.

They went back upstairs to get ready for dinner. She put on her one black dress. Downstairs again, she met Jacinda, Riccardo's sister. She was beautiful; soft wavy dark hair fell just past her shoulders. Colour added to her pouty lips, a trim figure dressed in elegant clothes. When she spoke in English, her accent was well rounded and bespoke of an upper-English education. However, there was scorn in her dark eyes. 'So you are the reason we seldom see my brother on weekends?' she said. She turned away as if she could not endure looking at her. Whatune wandered over to a small painting on the wall; the old man followed her. She looked at it for a long time, trying to place where she had seen it. Sarvas asked her what was so interesting about this painting. 'This was a part of a collection that was stolen after the war, I believe there was some talk that it may have ended up in a private collection.' 'Are you a collector?' he said suspiciously.

'No, I think I read about it somewhere,' she said.

They sat down to dinner, seated at one end of the long table. The food was good and in spite of nerves, she ate. She had a glass of red wine but refused a second. The family talked in fast Greek, which she could not understand, and so for the most part, she kept her eyes down and only answered when a question was directed towards her. These mealtimes were to become the hardest part of her stay in the 'big house'. After the meal, she excused herself. Explaining she was tired after such a long day having only been released from the hospital today. Riccardo said, 'I should have realised that you would become tired. Sorry, I'll come with you.'

In the bedroom, he became passionate and even though she was tired, she tried to perform as he wanted. She could feel he was disappointed with her lack of response.

'You could at least try to be more interested.'

She felt his anger. 'I am what I am, I'm not going to pretend or lie to you. I know you think I'm fire and ice, but I can only be me.' He sighed; in some ways, he understood and was glad because when she was turned on, because then she was hot. The trouble with him was that every girl he had ever been with had always been turned on straight away; now he wondered if it was real, or was she starting to make him doubt himself? Perhaps she was just a cold fish. He looked at her wondering why he found the idea of conquering her completely so enthralling. He did not like to lose.

That night, she had an unusually vivid dream. She was in Fiji at a village orphanage and school. Some rebels came and took a Christian nun hostage. She felt she was a watcher to a dramatic event. She woke up and did not know where she was. She sat on the edge of the bed and looked around. It took several minutes for her to recognise Rick's room. She got up and walked over to the full-length mirror and looked at the dark image of herself. Why does this keep happening? She could not shake the idea of what was about to occur in Fiji or if it had already happened. She tried to tell herself it was only a dream and not to be silly; however, she knew there was going to be no more sleep for her tonight. She went downstairs and sat in the lounge for a while until she noticed the sky becoming pale. Then she went back to bed and felt the warm comfort of Rick's body next to hers.

The morning breakfast consisted of bread, soft cheese, pastry, and coffee. Riccardo had arranged for her to be served tea as he knew she did not like coffee. He could not understand why because it was the best thing to start the day. He told her that Jacinda was going to take her shopping. The chauffeur in the black limousine would pick them up at 10.30 a.m. Jacinda made no comment, choosing to ignore her until she had to. Riccardo tried to make light of it saying it would be fun and she could spend insane amounts of money and get everything she wanted. He kissed her on the cheek and told her he would see her in the evening. She went upstairs to look at her computer; she told herself she would not look at the news, afraid of what she would find. Instead, she looked at fashion. She remembered a dress from a fashion magazine she had seen once and shown Rick the most beautiful dress she had ever seen.

Not that she wanted it as she did not have any place she could wear it; it was just nice. She looked at the colours of the season's fashion to gain an idea of what to choose. With that in mind, she went downstairs at ten thirty and found Jacinda waiting impatiently by the car.

They went to several shops, and Jacinda gushed at several frilly dresses. She hated them and would not get them. Jacinda was getting impatient. She suggested they try and have a coffee and talk about it. At a small outside coffee stall, they ordered what they wanted. She tried to speak with Jacinda. 'I get it, you don't like me. This was not my idea, but for the sake of harmony, we should try to be at least civil to each other.'

'Jacinda gave her an impertinent look, 'I think you are a witch, or you have something over my brother,' she said. 'What's wrong with the clothes I have been showing you?'

'They are too flowery and showy for me.'

'I have a flowered top on.'

'Yes, and it looks gorgeous on you, but I am not you, I like plain, classic clothes. My relationship with your brother is none of your concern, but I am not holding anything against him, and he can choose to end it whenever he likes, and I have no claim on him or his money. I know my place. I am sleeping in the nanny's room. I think that I should choose clear colours that match together so I can wear them differently. And I guess I need a couple of cocktail dresses.'

Jacinda sighed and said, 'Oh well if you really want to be plain Jane,

I'm sure we can get you something, but you could lose him to a better-looking woman if you don't look out.' They got back in the car that had been trying to keep up with them, and she ordered the driver to take them to another place. Finally, they found a fashion house that suited her and they bought a pile of different outfits there. The designer himself came out when he knew Jacinda was in the shop. He had taken charge of Whatune when he realised she had an open credit card and money was not an issue; he came up with just what she wanted. She chose "block" colours in blue, green, and mint green that blended together and a top with the colours in a pattern. A cocktail dress was in emerald and suited her skin nicely. He said he would be happy to design other clothes for her as he noticed she had standard figure size, and he would be delighted to send them to the house. She still needed shoes and accessories. Again, the designer came to her aid, saying she should just let him get them for her. She was happy with his because she had just about had all she could take of Jacinda. They gave the clothes to the chauffeur and climbed into the back seat.

'I need a drink.' Jacinda said and told the driver to stop off at a small bar. She ordered a cocktail and Whatune ordered a whisky sour. Jacinda lit up a cigarette and offered one to Whatune, which she accepted, even though she was not sure she could smoke. They sat in silence, both thankful that the shopping trip was finished. Finally, Jacinda said, 'Okay I don't like you, but I will call a truce for now.'

Whatune sat back and smiled. She could feel the softening of attitude coming from Jacinda. She did not know what to say, but she was glad of any relief from the tension. She thought maybe this was a part of Rick's plan to get them to talk. She made up her mind to be as helpful as she could towards Jacinda and ignore any snide comments that came her way.

There was another surprise for her that day. When Riccardo came up to their room, he was carrying a large box. He had a big grin on his face as he handed it to her. She opened it and saw the dress she had admired in the fashion book. She was astonished; it was a one off and must have cost the earth. 'It is beautiful,' she said. 'But what will I do with it?'

'I'm sure you will find an occasion to wear it, and on you, it will be stunning.' She slipped out of her dress and put it on and turned around for the zip to be done up. It fitted her like a glove, leaving little room for her to breathe. It was straight down to the knees and then flared out at the bottom. 'It was so elegant with many colours that reminded her of a church's stained glass window. All the hand-sewn beads seemed to shine. She had to stand on her toes, and she knew she would have to wear high-heeled shoes with it.

'Thank you so much. I know you must have gone to a lot of trouble to acquire it.'

'It is the least I could do since you spent a whole day with my sister,' he said.

Chapter 6

GOOD DOCTOR

The next day, she rang the Institute of Human Development and asked to speak to Doctor William McKlean. He came on the phone, and she told him she had been referred to him. Yes, he had been invited to see her and had received the paperwork about her from the hospital; he would be happy to see her. He suggested he could come to the house on Friday afternoon. His voice sounded soothing, and although she was initially frightened, she felt maybe he was the right person for her.

On the appointed time, he was ushered into the sunroom. She stood up and shook hands and sat down again. He had a dark suit on with a black tie and blue shirt. He was fairly tall and distinguished looking. She guessed he was around about sixty or seventy years old. He had an oval face, intense dark eyes, thinning grey hair, and a cropped beard and moustache. She felt he was someone she could trust, and this was rare because there were few people that she did trust, and even then she could be misled by some people.

He started by telling a little about himself. He was raised in the USA. His father was a philosopher and a theologian who preached at their local church. His mother had suffered from depression for many years up until she died at the age of forty. He had gone into medicine and became a psychiatrist, which he explained is a medical doctor who specialised in treating mental illness. He later went to England to study becoming a psychologist, who studies human behaviour. This was because of his interest in the paranormal.

He explained there have always been people who are deemed to have unique gifts of insight by their communities. This is not a new idea; however, the past experiences have been expressed as superstition, and little effort was made to find out about these people. Now there is a growing idea that this may be one of the next evolutionary steps for man. With new technology, one could see the changing patterns made in the brain through various situations.

He founded the Institute for Human Development twenty-five years ago. He explained that the institute was a privately funded research facility. The people who usually came to him were people who thought they had some form of extra-sensory perception (ESP) or had been referred to him by other agencies. They were put through some tests to see if there was any evidence of this. The tests were rated high if their score was higher than the laws of probability. If he found no proof of any form of ESP, he would tell them. Most people were concerned about the implications of this, but through counselling, they found answers to questions they had been asking themselves for a long time. His studies and the papers he wrote were mostly about people who did have some form of ESP. He found that individuals who had some skills, and had an open mind, and were willing to work to enhance or control their abilities were happy when they were offered a class at the Institute. The institute also offered meditation and free expression classes. So the people they initially tested and who had been through their training did, in fact, test higher the next time.

He went on to explain that the notion of parapsychology had been around since 1889 and was started by a man called Max Dessoir. 'Para' comes from a Greek word for *alongside*. Thus it means 'alongside psychology'. Parapsychology is a branch of psychology which studies behaviour transcending known modes of sensory cognition and motor activity. These abilities seemed contrary to common sense and the known laws of nature. A growing number of psychologists believed that the phenomenon had been demonstrated scientifically, but there would always be those who say it had not. The issue surrounding the division of thought was that, given the large numbers of people that had been involved, in thirty-one different countries, concrete evidence was hard to find because of the few individuals who utilised all their senses. There is the notion that ESP primarily comes from the unconscious mind. It is not a conscious decision to suddenly become a psychic. Studies showed that there was a significant portion of the brain that is utilised by the unconscious mind. Developing an awareness of the unconscious mind was a start to that process. Dreams were a way for the unconscious mind to work out the known problems of the day.

'This is interesting, but what has it to do with me?' She said.

He explained his perspective of the letter and MIR brain scans done at the hospital. 'I think you have been treated very badly by the hospital, and that is because they did not understand you.' He went on to clarify what he meant. 'You seem to have some issues that need to be addressed right now. The first is you do not have brain damage. There is no sign of brain trauma other than the fact that you did have a concussion that has now taken up. The lightened areas on your scan are not dead areas but rather areas with heightened level of activity. The incident in the doctor's office is one of his own making. He tried to push you too far, and you responded in the only way you could. Hypnotherapy uses guided relaxation, intense concentration. While the person's attention is focused in this state of awareness that is sometimes called a trance, there is a possibility for the individual to examine areas that are blocked out or ignored. The hypnotic state allows the person to explore painful thoughts, feelings, and memories they might have hidden from the conscious mind. It is important that the therapist is aware of the individual's state of mind before attempting to use this tool. The doctor did not do this. Then he shouted at you as if it was your fault and succeeded in frightening you.'

'I didn't do it,' she said, feeling defensive.

'Have you heard of Psychokinesis?' he asked. She shook her head. 'I believe you may have had this skill for some time but have never used it. I think when pushed to remember something too painful to accept, you threw what can only be described as a 'psychic temper tantrum.' At some point, the doctor realised what had happened, and that is why he has referred you to me.'

'I didn't intend this to happen to me. I find it all hard to believe,' she said. 'I don't know why I am different from other people. I feel you do have my best interest at heart. What can I do? I just want my memory back. It is like being a baby. I just don't know what to do. I have to relearn things all over again.'

He explained how a baby learns. 'Between the age of six months and seven years, a child's learning ability is at its fastest. They learn by watching what the people around them do and trying to copy it; it creates patterns in the Neurotransmitters in the brain. They build upon these patterns as they grow older; these Neurotransmitters join together to create more pathways. It is perhaps the same with you, except you already have the channels established. It is only finding ways to access the information stored in your mind. You told me you read a lot. What kinds of books do you read?'

'Mostly history, religion, and some nonfiction type of books. When reading on my laptop, I usually read current affairs. I suppose I am a bit like a baby then because I seem to find out things by sensing other people, and then I know whether to trust them or not.'

He asked her about her life as it stand now and she told him an edited version of the truth. He asked about her relationship with Riccardo Rodregious. She hesitated, not knowing the psychiatrist well enough, to tell the truth. 'I don't always understand him.' she only said.

'There are no easy fixes for you. It will take time and patience. I would like you to come down to the clinic for a few days to do some testing. Then we will know how to deal with some of your issues at least on one level. Then I would like to try hypnosis again but this time using "Sodium Thiopental" as well. It has been around for just under one hundred years and has helped many people overcome the most severe circumstances. It acts on the nervous system to calm anxiety and contributes to relaxing the mind and thus we will not have any outbursts like the one in the doctor's office. I promise you this: I will not make you do anything that will impact on your mental health.'

'This is all very scary,' she said. 'I feel as if you want to know me from the inside out. I will have to ask Riccardo about leaving, but I think he will say it's okay.'

'Are there any questions you would like to ask me?' He said. She shook her head. 'Here is my card. Call me and let me know when you want to come so I can have things ready. Now is a good time because our students are on a break and I can devote all my time to helping you.'

She stood up to shake his hand and noticed that they had been talking for three hours. 'I should have offered you some refreshment. I did not see the time.'

'It's all right,' he said. 'I will be home quickly. It is not that far.'

When he left, she continued to take in what he had said. He exuded confidence, and that led her to think he may just be able to help. She came to call him the 'good doctor' as opposed to the 'bad doctor' at the hospital.

When Rick came home, she took him up to the bedroom and told him about the good doctor. 'I don't really like the idea of someone poking around in my head,' she said. 'You never know what you will find there.' She showed him the card, and he said it was not far from their place on Highway 91.

'I will be amazed if he finds something surprising. You must go if you are ever to know about yourself. You can take my car, and I will use the limo. That way you can make a quick getaway if things go wrong.'

She thought of how kind he was to her, always offering to help in some way. She realised that her life could have turned out so different if she had not met him. He had a way of comforting her by making light of her fears.

Chapter 7

DARKNESS REVEALED

On a Monday morning, she drove to Vouliagmeni on Highway 91 and reached Emaus Street. The drive had taken about thirty-five minutes. She drove along the street until she saw a rendered fence with the sign on it. She pushed the bell at the gate and waited. The good doctor opened it for her, and she asked where she should park the car. He pointed to a place just inside the front gate. The institute was built in a two-story square with all the buildings on the outside and in the centre, was a garden with trees and walkways. Benches were placed in various locations for privacy. It looked like the monastery that it had been in times gone by. The only difference was that it had been modernised. She parked the car in front of the small suite that she was to stay in. She liked it right away as it had a comfortable style about it. The doctor suggested they get something to eat before starting anything. He led the way to a large refectory with tables and chairs. He explained that when classes were on, they had about twenty people staying there at one time. They also ran weekend workshops for people who worked. It opened into a large kitchen that had a server all in stainless steel. In the kitchen, he asked what she liked to drink; he poured a couple of cups of tea and got some ready-made sandwiches out of the fridge. As they carried them over to a table, he noticed she seemed to be shy and nervous. 'Don't worry, the first part is easy,' he said. 'You will spend the rest of the day just filling out forms and doing some questionnaires.'

The first forms consisted of name and any other information, like next of kin.

There were so many blanks. She put Riccardo's name down as next of kin.

The doctor smiled and said, 'I guess he will be paying the bill.' She made a mental note to say something to Rick when she got back to the house. The first test was an IQ test on general knowledge and some patterns. The personality questionnaire was a book long. The doctor told her to answer the first thing that came to mind and not to overthink it. Ordinarily, it would not be considered hard, but she found it so because of all the gaps in her understanding. It took about three hours to finish. The doctor suggested she have a rest for a while. He gave her a book called *Passions of the Mind* by Irving Wallace. It was the story of Sigmund Freud. He said it would help her to drift off to sleep. Back in the room, she took off her shoes and settled down on the bed to read. He was right, the place was quiet, and she slept on until he got her for dinner.

When she came into the refectory, she saw another man. He was lean, lanky, about twenty-five years old with dark-rimmed glasses. He had hair with the annoying habit of falling over one eye. The doctor introduced him as Tim. She was told he was a writer who was using the archives to research a book he was writing. He smiled at her and seemed about to say something but changed his mind and stayed quiet. The doctor told Tim he was about to test Whatune over the next couple of days. He nodded and continued to eat.

The doctor asked her a bit more about herself. Of course, Whatune is not my real name, we made it up because I can't remember my name. She talked about her ability to read people. 'I can always tell if someone is lying to me and most times I know why. It is like I know what they are thinking. I am not reading their mind. It's more what they are feeling. I kind of feel if they are faking it, sometimes I feel when people are sad or angry even though I am not sad or angry. It's very hard to explain, but if someone is concentrating on something like a puzzle, I can feel the intensity of their thoughts. It's as if they give off different vibes and I know. I don't have to be close to people doing this. I just have to think about them. Sometimes in a busy shopping mall, I can feel the mood of the people around me. This can get me into trouble because I react to their feelings and then they respond to me. On the other hand, it is good because I can sometimes help people.'

'What about your own feelings?' asked the doctor.

'I think I know what I am feeling. I just don't know how to deal with it.' She waited a while and then said, 'I am often afraid when there is no reason to be. I think safety is an issue for me.'

Tim started to talk about how his interest in the paranormal began when he was young and used to talk to his dead grandmother. 'I just thought she came down from heaven to tell me good night. To me, she was as real as you are now. I sang songs she taught me even though I was only two when she died. My parents thought there was something wrong with me and took me off to a psychologist. I was lucky because he believed me and told me that sometimes, young people can see someone they love for a while until the adult world crashes in and they forget. I have not forgotten, and I would like to find out more about it.'

They broke up for the evening because the doctor said she would need to concentrate the next day.

The next morning, they began the real tests. The first was easy; the doctor took a pack of ordinary playing cards and spread them across a table in a straight line. He asked her to choose a seven of hearts. He told her he did not know where anything was. She picked the wrong card. He shuffled the cards and repeated this ten times. She picked four out of the ten. 'That is not bad,' he said 'given that the law of probability for you to choose even one out of fifty-two cards.' He brought out a set of unique cards that had symbols on them and first showing her the cards, he moved to a chair across the room and held them face down and asked her to say what the symbol was on the top card. If you can guess above 20 percent, you are doing well.' Out of ten tries, she guessed right three times. Next, he got her to turn her back to him and held the card face up so he could see them and asked her to try again. He was surprised that she guessed nine out of the ten tries. He carefully wrote each step down on a form. They had a coffee break, and he asked Tim to help with the next step. He put Tim in a small boxed room and asked him to draw a simple picture. Then on the other side, he asked her to copy what she thought Tim had sketched. She did well at this; first was a sailing boat than a house than an apple followed by a vase with a flower in it. This one confused her because Tim had drawn it small on the paper and there were two elements in it. The doctor thanked Tim, and they tried another test. In this one, he placed her into a booth and put headphones on that had white noise in them and turned out the light except a small red light. He asked her to continue talking about all the things that came into her mind, any thought feelings or images, all of which he put on a tape recorder. Outside, he watched five different video clips. This sending lasted about thirty minutes. Then he brought her out of the box and showed her the clips and asked her which ones he had been watching and in what order. This tested whether she could read his feeling. She was surprisingly accurate above the norm. In fact, he thought she had produced the highest score he had ever seen. She told the doctor that she had a headache. It was not surprising given that she had to concentrate for an extended period. He suggested that she should rest and they would take it up the next day.

The next day, she was put on a computer with random numbers and told to try and move them without touching the keys. She could not do this, but when he wanted to get an answer to what they added up to, there was a difference. She explained to him that she was not good with numbers and when pressured to produce an answer she had used her eye to line them up in order only she could understand. She mentally pressed 'sum of'. And the answer came into her mind even though she had not visually changed the numbers around. In another test, he lit a fire in a grate and asked her to stand near it. She said she did not like it and suddenly, the fire went out.

The final test involved Tim again, with him in the library and monitors placed on him while she was in the lab area. She attempted to change his mood and thought. This was hard as she did not know much about him. She tried to imagine his face and thought of the grandmother who he loved. He, on the other hand, thought this was silly. Then he started to feel sombre for no reason he could explain. His heart and respiration went up at the same time. He was not happy with this experiment and said he did not want to do anymore. They met for lunch, and the doctor told them he had got all the information he needed for now. He thanked Tim for his help. He told her they would have their first hypnosis session in the afternoon after she had a rest.

Later that day, she went into the doctor's office. In one corner was a big cushioned chair that had an extension for the legs, another comfortable chair, and a coffee table. He told her to sit in the big chair. She said she was afraid something would go wrong. He promised her nothing would happen and he would explain each step as they went along. He produced a silver-backed blanket and elucidated that when one is in a state of deep relaxation, the body temperature tends to drop. He described what they were going to do; the session would last about an hour, and when she woke up, she may not remember. He said this is normal and not to be concerned. He explained that he was going to try to reconstruct her life, but it may not be in chronological order and that it was a bit like putting a jigsaw puzzle together. He told her he was going to give her a small injection to help her to relax further. He had asked her permission to tape the session as it was easier for him than trying to take notes and meant he could give all his attention to her. He assured her that there would not be a repeat of the last session and he would have full control of everything that happened and he would know if it was too much and he would stop.

'Now I am going to put on some music. Soft tinkering

music filled the air. I want you to listen and try to take long slow breaths. With each breath out, I want you to relax a bit more. Starting from now, each time you let the breath out, I want you to relax more. First, relax your head and shoulders.' He spoke slowly and waited for her to complete that task. 'Now with the next breath, I want you to relax your arms, with the next breath, I want you to relax your back, check to see that no part of your upper body feels tight. If there is, move it around until you feel comfortable. With the next breath, I want you to relax your stomach. You are already feeling calmer and quieter. Take another breath and feel your legs, make sure they feel comfortable. Your whole body is now feeling relaxed, and you are starting to feel sleepy. I want you to open your eyes and look at me. You feel safe and that you can talk to a trusted friend. Listen to the sound of my voice. Nothing you say can hurt you. I want you to tell me a story about you, but it is as if you are reading a book. There is nothing that can hurt you. I want you to talk about what happened in your life and what you felt, but it is as if you are looking outside yourself. The essential part of you is safe so you can let go and feel free to look at things without any harm coming to you. I am going to take you back to the day before you woke up in Riccardo's house. Do you remember what you did in the morning? What did you do?'

'Yes! I was coming into the port on a cruise ship. Everyone was excited at breakfast. I felt depressed. I know this trip is right for me and I am trying to get into the spirit of things. I go back and pack my bag. I only have one bag, and I put my passport and papers in the side pocket. I leave it outside my door for the porters to take through customs.' She stopped, and he said, 'What happened next.'

'After customs, I went through to have my papers stamped. And then I have to go outside to catch a bus to a hotel. There are a lot of people around, and I feel claustrophobic. At some point, I put my case down, and when I went to pick it up, it was gone. I went back inside and looked for someone in a uniform and tell him that my case is gone. They take me into a small room, and another man asked me a lot of questions. I did not remember the name of the hotel because it was written down in the side pocket of my case. I thought I would not need it. I was supposed to follow the tour guide. I stayed in the interview room for a while and then they said they would let me go. I was told to report to the Australian Council as soon as I could so arrangements can be made to cover me while I am in the country. They gave me a map of how to get around, marking where the embassy was and then I left there. I just walked and walked somehow I dropped the papers they gave me. I got tired and hitched a ride. I thought I was heading towards the city. But I was moving away from it. The people let me off as they were turning another way. I saw a bus stop and sat down beside the road. When a bus came along, I got on but did not have the right money, and because I think I looked bad, the driver said I did not have to pay. I stayed on the bus for a while, and I fell asleep and went to the end of where the bus was going. The town was by the sea, and I walked along until I reached a point. I felt so bad I just did not want to be alive. I thought that the best thing to do was to swim out to beyond the point of no return and I would drown. I took my clothes off and swam out. I got tired and floated on my back for a while until I felt stronger, then I swam some more. I knew that I was getting fatigued and thought that would be the end. I became aware of a thump, thump on the water and so I stopped. There was a boat heading straight for me. One thing I knew was that I did not want to be chopped up in a propeller, so I dived out of the way. The next thing was that the boat had stopped and someone threw out a lifebuoy. I knew I should not touch it, but somehow my sense of self-preservation is stronger than me, and I caught hold of it. I found myself on the deck with a man staring down at me. He seemed angry, and I hated him because I knew I would not have the courage to do that again and it was my one chance for an out. I felt sick and threw up. I started to shake. He said something to me, but I did not understand him. When the boat landed, he picked me up and put me into a car. He took me to a house and made me drink some terrible stuff. I was still shaking, so he gave me another drink. It felt hot as it went down to my stomach. At first, I did not notice the rug had come off, and he was trying to take my top off. I told him to stop. I tried to push him away, but he held me down. He raped me. I fought him as hard as I could.

All I could feel was the pain as he pushed inside me again and again. I wanted it to stop. I had to get away somehow. The only way was in my head. I let inside my head go black.'

'So the only way for you to escape this terrible rape was to wipe it out of your mind,' he said. 'I am sorry you had to go through this, it must have been terrible for you. I am going to wake you up now. You will remember nothing of this. The next time I tell you to relax and listen to my voice, you will remember how to go into this state straight away. When I count backwards from ten, you will wake up now and feel okay and that everything is right in your world.'

She heard the words three, two, one, and opened her eyes. It felt as if she had only been relaxing and thinking of her breathing. She remembered nothing.

'How do you feel?' he asked.

'I feel superb,' she said. 'When are you going to start?'

He smiled at her and said, 'We have finished for today.'

'I have a feeling that I have glimpsed just the tip of an iceberg.' I need to see you next week I can give you the results of the tests. I could come up to the house if you wish.'

'No,' she said. 'I always have a feeling someone is watching me there. I don't know why I feel this because it is entirely unreasonable. Some areas are worse than others. Funny, I never feel it in our bedroom so if I want to talk to Rick, I wait until we can be together in our room. I would rather come down here.'

He looked in his diary and asked if the next Monday would do about ten thirty. 'All right,' she said and left to drive back to the house. Funny, she thought she always referred to it as the house whereas the family thought of it as home.

That evening, she could not wait for Rick to come back. She wanted to tell him about the stay she had with the "good" doctor. She showered and changed into her black dress and waited in the bedroom looking out to the sea. He came in so quietly that she did not notice until he put his arms around her and pulled her back against his body. He did not speak, just kissed her neck as he undid the back of the black dress and her bra. Her clothes fell away, and she felt his fingers touch her breast. She leant her head back against his shoulder and sighed. She stayed there for a while, feeling her heart start to beat faster. He fumbled with his clothes, taking everything off before he turned her around, kissing her on the lips; his tongue sought hers. She closed her eyes, willing her body to relax. He pulled her over to the edge of the bed and sat down, pulling her down onto his knees, her legs either side of him, placing his head to nuzzle in between her breasts, almost like a child. She caressed the top of his curly head. With his passionate kisses, she barely felt him enter her, and when it did register, she felt a deep desire to move with him. It carried her away to some place where there was no fear or thought, only of being loved and wanting to return that love. They did not speak for a while, both relishing the moment. He nodded at the time and jumped up and said they were going to be late for dinner if they did not get ready. 'I was ready until you came in and messed me up,' she laughed.

When they retired to the bedroom, she told him all about what she had been up to at the Institute. 'I am afraid it will end up being very expensive. I have to go back next Monday, and then I will find out the results of the tests.'

'Please don't worry about money, I can afford it.'

'It's not that, it's that I seem to owe you so much and give you insufficient in return.'

'You do your best to give me what I want. But I really want you to be happy. Have you told the doctor about your bad dreams?'

'Not yet,' she said 'I don't really know him that well, and on top of everything else, he might decide to put me in an institution for the insane.'

Riccardo laughed. 'You probably are putting up with me.'

William McKlean sat down to start a new case file. He reached for a new folder and allocated a file number 786245 Whatune. He reread the hospital report, taking note of the irregularities between her story and the notes the hospital sent. He listened again to the tape.

He wrote that (1)she was unaware of the heinous crime committed against her and she covered up the other acts of violence. The time spent alone because of the fear he had implanted in her mind could almost be described as a mental hostage where the person held comes to think of the controller as good.

(2) There was no doubt in his mind that she had completely broken down and that the memory loss was total. At this point he considered her to be very vulnerable to the influences of others.

(3) The question was: did she need to be protected in a controlled environment?

(4) Avoidant personality disorder (APD). She had low self-esteem. Hospital staff observed her as shy, isolated, and lonely. She had described herself as feeling inadequate and felt extremely sensitive to what others thought of her. She expressed her inability to 'fit in' when she was with a group of people. She uses intuition to vigilantly appraise movements and expressions of those she comes in contact with. Tended to idealise the relationship she was in.

Did the rape cause the memory loss?

What part did the depression play in her decision to stay with Riccardo?

Were there other uncovered factors?

Why was she depressed in the first place?

When did she develop these skills? Was it from childhood or because of the isolation and mental torment?

He then reviewed the charts he had made during the testing.

IQ: her average mark was 135. When seen in the light of memory loss, it implied she is very smart.

Personality: Impulsive, but under stress, she may become logical and analytical. Kind hearted and felt for the suffering of others. She is easily swayed towards other points of view. (This may change with time and confidence).

ESP tests and anecdotal evidence indicated she is not a physic even though she scored higher than the average. There is substantial evidence she is an 'empath', and she utilised these skills over a long distance simply by concentrating on a particular person. This is the first person that has presented at this institute who employs their empathic skills on a daily basis. There are dangers in this because she has no control over how she reacted to the feelings of others. She could blunder into dangerous situations.

Is there any other evidence to suggest that she used Psychokinesis? This is walking into another dangerous area. I am aware she does not believe this was possible and that makes it harder to demonstrate as it seemed that she would have to be pushed very far for her to react and that reaction could be unpredictable and may cause her or others harm.

He then designed a strategic plan that would include counselling and hypnotherapy to bring about change in her behaviour as well as finding out what had caused her breakdown. He was aware of her sensibility to suggestion and realised if he was to help, he had to guard his own emotional reactions, particularly because she was an interesting case. It would not be advantageous for her if she picked up on his feelings and reacted to them instead of concentrating on her own. He believed that she would try to avoid things that were too hard for her. He made a mental note to get another MRI brain scan done using colour imaging to see if there were any other hot spots in her brain. He hoped there would be so he could demonstrate the indications of an 'empath' in pathology as well as clinically.

He carefully put the graphs together with the notes and filed them. Then he made up a box out of flat cardboard, marked it number 786254, and marked the tape number 1 then placed the tape in the box. He sighed and thought this was going to be challenging; however, he would have a good chance to study an 'empath' up close.

Chapter 8
MUSIC

Monday morning, she woke up with a migraine. She felt sick and could barely see. Riccardo told her to stay in bed. He pulled the curtains together, shutting out the light. He said he would tell staff to be quiet and get Faustus to ring Doctor McKlean and make another appointment. She loved it when he took control of everything because then she did not have to think. He asked if she needed any medication, but she told him that she did not like taking drugs and would get better in time anyway. He kissed her on the cheek, said goodbye, and told her to call his cell if she wanted anything.

She stayed in bed most of the day partly because of a headache and partly because she had just wanted to shut the world out for a while. She got ready for the evening meal and came downstairs at seven thirty. Riccardo was already there, sitting down, talking to Jacinda. He looked up when she walked into the room.

'I thought you may still be sick.'

She told him that although she still felt a bit 'jagged', she thought she would try anyway. She had a glass of wine and then they went to dinner. She could not eat much and just moved her food around the plate. She had another two glasses of wine. Now she felt light-headed. She excused herself from the table and wandered into the sunroom. She observed the grand piano sitting at the end of the room. She ambled over and lifted the lid and tentatively pressed a finger on the keys. Sitting down it seemed that all the music in her head transpired through to her fingers. She started playing; she heard a crash in the other room and out of the corner of her eye, she saw the old man, his face was as black as thunder. She decided to ignore him and just let the music flow through her. She played a Schubert piece than Beethoven's Piano Concerto No. 5 in E flat and Chopin's Mazurka in C sharp minor. He sat down on a chair opposite her. She played three pieces before she stopped and looked at him. Very slowly, he started to clap.

'You have brought music back into my home, thank you.'

He got up to leave then turned back to her and said, 'You can use the piano anytime you wish.'

He went into his study. She noticed Riccardo and Jacinda were standing there, looking as if they had seen a ghost.

'What is the matter?' she asked.

Jacinda turned to her and said in a harsh voice, 'Nobody uses that piano. It belonged to my mother and the only time it is touched is to dust it or when someone comes in to tune it.'

She felt their distress but could only say, 'I'm sorry.' She could feel she was going to cry and ran upstairs to the bedroom. Without meaning to, she had broken another rule. But where did the music come from? She had felt some kind of release from pent-up emotion when she played. She should have stopped as soon as she saw the 'the old man' but intuitively, she knew he did not really want her to end. She hadn't given a thought to how the others may be feeling or the shock she had given them. The fact that Rick did not follow her told her that he was mad at her as well. When he finally came in he sat on the bed beside her, he turned her head towards him and wiped the tears from her eyes that were by now red and swollen. 'Where did that come from?' he asked. 'I don't really know,' she said. 'You know that I have songs in my head a lot of the time and when I feel stressed more so. But blame it on the wine and an empty stomach.'

'It sounded good,' he commented.

'I wish I knew there must be a logical explanation,' she said.

The next night, the old man announced he had invited Ziehn Meapha, the maestro of the Greek Symphony Orchestra to dinner to hear Whatune play. She stopped eating and looked up in surprise. She knew better than to talk back to him and glanced over at Rick to see what he thought. He showed surprise but was also pleased.

She waited until they went into the bedroom to talk to him. 'I can't play,' she said.

'What do you mean you can't play?'

'I went to the piano today and sat there and could not play a note. I stared at the keys and nothing happened, I just do not know how.'

'Well! What happened last night?'

'You remember, I had a couple of wines without eating anything, I think I was a little drunk,' she said.

'You must do this, or my father will lose face. My Father is a proud man, and he will not forgive you if you let him down.'

'I just can't,' she said.

He looked thoughtful and then said, 'What if you replicate the actions of the other night?'

'You want me to get drunk?'

He thought for a while and thought of another plan. 'If all else fails, you can slam the cover down on your hands and break your fingers, then you won't be able to play.'

'I may not have the courage to break my fingers, what then?' He took her by the shoulders and shook her hard until her head was ringing; he glared at her and told her she had to do something. If she came up with a better plan, okay as long as she did something.

She could not sleep with worry about what she should do. She got up and walked down to the piano, sat on the stool and looked at it. From out of nowhere, she felt a deep-seated anger. She felt the fury in the pit of her stomach. She hated the piano. However, she would not do it any harm. She walked out the back to the rail overlooking the sea and yelled her anger. She did not understand where this anger came from. She felt it was something she had been carrying around inside of her for a very long time. Somehow this shadow had cast a spell over her entire life. It seemed as if it kept pulling her back to some unknown source.

The next evening, she dressed with more care than was usual, putting on a long black skirt and a white beaded top. She still did know what to do and hoped that wine would work. Rick came in and noticed her agitation. 'I really can't do this. It's impossible. I tried again today to see if I could remember anything, but nothing came to mind. Whatever happened before, it has gone now. I came up to my room and played a song about going to Heaven on the guitar.'

He took her in his arms, telling her they had a plan, he had confidence in her that she would work it out somehow. 'I can't face it,' she said.

'You are a brave person. I know you have a habit of finding a way through difficult situations and you never give up. I know you can do this.'

They went downstairs, and she was introduced to the 'maestro'. She could not look at him and kept her eyes lowered. Jacinda commented on her modesty, saying it was extraneous shyness. At the meal, she really could not eat anything but drank several glasses of wine. She tried to put off going into the other room by taking a long time pretending to eat. When she could not put if off any longer, she walked in and sat down at the hated piano she was prepared to slam down the top on her fingers. She felt the anger inside of her, and as she let it go through her, she started to play something that expressed her feeling. The piece was one from Tchaikovsky. She let her imagination take her to the Kazakhs thundering across the steppes. It is an unyielding piece, and her fingers flew across the keys finishing with a loud crescendo. She looked up at Rick standing by the piano, and he said mildly, 'Whatever did that piano do to you?' She tried to tone it down a bit playing Chopin: Prelude in E minor. There was another piece of music in her head, but she did not know what it was. She played as much of it as she could, but stopped after five minutes. She stood up and bowed to the maestro, Ziehn Meapha. Looking at Jacinda, she indicated if she had a cigarette. Jacinda looked towards her purse. She picked up the purse and walked out onto the back lawn, her hands were shaking so much that when she tried to light up a cigarette, the flame would not reach its intended target. Rick came out and took the lighter from her and held it for her. 'I did not know you did this,' he said, indicating the cigarette. He looked at Jacinda's purse in surprise because as far as he knew, she did not do it either.

'Yes, she does, and so do I sometimes,' she said. 'I am never going to play the piano again. And now I am going to bed. Please make up some apology for me.'

During the night, she had another nightmare; there was fire, and she was running and running. She cried and sat up. Rick reached up and pulled her down and told her it was only a dream and to go back to sleep. She stayed quietly by his side, not wanting to disturb him. But she did not sleep.

The next morning at breakfast, Sarvas Rodregious commented on her rudeness to Zielin Meapha. 'He wanted to talk to you.' He looked annoyed at her. She looked sad and said, 'I'm sorry.'

Riccardo kissed her on the cheek and told her he would be home early in the afternoon, and they would go out for dinner. She went up to the bedroom. When he was not there, she liked her little room and would spend the mornings on the laptop, playing the guitar or reading. She was a passionate reader and always had some book on the go. This way, she kept out of the way of other people in the house. At 9.45 a.m., there was a knock on the door and Patra, one of the girls who worked the first floor, poked her head into the room and told her that Mr Rodregious wanted to see her in his study. She brushed her hair and went down to see what he wanted. She knocked before entering and stood enquiringly waiting for him to speak.

'Sit down. I believe I owe you an apology,' he said. 'Riccardo called me when he got to work and told me you were drained after your performance. I should have known, as my wife used to feel the same way.'

'I do not need him to fight my battles for me. But I do owe you an explanation. You see, I really cannot remember. I sat at the piano a couple of times and nothing happened. Riccardo told me I was not to let you down, that you were bringing just about the most prominent conductor in the country to hear me play. We devised a plan for me to drink too much and hope I could do what I did the other night. I was terrified of what was to happen, and if I failed, I was going to drop the lid in my fingers and break them. I tried my best, and this caused me to shake and felt sick. That is why I left. I will go and offer Maestro a personal apology.'

He gave her one of his hard looks and grudgingly had to admire her attitude. 'He wanted to tell you that you play very well and that it must have taken many years to perfect your art. He thinks you must be a concert pianist of some repute.' She stood up to go then he said, 'I hope you continue to try. If you look in the stool, you will find some music there. Look at it, and maybe you can make some sense of it and play.'

Rick came back just after lunchtime and said they were

going fishing. This made her feel glad to be able to get out of that house for a while and not have to worry about what was expected of her. He drove the car to a small airport where there was a hangar containing a shiny *Gulf Stream G650* Jet waiting for them. He introduced her to Neil, the pilot. He was a young man with a small body, dressed in a khaki overall and a cap on his head, hiding most of his face. He had freckles on most of his skin and a lopsided smile. He shook her hand and went back to getting the jet ready for take-off. 'This cuts our trip by half,' Rick said. They climbed into the luxury plane and took off. He explained that this was a company plane that he used mostly for inter-country trips. It seated fourteen in soft leather seats and across the back was one long seat that was used as a bed. It had a fully equipped bar and meals area. Neil was on a retainer and was on call most of the time. However, safety regulations stated he was only authorised to fly a certain number of hours before he had to rest, and he was not allowed to drink for twelve hours before a flight. They flew to Messni airfield where there was a car waiting for them. It seemed that they were on the boat in no time. Again, she felt all the tension fall away. She wondered at how he could arrange things so fast, everything fell into place so quickly for him whereas every day was some kind of struggle for her. She tried to rationalise the last couple of days. What did it mean? Was it part of memory coming back, and if so, would it tear her relationship with Rick apart? It did not feel like a memory because there was nothing else, like seeing a room or place or people. She could not remember learning to play the piano. What about the anger? Was that real or was it just in her mind? After a while, Rick said they could go straight back, or they could spend the night at the beach house and fly back in the morning. He was aware of her fear of the house, but he said he would be good and not hurt her. He gave her his pleading look, which was very endearing and she laughed and nodded. He used the cell to arrange it. This meant they could spend longer on the boat, which they both enjoyed. They could eat fish and chips out of the paper with their fingers and just have fun.

The next Monday, she went to see Dr William McKlean again. This time she went in the big black car with Abrax, who was the driver. She decided not to feel intimidated by his insistence on doing the right thing by ignoring anything happening in the back of the car. She was determined to break his silence and get him to talk to her. She sat forward in the back seat and asked him about himself. She found out that he was married with three children and lived not far from the big house. He worked regular hours unless one of the family members needed him at night. Then he would take the next morning off. He did not work on Sundays unless he had to. Apart from driving, he was also a mechanic and kept the cars in order. He had been working for the family for ten years. He liked his job as nobody bothered him. He was essentially his own boss and the pay was good. When he waited for people, he had time to read. He liked to read racing books and books about the latest cars. He told her that the family was always changing cars and it was fun to work on the latest car.

They arrived at the Institute, and Tim ushered her into the doctor's office. The doctor was smiling and friendly as he asked her to sit in a chair opposite his desk. He had her file in front of him. He asked her about the migraines.

'I have them maybe once a month. They can last from a couple of hours to three days,' she said.

'And what medication do you take for them?' he asked.

She explained that she did not believe in drugs and, when possible, she would just lie down in a dark room and wait until it passed. 'The problem is if I am out. I get symptoms before my head starts to pound. I get something like multi-coloured rain in front of my eyes, and I feel sick. There is nothing I can do except put up with it.'

'I can give you something to take as soon as the symptoms appear and then you won't suffer so much. You only need to take them if you are out if you wish.' She sighed 'I suppose it would be a good idea to carry them, but I still don't like the idea of depending on drugs to fix things' she said. He wrote her a script and handed it to her.

She told him about the music and what had happened.

She explained to him how confusing it had all been to her. She talked about the anger she felt and her inability to understand the reactions of the old man. 'It would seem that music is a big part of your life,' he commented. She tried to tell him how she thought it was not a memory as such because although she heard the music in her head, she did not associate it with any place or people. She did not remember getting lessons.

The doctor explained again the way the conscious mind used only a small part of the entire brain. 'We now know a large proportion of the unconscious mind has a lot more to do with the way we perceive the world and the way we act than was understood before. The unconscious mind may understand and respond to meaning, form emotional responses, and guide most actions largely independent of conscious awareness. Thus despite the devastating experiences, a person may appear to have lost conscious control of feelings and thoughts. Decisions and actions can be monitored by the unconscious mind. Deeply held ideals can be infused in a person's actions through their unconscious mind. So even though you don't remember on a conscious level, your unconscious mind can take over. There is a notion in 'critical mass theory' that the more people think the same way, the more people will continue to think that way. It says that some things are inbuilt in us because of our race or background. For example, if your family had, over generations, all been musicians, some of that could have rubbed off on you. You would be more likely to make the choice of music as a career. You may not realise it, but the unconscious mind may well be guiding you much of the time. How do you feel about that?'

'So even if I don't actively remember, another part of my brain does. It is why if I let go of these tightly held feelings of 'I can't do it because I have forgotten', I haven't actually forgotten. This seems to be gobble-gook to me.' She felt more confused than ever; a person should at least know what their own mind was doing.

She talked about Rick's instance for her to play for the guest. 'He shook me by the shoulders and refused to accept any option but to play. I was terrified, and I did not want to break my fingers. I was sitting there on the piano stool, wondering what to do. I just tried to do something, and thank God it came to me. The maestro said I must have been trained for a long time to become as good as he thinks I am.'

'Maybe we should explore it in today's hypnotherapy session,' he said. 'Meanwhile, I think you might be interested in the results of your tests.'

He explained 'The intelligence quota (IQ) test shows that you are probably in the top 10 percent of people around the world. It was hard to judge since one must allow for memory loss in some areas. That 's right for you because it shows you are intelligent enough to work through whatever is bothering you. The puzzles you did, demonstrate that you have an analytical brain and can fix things by using logic. The personality test would imply that you are somewhat impulsive and only apply logic when pushed. Most of the other tests we did were about psychic ability. You are aware you scored quite high in most of the tests, but some were better than others. On reflection, I decided that you are not exactly a psychic although you could become one. I believe you are an 'empath' and the more we talk, the more I can see how this is impacting on your life. You told us at dinner, you can read people, and this is true, but you are reading their feelings, not their thoughts. Empaths have a sensitivity to the energy around them. That includes colour, sound, and movement. If you can imagine that we are connected together through energy. Everything alive from animals to trees gives off some sort of energy. There is also a correlation between trauma and someone developing sensitivity to the world around them. They become hyper-vigilant. Often they may pick up on the negativity of those around them more than calmness or joy. When this happens, it saps the person of their own energy. This can, in turn, lead to psychical illness such as fibromyalgia.

'Anger is more about boundaries being taken away. At some time in your relationship to music, you may have felt powerless. And the anger had stayed there. When abused, you may feel others' anger rather than your own.

'The issue for you is that you have no control over these

feelings. So when you played the piano, you correctly read the father's need to hear particular songs. You were able to accept on one level his joy at hearing the music even though his actions did not portray it. Do you understand what I am saying?'

'I think so, but it sounds like I'm a 'brainy mess' and not going to change anytime soon.'

'What it means is that you have some work to do to unravel the different passages through your mind. As I told you right from the start, there is no easy fix. I am sure together we can work through issues that may have bothered you even throughout your life.'

'What about the other 'thingies'?'

'You mean Psychokinesis? I'm not sure where that fits yet.'

'There is another thing I am supposed to tell you.' She spoke hesitantly and sighed as she launched into the dream area of her nights, the fear, lack of sleep, and the horror when she found out that what she imagined has happened or was about to happen. She tried to explain that these thoughts were different from other dreams. 'They are so vivid, and I cannot shake them off. I dream of things that have happened, but I have never heard of. Sometimes it may be two weeks before what I have imagined happens and when I read about it in the papers or see it on my laptop news; I think my information is better than the reporters. So, you see, I'm not sure if the dream is in the past or in the future. I have other dreams about fire and running, that happens often. I wake up, and I am crying and shaking with fear. I have tried to wake myself up during the dream by telling myself it is only a dream. I become disorientated, and when I fall asleep again, the dream becomes worse. I think Rick gets sick of my disturbing him during the night so I get out of bed and go downstairs and sit in a chair until morning and then I creep upstairs and go back to bed so he won't notice'

'How long has this been going on?' he asked.

'Ever since I started to remember.'

'That is a lot to take in,' he replied. 'I can give you some sleeping pills if you think that will help, but somehow I don't believe that you will take them.'

'I keep hoping it will bring back a memory,' she said.

'Let's have some coffee and a break before I begin the next part of our session,' he suggested. Yes, she was glad of a break in what was to her an intense session.

Back in the office, he told her to sit on the special chair again, putting the blanket over her. He asked if she would allow him to video this session and she nodded. 'Now we are going to talk about the role music plays in your life. I would guess that you started to play quite young, so we will talk about your life at about eight or nine years old.' He clicked on the music, turned on the recorder that had been placed ready for the session, and gave her a small injection. Sitting down on the chair next to her, he told her to think about her breathing. 'At the Last session, I placed a suggestion in your mind to remember how to go into a trance. Do you remember how to relax, look at me and listen to my voice?' She nodded. 'Now I want you to think about when you were eight years old, can you see that now? Remember that you are telling a story about you, but nothing can hurt you now. Tell me about what happened when you were eight and at primary school.'

'I went to a school for girls. It was the best school in the state. I did not like it there and tried to get expelled. I was not good at schoolwork because a lot of the subjects mostly bored me. I hate math. I got into a lot of trouble, but I think because my parents were highly thought of, the school overlooked my misdemeanours, and I just got punished. I was good at history, sports, and music. If my teachers wanted to teach the class a new song, they taught it to me first, because I have a strong voice, and I could lead the class. I learned piano and sometimes covered three exams a year. Someone came from the music examinations board and tested me. By the time I was nearly nine, I had reached what is called an associate in music, which is at university certificate level. Now the school told my parents that they would have to get a private teacher. Mrs Pierson was a dragon, I hated her. My mother played the piano, and I loved to hear her play. She never had much formal training, but she played with soul. I was supposed to practice three hours a day. I would put 'love comics' in the middle of the page and simply do scales. My mother never noticed what I was doing because she was busy in the kitchen making our dinner.'

'Now I want you to think about you as a nine-year-old, was anything different?'

'At the end of the year, they held the World Piano Competition in Sydney. My teacher wanted me to go. Mum was pleased and wanted to help me achieve this goal. She bought me my first grown-up dress. I thought it was beautiful I chose a piece to play. It was the Tchaikovsky piece, one my mother played and it always excited my imagination.'

'Was this the music you played for Zielin Meaphei?' he asked.

'Yes, I love it, and I often play it in my head. The 'dragon lady' thought it was too hard for me, even though I could play it in my sleep. They chose a Chopin Medley instead. The 'dragon lady' thought it was better to get it perfect rather than go for something more challenging. When we went to Sydney. They had a cocktail party for the contestants from all the other countries. I was surprised because they were all grown-ups in elegant long dresses. It was the first time I thought of myself as just a child. They got to drink exotic drinks, and to my mortification, my mother asked for a glass of milk.

One boy from Russia who was twenty-three years old was kind to me. The others ignored me. We were given strict schedules and told not to be late for rehearsals. On the night, the finalists played with the orchestra in front of the judges and a full house of people. In the end, they announced the prizes beginning with the last. I kept thinking they will call my name and then there were only two and I came second and the Russian came first. We were given flowers and a cheque. Everybody clapped, but when I went out, my mother took the flowers and slapped me across the face and said there were no prizes for second. I was not allowed to stay for the party and was taken straight home.'

'I was told that if I were to do better, I would have to try harder. I started to hate my mother and hate my life. My brother had a band and played at the local dance hall. I was not allowed to go because the young people there were too ordinary. I was not allowed to play rock-n-roll because it might ruin my ear. Every chance I got, I played pop songs on a small radio. Going back to school was hard because the kids thought I was stuck up because I had played with the orchestra and had my picture in the paper. At home, I used to sneak out whenever I could. I met a couple of my brother's friends, and when Mum and Dad were out, they would come over and bring their guitars and teach me to play. We planned to run away as soon as we could get some money together.'

'Did you stop playing the piano?'

'No, I still played, but I ceased to listening. I did what was necessary to keep me out of trouble, but every chance I got, I played the guitar. I started to write songs for us to sing. I vowed that when I left home, I would never touch a piano again I hated it.'

'When did you leave home?'

'I ran away from home when I was fifteen years old. I sent my parents letters from foreign ports that I asked sailors to post for me, and so they would stop looking. I never went back.'

'Did you feel that you had done a bad thing or that your parents might be worried about you?'

'Yes, sometimes, but I had spent most of my school life in a boarding school trying to learn how to be a lady. I learned early that having money does not make you happy. Also, they kept all the money I earned from playing. I felt I owed them nothing. In all the hard times we had, the boys in my band were kinder to me than my parents ever were.'

'I think we should stop there,' he said. 'I am going to count backwards to one. You are going to wake up feeling refreshed and well. You will not remember anything. You are not worried about this as this is normal. The next time I say look into my eyes and listen to my voice, you will find it easier and easier to go into a trance.' She woke up and smiled at him.

That night when they were alone together in the bedroom, Rick asked how the session went. 'I think I'm okay, just a little strange. He told me I have intelligence within the top 10 percent of people. So I'm smart enough to work out things. He said I'm not psychic, but I'm an empath. I read feelings, not thoughts. Like I said, I can understand people.'

He rolled over on top of her, looking into her eyes, and said, 'So you think you can read me?'

She laughed. 'Of course, but I see you with rose-coloured glasses.'

'What does that mean?'

'It means, my darling, I only see the good in you and forget the rest.'

'Did he say anything else?'

'He thought that I might have picked up on your father's longing to hear music and that is why I started to play. I believe he sees me as vulnerable and not very good at looking after myself.'

Rick kissed her and said, 'I know that.'

William McKlean reviewed the video before starting to write in case 786245. He began to write in his neat hand his views of the session, starting with the counselling session.

Music may be the key to recreating a sense of the

past. The client seems cynical about parapsychology, and she desired another explanation for the sudden development of the role that music had played in this event. She wanted to say that simply having more wine could induce her to recreate the music she hears in her head. She expressed that she used songs as a way of reducing stress. Again, she seemed to be unaware of the level of expertise it would take to transfer music in her head to her fingers. This would indicate avoidance behaviour as observed in the last session. She expressed a real fear of not being able to please Mr Rodregious and stated that again she would carry out the suggestion placed in her mind by Riccardo as being an appropriate action to take.

The more interesting thing was her willingness to confess to Mr Rodregious how her memory loss had affected her. It establishes a need to find someone to connect to, such as a parent figure. She tries to stand up for herself when she feels she has an obligation to do so. Further, this indicates that she has a strong sense of right and wrong. There is a need to develop a self-awareness of her actions and a deeper sense of self in general, which is hard to do particularly when she does not know her own name.

I need to research and evaluate ways to introduce her to her own identity. She confessed to having very disturbed nights and expressed what she believes are a perception of information about future places and events. Other dreams about fire and running need further investigation.

Hypnosis: (refer to video tape 1)

Client talked about extreme events occurring at age 8/9. There seems to be a lack of parental connection during formative years. She describes herself as rebellious. She did not achieve potential in academic classes even though she was capable of doing so, citing boredom as the reason. During this time, she learnt contempt for money and privilege. There does not seem to be any evidence of empathy at this stage. Her primary outlet was in music in which she excelled. She seemed proud that she could lead a class in singing. Her choice to leave home at 15 was not an impulsive act as it took some planning to achieve this end. At this age, she seemed to be self-willed, independent, and opinionated; in other words, a typical teenager. The difference is she took it to extremes.

Questions:

What changed and in what time frame?

Are deep-seated ideas still held today in some way?

What influences were/are prevalent?

Development of avoidance personality disorder

A week later at breakfast, Riccardo announced he would be going to New York on a business trip. He said he had been neglecting his overseas commitments to be close by to help Whatune settle in. She wanted to know what he would be doing, but he did not say. She asked if she could come with him, but he said that as she did not have the proper paperwork, she would not be allowed to enter the country. Anyway, he would only be gone a week. To her, this seemed a long time to be left on her own with this family. She sensed his irritation at her request, so she refrained from further comment. She could not tell him how she was afraid of the family and how alone and isolated she was when he was not there. He intended to leave the next morning and said a 'chopper' would pick him up at his home and take him to his plane. This was a novel idea for her. Where would it land? He told her that was why the back part of his home was all grass.

She waited for a time when there was nobody home before she tackled the issues of why she could play music from her head only when pushed but could not play otherwise. If she was as good as they say, she should be able to pick up a piece of music and play.

Left alone to her own devices, she decided to try to work out the music in the piano seat. She chose what looked to be the easiest one. She stared at the notes on the paper, trying to make sense out of them. Beginning with the right hand and finding middle C, she tried to trace the tune. It was like teaching herself to learn all over again. She was patient with herself knowing that somewhere in her brain, it was there. The problem was that it was not a song she knew and she wondered if she would be better off finding music she knew. She went looking for Nara, who worked as a general maid; she edulcorated all the rooms and appeared to run messages around the house as well. She was small, dark, and had a happy disposition, always friendly and nothing bothered her. She also knew all the gossip among the staff, and if one wanted to find out anything, she was a good place to start. Whatune asked her if there was any other music stored in the house. She led the way to a small storeroom at the end of the passage, produced a key, and opened it. Inside there were several boxes of papers and music. Sitting down on the floor she looked for one that she may know. She found some Christmas music and although it was not Christmas, she thought she could learn these. She took them back to the piano, stared hard at the words as well as the music. She could remember 'Silent Night' she hummed it and then played it. It worked; she could play it in no time at all. She found 'Brahms Lullaby' and found she could read the music and sing as well. She played it several times until she was sure of the notes. She felt determined to be able to read the music and not just play what was in her head. It was not as easy as she had first thought as she felt there was something inside blocking her progress. Could her love of music override her anger at the instrument itself? She did not have trouble with the guitar. She knew the symbols for frets straight away. She picked up a more complicated piece and tried that. The notes were right but the beat was not; too slow, she thought. She read it through tapping her fingers on her knee to get the timing right and then played it again. Slowly, slowly it came back to her. It had taken a lot of concentration to get this far.

She went into the kitchen to find something to eat. She did not want to disturb the staff as she could do it herself. She was unprepared for Adora, who was the cook. The kitchen was her domain, and family never came in. She met with Jacinda once a week to discuss menus and ordering. She kept household receipts and orders in a book and was meticulous about her job. Whatune introduced herself and dropped down on one of the chairs, explaining that she was just looking for something to eat. Adora told her she just needed to call or ring the bell and someone would take her order. Not to be put off, Whatune told Adora that she liked doing things for herself. She loved cooking and hoped that they could become friends. Adora was not your typical cook in that she was young and educated, having gained a diploma in nutrition and nourishment at Patras Technological Institute. She was dressed in neat but functional clothes comprising of a white shirt and navy blue skirt over which she had placed a plain blue apron. Her brown hair was tied up in a ponytail, and she had no makeup on and did not need it as her skin was clear and smooth. Of course, she knew all about this odd person in the home that refused to conform to convention. There was speculation about Riccardo's affair and some bets on how long it would last or if they would marry. Whatune noticed a small ginger cat at her feet and picked it up and gave it a cuddle. 'What is its name?' she asked.

'It just wandered in here one day when it was still a small kitten, and I did not have the heart to put it out. I just call it Ailuro,' she said. Adora thought she would like having this one as a friend; just because she did not put on any airs and seemed genuinely nice. 'I could get you something out if you wish.'

'No, it's not necessary. Just point me in the right direction. I'll even wash up, so you will not know I've been here.' She laughed. Adora asked her if she liked Greek food.

'Yes, very much, but I like to cook Italian, Chinese, and Indonesian as well.'

'We must trade recipes then,' she said. Adora watched as Whatune prepared some lunch and made a pot of tea. Then to her amusement, she sat down at the kitchen table and had no intention of going into the dining room. Adora got out another cup, and they drank their tea together and talked about nothing much. Adora had indeed found a new friend. True to her word, she washed up before going back to tackle the piano.

By the end of the day, she was happy with the progress she was making. She put the music away and played and sang a couple of old songs that she knew.

As both the old man and Jacinda would be out for the evening, she had an evening meal alone and retired early, hoping she could get some sleep. She decided to sleep in the single bed in the nanny's room. She liked this place; it felt snug and comfortable. She thought it had good vibes or something. She settled down and slept about two hours and then dreamed about Rick.

He was in a room with two 'suits'she did not know. An Asian-looking man was sitting across from him. They were having a heated discussion about some containment of guns. It has something to do with orders and consignment numbers. She felt Rick was being threatened and was sitting on some kind of edge. She woke up and thought, 'How strange. Why would he be even talking to this man? And why would he need bodyguards at a business meeting?' She wanted to put it from her mind, but the questions kept coming back. What did she know about his business? She tried to think over anytime he had said something about his work. He was in import and export, he owned some ships, was part-owner in some other business enterprise. He worked hard keeping everything going, most of which his father had started, and he was in the process of taking over. He also had some companies that he owned in his own right.

She knew that was the end of sleep for a while. She crept down the steps and into the sunroom, closing all the doors so as not to wake anybody. She just wanted the music wash over her, making her forget the dream and things that were none of her concern. She thought about the boat and the sea; she played a new song that she made up as she went along. Then she thought it sounded quite good and maybe she should write it down. She thought she would get some music paper and pencils tomorrow. She looked at the sky and realised that it was today and she had better go to bed for a while. However, as soon as she got back into bed, she started to worry. What has he got himself into? She hated anything to do with guns and thought the world would be better off if nobody made them. In her eyes, killing was wrong no matter what the circumstance. She wondered if security guards carried guns. Now she was getting fanciful. 'Of course, they don't,' she thought. 'It's just all those muscles that make their suits bulge.' She fell asleep for two hours and then got up in time for breakfast.

Going to breakfast, she tried to put a positive spin on the day. She told the old man that she had indeed learned to play music. She asked if she could shop for some music paper and pencils.

'Just write a list of what you want, and I'll have Abrax get them for you,' he said.

Jacinda announced that she had a meeting with her charity group today and they were thinking of doing a concert for refugees. This meant that everybody would be out of the house again and she could write down the music from last night. Also, she looked forward to spending some time with Adora. After breakfast, she went back to bed for a while trying to catch up on sleep before she attempted to write down the music she had played last night.

The good doctor rang in the morning and asked if she could change their meeting for the next day. She agreed and thought she ask Rick if she could use his car when he rang that afternoon. It would be fun if she could go out on her own and she knew how to get there.

When Riccardo rang, he sounded groggy and grumpy. He asked how she was getting along and she told him she was fine. She said she had an idea for a song she wanted to write down. She said she was concerned for him and wanted to know if everything was working out as he wanted. Riccardo assured her that his business was going well, he had a big night, the night before and laughed that he was getting staid and not as used to 'all-nighters' as he used to be, and he would be home in the next couple of days. She told him she missed him and did not want to sleep in their bed and had been using the nanny room. He thought that was funny as he thought she would have liked the luxury of having a big bed all to herself.

Chapter 9

THE CONFRONTATION

Dr William McKlean prepared for his interview with Whatune. He requested this time mainly because he wanted to talk her when she had some time away from Riccardo. He was concerned about Riccardo's influence on her. The fact that she was prepared to break her fingers because he suggested it was worrying. Looking back at the notes, he saw that her main contact had been with him and that she was in a sense isolated from other social interactions. He needed to investigate at what level the abuse was still going on. How was she dealing with it? He realised that she would be better off if she would cease the relationship altogether to concentrate on developing and controlling her other skills. Because of her sensitivity to emotion, he needed to keep a non-judgmental approach to anything she may express.

She set out to visit the institute driving Rick's car again. Dr McKlean answered the door and ushered her into his room. He told her that Tim had finished his research, but the other members of the staff were back, and she would meet some in due course. She sat down opposite him and noticed a change in his demeanour. He asked her how she had coped with Rick being away. She told him she was fine. He looked at the tape on the desk and turned it on.

'I want to talk to you about your relationship with Riccardo,' he said. 'Do you know that I received all the files from the hospital when they transferred you into my care? I am conscious of the fact that your story and the data are somewhat different. I think you have left out information that would help me to help you.'

'I don't like talking about those days,' she said.

'I understand that it may embarrass you, but you need to voice exactly what went on. For instance, I know you were not living in the house without his permission, but that is what you both led the hospital staff to believe. I know he abused you sexually.'

She told him about the agreement they came to, about the locket she wore around her neck, and tried to explain about the depression and fear she felt all the time. 'I really just wanted to be dead' she said, 'and I did not care what happened to me. He hurt me, but it was my fault because I let it happen. I was not strong enough to oppose him. But faced with the possibility that he might unintentionally kill me, I bolted.'

'I want to make sure I understand you right,' he said. 'You believe in this contract that you signed in your blood?'

'Yes, and part of that contract is I will never say anything that will get him into trouble.'

'And now, what do you believe?'

'Things are different because there are other people around and so our emotions cannot get out of control. Anyway, I really care for him, and he has told me he loves me. I'm not sure about how I feel about that, but I never lie to him, and so I don't say I love him.'

'How do you describe him, what would you say when I ask you to tell me what he is like?'

'Well, he's attractive to look at, has a pulchritudinous anatomy. I think he can be kind, but he is spoilt and used to getting everything he wants. I don't believe he cares much for people who work for him. He has been brought up to assume that money and power can solve everything. But on the other hand, he works hard to keep everything running. He has a sophisticated, urban way about him that hides some sort of anger or discontent. He can be kind to me and then sometimes he will hurt me. There are times when he comes home from work angry, and he takes it out on me. I don't know why he is like this. He tells me he loves me. Sometimes I think he likes the idea of inflicting pain as a way of control.'

The doctor challenged her by saying, 'Can you understand that this relationship is not the usual kind of relationship?'

She said stubbornly, 'He saved my life, I owe him.'

'Or is it just convenient to stay there?'

'I have thought about it, and there may be an element of truth in that, but I don't think I would stay if that were the only reason. Sometimes Rick gets a little rough with me, but then he is also kind to me. Did you know the old man offered me a lot of money to get out of his life? If I didn't care, I would have taken the money. Besides, I think I am getting stronger now, I don't want to be dead, and I am trying to develop my music, and that makes me hopeful that in some way, it will all come together.'

'What is the most important thing you want to get out of coming to see me?' he asked.
'I want to get my memory back; I want to know who I am and I want to know for certain I haven't harmed anyone. I want to be a whole person. I want the dreams to stop, and I don't want to know if people are going to die.'

'That is what I thought,' he said. 'Of course, it is a big task because you cannot change who you are. You can learn to manage it a lot better than you are now. Just as you said you will not lie to Riccardo, I don't want you to lie to me. If you are to get through this, you have to trust me and believe that what you say in this room stays in this room.'

She felt tears coming to her eyes; she was not sure if they were out of self-pity or relief that she could talk to someone. 'I want to make it work between Rick and me,' she said. 'Sometimes I feel as if I am all alone in this world, even when there are people all around me. I wonder why that is?'

He tried to explain the impact of having unique skills which could make one feel different from others, and that was because they were different. 'How you developed these skills is still a bit of a mystery. I can surmise that the time you spent alone without any memory to guide you may have enhanced your perceptions of your world, but at this point, I don't know,' he said. He stood up and told her he would see her in two weeks. 'In the meantime, I want you to think about making independent decisions, not rely on Riccardo to provide you with all the answers and question what he tells you to do, particularly if it goes against your own instinct.'

'I'll try.' She smiled.

That night, Rick came home, and she was happy to see him. He bought her a diamond bracelet for a coming-home gift.

Chapter 10

HEARTBREAK

A week later, Jacinda announced they had set a date for the charity concert. Whatune asked if she could do something. Jacinda sneered at her, saying, 'There is nothing you could do except get in the way. We know how to run a charity concert, and we have famous guest stars.'

'I would really like to do something, perhaps I could sing in the break. Nobody would notice that much, and you don't have to put me on the program, but I would feel as if I had done something,'

'No.' Jacinda said emphatically. Riccardo spoke at the table. 'She can sing, you know, and how can it hurt?' They both looked at their father to say something.

'They tell me she can sing,' he said.

After dinner, the 'the Old Man' came and sat on the chair opposite the piano and said to her, 'They say you can sing, so sing.'

She sang 'Ave Maria'.

She was not prepared for the reaction she got. Out of the corner of her eye, she saw great tears rolling down his face. He did not bother to wipe them away; they just dropped on the front of his shirt. She felt his heart break. It was as if years of grief came over him in a few minutes. When she had finished the song, he got up without a word and went into his study. She looked enquiringly at Rick.

'It was a trick of the light. You were not to know that was one of my mother's favourite songs and you sang it exactly the same as she did. In the half-light, it seemed as if she was sitting there. She used to wear her hair down in the evenings at home like yours is now. I have never seen my father cry before. I suggest that if you play for Father again, you put the overhead light on.'

'I don't know why I sang that song,' she thought. 'It is not as if it is one of my favourites. Maybe it is something to do with this empathic thing, and I sang what he wanted to hear. Could it be true that I can read people more than the average person?'

When they went up to the bedroom, she noticed that Rick seemed edgy. He hugged her and said, 'You always surprise me. You have come into our lives like a whirlwind, and you turn everything upside down.'

'I'm sorry,' she said. 'I don't know why I sang that song, it just came to me.' She buried her head in his shoulder and sighed. 'I do not mean to upset things, it just happens.'

'I know. I just wish you wouldn't sometimes.'

The next morning at breakfast, she noticed that the old man had changed somehow, something in him had shifted. She could not work out what it was that was different. She hoped that it was because he was able to cry for the first time since his wife had died. She could think of nothing to say to him and thought it best if she pretended that nothing had changed. She wondered if the others noticed or was it just her.

It was about mid-morning when Jacinda knocked on the nanny's room door. Whatune jumped, not expecting anyone to interrupt her morning perusal of world news. Jacinda looked upset and started to verbally attack her at once. 'So this is where you stay.' She said sarcastically. 'I want to know what you have done with my father. You are a witch and somehow have changed him just like you have done to my brother,' she fired at her.

Whatune asked mildly, 'What is wrong?'

'You should know. I got called to father's study, and I am told that I must let you play at the concert. So, you can have your chance to sing during the break. I will not acknowledge you on the program. You can't rehearse with the cast, and you can only have one spotlight.'

'That is all I want. Thank you.'

Jacinda peeked into the room curiously, 'I thought you lived with my brother? Don't tell me that you really use this room?'

'It's none of your business,' she said, closing the door firmly, not wanting any more conflict. She took a long breath and thought she would not let Jacinda get to her. Why had the 'the old man' come to her defences?

It was not like him; he never admitted he was wrong about anything. Had he changed his stance on her? It would be nice if he had; she could imagine one less person she would have to watch for.

Three weeks after the confrontation with Jacinda, the concert was held in a large concert hall. It was a black-tie affair with a party arranged back at the house after the show. Whatune was nervous; she tried to keep out of everyone's way by staying home until the last minute before she would sing.

She took Rick's car and parked it around the back of the concert hall. She showed the security guard her ID that Jacinda had given to her. She had on the black skirt and white shirt she wore for Ziehn Meapha. She waited in the wings until all the lights went out and all came back on again. She asked one of the stage hands to put a stool in the centre front of the stage. Then she walked out and sat on the stool and played and sang three protest songs. Each song had been carefully chosen to make people think about what the concert was about. The last song was called 'Wake up your mind.' About half the people had started to walk out, and a lot of people just sat down again. It seemed as if she came alive on the stage; although shy, she became outgoing, and her personality came across as compelling.

Jacinda's partner was one of the committees; a tall, distinguished man in his late fifties called Paul. He stood up to go out and then fell down in his chair.

She looked at him in surprise. 'You look as if you have seen a ghost,' she said.

'I have,' he said. 'There is only one person I know who can sing the saddest songs with the sweetest voice and that is Marion. I thought she was dead. I must talk to her.' Jacinda told him she was her brother's girlfriend, but they must get out the front to mingle if they were to get any money. 'You can talk to her at home later. I am dying to know all the dirt you have on her.'

As soon as her song was finished, she went back to the house and changed into a short dark-green dress. She went down and drank a whisky dry for luck. The lounge room had been changed; the chairs had been pushed against the walls. Thus, it created a place where a lot of people could mingle. Jacinda had hired a band that was setting up. She went over to talk to them. They had a keyboard, and she played on it for a while. Then she borrowed a guitar and sang a song into the mike just for the fun of it while they tested the equipment. She had just got another whisky dry when people started coming in. She slipped out the back to have a cigarette.

Jacinda and Paul came out to find her. 'It seems you were a great success tonight,' Jacinda said. 'By the way, I believe you know Paul. I've got to get back, but you two should stay and talk.'

'Marion, I can't believe it's you, where have you been?' She looked confused, and he said. 'Surely you have not forgotten me? You know who I am, don't you?'

'I think I may have seen you in the papers, but I don't recognise you.'

'People don't forget their first boyfriend.'

'I have amnesia,' she said. 'Where did we meet and how long ago was that?'

'You were very young, and we were in Germany, you had a band and played in one of the clubs there. You knew me there with an emphasis on the biblical meaning of *knew*. You broke my heart.' She did not know what to say. 'Is Marion my real name and what is my last name?'

'We never got that far to worry about last names.'

She needed to get away from him; it was getting too weird. 'I need to find Riccardo,' she said and ran as fast as she could to the house.

When she found him, he was talking to a group of older people. 'May I join in.' She said but at the same time pulling his arm away. Surprised more than irritated, he turned to her. She whispered in his ear. 'I just met a person who said he knows me. He said my name is Marion.' Riccardo excused himself from the group, and they went to look for the man. He was hugging and kissing Jacinda, who was laughing and flirting with him. Riccardo was holding her hand firmly as they approached. Paul looked up enquiringly. Riccardo asked him if he knew his girlfriend. He grinned at them saying, 'I was her first boyfriend when she was playing with a band in Germany. One usually does not forget the first, yes?' 'Are you sure that this is the same person and her name is Marion?'

'Of course, she made records, and you can look them up if you don't believe me, I think I might even have some at home. I could look if you like.' He turned back to Jacinda, giving a big display of affection and ignoring them. Marion felt he was not sincere in his attentions towards Jacinda, just playing around. Marion looked at Riccardo.

'I don't know what to do,' she said. I want to put a sack over my head and hide.'

'No, my dear, this is the time to flaunt it. People have asked me if you will sing again. I will introduce you to everyone now, and you will sing with your head held high, and we will get it over with in one hit, right? Be a good girl and get your guitar and give it to them.' She felt dazed. How could she stand up in front of these people who knew her by a name they had made up and pretend it was all a joke? She thought to herself, 'I must love him to do something so silly.' But she knew she would do it for him anyway.

She came back with the guitar and Riccardo introduced his friend Marion to the crowd. She sang two songs that came to mind. Her pure voice stopped the noise, and most people just listened to her sing. A couple of people asked if she could sing particular songs. One she knew was 'Danny Boy'. She put the guitar down and sang without any instrument. Another request she knew she started to play it and a big lump came in her throat, apologising saying she had forgotten the words. She sang one other song and stopped.

People clapped and then turned back to what they were doing before she started to sing. She thought her ordeal was over. Riccardo gave one of his rare public displays of affection by kissing and hugging her.

Paul managed to escape and came across to her and told her why she could not sing the song he had requested. 'It was because you wrote that song for me. He said. I believe you have not actually forgotten me. Anytime you want more just call, and we could make great music together'.

She did not answer him and just walked away. Her mind was in turmoil, thinking, 'He just hit on me.' Should she go to him anyway, if he had the answers? She felt she could not trust him; now more than ever, she should trust that instinct to guide her.

The Ziehn Meapha came over to speak to her. She had not seen him in the crowd and was pleased to have a chance to talk to him. 'That was captivating.'

'I am so happy to see you again,' she said. 'I have wanted to get in touch with you for a while. I did not know where to find you.' He gave her a card and told her he would be happy to see her again. She agreed to give him a call and make an appointment to talk to him. She said she was sorry about the last time they met and thought she owed him an explanation. He brushed it off, telling her that Sarvas had said about that night, and she was not to worry about it.

'I have an idea I would like to put to you. Maybe we could do lunch?'

He smiled and told her please call.

She felt that she could not cope with the crowd anymore and as soon as she could, she went up to the bedroom and lay down on the bed, intending to talk to Rick when he came up. However, she quickly fell asleep and did not hear him come in. She half awoke when she felt him removing all her clothes. The cool air brushed her skin, and she felt his naked body touching hers. She wanted to sleep, but his persistence soon brought her awake. His kisses sent shivers all the way down to her toes. She felt happy to have him close to her again, and she revelled in the pleasure he gave her.

When she could catch her breath again, she thanked

him for helping her through the night. 'Are you upset in any way about that vulgarian Paul?' she asked.

'No, I don't care what your name is. Anyway, Marion suits you.'

'You introduced me as a friend. I thought we were a bit more than that.'

'I had to do that for convention's sake. A lot of the people there are my father's guests, and I would not upset their high moral code to explain things to people if they asked.'

The next morning was particularly trying for Marion. It was hard enough to learn a new name for herself, without Jacinda enjoying her discomfort. She could feel Jacinda's contempt for her; she tried to keep her eyes down and played a song in her head. The old man was silent, and Riccardo seemed preoccupied. She wondered what the matter was but decided not to go there.

'Now I know all about you,' Jacinda quipped. 'Paul told me that you are lying and you have not forgotten anything, and he said he could prove it. He requested a song, and he told me you could not sing it and nearly cried because you missed him. Why am I not surprised your nickname was the Ice Maiden, and what were you doing in a nightclub with a bunch of boys so young? You put on a face of an innocent child and all the time you are sleeping around.'

The old man looked up and said, 'Enough.'

Marion knew that he was feeling angry because of the tension between the girls. He hated there to be any unpleasantness at the table. Jacinda looked down at her plate with a sour look on her face. She was not about to give up that easily. She tried to put a smooth voice on and announced to all that the charity concert had been a great success and that they had raised more money than they expected. Some people had come back after they have bought a ticket and written a cheque and had given again. Riccardo looked up and suggested that it was because the songs Marion had sung attacked their conscience. Jacinda shrugged as if to say, 'Have it your way.'

The old man announced he would be going into the office that morning to get ready for a board meeting. Riccardo said he may not be home for dinner as he had a lot of work to catch up on. Marion thought she would have to put up with verbal sniping from Jacinda; however, she would be out all day sorting out the funds for their charity and then she was going to dinner with Paul. Looking across the table to see if she could get any sign that her comments affected her enemy. Relief flooded into Marion as she realised she would be home alone the whole day.

Marion felt easier when she could escape to her room and read the news on the laptop. She waited until she was sure that everyone was out of the house before she made her first call. It was to the good doctor and told him about the evening. She explained she had no idea about being in Germany or Paul. She said about the invitation Paul had made to her. No matter how much she wanted to know about herself, she would not meet him. He was just creepy. She also told him she was afraid to say anything to Rick because he might take it the wrong way and get angry. The doctor was soothing telling her that a first name was a start and not to worry about anything else. He said there may be a way he could extract the second name when he felt she was ready. He suggested that she write down the names of songs as they came to her because later they might be able to place them in a time frame.

She wandered down to the garage to see if Abrax was there. He straightened up as soon as she entered the room. 'I did not mean to startle you,' she said. 'I was hoping you could help me. I think you might find it a bit strange, but I don't know the city well. I want to take someone out for lunch, and I don't know where to go. I would like somewhere nice but not too flashy. Could you help me?' He smiled at her; of course, he would help, would she like him to decide? 'Yes,' she said. 'Do you know if anyone wants the car tomorrow?' He checked his diary and stated that they needed it in the evening as there was a board meeting but not during the day. 'Do you mind helping me?' She asked. She showed him the card Ziehn Meapha had given her and said she wanted to take him to lunch. He suggested that they pick him up at 10.30 a.m. and that would give them time to get settled and have lunch before a rush begins. She thanked him again and walked back to the house and rang Ziehn Meapha and asked him out to brunch. She told him she would pick him up at 10.30 a.m. the next day if that was all right by him.

The next day, she felt anxious about taking Ziehn Meapha out. It was something she had never done before, and she had not consulted Rick about it. The doctor had suggested that she should make some decisions for herself and this was what she was doing. Taking Abrax and the limousine seemed to be a nice touch. She fussed over what to wear; she hated dressing up, but at the same time she wanted to appear smart. This was the single biggest thing she thought she would ever do.

She arrived at the building which was a grey nondescript-looking building, where maestro had his office and went in to get him. There she had a chance to really look at him. The room was big enough, but it was cluttered. There was a piano on the back wall and stacked on top of it were piles of music. A large desk was situated in the centre of the room, and it too was cluttered with all sorts of timetables and files.

The room suited him. He was not tall and had dark greying hair, blue eyes and glasses that were clear rimmed, and a generous mouth. He was dressed in a blue suit, white shirt, and pale blue tie. Most of important for her was that he gave off a generous and kind feeling. There was nothing pretentious about him, but he was the type that would not stand nonsense and would call things as he saw them. In other words, he would be straight with her, and this is what she needed. He greeted her warmly, and she told him she had a car waiting. Once in the car, she confessed that she had let Abrax make arrangements for her as she did not get out much.

The restaurant was small and intimate with booths where customers could talk without being bothered. The decor was old fashioned with red-and-white checkered tablecloths and flowers on every table. The menu was in Greek, and she had to ask him to order for her. She told him she liked most Greek food, so he ordered quesadilla and salad and the same for her. She asked him to get a bottle of red wine to go with the food.

'Now I am curious,' he said. 'You seem to have gone to a lot of trouble to take an old man out.'

'There is a lot I want to say to you, it is hard to start.' She told him about herself and her connection to music. She reminded him that he said it must have taken a lot of years to get to the standard she played at. She explained that she could not remember how to even read music and how she had to relearn it all over again. She went on to say that she did not sleep well and had taken to going to the piano in the middle of the night. At first, it was just to drive the dreams away and then she started to write down the music that she played. She now had a big box full of music. Every songwriter dreams of writing a symphony at some time. 'I have written one.' She held her breath, wondering what he would say. He just nodded and let her continue. 'Now the question is what to do next. I believe from what I heard on the news that there is 45 percent of people out of work. I am sure that must affect you.'

'Of course,' he said. 'In fact, it has come to the point that the orchestra may have to disband. I have agonised over this, knowing that these people need work to help their families and I don't want to be the one to put them off, but there is simply not enough work.'

She took a deep breath and said, 'What if I could get the funding, would you be willing to stake your reputation on an unknown writer, particularly if you could keep the orchestra together?' He did not comment straight away, and they continued to have brunch, which was delicious. Then he said, 'Tell me about it.'

She expanded on the theme of the music. 'It is a story of the sea and seabirds. I have a great affinity to the sea. It is a story about pride, hope, and dashed hope then one's ability to rise above all odds and succeed where others would fail. It is a joyous event meant to raise the spirits of those who listen. In a way, it is my story put to music.'

He mused about the thought of bringing something fresh to a staid audience. 'Of course, I would like to see the music and hear you play it before I decide to take such a risk,' he said. 'I know you have a lot of talent and if you think it is good, and then it probably is good. If you could raise the money to fund the orchestra in rehearsal, it would help all those who are trying to support their families. As to my reputation, I am an old man, I don't care what people think of me.'

She felt ecstatic; he would hear her out, and that is all she wanted, for now. 'Let's have another glass of wine to celebrate our collaboration in a new adventure.' She gave the waiter her card and called Abrax to pick them up at the front. She found it hard to contain her joy on the drive home because she was sure he would love it. At home, she went into the kitchen and told Adora that she could make her own evening meal and that she should take time off. She danced around the room and decreed that as nobody was going to be home, she could help herself.

The wine had gone to her head, but she did not care. She went to the piano and played her seabirds song. Then she sat down with a piece of paper and wrote a timeline. She intended to ask Rick for a loan of money, and she would insist that it be drawn up into a contract. She knew he would give it to her if she asked but she wanted to be independent. She had an idea that she would not say anything to anybody until she was sure she could pull it all off. She would have to choose her moment.

Her ambition had grown, and she started to think of making a recording and selling it. What if she made a videotape to promote it? They may be able to sell it overseas. She stopped herself from dreaming and thought about concentrating on the job at hand.

Chapter 11

THE UNWELCOME GUEST

The next day, she came down to earth with a thud. She was playing the piano when a man appeared at the side door. He said he was looking for Riccardo. She told him he was at work and would not be home until 6.00 p.m. He walked into the room and introduced himself as Nikator. He spoke in a broken form of English that she found hard to understand; however, his meaning was clear. He seemed to 'slave over' her, and she felt disturbingly uncomfortable. He was a big man, wide as he was tall, with a big stomach that hung over the belt that held up his jeans. He had light brown wavy hair. Hazel eyes that were almond shaped and spaced wide apart and a full mouth, suggesting he laughed a lot. He had the overall appearance of an overgrown schoolboy. She told him her name and suggested he come back at 6.00 p.m. But he just dropped into a chair and said he would wait. She turned around to continue to play when he said, 'Where can a man get a drink around here?'

She sighed and got up and asked what he wanted. 'A beer if you can,' he said. She went into the fridge to the kitchen and found a Heineken and brought it out for him. He was intent on engaging her in conversation. 'What do you do around here?' he asked. 'I live here,' she murmured.

She instantly did not like him; he seemed presumptuous and arrogant. She wondered how he had managed to get in past the security should she call them or should she call Rick. She decided on the latter as she did not want to cause offence. She went to another room and called the office. The phone switched to voice mail, and she left a message. Within a few minutes, Rick was on the phone, and she told him about Nikator. He did not sound too pleased but said he would come home as soon as he could get away. In the meantime, she was to entertain him and keep him happy. She suggested that he should maybe bring home, some more beers.

She went to find Faustus. He was sitting in a small office, reading. He stood up as soon as she entered. She told him that they would have a guest for the night as it seemed as if Nikator had no intention of moving anytime soon. Reluctantly, she went back to talk to him. He told her he was on holiday from Thessaloniki, the capital of Macedonia and the second largest city in Greece. He told her he was proud of his Jewish heritage that had been passed down in spite of wars and bigotry. He told her about his great friendship with Riccardo. 'You are not from around here,' he stated. 'Where are you from?'

She tried to look vague and said she had been travelling

from different places. Quickly she said, 'Do you like music?' hoping to get him onto another track.

'I heard you play when I came in, and it was a bit too high-brow for me,' he said. 'I can play the guitar for you if you like,' she said hopefully.

He nodded and she went to get it. She played some flamenco type of music, and he seemed to like it. 'You are good, and you look good too, I think I am going to like you,' he said. She tried to think of something else to do with him. She realised she was no good at being a hostess and wished someone else was there who could help her. 'Would you like to walk in the garden?' She was feeling desperate now, wanting to get as far away from him as she could. She was giving into unreasonable fear brought about because of the feelings he was giving off. She perceived that he saw her as a sex object.

'Only if you get me another beer,' he said.

She was hoping there was another in the fridge but there was not. She went back to tell him Riccardo would bring some home when he came. 'Yes, we will walk then.' He swung his arm around her waist and pulled her closer to him. Fear was welling up in her; she could feel his intent. She wondered if it would be any use to run away from him. Just then to her relief, she heard the sound of the car. 'Riccardo is here now.' She thanked God and all her lucky stars that she was saved from this brute. They went to meet the car and as soon as Rick got out of the car Nikator gave him a big hug, kissing him on both cheeks. 'My friend, I have come to save you again, this time from the boredom of having to work all the time. I have three days off, so I come to see you. This lovely lady has been keeping me company until you came home.' Quickly, she butted in and said she had work to do, so she would leave them to it. She moved as fast as she could without being rude.

She went to their room and stayed there until Rick came in to get ready for dinner. He was not happy and glared at her. 'When I was doing National Service, I did something rash and could have been killed. Nikator saved my life, and I owe him. He likes you, and you must be nice to him.'

'Of course, I'll be polite to him, but I am not going to go to near him.' Rick grabbed her by the shoulders and shook her hard. He was infuriated now. 'You will do as I say and be very nice. It is only for a few days. Do you understand me?' Shock ran through her. She knew what he was asking her to do and it made her feel sick. This man wanted to touch her and maybe even do more, and he was going to let him. He said he loved her then; how could he even suggest that she be very nice? Maybe he did not understand this man's intentions, but she thought he did because that was the kind of man Nikator was. Even though the weather was warm, she put on as many clothes as she could to cover up as much as she could. And they went down to dinner. During dinner, he did not hide his thoughts and stared at her steadily. She kept her eyes down and did not say anything. She wondered if the others had noticed or if the things she was feeling were of her own making. Riccardo had agreed to take a few days off and suggested they go fishing. 'That sounds just the best thing,' Nikator said. For a moment, she thought that they would go together and she could stay at the house. But that idea was soon dashed by Nikator telling them that the three of them would have a very good time.

Nikator said after dinner he would like to go for that walk in the garden that she had promised. She was about to say no when she saw the look in Rick's eyes, challenging her to refuse. She thought she was going to get 'it', whichever way she chose. So to save face, she agreed. She walked quickly around the grounds, telling him everything she knew about the flowers. When she was out of breath, he grabbed her and pulled her to him until their bodies were touching and he tried to kiss her; she pushed him away, but he pulled her back and pushed his hand up to her breast, his lips closing onto her neck. With power she did not know she possessed, she pushed him away so hard that he stumbled a couple of feet away and she ran into the house. She did not mean to push him so hard; how was it that she could drive such a big man so far? She went straight to her room and sat on the bed, shaking. And this was day 1. Whatever was she going to do at the beach house when there was only one bed? She went into the nanny room and fell asleep. She did not hear Rick come in and go to sleep. She dreamed of the three of them in the bed fighting for a piece of each other and woke up, crying. Rick came into the room and put his arms around her rocking her back and forth as one would do to a baby, telling her it was just a dream and everything would be okay. He stayed beside her in the single bed for the rest of the night.

In the morning, everyone acted as if nothing had happened. The three of them drove down to Pilos. Riccardo called ahead to make sure the boat would be ready to go. She had put her bathers on and a pair of jeans over that, a long-sleeved T-shirt and hung a towel over all, a big hat pulled down as low as she could get it, and to complement that, she had a big pair of dark glasses. She felt like the abominable snowman because she had so many clothes on and she wondered what would happen when it got too hot to keep it all in place. Riccardo ignored her, but he thought she's got pluck if she thinks she can carry this off.

Nikator acted as if this was the biggest adventure of his life and insisted that he get some beer and wine for the trip. He already knew he was going to enjoy this journey. He had big plans to get something from the friend whose life he saved.

While he was buying the drinks, she turned to Rick and said, 'If he tries it I am going to kill him. I am going to sleep with a big knife, and anybody tries anything I'll use the knife and I mean this.' He did not have a chance to reply because Nikator came back to the car. Riccardo's body felt tense, and he realised too late that this was the worst of ideas. He would have to take Nikator aside and warn him to be careful. Then he would have to take her aside and 'belt the shit out of her' if she made things so uncomfortable that he could not get rid of his 'friend'. It might be a game for his friend, Riccardo thought, but it was not to him. What if he had to choose? No, she must be obedient to his wishes, but she also had a right to defend herself. There was a place where it has to stop. A slap and a tickle were okay, but he could not take her.

Out in *Yolanda* where the water was so clear, one could see the fish swimming; the boys set up the lines. Marion said she would just watch.

Riccardo was used to her quiet ways and was not bothered if she just sat and looked at the sea. Anyway, there was not enough room for the three of them to fish at the same time; he started to calm down. He had thought of how he would handle things, so now he was able to make light of the day. He waited until she went below to make something to eat before he spoke to Nikator about her.

'I can tell you like Marion,' he said. 'I should tell you that she is my girlfriend and she is special.'

Nikator looked at him, not believing him. 'You have so many girls it is hard to keep up. I did not think you would mind sharing.'

'I'm in love with her and will probably marry her,' Riccardo replied. 'She is a little strong-willed, and I am afraid if you try anything with her, she has threatened to kill you.'

'I don't believe she could do that.' He laughed and said, 'I am sorry if I misunderstood your relationship. I wouldn't have thought she was your type. Not mine either. A bit too posh and stuck up, if you ask me.'

'She is a lovely lady, kind, and I trust her, which is more than I can say for other women I've met.'

'So you want me to treat her as a sister?'

'That would be a good idea.'

'That doesn't mean that I am not going to try and win her over,' Nikator challenged.

Riccardo said, 'Don't say I did not warn you.'

She brought the men sandwiches and cold beer. They both smiled and thanked her. She felt something had changed. The air between them was evident; maybe Riccardo had said something, and now she was able to relax. She pulled her hat down and closed her eyes. It was a shock when she noticed the boat was coming towards the town and she was lifted and thrown overboard. The next thing, Nikator jumped in with her. She splashed about for a while getting, her hat and towel and throwing them in the boat. Then she swam around the other side; she could easily outswim him even when he tried to catch up. Riccardo was laughing so hard he could barely pull her in. She picked up the fish bucket and poured it over his head.

Nikator climbed in on the back of the boat in time to see her display of temper and laughed too; he could understand why Riccardo was in love with her.

It turned out to be a reasonable period for them. She decided to let things go for the moment for the sake of peace. They let Nikator sleep in the bed because of his size while they slept on the couch together. Rick sighed. 'Just like the old days.' Nikator tried to kiss her a couple of times, and she let him peck at her, but when she felt his intent was to see how far he could get, she put a stop to it.

Pantos, the boy from the town, was happy because they kept him busy running errands for them and he got to drive the car for two days straight. His family was happy because of the fresh fish, which they cooked with olive oil and lemon juice. They mostly ate out as Riccardo did not want Marion to be seen as just the cook, although he did not tell her that. He knew he had done the wrong thing by her and could in some way understand her anger. He realised that he would have to make it up to her for what he had expected of her. When it was time to drive back, everybody seemed to be in good spirits.

But both Marion and Riccardo were happy to see Nikator

go back home. Something was bothering her, though; she realised that under the urban guise, Rick still had the potential to become violent. But it was more than that; he was prepared to go along and let Nikator sleep with her if that was what he wanted. He was the jealous type, so it seemed inexplicable for him to even think along those lines.

He came home early in the afternoon; she was reading on the small bed in the nanny room. 'I have something to show you. Come with me.' He grabbed her hand and pulled her to her feet then led her outside. Sitting in the driveway was a shiny white car. He gave her the keys. 'This is my way of making up to you for what happened with Nikator.' He had a big smile on his face. Suddenly, she was outraged. How dare he think that buying a car could make up for the fact that he was willing to let her become a plaything for a friend? 'That's it. It's over,' she said. She took the necklace off and gave it to him and walked down the driveway.

She did not care where she was going; she could not see for the tears coming out of her eyes. What a fool she had been to think Riccardo would ever change. The good doctor had warned her about him. She did not want to believe it. Getting a car was nothing for him. Being truly sorry and understanding why would have meant more. It felt a bit like déjà vu just walking along not knowing where she was going. She thought she should get off the road in case he came looking for her. This time, she was definitely not going back.

He was left staring after her, wondering what he had done. He had just bought her a new car, what was so bad about that? He did not chase after her; he was sure she would come to her senses and come back. If not, he would find her some other way. Let her have a cold night out under the stars, and she might come back. He walked back into the house and poured himself a stiff drink. At the evening meal, his father asked him where she was. 'She has left me, again,' he said.

'We will talk in my study after dinner,' his father said.

In the study, his father poured two double malt whiskies and sat down. 'Do you want to talk about it?'

'Not really, I don't understand what I've done. I just bought Marion a new car and instead of being happy, she stormed off.'

'I think the question you should ask is why did you get her the car, given that she does not have a license?'

'I may have been a bit harsh with her.'

'You should know by now that she does not value anything to do with money.'

Riccardo looked perplexed. 'You always said that everyone has a price. So what is hers?'

'I don't know, son, but I think it has something to do with a moral stand.'

'I love her, you see, and I would marry her tomorrow, but she turned me down.' His father looked at him with sad eyes and said, 'She told me and I believe her that she would do nothing to bring this house into disrepute. I think she is waiting until she can find out about who she is. I have come to respect her integrity. Where would she go?'

Riccardo looked at him, thinking about the locket and what it meant. He thought she would just walk away and never say anything to anyone. People would ask questions. How would he answer them? Finally, he said to his father,

'I think I had better find her. I'll try that doctor of hers maybe he will know where she would go. Thank you for listening.' He got up.

He rang the Institute and asked to speak to Dr McKlean. When he came on the phone, he asked if she was there. The concern in his voice convinced him that she was not there. He asked what happened and when he heard the short version, he became more concerned. He suggested that they call hospitals and even the police. He thought she may try to harm herself. Up to that point, Riccardo did not think of this. Now he began to worry. The police were no help saying she had to be missing for at least twelve hours before they would think of writing a report. She had not turned up at any hospital.

It would be three days later in the late evening before

the doctor rang and said she had arrived there barefoot, tired, and dirty. He asked Riccardo to leave her with him for a while, and he might be able to sort things out. He told him not to call or come until it was okay. 'I think we should meet,' he said. 'Will you meet tomorrow morning early for coffee?' Riccardo agreed, and they set up a place to meet.

'I am going to put you to bed in the same room you stayed before,' the doctor told her. Have a shower, and I will get you some soup. I will be back in five minutes. After she had showered, she jumped into bed with nothing on as her clothes were a mess. It struck her as ironic that she always seemed to have no clothes. The doctor brought her a cup of hot soup. She could only manage to drink about half. He said for her to relax look at him and think of nothing. She took a deep breath and let it out slowly. She found herself drifting off. He suggested she would need twelve hours of dream-free sleep. 'Your body will wake you up, and you will feel fine, and you will be able to talk to me about what has happened to you.' As he was walking out, he scooped up her clothes and would get Helen, his assistant, to wash them for him.

The meeting with Riccardo was terse and direct. The doctor told him he had the case files from the hospital and knew what had happened at the beach house. He also told him that he knew he had raped her; it could explain why she had a complete mental breakdown. He told Riccardo that Marion had been careful to protect him. She would not say anything against him and would lie about their relationship, saying that he was kind to her. But the evidence from the medical examination said otherwise. He explained about her unique skills that could help or hinder her mental health. One must think of her as a gentle child who is trying to find her way. He explained that Riccardo was required to take care of her because it was essential for her mental health.

'I love her,' Riccardo stated. 'I don't want to hurt her.' The doctor asked about the contract, and when Riccardo said it was a bit of fun, the doctor told him that she took it seriously and would follow it to the end. 'If you are really serious about her, then you need to see things from her perspective. And if she is a bit of fun, then let her go.'

'I have no intention of letting her go. I want her around forever, even though sometimes she is more trouble than she is worth, and besides, my father likes her, and that is a big plus.' The doctor stared at him intently.

'I have even considered having her placed somewhere for her own protection until she can deal with the multiple issues she has. However, if we work together, we might be able to save her. I have an idea on how to get her full name, but I am not sure this will restore her memory. I will find out this afternoon how things stand and think if you can give her some time, I will try to encourage her to go back to you. This is against my better judgment, but I think she loves you too and human contact is imperative, as is safety. Do we have an understanding about this?'

'I'll do as you say,' answered Riccardo.

Marion woke up around 11.00 a.m. the next day. She looked around, wondering how she got there. She got up and noticed her clothes were at the end of the bed. Someone had washed them. She showered and dressed and wandered out to see if she could find anyone. There were quite a few people gathered together in small groups. She did not want to approach them, so she walked up to the doctor's office. She knocked on the door; nobody answered. A woman approached her with a big smile. 'My name is Helen and William told me to keep a lookout for you. I am his assistant.' She was middle aged, slim, and dressed in sensible clothes and a white coat over the top. She had pale skin that rarely saw the sun. She looked like she spent her days behind a desk. She had a kind of serenity about her as if nothing would worry her. 'Would you like something to eat?' Marion nodded, and she took her along a passageway to her room and through to a small kitchenette. She pulled out a tray of sandwiches and a bottle of chocolate milk and placed it before her. 'William will be back soon, as he knows you are waiting for him.'

When he came back, he took her into the office. 'You had us all worried,' he said. She looked defensive and told him how she had lost her way. Not that she had set out to come here; it had just happened somehow.

'You had a fight with Riccardo, and you have left him, is that so?'

'Yes, but it is more than that. I know he is not going to change. He hurt me and then tried to make it up by buying a car. I hate it when he first treats me like dirt and then thinks he can fix it with expensive presents. That is all he knows.'

'How does that make you feel?'

'I feel already bad enough about our relationship. Riccardo indicates that he does too, in some way, because he introduced me to his friends as a friend, and we are more than that. But what he wanted me to do with Nikator was hurtful and shows me he does not even respect me.

Because now I am a bit stronger, I could tell him, no, but I should not have been put in that position in the first place.'

The doctor looked at her a long time before he spoke. 'You sound angry. This is a good thing as it shows that you are feeling better about yourself.'

'Right now I hate him.'

'Do you have any plans for what to do with your future?'

'I did have plans, but now I can't do anything about them.'

'I talked to Riccardo this morning, I am sorry to say that he does not really understand why you are upset. He said he loves you and wants to make things right. He is okay with the idea that you can stay here as long as it takes and he won't bother you, but am I to believe you want to have no further contact with him? Or do you have some feelings about him but can't find a way across the divide?'

She started to cry; confusion ran through her mind. She did not know what she really wanted. The thought of not seeing him forever was unbearable. She thought she needed him. She needed to feel him close, but she also needed to feel safe, and he would never be safe. 'I think the bridge between us is too wide,' she said. 'Nikator was just the catalyst for something that has been brewing ever since we met.' And then she cried harder. 'I think you should rest for now and we will talk later. Maybe there is a way to close the gap between you if you both want to work at it.'

'Do you think he is capable or willing to at least examine his views differently?'

'I am sure that in this contingency and given the right motivation,' he said.

Marion stood up to leave the room, viewing his ideas as a way of giving her some hope. She would grasp at any straw in a rainstorm to keep herself afloat.

In the evening, they went to the refectory for the evening meal, which consisted of a lamb stew and rice. There were groups of people sitting at the tables. As she walked in, she was conscious of all the eyes looking in her direction. The good doctor stood up on a chair and rattled off a long sentence in Greek. In the middle of it, she thought she heard her name. He sat down beside her and Helen went to sit with another group. 'It's best to get rid of speculation before it starts,' he said. 'I told them you are staying here for a while but that you are not part of the groups.'

'Are they all like me?'

'In a way yes, different groups are put together to see if we can develop their skills. So you might feel something coming off them, but it is only curiosity. This is a good time to think about how you can screen those feelings off.'

'I don't think they like me.'

'The point is for you to close that part of your mind that creates confusion because you don't really know what they really feel as an individual.'

'How am I to do that?'

He smiled at her and said, 'That is something you have to work out for yourself. It does not come with an instruction book to only say do this and change will happen.'

At the end of the meal, Helen appeared with a battered old guitar, and again he stood on a chair and spoke to the room. 'I have not heard you sing, so I have told them if they want to stay, you will sing for them.' She took the guitar and tried to tune it; it was not good, but then it could have been worse. She sang a couple of songs, and she got such an enthusiastic response; she sang a couple more. She put the guitar down, and the good doctor told her that she had a sweet voice. Somewhere in her heart, she knew this was not so; it was more luck than anything. It was hard to find anything good to think about herself at this time.

They went back to his office, and he told her he was going to see if he could find out her name. He would use hypnosis and a small injection of Sodium Thiopental to relax her more. He bought out the blanket and made sure she was comfortable. He was only going to use a pad this time and said he would write down what she said. In a quiet voice, he asked her if she remembered all he had told her before. She nodded. 'So we start. Take deep breaths and look around your body to see if any parts feel tense or tight. As you breathe out, let yourself relax more. Take another breath, and as you breathe out, you will find that your limbs are feeling heavy. You are at peace. There is nothing to worry you. You are safe, and you can let go completely. Open your eyes and look at me. You are aware of the sound of my voice, and you can express out loud your thoughts. You are safe, and nothing you say can hurt you. I want you to go back to the day you arrived in Greece. You are packing your bag. You are going to leave the boat. What is the last thing you do?'

'I check to make sure that I have my passport and visa.'
'Look down at your passport, what colour is it?

'It is blue.'

'What is written on the front?

'Australian emblem and written underneath is Australian passport.'

'Open up the passport, do you see a picture of you?

'Yes.'

'Underneath the picture are a name and a signature, can you read the name?

'Marion Redford.'

'I am going to give you a piece of paper, and I want you to sign the signature. He handed her the pad, and she scribbled her signature. 'Under the photo, there are a group of numbers, can you tell me what they are?'

'I don't know, there are a lot of numbers, and I do not take a lot of notice.'

'Now you are putting the visa into the passport. You look at it, what are the numbers on the top?'

'I don't know.'

'Is there anything you can remember about the visa?'

'The reason for being here is holiday, and it is for three months.'

'What do you do next?'

'I put them in the side pocket of my case.'

'What do you do next?'

'I leave my room and follow the crowd.'

'How are you feeling?'

'I feel like a sheep, just doing what everybody else is doing.'

'Are you looking forward to your holiday?'

'No, I don't care. It is supposed to be good for me.'

'Are you unhappy about anything?'

'No, I don't feel anything.'

'Would you say you are depressed?'

'Yes, maybe that is it. I don't really want to talk to anybody.'

'Can you tell me why?'

'No.'

'Where did you come from to get the cruise ship?'

'London.'

'Did you fly to London from Australia?'

'Yes.'

'Was there anybody with you?'

'No.'

'Did you only have one case? What did it look like?'

'Yes, it was red/brown and had a handle on the top so you could pull it along.'

'Did you have anything else in the side pocket?'

'I had a brochure of the hotel I was staying at.'

'Did you go to the hotel?'

'No, I could not remember the name.'

'Thank you, now I am going to wake you up. You are feeling fine and relaxed. I am counting backwards from ten, nine, eight.'

She woke up feeling well and happy. 'What did you find out?'

He looked pleased with himself as he showered her the paper. I even have got your signature.

'What does this mean for me?' she asked.

'I am sure Mr Rodregious will now be able to sort things out and get some papers for you. Do you feel different?' he asked.

'Not really, but I am happy to have a name. I still can't remember anything I said.'

He reminded her that often, people who have this drug do not remember what they said and sometimes what they say is open to interpretation. 'I think we have it right this time. I am going to photocopy this and give you a copy for yourself. It may help to keep looking at it. It seems that you had problems even before you came to this country and that is something we will have to explore another time.'

When he came back and handed her the precious piece of paper, she looked at it and said, 'There is only one person I want to share this with, and I'm not talking to him.'

'I understand. You can call him anytime you want. Nothing is stopping you.'

'I am so confused,' she said. 'You thought it would be good to break from Riccardo and now you seem to want to get us together. Why is this?'

'I have not said this, although I may have thought it. It is up to you, what you decide to do. If you don't want to talk to him I can call for you. I think you should sleep on it. Do you want me to give you something to help you sleep?'

'I don't do drugs. I'll be okay. I'm used to not sleeping well.'

The next day, she was up at 4.00 a.m. she could not sleep anymore; she showered and dressed and went to the refectory to make a cup of tea. At that time, there was nobody about, and everything was quiet. Her mind was still in turmoil; she could hardly register what she was doing. In her mind, she could not see life without him, but at the same time she had some self-respect, and she realised she did not want to be abused again.

She found a bun and put it in the microwave to warm. The butter was on the other side of the large counter. Without thinking anything, she just wanted it to come closer. She stretched out her hand, and the butter moved into her reach. Helen walked in at the same time, but Marion was too preoccupied to notice.

Helen backed out the door and came back in making a loud noise to let her know she was here. 'What are you doing up at this time.'

'I just can't sleep.'

'Can I help?'

'I am here because I can't live with my boyfriend and I don't seem to be able to live without hlm.'

'That must be hard for you. I'm sure William will help you find the best answer.' Marion looked at Helen anew and asked, 'Is he married?' 'Married to his job I think,' she said.

'How long have you been with him? I feel you are very fond of him.'

'I have been here for twelve years. I am told you can read people, so please don't say anything.'

'I don't do things like that, I'm sorry if I offended you.'

'Do you have a computer here? I can get the news in English here on a computer.' Helen said she could use hers in her office, it was open. She waited until she left and made a mental note to tell William about the butter.

At ten thirty, Marion spoke to the good doctor. He asked about her dreams.

She did not dream last night, she said.

He explained about psychic dreams. 'Everybody dreams, but most people forget them, some humans have a heightened ability. Ninety percent of psychic dreams are about people who are close to them and they pick up on these feelings from their waking life. When a person mentally grasps random events that have not taken place, we call it 'precognitive experiences'. Although there is a lot of antidotal, evidence, there are no studies that can prove beyond doubt that these dreams exist. However, there are many theories. One theory is the precognitive experience itself discharges some type of strong psychokinetic (PK) force that brings the envisioned future to pass.'

She asked, 'Would that be a bit like a self-filling prophecy?'

'It could be. Another idea is that the past, present, and the future are all the same.'

'I think that sounds more likely, almost like parallel worlds.'

'Or,' he said, 'like you have told me before when you feel that you actually are there, your mind is able to go outside your body and see things that are happening. This may be a possibility for you. Again, it is not proven.'

'If I know beforehand and I know the people, I try to change it by changing the circumstances. Sometimes, it can work because the people do something different.'

'Mediation is the key to clearing your mind, but you may find it increases your skills. There are a lot of people that confuse premonition with recognition as being the same thing, but they are not. In some ways they are similar. Premonitions are a mixture of sounds, random images or feelings that flash involuntary in your mind. Whereas recognition presents itself in dreams using types of symbols, events, or odd feelings. About 70 percent of this is in dreams. There is no way of stopping these unbidden thoughts unless you put yourself into a more or less coma state each night. A good way to deal with it is to keep a dream journal and write down everything you remember because there is a percentage of your dream that is symbolic. By decoding your dreams, you might find some missing passages of your life.'

'Sometimes my dreams are so frightening I just want to forget.'

'Try instead of forgetting, look at how you are feeling and what is going on around you. I would like you to try this idea for a month, and we can see if we can work it out. On to the different and more pressing topic, what have you decided to do about your life? Do you choose to call Riccardo? What would you like me to do?'

'I don't know what to do,' she said. 'I miss him, but it

seems impossible to me. I want to share my news with him. I know if I see him, I will go back to him. And things will start all over again. Maybe I should join a circus and become a travelling fortune-teller.'

He smiled at the thought of her loose on the unsuspecting public. 'I don't work in conflict resolution for couples usually,' he said. 'But this time, it might be worth it as you both want to sort things out and I perceive there is good will on both sides. Would you like me to call him and make a meeting for after he finishes work?'

'Do you think it is the right thing for me to do?' She asked. He gave her a thoughtful look, 'You need someone to take care of you until you can develop strategies to deal with your empathic thoughts. This is not the place for you to stay as you saw last night you were picking up on a group of feelings and not able distinguish between them and what to take on board. The only time you relaxed was when you were singing. The only other place would be a nursing home, somewhere you could have a quiet time.'

'Do you think I am insane?'

'Of course not, but you have had a breakdown, and at this point, I don't know where it comes from. In spite of some abuse from Riccardo, he has looked after you, and if you get stronger living where you are, you will be able to stop this. I don't think he means to harm you nearly as much as you fear. I agree his way of saying sorry did not work for you, but it would have worked for most people. This is all he knows, and you can teach him what you really want. Shall I call him?' She let out a long sigh; somehow, she felt backed into a corner. She had no other place to go, so she agreed.

He arrived at 6.30 p.m. Helen announced, 'Mr Riccardo Rodregious is here.' He looked fresh and at ease. He came in and sat down as if he did not have a care in the world. She could feel he was anxious and not sure what this was all about. The good doctor took the lead when it became apparent she was not going to speak. 'We have some good news that Marion wanted you to be the first to know.' He handed over the paper from last night's session.

'This is the best news because now I can do something about settling this with the proper authorities.' He smiled at her, willing her to be happy.

The doctor continued,' I have had a long discussion with Marion, and she is willing to give you another go. Do you still want this relationship to work?'

Rick looked at her and said, 'I'm sorry I hurt you. I thought I was making things better with the car. It seems that Father understands you better than I do, but I want to have you in my life always.' She could feel the tears welling up in her eyes. She knew she could not stay mad at him for long. He saw the change in her face. He jumped up from the chair and hugged her, pulling her to her feet and kissing her on the cheek. He was happy and did not care who knew about it. The doctor watched the scene play out, wondering how long this tumultuous relationship would last. But for now, at least she would be as safe as she would be anywhere.

Rick said, 'If that's all, we will go.

'I want to see you in two weeks,' he said to her. 'We have a long way to go before we are out of the woods.'

They came out to his car, and he told her he would take her home to change clothes and then he was going to take her out for supper. 'There is so much I want to say to you, but I am afraid I will get my words mixed up, so will you be patient with me and let me talk to you without exploding?'

'Of course,' she said. 'I feel I am probably a bit of a nut case. The doctor was even talking about locking me away for my own protection. He is on your side and thinks you can look after me better than a hospital. If that is the case, I'm sorry to be so much trouble.'

'Don't be crazy, let's wait until we can sit down and do this thing properly,'

When they got home, he was tempted to take her clothes off and forget to put them back on. He restrained himself while she appeared to be having trouble deciding what to wear. He went over and picked a red dress and handed it to her while covering his eyes with his other hand. This made her laugh. 'I kind of feel the same way,' she said.

They went to a restaurant that seemed to be made up of lights. Bright chandeliers hung from the ceiling; white tablecloths, crystal glasses, and shiny silver made everything seem bright. People were waiting for a table, but Rick just walked in, and they were shown to a table close to the wall and as far away from the centre as possible. He did not appear to ask for anything, and the waiters seemed to know what he wanted. By way of explanation, he told her that he came here often. She was shown a menu, but it was Greek to her. And he did not look, just nodded to the water. Some wine appeared and glasses were poured before he started to speak. 'I am sorry about my friend, in fact, he is no real friend of mine. He saved my life as I said and has never let me forget it since. I usually just try to get rid of him by giving him something and have a couple of beers with him. He tends to bring out the worst in me, and I took it out on you. I actually did not know what to do. I was ashamed of the way I acted. I know you responded as graciously as you could and found you had to defend yourself when it should have been me that put a stop to it straight away. I did talk to him, and then he toned it down a bit. I should have known you well enough to just come out with the truth. I promise you it won't happen again.'

'I am sorry too,' she said. 'At the time I could see no way forward for us. In spite of what the doctor says I am getting stronger and the stronger I get, the better I can stand up for myself. When I was away from you, I could not imagine a life without you. You know I can't stay mad at you for long because you are so damned cute.' He laughed and said, 'You're not bad yourself. So does mean that we can go home and make mad passionate love to make up?'

'Hmmm, I am not sure of that just yet. While I've got you at a weak moment, there is something I had wanted to ask you.' She waited until the meal was served and then said, 'Would you loan me 50,000 euros?' He looked surprised. This was the last thing he had expected. 'I guess I can give you that, but why?'

'I don't want you to give me money. I want you to invest it. I want to have a loan agreement made out that I pay back by next year.'

'I'm not a bank,'

'I know. I can't tell you much, but I promise I will soon.' He looked at her wondering what her devious mind had come up with. He thought it would be fun to see what she did with it. He had no doubt it was for a good cause because she was not the type to go on a spending spree. 'You never use your clothing allowance I put in the card for you. Why don't you use that?'

'Because it has to be in a separate bank or it will be harder for me to work out payments.'

'All right, I relent. You can have what you want. Is that

all?'

'No,' she said. 'I still have to find a way of making things right with the government.'

'That isn't a problem. I'll have an uncle who can fix things in a flash. How did you sign your name?'

'I was under the influence of some drug he uses. I don't think I can repeat it. I am going to have to practice it. Isn't that funny?'

'Maybe, for now, you won't have to use it. We always can get it into the computer, and you can sign forms that way. I'll make sure you have an international driver's license as soon as I can. You won't have to sit a test. I'll just pull some strings so you could have that in a week, and then you will be able to drive your new car. Meanwhile, Abrax is looking after it as if it were a new baby.'

'He is a nice man,' she said.

'Do you really want to wait around for more food or can we go home now.'

'Yes.'

It astonished her how fast life settled into the same pattern as before because she perceived something had changed. She did not know if it was she that had changed, he had changed, or both. She felt a sort of peace within her. Maybe because she was busy with developing the music with the maestro and the orchestra. They were in full rehearsal now, and she found that she had to keep rewriting different segments as people would come up to her and say this will not work. She loved the collaborative effort, and that everyone was participating. Everyone was using their own creative ideas to make it better. Maestro could see how adaptive she could be and so each day became a pleasure, not having to worry how to find work to keep everyone together helped, although the orchestra still played at as many functions as they could to make money spin out as long as possible. She told him of her ambition to record the music and make a video as well. He would be just as happy to be able to present it to the community. She insisted that they copyright it in both their names for twenty-five years so no one else could use it unless they paid. He marvelled that she had a good business head on her shoulders as well as being able to write this music. Each afternoon between two and five, she would turn up to see how things were going. They made a pending tape to show the group how it sounded overall. She asked for any feedback that might enhance the music. Nobody made any more suggestions. Then she told them of her great plan to have it made into a visual tape to sell CDs so it would not be just one concert but a resource you could take to the world. Some expressed surprise that this was possible. She told them now was the time to think big. It was the best way they could keep together and ensure that there would be work for some time to come. She wondered how she knew all this stuff.

A week after this meeting, she decided to add some lyrics to the music. Then she had a nasty surprise at the house. Nara, one of the maids, said something to her that did not make sense. She asked for all the gossip going around; Nara was usually fun and did not mind a chat, but this time she looked embarrassed. 'What are they saying about me?' Marion asked. 'That you have another boyfriend, and meet him in the afternoon before Sir comes home.'

'Do you know how the rumour started?'

'I think Jacinda may have said something.' Marion thanked her for being so kind as to tell her. She promised not to tell anyone who said so. When Jacinda came home, she confronted her about the stories being told about her. It's just nasty and not necessary. She waited until Rick came back and asked him about the rumours. Yes, he had heard but was trying not to act jealous. 'Why did you not simply ask me? I told you I will not lie to you.' That afternoon after tea, she asked if she could meet the old man in the study.

When she entered in, she did not know what to do. Just state the facts or express her concerns about Jacinda. She knew he hated any friction in the house. 'There have been some rumours about me going around the house. They say I have a boyfriend. Will you give me the honour of inviting him to the house, staying, and listening to something?' He gave her a worried look, and she could see him weighing whether to trust her judgment.

Finally, he said, 'The first time you came into this study, I told you to fly below the raider. In other words, I don't want you to cause any trouble. Somehow you seem to be able to upset people all the time. I don't think you mean to do anything wrong, but around you, things get complicated. I am prepared to accept this one thing as long as it doesn't end up in a fight with Jacinda. You see, I have heard rumours too.' She jumped up and said thank you.

In the evening, Ziehn Meapha came over. She was waiting for him to come and brought him directly into the lounge. He hugged Sarvas warmly and kissed him on both cheeks. The old man glowed at him. 'Welcome to my home. Are you Marion's mystery man?'

'Yes, we have something to show you and your family. You are the first to see the product of our labour.' She fussed over getting the TV and recorder in the right position and put the CD in. Then they sat back to look and listen to the music. No one said anything until it was finished. Marion held her breath, what would they think? Would it be good enough? Or was she deluding herself?

'That is truly beautiful music but not one I recognise,' the old man said. Marion looked at him in the eyes. 'That is because I wrote it and you are the first to hear it. This is what takes me out in the afternoons.' She looked at Rick for support; he seemed stunned. 'I have great plans for this, but we may run out of money.'

Sarvas said he would be happy to put any extra money to finish the venture. Jacinda was quiet and did not make any comment. Rick looked at Marion and asked

'When did you have time to do this?'

'Usually, when I can't sleep, I come down to stop my bad dreams. I concentrate on the music. This is the first run, and there is still work I want to do before the finished product comes to the market.'

She thought it had the desired effect; it stopped the rumours in their tracks.

Like the doctor said, if you get in first, it prevents people from speculating.

Ziehn Meapha beamed at her. The seabird song was truly like her; it was as she had said, 'joyous and uplifting', and the family felt it too. This meant a lot to him because of the Rodregious family's devotion to the arts. If they liked it, that was a big start, and any extra money would be good too.

A couple of days later, there was another event to disrupt the household. Marion was sitting in the sunroom reading when she heard or felt something. She knew it came from the study. She jumped up immediately without thinking and called as loud as she could for Faustus to come quickly. She did not wait; she just ran into the room. The old man was half out of the chair, and he looked strange. She noticed his lips were bluish. Faustus came in behind her, and she got him to help lay him down flat on the floor. She was shouting at him to call an ambulance and go to the gate and bring them as soon as they came. Hurriedly, she took off the tie and unbuttoned his shirt. She checked for a pulse and could not find one. She moved his head back and gave him five quick breaths, hoping that would start him up again. She knew from the look of him that he was not breathing. She felt for a pulse again and when she could not find one she started cardiopulmonary resuscitation. She put one hand over the other, placing the heel of her hand in the centre of his chest and pumped his chest, keeping her arms straight. After counting to fifteen compressions, she gave him two quick breaths. She did this cycle for what seemed an hour. She was nearly at the exhaustion point, and her lips were bruised from the effort when the medics came into the room. One pushed her out of the way, and they used a defibrillator to restart his heart. Marion and Faustus stood there wondering what to do. The medical team worked fast and efficiently to stabilise him before putting him on a stretcher to take to the hospital. One of them turned to her and said she had saved his life. She was in shock, and she forgot to ask where they were taking him. Other people were standing around, but she hardly noticed them. She thought only to call Rick and ask what to do. He answered the phone straight away, and she told him his father seemed to have had a heart attack. 'Where is he?' 'I'm sorry I forgot to ask,' she said.

'That was a dumb thing to do, don't worry I call around

and find out.' He hung up the phone. It was only then that she sat down and cried. Someone handed her a cup of tea, and she drank it without thinking. She asked Faustus if he knew where Jacinda was. He only knew she was not expected for dinner, but he did have her cell number. 'Can you get it for me?' It was a call she hated to make; she would just have say the same thing she said to Rick. Jacinda started to scream thinking her Father was dead. 'He is going to be okay, we got his heart going again, and he is getting treatment.' 'Where is he?'

'I forgot to ask,' she said, expecting abuse for not asking. 'I have called Rick he probably knows by now,' she said. Jacinda hung up the phone.

Nobody came home, and nobody called until the middle of the next day. She had fallen asleep on the couch and woke up feeling sore, her lips were bruised, and her arms were sore from the effort. She could not eat anything, and people seemed to stand around, not knowing what to do.

Rick finally rang and said his father had a blocked artery and they had done surgery on him, and he was going to get better. He was told that she had saved his life by doing CPR until the medics had arrived. How long did she do that? She did not know, only that it seemed forever. 'I'll come home soon,' he said.

The old man stayed in the hospital for a week before

being discharged. Everyone appeared to be unable to cope with the thought of his near miss. When he came home, he was cantankerous and ill-tempered about everything and everybody. He snapped at the table for little things, making meal times even worse than they had been before. When it got so bad that she hated even the thought of eating, she asked if she could see him in his office. She went in there thinking he would criticise her. She did not wait to be asked to sit; she just did. 'I know you have a bit of a fright,' she said. 'Now is the time to get over it. You are not that sick, and if you actually did what the doctors have told you, you would be better than you have been before.'

He glared at her, 'How dare you.'

'I dare because I care. You know what I am saying is true, and if it helps, I will go for walks with you.'

'I only give you license to say this to me because you saved my life, but if you think you can come in here and lecture me about what to do, you have another thing coming.'

She gave him a sweet smile and said, 'Then I will take it that we will go for walks in the evening together and you can show me the sights that I might have missed.' With that, she jumped up and left the room before he had time to say no.

Rick wanted to know what she was up to and she told him what she had done. He shook his head wondering how she was able to judge his father so well. 'I have neglected you, and I have not even said thank you for saving my father,' he said.

'It was just luck that I knew what to do. I didn't have time to think. I don't even know how I knew there was something wrong. I just acted out of instinct,' she said. 'If I thought about giving him mouth-to-mouth, I may not have done it. It's not something I want to think about.' He smiled at her. 'This time, thank God you have this empath thing.'

True to her word, she made sure they went for a walk in the evenings. Sometimes they would drive the car to a park or place he wanted to show her, and they would walk around. She was initially concerned that the 'suits' always came with them, but eventually, she got used to them being around. She felt she had somehow acquired a father that she never had and told him stories about what she was doing. He tried to teach her Greek, but somehow she did not get it. He asked her about her relationship with his son, but she said she did not know enough about herself to commit to a marriage. She told him that she believed that marriage was forever and she did not believe in divorce, so they had better make sure it would work before committing to it. He agreed there was a sense in what she said.

Rick was working harder, taking on the responsibilities that were usually assigned to his father as well as his own tasks. When he came home, he was drained and did not even make a pass at her. He would fall into a dead sleep and not even move in the bed. There looked as if he had no time for anything else. She thought she needed to get the old man back to work for everyone's sake.

On her next visit to Dr McKlean, she told him about the heart attack, the walks together, and the need to get him back to work. 'It seems as if you have stepped up to fulfil a void in that house,' he commented.

'I am quite busy now because we are planning to launch our new symphony soon and I am involved in finding merchandising that we can sell. The visual video is good, and I don't want to leave anything out. This makes it hard because it turns into a movie and that is not what I intended. But adding lyrics and a singer has made it more, I think, well better because it can take the orchestra to a new level of entertainment. We could make it into pop art. It all makes money. Being busy takes my mind off other things that bother me.'

'You have built up a relationship with Mr Rodregious. How is the family dealing with that?'

She looked sad and said that she had thought Jacinda would be jealous, but she does not seem to notice or care. 'It is as long she knows he is there, she does not appear to worry. I think his children are a bit scared of him. Whereas I know him for whom he is. He can't hurt me, and I say what is on my mind. Sometimes Rick is shocked when I tell him what I say. He is really sagacious, and I listen to him. That is because he feels like a father to me.'

'Have you done anything about the dream journal?' he asked.

'Not really, I am still having strange dreams, and they wake me up. I try to ask myself how I feel and all I get is confusion. I have stopped for now. Would you like me to send you tickets for opening night? You could take Helen. I'm sure she would like that.'

'Yes, of course, I would love to hear your music. However, I see that you have put your issues on the backburner for a while and this is a bad idea because they will come back and maybe even worse. You need to deal with them.'

'I will, I promise, just not now. Be happy that for a while, at least I feel normal.'

The day for the opening night arrived, and she was always worried that something would go wrong. She called Ziehn Meapha several times to make sure that everything was right from his end. She called the caterers to ensure that the cocktail was all set up. She felt sick. It started with the usual blindness in her eyes, nausea until it was a full-blown migraine. This time she could not wish it away. Rick came home in the afternoon to see if there was anything he could do to help, but when he saw her condition; he felt he had no choice but to call a doctor.

The pain she felt was the worst she could remember. He said he would have to give her an injection to ease the pain; however, there was no way she would be able to go out that night. She felt shattered. Rick offered to stay home, but she said she wanted him to be her eyes and ears. 'Listen to everything people say; I want to know what happens. I am so sorry for Ziehn Meapha. I am leaving him out on a limb with no one to blame if it all goes wrong.' He helped her to change for bed. Each movement made her feel worse; when she was lying down, he kissed her and told her everything was going to be great. He waited until the drug took effect and she was nearly asleep, and then he left.

The next morning, she awoke only to find that the headache was still bad. Rick was asleep beside her, and she moaned as she tried to turn over. He woke up straight away, and she said, 'Well? Was it great? What did the people think of the backdrop? Did anyone buy the CDs?'

'It was everything you knew it would be,' he said.

She was crying both with pain and relief. 'I'm going to call the doctor again. You are still not well.'

The doctor suggested she should go to the hospital; however, she refused, and thus he ended up by giving another injection and insisting if it was not better by that evening, she should go to the hospital. Faustus fielded all calls that came in for her and the old man even came up to make sure she was all right. She felt paralysed, unable to move lest she incurred more pain. Through it all was a sense that she had done her job and the music would take on a life of its own from now on, she did not have to worry. There appeared in the corner of her mind a stern figure threatening to take away her newfound peace. She tried to push him away, but he came back.

On her next visit to the good doctor, the first thing she asked was his impression of the concert. He told her he was disappointed to find that she could not go because of a headache. He said it was exciting music; he did not attend many concerts and could not comment if it was great or not. He had bought the CD and found it was like watching a movie about music and a seabird and he thought it was clever how she had interwoven the two together. He liked the songs as well, and the male singer had an extraordinary voice.

She told him of the headache and how bad she felt for several days after. The doctor they had called had given her morphine, and it had worked at the time, but it had left her feeling depressed. 'I hate taking drugs as you know, but if I had realised what he was giving me, I would have refused.' She explained that while she had been busy, she could push other things out of her mind. 'I thought that maybe it is time to put the past behind, perhaps it was not meant to be that I remember what happened before. Do you know it has been three years since I first woke up? That is my lifetime. I think I have changed into a different person and even if there was another life to go to, would I really fit in?' She told him of the dark stern figure she sometimes saw in the corner of her mind. 'I think it is some kind of warning, but I can't imagine what.' The doctor listened, nodding his head.

'You are still emotionally fragile,' he said. 'My concern for you is that you may slip back into the place where you were before. I know you will think this is a bit harsh, but pushing things away may only be all right for a while. Until you understand the dreams you get, they will continue, and you will still be buffeted by the feelings of others until you can learn to control your emotions.'

'But,' she argued 'it was my feeling that saved the old man's life. The thought of giving him mouth-to-mouth resuscitation makes me feel sick. If I had thought, I would never have done it. So there is some good in having them.'

'It is up to you', he said. 'You have to want to do something about it. Maybe you should take some time to think about it. I am always here, and you can come to me anytime. How does that sound?' She thought for a while, not wanting to break off contact with him, but at the same time now things were going better, she did not want to divulge the past that may give her more grief. 'I think I should go on seeing you if that's okay,' she said. 'But maybe I should come once a month, instead of every two weeks. I know I should work on that journal and it is really fear of what I might find that stops me.'

'If that is what you want to do, then I'm happy with that,' he said. 'But remember, the moment you feel you are in trouble, please call me, and we can talk even over the phone.'

Chapter 12
ACCOLADE

They were in bed one night when Rick spoke to her about her status in the country. 'You have been issued with a new passport given yours was stolen, that one has now been cancelled. It should come in the mail soon, and I have gained you a temporary visa. This means that when it runs out, you have to leave the country and reapply to come back again. Another idea is that you change your citizenship status altogether and apply to become a Greek national.' He put on a sad face and said, 'Do you want to leave me and go back to Australia?'

She tried to take in all the implications of this. 'I've only just found out that I am Australian. I think I should at least visit before I give up all my rights to that country. What if we don't work out? Is there another way?' He looked at her thinking she was smart enough to see all sides, and he had to admire that.

'I think you might be able to get dual citizenship, but you might have to have Greek parents or be married to a Greek.'

She studied him, looking into his eyes, what to do. 'I don't know yet, so I'll just have to go with you on your business trips and reapply to come back each time.'

He rolled on top of her, smiling broadly and said, 'you devious little thing, that's what you wanted all the time, isn't it?'

'I don't think separations are good for relationships. Look at what happens to movie stars, their relationships always fall apart. I don't want that to happen to us.'

'Fine,' he said. 'I'll see what we can do to make it work. You will have to be patient until I find an answer. My uncle has some pull, he might be able to help, and I know he likes you and would not want to see you go. Meanwhile, I have another business trip next week, and no, you can't go on this one.'

She waited until he came back before she told them about the film industry awards. During the evening meal, she announced that the maestro had nominated their film for an award in short film section. They were now in the finals. 'He has asked me to go with him to the awards night.' She looked across at Riccardo to gauge his reaction. He appeared surprisingly pleased.

'Now you can wear the dress that had been sitting in the cupboard waiting for an event worthy of it.'

She told them she would be away for two or three nights.

'I'll get you booked into the best hotel and just remember

to have fun,' Rick said.

As the night of the awards came closer, the more she fearful she became. She thought she could not go through with it. Something was going to happen. She thought Ziehn Meapha should be able to handle it by himself. Then she realised how selfish this was. She missed the opening night and had not paid much attention to it since. As far as she was concerned, her job was finished; she just had to sit back and reap the rewards from the royalties that came in. Soon they would have enough money to pay Rick back. She knew she would have to go. She had seen enough movies to have an idea what she was in for; all she had to do was keep a clear mind.

Everything was ready for her to go. She spent some time with Rick in their room before Abrax would take her to the airport. She told him how scared she was and he reassured her that she would be just fine. Zielin would look after her, and if she had enough confidence to go to him in the first place, she should have enough faith in him to take care of her. 'Remember to keep your head up high and smile no matter what happens,' he advised.

When they arrived at the hotel, she was shown to her suite on the eighth floor. She looked around, and it was beautiful; several vases of flowers were around the room, and she guessed they were from Rick. The sitting room was coloured in soft peach. All the lighting was indirect thus making the room glow without the glare of an overhead light. The bedroom continued the tone; even the silk sheets were peach. It was big and spacious. It was just like him to think of things that would make her feel better. Ziehn Meapha's room was on the floor lower than hers, but he said he would come and get her when it was time to go. She phoned down to the concierge desk and asked if they had a hairdresser and could one be sent up. Feeling very nervous, she tried to order what to do to get ready. Finally, she put on the dress. She looked at herself in the mirror. The dress was made to appear as if like a stained glass window sewn together with black beads; it sparkled every way she turned. It had a high neck, long sleeves, and cut low in the back. She had lost a little weight but the dress just looked better. Ziehn Meapha knocked at the door, and when she opened it, he looked and went 'Wow! You look beautiful.'

As they were walking out, she told him about the time Rick had bought the dress and how she thought she would never have an occasion to wear it. There was a limousine waiting to take them. When they had got in, she told him to hold her hand tight and not to let go because she was nervous. She had good reason to be afraid because as soon as she stepped out of the car, the noise was deafening. She felt overwhelmed by the sound and the feelings rushing at her at once. Lights were going off in her face, and she felt as if she would faint. Ziehn Meapha managed to get her inside and seated and then he went for some cold water. It seemed there was every drink on the table except water. He put some ice in a napkin and placed it on the back of her head. 'Why didn't you tell me you can't cope with crowds?' he asked. 'I did not know.' She tried to explain an empath, but he did not understand. She thought about Rick and said to herself, 'Keep your head up high and smile.' She sang a song in her head. For a little while, the noise in the room died down. But once the proceedings, started the noise got higher and higher. Everyone appeared to her to be yelling, 'Me, me, call me.' The emotion was so strong she struggled to hold herself together. Thus when their section was announced, she did not hear any of it. Her name was called out, and Ziehn Meapha grabbed her hand and pulled her with him onto the stage. Someone kissed her and put something into her hands. She said thank you and let Ziehn Meapha do the talking. As they went back to their seats, things seemed to become quieter. She drank a couple of glasses of champagne. When she calmed down a bit, he handed her an envelope. She opened it and nearly fell over. There was a money order for 25,000 euros. She hugged him until he said to stop. It was the first the time she had become animated. 'Do you know what this means?' She asked him. He shook his head. 'It means we now have enough money to pay off our debt to Riccardo.' She gave it back to him and told him he knew how to handle the money side of their project, and she trusted him to do the right thing. 'Now you will have a lot of money in your own account,' he said.

'I know that I don't have to do anything and I keep

getting paid, isn't that great?' She smiled. They had to go behind the curtain to have a group photo and more champagne. She lost hold of his hand, and the noise was getting louder. A lady came up to her wanting an interview; she tried to get away, but she kept pressing forward until Marion was against a wall.

'You just have to tell me', she was saying. 'What do you want?' 'What is it like to be with a Greek God?

'What are you talking about?'

'Riccardo Rodregious of course, this is such a romantic story. It has all the elements of a Greek drama. Don't you know you are the envy of every woman in the room? You are definitely the best-dressed woman here, and you have saved our old orchestra. You have even made them famous.' She tried to smile and said, 'I just write music. They are the ones that should get all the accolades.' She pushed her way through the crowd to where Ziehn Meapha was standing surrounded by people. 'I'm sorry, but you have to get me out of here.' He put his arms around her, hoping to protect her from the crowd, but he could not stop the noise in her head. They were about to leave when one of the organisers came up to her and told her she would be on the morning TV show. A car would pick her up at 6.30 a.m. By the time they got back to the hotel, she was crying and feeling like she was going to throw up. Ziehn Meapha had to get the manager to help her up to her room.

'Is she drunk?' he asked.

'No, it is something to do with the noise,' Ziehn Meapha said. 'She has a car coming for her at 6.00 a.m. Can you arrange for someone to call her room and wake her up?'

Chapter 13

FEAR HAS A NEW NAME

The next morning, someone knocked on her door saying it was time to get up. She jumped up and showered and dressed and was ready to go down when the car arrived. When she alighted from the lift, there were several reporters flashing lights in her face and yelling at her. She smiled and hurried through to the car. The same thing happened at the studio. She felt like she was being pushed around. First, her hair was not good enough, and they redid it. Then they reapplied makeup and rushed her to a chair that would turn around on cue. The reporter who was to interview her only wanted to talk about Riccardo. As firmly as she could, she said she did not talk about her private life. 'But I am happy to tell you a more interesting story about how the film came into being.' By the time she got back to the hotel, she was a wreck. She took the phone off the hook and would not answer the door to anybody. She went into the bedroom and put the pillow over her head and tried to blot it all out. The noise was still in her head as if she was still in the crowd. Her fear was that she would never get it out again. She could not face the crowd, flashing lights or questions anymore. She thought the only way to escape was to throw herself out of the window.

At home, Riccardo turned on the TV to watch a replay of the news. He saw they had won their section awards and there were pictures of them going into the event. Then in the morning interview, he knew in immediately that she was in trouble. He called his father and said he would have to go and help her. 'I'll go into the office now and cancel appointments and try to get some help. If it is all right with you, I may be away for a day or two. I think I will take her to the Genève house until things settle down.' His father nodded and said, 'If you like I can go to the office and keep things running. Do all you can to help her.'

Riccardo left straight away and on arrival at his office started barking orders to his security. 'Call Neil, and get him to have a helicopter ready.' He rang his French security office and asked if George and Flynn were available. He then directed them to the house in Genève, on Ch. De Bellefontaine. He called the hotel and requested to speak to her. The manager came on the line and told him he was worried about her as she would not open the door and had taken the phone off the hook. Riccardo said not to worry as he was coming and would fix things up. He called the institute and spoke to Dr McKlean; he told him that she had some kind of meltdown. He asked if it was possible for him to come to Genève. 'It will not be possible this week, but I may be able to come next weekend. Meanwhile, I can speak to her on the phone.'

'Thank you.'

He arrived at the airport and jumped in the helicopter to take him to the hotel. Then rang the manager to let him know when he would come. He told him he would pay extra for all the kindness he had done for Marion. When he arrived, he went with the manager to her door and knocked and called out to her. She did not answer, and so he asked the manager to open the door with his master key. He thanked him and said he would call him again when he had things ready to go. He strode into the bedroom and found her still dressed but with the pillow still over her head. He shook her, and she jumped; realising it was him, she threw herself into his arms and cried and kissed him all at the same time.

'I've come to rescue you since you seem unable to look after yourself.' He looked at her tear-stained face and said, 'You're a mess I think you should have a shower and clean yourself up. Better still, I think I could do with a shower too. I'll race you to who can get their clothes off first.' In the warm water with his arms around her, she felt safe again. She felt his passion rising, and she wanted him too. They were still wet when they fell on the bed to make love wildly and were quickly spent. She looked over at him and said.

'They tell me you are a God in this country, you are not

a God to me, but you are my hero, and I do love you. I don't know why you keep saving me, but I'm glad you do. But I don't think I can go through the crowd again. The noise from them is terrible, and I feel it all.'

'I know', he said. 'I've called your good doctor and talked to him. You have a kind of 'sensory overload'. I have made plans for you to go to a safe place and you can speak to him there. I am going to call the manager, and we are going up to the roof and get a helicopter. I am taking you to my Genève house. I hardly use this residence, so it is like a safe house.'

She gave him a cynical look and said. 'Don't you think you should put your clothes on first?' He laughed and said, 'That's my girl.'

However, when she went on to the roof and saw the helicopter, she was scared of it. Riccardo just held her hand tight and pulled her in then he showed her how to strap in. 'You'll be all right. By the way, Father sends his best wishes.'

When they were safely on their way. Rick called a cell number to see if his men had arrived and opened up. They had, and he advised them of their estimated time of arrival. He asked them to look in the cupboards and see if there was anything to eat; if not, could they get something. He explained that Marion only drank black tea with milk and red wine. It was late in the afternoon when they turned on to the Quai De Cologne, which ran along east side of Lake Genève. They passed an enormous water sports centre and then turned off onto a small road called Ch. De Bellefontaine and into another even more minor road that led to the house. The house was a large three-story place with a gable roof, and she counted six chimney stacks. It looked about 100 years old. The front entrance had a horizontal half-circular portal and around the house was a vast stretch of white paving. The extensive grounds were surrounded by a tall hedge and lots of trees. It afforded a lot of privacy and careful security.

Inside of the residence was filled with old-world charm, plush wallpapers, and big comfortable chairs. Marion could easily imagine a large family living with several generations in this house. When they entered the house, she met two men dressed in suits.

'This is George and Flynn; they are to be your minders. This is Marion Redford.' Riccardo said.

'She shook hands and said, 'How do you do?'

She was silent for a while as she appraised each. Both were good-looking. George was the tallest of the two he was well built with broad shoulders, he had red/brown hair cut short, and light skin that matched his ginger hair, and his face was square and open. His blue-grey eyes seemed dangerous. He was in his mid-thirties, and when he spoke, it was with polished English accent. On the other hand, Flynn seemed younger in his mid-twenties was a little shorter and wiry; he had dark spiky hair. He had an afternoon shadow across his face. He had bright blue eyes and a cheeky smile that was very engaging. He spoke with an Irish accent. Rick watched her look them up and down and laughed.

'All right you can look, but you must not touch.'

She pulled herself out of her gaze and said sorry. They went into, the lounge room and Rick opened a bottle of red wine and handed her a glass of wine.

'Sit down for once and let us look after you,' he said.

The boys went into the kitchen and put together a platter of bread, cheese, olives, and cold meat. While they were in the kitchen, he said,

'I want you to take special care of Marion because she is special to me, and I think she is the one I am going to marry. Try to do all you can to make her happy. Call me if you have any concerns.'

They came back and put the platter on the coffee table, and Rick poured three shots of bourbon. He told her he could not stay, but the boys would look after her, and he would come as soon as he was able. He expressed the notion that it would take two weeks for her to become last week's news and the press would move on to another topic. He pulled out a picture from the inside pocket of his jacket. It was of her from the front page of the paper wearing the dress. And then he looked down at her weekend bag. He picked it up and pulled out the award. 'It's all over this bit of plastic.'

'It is not plastic, it's crystal,' she chimed in. It was shaped in the form of a flame with the award's name and date embedded into it. It was standing on a piece of wood with her name and the name of the film *Seabird*.

Flynn took the picture and looked at it. He grinned at her, saying, 'I bet it's more about the picture and the dress, it's a stunner.' Rick said he had to go and stood up. 'Don't forget to be happy.' They both said, 'Yes, sir.' She went to the front door and kissed him then came back into the sitting room.

She poured another of wine and said, 'I guess it's just us now.' Why do you call him sir?'

George said, 'It is because he is our boss. He owns the security company we work for.' She looked at them inquiringly, and although she was tired, she was also scared of going to bed for fear of having another dream. She tried to calm down and engage them in conversation. They were polite and careful.

'As long as we are here, we will call him the boss, and if you call me madam, I'll jump on you. In my eyes, a madam is a lady who runs a house of ill-repute, and I am not one. My name is Marion. And another thing,' she said. 'Can you lose the suits? Do you have other clothes to use?'

They laughed. 'Of course,' Flynn said. 'I hate these clothes as much as you do. I am happy to oblige, my lady.'

She dug into her bag and pulled out her cell and called the doctor to let him know she was all right. 'It was the worst thing, all the noise swamped me, and people kept flashing lights into my eyes. I have never been so frightened in my life. I now know what you mean when you say I have to get it under control. I will see you soon.' She looked over at the boys. 'I am going to bed now. I will see you tomorrow.'

She went to bed and fell asleep straight away. She slept soundly for two hours and then had a terrible dream. Dead bodies were falling on top of her; she could not breathe. Standing in the corner of her mind stood a tall, dark figure. She started to scream, 'Leave me alone and get away from me.'

Flynn, sitting in the kitchen reading the paper heard her cry. He pulled his gun from out of the back of his pants where it had sat most of the afternoon comfortably and ran up the stairs two at a time. He opened the door, switching on the light and looked around. There was nobody there. She was sitting on the bed rocking back and forth; her whole body was shaking. He quickly put the gun away and sat on the bed, asking her what had made her call out.

'I just had a nightmare that is all. It frightens me because it is so vivid. I did not know I yelled out, I'm so sorry I scared you.'

'This is my job,' he said. 'No worries, no one will get to you here, you are safe.'

She looked at him bitterly and said, 'Except what's in my head.'

'Come downstairs, Marion, and I'll make you a cup of tea, which will settle you.' While she was having a cup of tea with him, she said 'He did not tell you I'm crazy, did he?'

'A bad dream does not make you crazy. From the little I've heard about you, the opposite is true.'

'Oh,' she said. 'Well, I guess you will make up your own mind soon enough. I'll go back to bed and try to sleep. Good night.'

She was up early the next morning; going into the kitchen, she saw George making bacon and eggs. He was dressed in brown cargo pants and a tight khaki T-shirt that showed off his muscles. She smiled and said, 'an English breakfast that smells like heaven.' 'Would you like some?' he said.

'Yes, please,' she said. He handed her a plate and put some more on for himself. 'I hear you had a bad night?'

'No, just a nightmare, I get them sometimes. Flynn came to my rescue. Now that I think about it, I believe he had a gun. I hope not because I hate guns.'

'You will have to ask him about that,' he said.

'I think I will probably have to ask both of you. You don't get off that easily.

Is it considered a necessary part of your job?'

'Well, may depend on where we are.'

'I think I should tell you that one of my little problems is that I can read people, and I know when they are trying to avoid an issue, like now.'

He smiled at her, sat down, and started to eat without comment. She said,

'The strong, silent type, yes? It's okay, we can talk about it later. We have two weeks of enforced confinement, so we have to get along. I just hope I don't drive you mad before the end.' She was thoughtful for a while then said. 'You don't look the types who usually do babysitting jobs.'

They finished breakfast and did the washing up together. 'What kind of food do you like?' She asked. 'I like to cook and can cook just about anything, so give me a list of your favourite foods, and I will make them for you.'

'I'm sure the boss has arranged a cook.'

'That's all right, I'll just get them to take a holiday on full pay, and nobody will be the wiser.'

Flynn was up at 10.00 a.m. and came in dressed in jeans and a blue check top. He had not shaved and looked as if this was his usual look.

'Would you like me to make you some coffee?'

He nodded, and she went and got it for him and some toast with cheese. He sat down and looked about. 'What are we doing?'

'I know what I'm doing,'

'I am trying to open the lines of communication with our silent friend. Did I see you with a gun last night?'

'I thought you were being attacked.' he answered.

Marion tried to explain that she had never had anything to do with bodyguards. 'Is it really necessary? I would prefer if you just leave them in your rooms. I have an idea that between us we could tackle any intruder.'

Flynn shrugged and explained to her that if it made her feel better, they would do as she asked.

'My plan is just to be quiet until I get back on an even keel again. I hate to say this, but I think you guys are superfluous to my well-being and I feel it is just to keep the boss happy that you are here. To make everybody happy, can you just think of it as a holiday from your real jobs?'

Flynn's eyebrows shot up, and he gave George a query look. George just shrugged.

'What types of food do you like, Flynn? If we can work out what to eat, I will get you to go to the shops with a list. I don't think I can face a crowd yet. I bet you hate shopping as much as I do, but someone has to do it.'

They sat down and worked out a list of things to get that would last them for several days. It covered several types of dishes, all which Marion said she could cook.

'I smoke and drink, but I don't know what to get here. I like good wine. Maybe when you report to the boss, you could ask him what to get. Don't look so surprised. Of course, I realise that he will want you to report on how I am doing, he's like that.'

They flipped a coin for who would go and she gave them the list, her card, and ID numbers. Flynn had to go, and he took off in their car. There was a small shopping centre in a village setting just a short way from the house.

'Are you always this organised straight away?' George asked.

'When you have lost your memory, you learn fast to use the KISS principle.'

'I'm sorry, I don't understand.'

'Keep it simple, stupid.' She laughed at him.

He was saved from further conversation by the arrival at the gate of a courier. He went down to the gate and collected several boxes of different sizes. He could only carry two up to the house and then go down to get the other. Rick had sent her some clothes, her laptop, and guitar. Now she was happy unpacking her guitar first and making sure it was in tune. She sang him a couple of songs.

'This is my life,' she explained. 'It helps to keep the demons away.'

As she dived into another box, she found a DVD of her movie. 'Great! Now you can see it. This little bit of plastic is going to make me a lot of money. I have already paid off the money I borrowed from the boss, and now all the money that goes into the bank is mine. I get a big piece of the pie because I wrote it, I scored it, and I produced and directed it. No middle man. I even designed the cover. This is what happens when one can't sleep. When Flynn comes back, you can watch it while I put things away.' Then she asked if he would mind carrying the box of her clothes up to her room.

'Of course not, we are here to help.'

Their first night set the tone for the rest of their stay. She cooked a Chinese feast that was good. They had some wine and told silly stories. She found out that they had worked together for some time and their security post in France was only part of what they did. She also discovered that the boss had many security companies in various regions of the world and visited each one at least once a year but more likely every six months. That he owned several ships and was involved in import and export. She explained that she had only been alive for three years because she could not remember anything before. She told them about Nikator from Thessalonica and how she had to fight for her virtue. Everything seemed funny; it was easy to believe she was half crazy and easy to trust her because she appeared to have a native code of values which she seemed to stick to.

Flynn put a call into Mr Rodregious the next morning, telling him about how she had settled down. 'She is a bit bossy sometimes.' Riccardo laughed.

'She is the only person who has ever told my Father to go to hell.'

Flynn suggested if they knew a bit more about her, it might help. 'Ask her doctor when he comes up' was all he could suggest. 'Don't let her put one over you because she is as smart as a whip. Good luck.' And he hung up.

Every night, she seemed to wake up worrying about something she could not express. She would come downstairs and have a hot drink and would talk to whoever was up. It suddenly dawned on her that either one was up all the time. This time it was George. 'Why don't you go to bed?' she asked.

'We take it in shifts, usually every four hours.'

'You mean you have to watch me 24/7? I'm so sorry, I did not realise.'

'Don't worry; we get paid big money for it.' 'I'm not worth that much.' She said.

'You are to the boss.'

'Am I hard to live with?'

'No, like you said it's just a holiday.'

She sat down thoughtfully and said, 'You know what the boss told me? He said that I came into their lives like a whirlwind and turned everything upside down. I am told to fly under the radar, not to be conspicuous. However, I am always doing the wrong thing. I could not sleep, and that is why I got to write my music. Then I went and made a movie, and look at the trouble that brought me. I don't know why things just happen to me.'

George had not seen her so circumspect and wondered if she was depressed, but she jumped up and said, 'Here I go again, I am going to sleep.'

The good doctor was due to come up to see her, and George offered to collect him from the airport. It would be a good chance to ask him about her. At the airport, he held up a sign with Dr William McKlean on it, and soon the doctor approached him. He only carried a briefcase, so they did not have to wait around. As soon as they drove off, George told him they were her minders and were having some trouble understanding her needs. He wanted to know what was wrong with her.

The doctor explained to him that he could not talk about

her case as it was privileged information, but he could say about the Institute of Human Development. 'We work with people who have special skills such as ESP. I'm sure you have heard about the idea that people can read minds or bend metal and the like? Not all of it is true, I don't know anyone who can bend spoons with their minds, but everyone has at some time in their lives experienced some form ESP, not all people have it all the time. For those that do, it is not easy to control. We are not sure how it develops or if one can, in fact, stop it altogether. We also work with people who have dreams that tend to come true. Again, for the individual, this can be a truly frightening experience.'

George thought about this for a while and then said,

'Two things seem to rule her life, and they are fear and safety. Her sleep pattern is terrible, and she tries to push it aside as if it was nothing, and I know it is not. She is a lovely lady. She is kind, funny, and wants to please. Most of the time, she is fun to be around, but as her minder, I would like to help her.'

'By providing her with a safe haven, you are helping,' the doctor said.

George did not want to push any further and thought to get Flynn to drive him back and see if he could find out more. He was especially worried about her notion that she could read people. She could compromise them without knowing.

The visit lasted only two hours as this was all the time the good doctor could be away from his other students. He noticed that she seemed depressed and asked her to tell him from the start what had happened to her.

'I know now what you were talking about when you said I need to control my emotions. The only time I felt this before was when I had my first date with Rick, and we went to a party where everyone was trying to outdo each other. I took it as a lot of noise then. I did not realise that sometimes I can't tell the difference between spoken sounds and the noise other people are making in their heads. At the awards, everyone seemed to be selfish and self-centred, and their emotion was focused on their own needs. I could hear it all as noise, and it was so oppressive I thought I was going to drown. And the next morning was the same. There was a lot of noise and lights flashing in my face. If Rick had not come and saved me, I could not have got out of the hotel, and I think I would have thrown myself off the building. He has brought me up here to be safe, and I have two kind men who watch over me all the time. They are interesting and make me laugh.'

The doctor was scribbling notes, and she had to wait until he finished writing. He looked up smiled and said, 'Now you know why I use a recorder. Please tell me you are keeping that dream journal?'

'No, but I will. My dreams have changed. They seem very busy, and a tall grey man is standing to one side with a stern appearance. At first, I thought it was you telling me to work on getting my life together. But now I think he is some kind of warning. I don't know what.' The doctor looked up and said, 'How do you feel when you see him?'

'I am frightened of him. I wake up and try to get him out of my mind.'

'I want you to try something for me. I want you to go to a place where there is not much noise and try to focus on something else, like your own thoughts and screen out others. Is that something you can see yourself doing?'

'I can try, but even here, I can pick up on my minders when they are being elusive and not telling me the truth. Their emotions give them away every time. It's kind of like being your own lie detector. I know that is not normal.'

'Maybe you should start by practising with them first and then go out. How long are you going to be here?'

'I think two weeks but maybe longer. I know they report back to Rick, and I hate it that I have to be watched.'

'When you come back I think you should attend the clinic more often. We will talk about it then.'

Flynn drove the doctor back to the airport. He said, 'How is our girl then?'

'She has had a setback, but thanks to you, she will recover her equilibrium soon. You are doing a great job and probably saving her sanity in the process.' Flynn asked casually, 'Does she really have all these things she said she has?'

'Yes, she is a rare person. And like people with special skills, she has to learn how to control them.'

'Why would someone get this? Are they born with it or do they develop it?'

'Flynn, if I knew the answer to that question we could make money just by turning on whatever hormone that turns it on.' He dropped the doctor off, and he was happy that he had got out of him the answer that was worrying them.

What the hell they were going to do about it was another matter.

The next day, she was full of joy; she told George and Flynn that the doctor had said she was in good hands. He liked them and had confidence in their ability to keep her safe. He suggested she should go out into quiet places to help her get back to where she was before. She thought a night out would be good for all of them. In the small village a couple of miles from where they lived, there was sure to be a tavern where they could have a meal and a quiet drink.

It was a warm day, and they thought they would take the cover off the swimming pool. As she was coming down to the pool, she stopped and watched when she saw them fighting. She felt no anger in them and they seemed to even like it. 'What are you doing?' she asked. 'Just keeping fit,' answered Flynn. Both had shirts off, and both were very fit; George was bigger and had a longer reach, but Flynn seemed to be tougher and quicker, and thus it seemed as if they were equal. When they sat down to dangle their legs in the water, they were hardly even out of breath. 'I would hate to meet you on a dark night.'

'There is a gym in the basement. You should try it, George stated.

'I know I'm not fit and have not been doing anything, but I bet you I can outswim you.'

'You're on,' said Flynn. 'Four laps of the pool.'

She raced him up and down the pool and could easily outswim him. Laughing, she thought that it was because she was Australian and most children are taken to the beach before they could walk. 'I would like to do something to defend myself. I don't want to become a fighter, but surely you could teach me some moves.'

George promised to teach her self-defense. 'I know, I can teach you to play guitar in return,' she said.

That night, they went out for the first time. The boys played 'scissors and paper' to see who would stay sober; George lost, and that meant George could only have two drinks and Flynn would take the night off. They found a quiet place that had a small band playing some kind of unknown type of music that she had not heard of before. She asked what it was. George spoke to them in French and was told it was the music of the mountains. It was quite lovely, both lively and melodious at the same time. One of the string instruments was unlike anything she had seen, with a long fret and four strings. It was painted blue and had flowers painted on it. Her interest in it kept her from worrying about anything else. The food was French style and delicious, and the wine was also French. After the meal, they sat back to relax and watch Flynn try to pick up a couple of girls.

'His life is all about the next fuck,' remarked George.

'Oh well, I hope he makes it then.'

'He will he always does.'

'Don't you try to?' she asked.

'I actually have to know their names before I start.' He laughed.

After she had several glasses of wine, she jumped up and went to the band and indicated she would like to play. They handed over the instrument, and she tried to focus on it. She had been watching all night and very quickly she played simple chords and sang into the mic. Everybody was surprised; she sang a soft love song part in French and part in English. The room was quiet as most people had gone home, but those who were there clapped. She sat down. 'I think we had better leave now,' she said. Flynn had disappeared, and Marion and George walked home hand in hand in peaceful silence. Flynn came back the next morning bleary-eyed and a happy smile on his face.

The next day was Saturday, and Rick came early. She was so glad to see him. She asked if the boys could have time off so they could have the house to themselves. He agreed, just as well as they both looked a little sleep deprived. He told her he had to leave on Sunday evening so they could have all that time in bed because he had missed her. She told him about the good doctor's visit. And that she was getting along fine. But she wanted to come home. He told her another week and she could.

'Did you mean it when you said those three little words I love you?'

'I told you I would not say it until I felt sure I meant it. It just took me some time to realise why I love you. At first, I just wanted to die, and you made me feel again.'

After making love, she slept through the night for the first time in a long time. She had not wanted to feel the tide of passion, it had been fear that had held her back. Now she seemed to have been set free. When she woke up, she went and made him toast and coffee and sat on the bed and watched him.

Riccardo said; 'I have something to say to you, and I don't want you to interrupt me until I have finished, okay?'

She nodded. He pulled her down beside him so he could look her in the eye. 'As you know, there has been much made in the press about our relationship. You know I want to marry you, but I understand your hesitation. I want you to say yes to getting engaged. It could be a long engagement if you wish, but it sounds better to say my fiancée rather than my girlfriend.' He dug under the pillow and pulled out a small box and opened it. It was the prettiest ring she had ever seen. In fact, it was more like a large round sapphire with diamonds set all around it. She looked into his eyes and saw a pleading look. She leant over and kissed him softly and said, 'Of course it is yes.'

He put the ring on her finger and thanked God it fitted.

'Have you told anyone yet?'

He paused and said not exactly.

'Well, your father will be pleased, and you realise Jacinda will be as mad as hell.'

The boys came back about mid-afternoon, and he said he wanted to talk to them. They went outside on the veranda, and he told them to try to get the computer away from her for a while as he had been caught buying the ring and their engagement had been announced in the news before he had time to ask. 'You may have to stay an extra week to let the fuss die down.' He asked if they had pressing business in France. As far as they knew, they had not and would be happy to stay on for an extra time.

'She seems to have built up a bond with you and that is important for her at this time. How would you feel about coming over to our team for a while?' George said they had certain stipulations in their contracts. He told them he knew about the contracts as he had approved them in the first place. He would continue with the contracts as they were. They would still be a part of the French Security Company and would be paid by them.

Chapter 14
LEFT FOR DEAD

As part of Marion's get-fit program, they decided that she should walk for at least one hour each day. The area around there they lived had several pleasant walks. The one that was her favourite was up a winding path, through trees, to a small hill that overlooked Lake Genève and the mountains beyond. Usually, they walked in the morning before she got tired. When she slowed down, they would encourage her to keep trying. It started as a slow walk and each day they decided to pick up speed. The boys could run up and down to where she was a couple of times and would keep yelling at her go faster. Slowly she believed she was getting better. It was important to change routes, they would say, for security, but she preferred this one. At other times, they would walk to the village not far from the house.

It was during one walk that they encountered an event that would change the way she would think about them forever. Walking along the path, George was in front then Marion and Flynn. Suddenly, five men came out of the bushes. They were dressed in black and had black balaclavas over their heads. They each had machine guns and started to yell at them in French. Everybody stopped and for a minute; nobody moved. Then they pointed their guns, indicating the trio were to continue up the hill. As they neared the top, they saw a black van. Flynn caught up to Marion and whispered in her ear,

'As soon as I give you a push, jump in the van, lie flat, put your hands over your head and don't look.'

The man walking behind saw him talking and hit him over the head. He stumbled but got up again. George had slowed their walk down to almost a stumble. When they were near the van, Flynn gave her a push and said, 'Now.' She did exactly as he told her, except she looked. By this time there was a man on each side of the boys and three men standing ready in front of them. The boys glanced at each other and acted in unison. They kicked up with their knees and slammed down hard with their arms and grabbed the guns. They then dropped to the ground as if to make themselves as a smaller target as possible and fired the stolen guns at the men standing in front from lying position.

For a moment, all guns were going off and then all was still. George stood up and went over to the ones lying on the ground in front of the van and fired a shot at one who was still alive. The men on the ground beside the van were still alive. One was not moving, and the other started to grown, and George hit him with the end of the gun. Flynn poked his head in the van and said, 'you okay Marion?' He helped her out.

She was speechless. She was unable to comprehend what had happened. She thought to seek clues from the boy's, but it seemed that they were not emotional about the event. They had just reverted to a style of training. George pulled out his cell and called the police and an ambulance. They took her down the bottom of the hill and sat her down and waited for the police to arrive. When they came, the boys walked them up the hill and talked them through what had happened. An officer tried to talk to her, and Flynn told him in French that she only spoke English. She was put in an ambulance, as she was leaving, she saw the boys being pushed into a police car. They took her to a medical centre where she was put into bed. Her head was spinning out of control, and she started to shake. They took her temperature and blood pressure and then took a blood sample. After a while, someone and gave her some pills to take. She took them, and they put her to sleep. She slept through the next day and then she was woken up by a policeman. They took her to a police station. She asked if she could see her minders and was told no. She sat in a room by herself for what seemed forever. She felt sick, hungry, and tired from the effects of the drug. When a policeman dressed in a suit came into the room and sat down and asks her some questions, she told him that she was Australian on holiday and someone had just tried to kidnap her. He spoke to her in careful English.

'I know who you are. What I want to know is what a lady like you is doing with a couple of killers like them, and what part did you play in this?'

She said they were not killers, but they were security guards hired by her fiancé to protect her. She told him that she ran and lay down in the van and put her hands over her head. She heard lots of sounds but could not decipher it. 'I was just terrified and thought I was going to die.'

'Why do you think you need to be protected?'

'My fiancé is wealthy, and I have just won a movie award. Maybe they believed they could get some money for me.'

She looked at him quite distressed and asked if she could have something to eat and drink, please. He softened his tone and said he would get her something. He bought some coffee in a cup and placed it in front of her. Some food will come.

'You see, I have three dead bodies and two critical in hospital. Were these men of yours carrying weapons?'

'No,' she said. 'I am truly against guns of any form, in fact, I believe strongly in non-violence.'

'Do you know what army they belong to?'

'They do not belong to any army. I told you they are security guards. They were hired to look after me because I have been sick. They have been just babysitters.'

'I'm sorry, but I don't believe you. How could two men do so much damage?'

'I think we were all scared and did what we could to stay alive.'

'What agency do they work for?'

'I think my fiancé part owns the company. But I don't really know. I don't know anything about his business.'

'I think you are either ingenious pretending to be stupid or foolish trying to be clever. What do you say to that?'

'I know I have had a nervous breakdown, and I have not been well, so I think that makes me stupid. I was so scared that I hid my face in my hands and all I could hear were guns going off. I did not know until after who shot who.'

'One shot was at close range; do you know anything about that?'

'No. When I got out of the van, I noticed some holes in the van. If I had been standing up or even looking up, I would be dead now.' Someone came in with a plate of biscuits and put them in front of her. She looked at the policeman in front of her and asked, 'What are you going to do about this?'

'I think it is probably a kidnap attempt. The question is why? I think your bodyguards used excessive force. However, it is going to be hard to prove given that they had no weapons. You and your bodyguards will be free to go for the moment. We will attempt to interview the others if they wake up. Your passports will be kept here, and you are not to leave the country until we have cleared up a few things. If we find that they killed the others after the incident, they will be charged with murder. I don't think you had much to do with it. But you may be called as a witness. A police car will take you back to your house. I don't know when we will release these bodyguards. We are waiting for confirmation that they work for the company they claim to. In the meantime, do you feel you need police protection?'

'No, I just need them to help me.' She started to cry softly. He softened towards her and said he would try to hurry things so they could come home and look after her. She thanked him for his kindness and understanding. And she went with a police car back to the house.

An hour later, the boys were dropped off. They were required to hand in their passports. When the police had left, she sat down at the kitchen table where she had prepared some leftover food for them. She looked at them and said,

'I am "bloody" angry at you. You see, I did look, and I have just spent four hours being questioned by the police. It is just as well I can read people because I have lied through my teeth to protect you. I know that you are not just bodyguards. I don't know what outfit you work for, but I have seen enough news and watch enough movies to know a specialist soldier when I see one. Why did you have to go and shoot that guy at close range? That is where the hole in the story becomes unravelled. I don't believe for a minute that this was a kidnap. I think they were after you for some reason. But for convenience's sake, we will say it was a kidnap. The police think I am just a crazy lady who doesn't know what is going on. I told them you were just my minders trying to help me get over a breakdown. It is true it happened so quickly that I did not have time to think. And it is true I was in shock, and that is borne out by the fact my blood pressure went through the roof. So I could use that part, and the guy who was interviewing me has a soft heart particularly for women. However, I think they are going to call the boss and find out about the security company you work for and what you do. I am so glad that you did not have guns because that would have made things harder to explain. So I hope your work part is in order. If they try to put me on the witness stand, I will continue to say I saw nothing. So now you know where I stand. What about you?'

George looked grim but said mildly 'I am sorry this happened. You don't really know that it was not a kidnap attempt. That is only a guess. I went and shot him because it was a humane thing to do. He was going to die anyway but in a lot of pain. And he could have got off another shot before he died.'

'The thing I don't understand is neither of you felt anything like it's just a job. While I mourn the loss of life, no matter whose life it is. You don't seem to understand that when a person dies, it is always hard even if it is for a minute. I can feel you are not sorry now.'

Flynn got up and put his arms around her, saying, 'It must be hard to be so sensitive. I am sorry, but not for the reason you think. I regret the fact that these people thought it is fine to hold us up for whatever reason and they paid a high price for their trouble. But if that is the way they choose to live their life, then they must expect to pay the price.'

She said, 'The next question is what we are going to say to the boss. I don't lie to him. However, I don't have to make too much out of it either. I think he is going to be hopping mad. Have you called him yet? I don't want to be the one to tell him.'

George said it was their responsibility to deal with the fallout. 'Just do what you do so well, be sweet and kind, and we will handle the rest. I should say thank you for sticking up for us. There was no need to do so really.'

'I disagree, because if I said what I actually saw, you two would be still in jail. The policeman said something about excessive force. Anyway, it's over now but for the shouting. I don't think the police have much they can hold you on given that you were unarmed and they had big guns and hoods over their faces.'

Rick came up late that night; he looked stressed and

upset. Marion had agreed to remain calm no matter what and she knew him well enough to know he would want a long explanation of what happened. She told him that she had done exactly what Flynn had told her to do, and if she had not done so, she probably would be dead.

'They were careful to protect me all the time, and I think they might have died for me.' 'Why were you there in the first place?' he said.

'I missed my walks with your father, and I needed to keep fit. They were only doing what I asked them to do.'

'You appear to have developed some sympathy for them.'

'Are you jealous?' she teased him. 'They are kind of like the big brothers I never had.'

He sighed. 'I was thinking of keeping them on with our team in Greece, but not if they are going to be trouble.'

'I would like that it's not my fault I got into trouble, and they did save my life.'

'Darling,' he said 'you are always in trouble.'

She was surprised that he was so kind.

'I am so glad that everything turned out and that you are all right.' He said, 'I don't know what I would do if anything happened to you.'

'When I get back, I am going to fix things and do

everything the doctor tells me, so I won't be any more trouble. I am going to be the perfect fiancée.'

He had a laugh. Anyway, one could not say she was dull. He thought about what Brian had told him: that he would be in for the ride of his life.

She waited while he took them outside and talked to them. She was grateful he seemed reasonable and did not make the big scene she had expected. When he came back in, she asked him if he would stay. He explained that since she had induced his father to go back to work, he was causing more upset in the company. 'There can only be one boss, and when he counter commands what I've put in place, our people don't know what to do. I've done all I can do. There is nothing more I can do here. I'm sure you will be home soon.'

They did not go out for walks again, and she had to be content with using the gym. Flynn took her down, and she tried using the boxing bag. Even though he was holding it, it still swung back enough to knock her over. He sat down on the floor laughing. 'I think that is not for you.' There was equipment for running; he put that on the lowest level. However, it took her off the end, and she landed on her bottom on the floor. He picked her up kissed her on the cheek and said,

'Don't worry, I'll find something for you to do.'

Next, he tried weights; she was to hold on to a bar and slowly move her arms up and down, but she could not control it, and it lifted her off the seat. He caught her around the waist as she fell on top of him. He started laughing at her again while she was becoming indignant at him for making fun of her.

'Has anyone told you that you look cute when you are angry?' He laughed. He thought for a while and said, 'I know, I bet you can skip.'

He got out a rope and showed her how to use it. To her relief, she found she could skip. At first, she got tangled up a bit, but she got the hang of it. He found another rope and showed her different ways to use it. 'Each way has a different purpose,' he explained. He was light on his feet and could dance the rope easily.

'It comes with practice.'

She felt slightly better that at least she could do something. 'You are going to tell George about this, aren't you?'

'Of course, we don't want him to miss out on the fun, do we?' She stamped her foot and said, 'It is not my fault I tire easily and am not as fit as I should be, I do try.'

'She noticed that the boys had increased their security measures since the event. She was pretty sure they were now keeping their guns close. She wanted to ask but was afraid of the answer.

There was one good thing to come out of it. The tall, stern man in her dreams had vanished. She tried to explain one night to Flynn about the dream journal that she was supposed to keep. 'It is because I have different types of dreams. It terrifies me when I have some dreams that are so real that I know they are real. Sometimes they are things that have happened and sometimes they are things that are going to happen. I try to make a difference by changing what people are doing and sometimes that stops a bad thing from happening. The good doctor thinks they also hold the key to my past, like a jigsaw puzzle. I think now that the man in the corner of my mind was a warning. I did not understand it and thought it was like the good doctor telling me off for not writing in the journal.

'Why don't you write it down then?' he asked.

'It is because it is like reliving it again, and I am trying to get it out of my mind. So I get up and make a cup of tea and try to forget it. Do you remember the first night we were here? My dream was more about what I had experienced and the way it felt to me, I ended up screaming because it was so bad to me. Some dreams are silly. Like now, I dreamed that I had a pain in my leg, I went to the doctor's office to get help, and other people started to come in. All were very sick with either severe colds or parts of their bodies half cut off. I decided to walk away because I was not that bad, even though I had trouble walking. I woke up and had a cramp in my leg. I am not bothered by this because I have an explanation for the dream.'

He suggested, 'While we are here, why can't I help you?

You can tell me, and I will write it down.'

'Maybe that is a good idea. It won't hurt to try.'

'Let's start with tonight. Do you have a book?' 'I'll get it,' she said.

They waited a week to hear from the police, each day hoping that they could go home. Marion called Rick to give him some news. She felt upset because he could not get away, even though she understood the reason for it. She asked George and Flynn what they were going to do about the boss's offer to join their team. 'I have an idea that it may entail more looking after me, which I know is not that exciting, but it is safe, and I believe you need a safe place when you are not doing what you do. And don't give me that look. Let's agree that I know and won't say anything about it.'

Flynn said, 'I'm happy to look after you, Marion, I can't answer for him.'

George stated that he thought he would take up the offer, but there were things that he would have to sort out first. He suggested that it might take a couple of weeks to make a move to another country.

'I am sure the boss knows how to pull strings to get you there, or he would not have made the offer,' she said.

George had a different approach to fitness than Flynn. He thought she should learn something about self-defence. Although she was a self-proclaimed pacifist, she did not want to be in a position of feeling utterly helpless again. 'I would like to be able to do what you did and stop someone in their tracks if I had to.'

'In that case,' he said, 'you need first the element of surprise and next you go in hard and dirty. The best way for a woman is to kick them in the nuts and then hit them over the head.'

'I would not want to kill anyone or even maim them. I just want to stop them.'

'We could try a few throws first and then see if you can knock me over. Somehow, I don't think you could, but we could try. The first thing you need then is to know how to fall without hurting yourself.' He started by teaching her how to fall and roll. This took about fifteen minutes, and she was exhausted. He suggested they try tomorrow and each day until she got that bit first.

Upstairs, she pulled out the guitar and sang a song. 'This is what I can do; now I will teach you how to play the guitar. It's a fair exchange, don't you think?' She showed him how to place his fingers on the C chord and strum, and then she did the same with the D chord. Then she instructed him how to change from one to the other and continue to strum. At first, his fingers were all over the place, but after a while, he got the idea. 'Like everything, it is just about practice.'

Two days later, she received a call from the police to come back in for another interview. Flynn offered to drive her. Sitting in the car, she said she was worried about what they wanted. 'Talk to me, Flynn, it may help to take my mind off it.'

'What do you want me to say?'

'You know so much about me. Tell me about you. What were you like as a child?'

'Well, there is not much to tell, I came from Northern Ireland. If you know much about the history of our country, you know its war between the Catholic and Protestant people as long as anyone can remember. I was a Catholic kid in a rough land. I learned to fight early to protect myself. I got into lots of scrapes with the law, and when I was seventeen, I was in a lot of trouble, and I was given a choice: the army or jail. I took the army. When I left the army, I was no better off except I am no longer the Catholic kid.'

They arrived at the police station. Flynn came with her as she went up to the desk and said, 'My name is Marion Redford.' The policeman came out and took her into the interview room. Flynn had to sit on a bench and wait. She sat opposite the man she had spoken to before. He had a file in front of him. 'I need to ask you a few more questions. You see, I don't think you were really straight with me. We have checked you out through Interpol and found out that you have been living illegally in Greece for two and a half years, and that this passport has just been issued. So you were deliberately evasive about this. I am wondering what else you have not said.'

She looked at him and considered whether something was wrong with her statement.

'I did not tell you any lies,' she stated. 'I said that I had a breakdown. It was a complete breakdown, and I lost my memory. I also had my luggage and papers stolen, I have only just found out what my name is, and that is why I have just received a new passport, and the one that was stolen has been cancelled. I still haven't recovered. I just wish I could be of more help to you. I would not like it to happen to anybody else.' She felt as before that he softened towards her.

'What we found was there seems to be no record of you anywhere. Is this your true name?'

'It is as far as I know,' she said. 'Does this mean there is no one anywhere in the world looking for me? Do you have any idea what that feels like to me?'

'He got up and left the room and came back with a brown case. 'Do you recognise this?'

'Not really' she said. 'A case is a case to me they are all the same, just something to put your things in.'

'I suggest you open it and examine the content.' She opened the case while he watched her intently. Inside there were some clothes packed neatly, a small roll of jewellery, and some toiletries.

'Look on the side of the case,' he said. Marion slipped her hand into the side pocket and found a passport. She opened it, and her face became white, and she sat down with a thud and said, 'This is me.'

He saw how pale she went and realised that this had come as a shock to her. He went and got a glass of water. She sipped at it, and she waited for him to continue. 'The men involved in the incident with you were French nationals of Middle Eastern origin. Now do you have any idea who they are?'

She looked at the passport and said, 'As you can see, I have never been to France.' She was thinking out loud. 'Why don't I recognise these as mine? What is so wrong that nobody wants to claim me? If you do not, believe me, what hope have I in convincing anyone else?' She looked at him and tried to explain that even faced with clothes that must be hers she could not recognise them. She stated she felt happy that he had found her passport because it might bring her one step closer to understanding who she really was.

'Because of your mental volatility, we will not be able to use you as a witness at any trial.' He said. 'So and your minders are free to go.'

'Have you questioned the men?' she asked. 'Did they say why?'

'These people are not going to say anything. We can identify them from photographs. I am sorry that this has spoiled your stay in our country. They will be charged under the terrorist act. I do hope you are able to put it behind you and get better soon. I have checked out your bodyguards. It appears that they were army trained, but that they are no longer in the military records. A look at their worksheets from the French Security Company shows consistent employment that they undertake a number of security tasks from pop concerts to diplomatic protection for foreign dignitaries who come to France.'

He handed her back their passports. She went out front to Flynn, holding the case and their passports. On the way home, she said that they could return to France whenever they wanted to. 'Don't worry we will not leave until after you do.' She commented on the nice car, and Flynn explained that it was George's car, and he always had nice cars. In one way she felt she would be sorry to go back to the life she had with Rick because she would miss the free, easy way of life they had here, and she would miss them.

That night, they went out for dinner at the tavern. It would be their last night together, and she wanted to make it a good evening. The boys were drinking 'shots'; she had one but did not like the strong taste, and one was all she could handle without getting blinding drunk.

Flynn thought it funny and said. 'See, Marion, you can't cut it with the men.'

'Okay, but there is something I can do better than you.'

She jumped up and went to the band and asked the man with the blue instrument if she could use it again. He was happy to oblige as he was impressed the last time. It usually took a lot of practice to play, and she had done it in one night. She sang a couple of sentimental love songs in her pure voice that made the listeners feel as if she was singing just for them.

Walking back to the house, the boys were pretending to be very drunk although she knew they were not that bad. She knew they would not let their guard down even for a little while.

She said good night and went to bed. She had another vivid dream, this time it was about the boys. She got up hoping Flynn was there, and he was. She sat down at the table with her book and told him about the dream. 'I must have been thinking about you,' she said. 'I don't know if this is the future or the past, but in either case, you should not be there. I was in a place in a kind of dessert. People were living in a tent. There was one woman who was different from the rest. She was taller than the others, maybe of mixed race. She had gold bangles on her arm, and one was like a snake. There was a man there who had two bullet holes in him. One was in his shoulder, not too bad, but the other was in his right side and had hit his bowel and would kill him. I felt his confusion about whether he was doing the right thing or not. I don't know why you were there, but these people were not involved, and their lives were at risk. I woke up because I think there was a blast of some kind. If you recognise the woman, then it is in the past, and I cannot do anything about it. If you don't recognise her, it could be in the future, and I would say to you don't go there.'

She looked at him and said, 'Why aren't you writing this down?' 'Because you show this book to your doctor, don't you?' he said.

'So it has happened then,' she stated. 'And people got hurt because you were there.' She looked into his eyes and saw a helpless look as if to say it had to be.

She felt torn between the person she knew him to be and the person that she thought he was.

'I am going to miss you so much because you are the only person who understands me. Promise me I will see you again.'

'Of course, I said I will come over and be your babysitter.' He had an urge to kiss her and thought better of it. Then he realised she probably knew. 'You had better go back to bed before you get both of us into trouble.'

The next morning, they were told that Neil would be coming to pick her up as the boss was away on business. They would stay behind to make sure the house was clean and adequately shut up before going back to France. Flynn told George about the dream. George thought she could be dangerous; to be able to describe a scene with such accuracy meant that she could do it again and he wondered what they should do.

'We should report it, you know. But of course, we won't because we don't want her life to become more complicated than it is. But now we should keep an eye on things. We can't afford to let this get out of hand. We will also have to take note of whom she talks to because she could inadvertently say something that could endanger us.'

Chapter 15

A NORMAL LIFE

She arrived back at the house mid-morning. After welcoming her back, Faustus told her nobody was home. He and Nara helped her get things upstairs and unpack. Riccardo would not be back for another two days. He had gone to Tastus in Syria. She tried to call his cell. But it was offline. She went to her little room and looked it up. There had been a lot of trouble in Syria, and she was worried he would be caught up in it.

During the evening meal, the old man asked her to show them her ring. He expressed his joy about their engagement. Jacinda also said she was happy for her. Marion felt that this was genuine and although they would never be close as least, they could be cordial to each other. He asked her how she liked staying in Genève and she said that it was good for her and she felt better than she had felt for a long time. She did not mention that there had been anything wrong as it appeared he did not know about it. She asked the old man if he was looking after himself and was he still going for walks. He explained that he had been waiting for her to come back. She smiled at him and said they could continue to walk together if he wanted.

The next day, Rick called her to say he was on his way home. She felt relief fold over her that he was safe. When he came back, he introduced her to Abdula. He was going to be her bodyguard for the moment. He was of medium build, skin the colour of wood and dark eyes. He had curly black hair and a short beard. Rick told her she was not to go outside the house unless he went with her. She complained that she did not need a bodyguard.

He told her that his sister did not go out without one.

'I have never seen her with one.' She said.

'That is because she has a shadow and refuses to acknowledge his presence. You, on the other hand, would not like that and would be upset if you knew someone was following you, and you would insist that you talk to him. I know you; you want to be friends with everybody.'

That night in their bedroom, he told her he had to go to Syria to close their office there and make sure all the paperwork and computers were removed. He had repatriated all their staff to the French office. She had to ask why he had a security office there in the first place.

'It is a perfect place for an office because everybody who is anybody needs protection. The office had flourished, and they were doing well up until recently and then nobody was safe.'

'Do you always cover your back so quickly?'

'Of course, I would be a fool if I did not keep an eye on everything. I work hard to ensure what my business is going well. That is why I must go away a lot. I don't just trust to luck that people will do the right thing. Sometimes this hands-on approach can make enemies, but I can live with that. By the way, you did not say anything to Father about the incident in Genève, did you?'

'No. I realised that he did not know. How is it that you can go anywhere so easily?'

'I am a diplomatic attaché for trade. That is how I can arrange things so fast.

Handy, isn't it?'

For the next couple of weeks, things settled down into a pattern of living that was conformable for everybody. Rick was attentive, and she got to know Abdula. She found they had some things in common. They both liked to read, and although he took work seriously, he did it in a way that was not onerous. He found she was a person of the 'book', and even though not a Muslim, she understood the words in the Holy Quran. They could discuss passages of both Quran and the Bible and put them in a common way. Rick was right, there was no way she would not include him in things she was doing.

She went to the Institute to see the good doctor and

introduced him to Abdula, who waited outside the office for her to finish. She had a chance to catch him up on the events of Genève.

Marion told the doctor about her engagement and how she felt about Rick.

'For a long time, I must have been depressed. I remember I noticed there was a dark side to Rick and he hurt me but I did not care. I did not want to feel anything. I unintentionally kept a kind of emotional distance, and I would not say I loved him. He did notice and thought I was just not good at sex, I think. He tried ways to make me more responsive, and I kept him at arm's length. Then quite suddenly while we were making love I realised I did love him. I let go, and I could feel all of him. I think I came alive again.'

Marion expressed disappointment having got her case back but could not recognise the things inside it. She had not opened it since coming back to the house.

She showed him the dream book that Flynn had been helping her with. She explained that after the incident of the kidnapping attempt, the dark man had gone away for a while.

'I feel as if Flynn understands me better than anybody else.' Some entries were silly except one common element that often happened, which was where she dreamed about a wall of fire. He asked how she was going in the effort to screen out the feelings of others. 'I think that it is only certain emotions that I get hooked into. I don't notice the feelings of ease as much as tension. However, if someone I know is upset, sad, or anxious, I feel it more. So there are times when I can be normal, just like everyone else. Now I know nobody is looking for me for a crime, I feel better, and I wonder why I worried so much about this.'

He asked her if anything else unusual had happened around her. And she answered not as far as she knew. He told her that next visit they would work on trying to put together some more of her past. 'But for now, continue to do what you are doing, and please write everything down in the journal. Even if you have a daydream about something you think might be worth mentioning.'

After the session with the good doctor, she went to have something to eat with Abdula. She wanted to know why he did not like working with anybody else. He told her that he found it hard to trust people because he had seen his family torn apart because of different beliefs. He had watched friends being killed for no reason. Thus he trusted only himself to keep safe, and he knew he could keep her safe as well.

'I know that must be true because Riccardo would not have given you this job if he did not think you are the best at what you do because he is very protective of me. I hope you can find the peace you seek here.'

Rick came home in the evening and told her that both

George and Flynn had agreed to join their staff. They will be coming next week. That meant Abdula would be going back to the French office to work. 'I should tell you that they are not always available and there will be times that they will be going away. This means you will have to do with other staff members. But if you want to have them as your minders, then that means some inconvenience.' She told him she understood that they had their reasons. He looked surprised and wondered how she could understand when he did not really know himself, except it was in their contracts.

The next week, she again took Abdula out for lunch. This time she chose an upmarket place for tourists. She found out he was a vegetarian and did not drink. She asked if he would keep in touch with her as she felt that they were friends and if there was anything she could ever do for him, he only had to ask. 'I am not big on lost causes. I have only one charity that I give to. I don't make a big thing about it, but I believe it is right. It is called Medicines Sans Frontiers or doctors without borders. They treat anybody, no matter which side they are on. I only wish that the world could see that killing is wrong, no matter what.'

That night, she told Rick what she had done. 'It seems I have a problem with letting go of people.'

'That is because you think all people are the same and they are not. My sister knows where people are in this world, and servants are there to help you, not the other way around.'

'But they are still people with feelings and pain just the same as me and you. To work for someone else is an honourable thing. I think the populace who work for the benefit of others are in fact better than people who just use them.'

He smiled at her. 'You do have some strange ideas.'

George and Flynn arrived and settled in at the gatehouse. Marion could not wait to see them and walked down and knocked on the door. George opened it, and she gave him a big hug.

'Welcome. I am so glad you decided to come.'

Then she saw Flynn; she felt a bit shy but did not know why. She gave him a kiss on the cheek and said she was happy he was here.

Flynn said, 'You can come in if you like.'

She had never been to the gatehouse. It was a big area that housed a workroom and sleeping quarters for six people; the bedrooms were small but functional. A kitchen area had a round table and a sitting room with big comfortable chairs, TV, and game consoles. It was the workroom that caught her eye as there was a line of computer screens showing different parts of the house and grounds.

'Now I understand,' she said. 'I have always had the

feeling I was being watched. I felt it more so in some areas than in others. I always talk to Rick in our bedroom because there I felt safe from the eyes. I thought it was just me being mad, but someone was watching. Doesn't it bother anyone else in the house?'

Flynn said that that was a normal part of security; people who have lived with it all their lives don't notice. She looked as the screens moved around different places, including the piano. 'Do they listen as well?'

'We can turn the volume up, but usually, there is no need. If someone comes into the rooms and acts in a threating manner, we may turn it up to assess the risk.'

Flynn explained the men who handle this part of the job don't live here; they just come here on shifts and go home to wives or girlfriends. 'We look after it sometimes. Otherwise, we live like monks. No girls are allowed to come here.'

'Poor you,' she exclaimed. 'What would you do, I guess you make the most of every opportunity.'

'Yes! It's tough, but someone's got to do it.' Flynn gave her a cheeky smile.

'Did you have a chance to meet Abdula?' George said they had met him before and liked him. 'He was good to me while he was here. I asked him to keep in touch. Do you think he will?'

'I'm sure he will.'

'I had better go back now. Can I come again or do I have to call first?'

'Whatever you want, you can get Faustus to have us come up to the house anytime you want.' Flynn offered to help with the dream book if she still needed to, just not in the middle of the night. She laughed and said she could continue to teach George the guitar.

As she was walking back to the house she thought her little world was complete; she felt safer knowing that they were there and would understand her. She had someone who was on her side in this sometimes confusing household.

It made Riccardo happy to see her appeased by the new additions to the staff. When she was content, it made him content as well. Like his father, he hated friction around his home. It had the added value of keeping her out of trouble, he hoped.

A couple weeks later, Rick told her that he had a business trip to America. He planned to be away for four days and would be taking George and Flynn with him. She asked tentatively if she could come. He told her she may be bored as he would be working and would need the boys with him.

'It's okay, I don't mind, I am happy to wait for you. And it would get me out of the house for a while, and you can't work all the time. I'm sure we could spend some time together even if it is only for the night.'

Faced with that sort of logic, he relented and said she could come. 'I noticed you have not opened your case yet. Is there any reason for this?'

'No, I don't know why. I did open it at the police station, but I could not recognise anything in it. I know it is mine because it had my old passport in the side pocket and the picture in it is nearly the same as the one I have now.'

He was resigned to the need for patience. He suggested they try now and see what's in there because she could use the case if she were going away. Together they opened the case up, and she pulled out the clothes. He noticed that nearly all the clothes were designer clothes and looked quite new and expensive. She tried a Chanel suit on, and it was a little loose; otherwise, it fitted her well. She undid the jewellery roll and found several beautiful sets. The diamonds looked real, and there was a set of emeralds as well. She also found an opal ring that sparkled when turned to the light. 'These clothes are better than the ones you wear,' he said. She felt like she could cry. Why then did they mean nothing to her? Whatever happened to her must be blocking her from even remembering her own clothes. 'I just wish I knew. I suppose I should talk to the doctor about this.' He suggested that she should wear them and see if she felt different. She smiled. 'That is a good plan.'

She was excited about the coming trip. She told George she was looking forward to having them together on the plane for a long time. 'I think it takes about twenty-eight hours, and that does not include any stopovers.'

A couple days later, she went with Flynn to see the doctor for her next visit.

He drove her white sports car. 'This is nice,' he said.

The doctor said it was good to see Flynn again. Then he looked at her up and down, and he commented on how impressive she looked.

'These are my own clothes.' When she was seated at the desk, she explained how upset she felt when she could not recognise anything about them. 'Even faced with evidence, I don't understand why something doesn't come back. I should remember when I bought them, but I don't.'

The doctor explained again about retro amnesia and the fact it could last many years. Whatever had happened to her must have been so dramatic that she may have bought them in a daze and not have taken much notice. 'You can't recall if you never took it in, in the first place.' He wanted to do a hypnotic secession with her, but she said she could not settle down because of the impending trip and suggested that they try when she came back.

On the way home, she suggested they stopped off for a drink. She was direct as usual and asked Flynn why he seemed to be keeping his distance. 'You know I can tell when you are evasive, so don't try. Just tell me.'

'My job is to look after you, not to get too close,' he said.

Marion looked at him as if she could see through him and he felt the intense gaze. 'There is more to it than that. What's going on?'

'There are a couple of reasons why we should not get too close. One is I think you already know, I like you a lot, more than I should considering that you are my boss's fiancée. And the another reason is that you know too much about us and that places all of us in danger.'

'What kind of danger? I told you I would not say anything about what I think of you. Nobody is going to believe I had a dream. I'm sorry, I did feel something the last night we were together, but I thought it was only me, I am very fond of both you and George, and you are like brothers to me. I love you both. In my eyes, you are not just servants, and in some ways, more than just friends. I need to have someone I can trust too, and you should know I would not do anything to put you in danger. I think I might be good at keeping secrets. I tell Rick everything that is pertaining to our relationship and would not lie to him. What I think I know, I don't say. I would not even look it up, even though I can. I like to hack into places that I should not go. I have set my laptop up so that if anybody tries to hack back, my laptop will self-destruct. I am very careful with changing my password numbers and codes. I could find out more, but I choose not to. I guess that you will have to trust me to be discreet. I hope that clarifies things better for you.'

'Yes, it does, Marion, but it still doesn't change the way I feel about you.' She lit a cigarette and said,

'I think we are going to have to live with that.'

The trip to America was exciting. Going over there was long and a bit boring because Rick had to work on his laptop and did not want to be interrupted too much. George had a book which he was engrossed in. And Flynn was just sitting and doing what he called 'zoning out'. She then spent time playing on her laptop and catching up on world news. And getting food for them when she thought it was time for a break. They would stop then for a while and just be sociable, which was nice.

Rick owned an apartment in a tall building in New York. It had a view that swept across the landscape, which was buildings as far as the eye could see; however, at night it was like a fairyland. George and Flynn were to stay at a hotel nearby. Neil nearly always stayed at whatever place he could sleep at near the airport. Rick got up early and was ready for the day's meetings. He had picked up a history book of Manhattan for her to read. When he left, she settled down to relax and read. A worrying thought came into her head, and she wondered if he was going to see the Asian man again. She did not want to bring it up with him as she did not want him to think she was prying into his affairs. He called at lunch time and said he had one more meeting and then he would be home. 'I suppose you want to go shopping,' he said.

'You know I hate shopping even in New York, but I would like to see the big lady at the harbour.'

'You mean the Statue of Liberty?' Rick asked if that was wise given she was sensitive to crowds.

'I am sure I'll be okay,' she said.

They came back around 3.00 p.m. to pick her up. They had a cab waiting, and Rick explained that this was the easy way to get around. She had her book, and they joined a group to go up. She said she felt well and there was no extra tension around to upset her. They all enjoyed the experience as none of them had been there before. She had the feeling of a holiday and thought she would be able to tell the doctor that she could do this. Later, they all went out for dinner and the holiday mood continued.

Watching the banter around the table was fun. She could see that Rick was relaxed and comfortable acting socially in the presence of his staff. She realised this is what was missing in his life. He either had business acquaintances or people who just wanted to be seen in his company.

The next day, they flew to San Francisco for more meetings. They stayed in a nice hotel and while he was out, she decided to have a hairdo. In the afternoon, he took Flynn with him and suggested she sightsee with George. They caught a tram at one end and travelled all the way to the bay. They found a coffee shop and had the best coffee she had ever tasted.

She asked George to tell her a little bit about himself, citing that he knew all there was to know about her and it was not fair that he would not say something about his life. He was as usual somewhat non-committal about it. He said he was good at school and attended a public school. His parents are both academics, and so in that sense, life was relatively easy for him. He told her that his parents used to fight a lot and when he was younger, it used to frighten him. When he was about fourteen years old, he decided to stop being concerned about what other people could do to him and that nothing would ever frighten him again. He would trust himself and nobody, or nothing would have that kind of power over him again. He had attended University, achieving his A-levels in languages. He then went to Royal Military Academy at Sandhurst.

'So you are in the army then?'

'I was,' he said, 'and I did a tour of duty overseas as well. I am not in the regular army now.'

'How many languages do you speak?'

'I can speak six well and can pick most others up when I need to.'

'You should be good at music then because it requires you to have a good ear for sound, and you get that when you listen to the different sounds of language. Have you ever thought of being in the diplomatic core?'

'I like what I do,' he said.'

She thought she should not push him for more information right now as he might clam up altogether.

Changing the subject, she said,

'We they have a chance to see the Mission district which is where the 'Mission Delores', the oldest building was situated built in 1791. It is supposed to combine the cultures of many countries and is known for its arts and food.'

They caught a cab and spent a delightful time exploring this famous area. They forgot the time, and the boss called to ask where they were. They suggested he come down to meet them and grab a bite to eat at one of the shops here. They met up at a quaint drinking place and then went on to eat at another location just because the aroma coming from it smelt so good.

It seemed as if the party was just beginning when he said he did not want to stay too long because of the long flight home. Before they left, she could not resist borrowing a guitar from a street group and playing flamingo-style and sang a song about the Bay. They clapped then Rick looked at her and said, 'You just can't help yourself, can you?' She just laughed.

Coming home and back to the routine of the house felt good because of the break; she could appreciate the life they led. She had missed the old man more than she would ever admit. She hugged him when she saw him and although he said not to go overboard, however he appeared pleased. Rick could not get over the fact that they got on so well given how hard he fought his father for her to stay. His sister seemed to have become resigned to the fact she was there to stay and nothing she could do to would remove her.

Chapter 16

MARRIAGE

Riccardo thought it was time to tackle the question of marriage again. He decided to put to her all the logical reasons why it was a good idea. He planned to wait until they were having a good night in bed together. He realised that it was a touchy subject because of all her insecurities. But now that they had established she was not wanted for anything in any country, which was the reason she said she wanted to wait, there was no bar to marriage that he could see.

On a night when he felt that they were particularly close, he told her he loved her and could not see a life without her.

'Will you marry me?'

Before she could answer, he said, 'I have thought that if we were married, you could apply for dual citizenship. It would make it much easier for you to come on trips with me. Father would be happy because he already thinks of you as a daughter. I promise to look after you always even if you get old and fat.' He knew that would make her laugh.

'It's a big step,' she said seriously. 'Do you really think you can put up with me for life?'

'Of course, I don't expect you to change, and I don't think I am going to change either, but we seem to complement each other. I like it that you are a bit different and you always manage to surprise me.'

'I like it when you are so masterful and take over. Somehow that makes me feel safe. I can't imagine my life without you either. It does seem that the time is right for us to marry has come, so I am going to say yes.'

He hugged her and said, 'When?' She thought for a bit and told him that now that had made up their minds, there was no point in waiting.

'There is a lot to do, and we have not thought about how we do this thing.' She looked at him and laughed.

'Why don't we just go to a church and say we want to get married?'

He tried to explain that in their culture, it was not that easy, marriage was a big affair. Families and extended families were all involved. It requires a lot of planning. 'I think the best is that we hire a wedding planner to make all the arrangements. That way you will not feel the need to oblige all the pressures that people will put on you.'

'Is it really that bad?' She asked. He laughed, 'Remember,

you are marrying a Greek God. People will expect it to be a big affair.'

'Now you are making me afraid. Am I going to be able to deal with it?'

'Yes, because I will be there, holding your hand.'

'I don't have any family; won't that appear strange? I know, the boys can be my family, they can be my brothers.' He shrugged, 'If that makes you happy, it's okay with me. We can set a date for three months if that's okay with you?'

'We will tell Father and Jacinda in the morning and ask them to help us. Jacinda is a great organiser, and I bet she knows the best wedding planner around. She could also be your bridesmaid, which would make her happy. Do you mind?'

She shook her head. She did not really care as long as it was settled and over. She made up her mind to talk to the doctor about it and find out of there was any way she could get through a big day without falling apart.

The next morning, they told the family about their plans. Jacinda said she had been expecting it and wondered why it had taken her brother so much time to get to the point. When he went to work, she walked down and told the boys the news and now they were officially her brothers. She could not wait to call Dr McKlean and tell him about it as well. He did not say much; only they would talk about at the next session. She was disappointed at his lack of enthusiasm. She sighed and thought she should talk to Jacinda about being her bridesmaid. She found her in the library with her secretary. After poking her head in, she thought she should withdraw and come another time, but Jacinda called her to come in.

'We were just talking about you. I think you must be pretty excited at getting my brother to marry you.'

'Yes,' she replied. 'It is a big thing. I come first to ask you if you will be my bridesmaid?'

The smile on Jacinda's face was all she needed to know. Rick was right, it would make her happy.

'I understand getting married here is a big thing. I know I cannot do it alone and we thought to get a wedding planner. Riccardo said that you know all the best people to arrange this, and he told me you are a great organiser. I am hoping that you will get me through the rough patches.'

'Now that you are going to be my sister-in-law, I have to help you all I can. Do you have a dress picked out? Getting the right dress is everything and it can take a lot of time. You have not even had an appropriate engagement party yet, to introduce you to our family, which is quite large, and all will want to meet you. I will organise one as soon as I can. Otherwise, people will think there is something wrong with a rushed marriage.'

'I have not even thought of a dress. I don't think I should wear white because I have been living in sin for a while. I am not even sure that I want a long dress. I don't really know what to do.'

She could feel Jacinda's impatience and tried to amend it by saying 'Maybe you could introduce me to a good designer?' Jacinda brightened up at that and stated she would get all the information they needed that day and they could talk about it tomorrow. Relieved that that was over, she felt free to go to her room and play on the laptop.

She was interrupted by Faustus who said he had a call from Carl De Silver. He said he was a friend and was staying at the Grande Bretagne Hotel in Constitution Square PH 21 0333 000. He wanted to talk to her a soon as possible. He handed her a slip of paper. She thanked him and wondered what to do. Then she had an idea to get one of the boys to check him out first. She called down to the gatehouse to see if someone was free. George said he would come straight up. She met him in the sunroom and showed him the piece of paper.

'I have a bad feeling about this, so I was wondering if you could check him out through your connections before I meet him.'

'Of course,' said George. 'How far do you want the check to go?' She thought for a while, suddenly becoming aware he could be anybody, and she would not know.

'How far can you go in a day?'

'Quite a bit, if that is what you want.'

'If he checks out, then I will meet him tomorrow afternoon.'

The next day George had found out that Carl worked for a TV station in Australia, that he was also one of the members of the first singing group she was involved with. He had a clean police record and was married but had no children. He seems on the level. 'However, I recommend that I come with you to be sure you feel okay with him, and if not, just give me the nod, and I will end the meeting.'

'I think this is my past catching up with me, I'm scared of what I might find. I know I have to face it, whatever it is, but I'm glad you will be with me.'

Carl was in his late thirties; his olive skin and almond eyes hinted at his mixed race. He was handsome, well groomed, and had the body that showed he was careful with diet and exercise. He had a friendly and open face, one that instantly says, 'Trust me.' They met in his hotel suite; he asked them in and asked what they wanted to drink.

'I seem to remember you like scotch,' he said, looking at her. 'I was amazed when I saw the story of *Seabird* in the paper. Then when the story about your engagement came out, I wanted to see you. I hear you have lost your memory and I can't imagine what that is like. I was so mad at you for so long and then I heard you had died. And now here you are with a minder to watch over you.

By the look on your face, I understand you have no idea who I am.'

She took the drink from him and tried to get a sense of what he was feeling. There was no real hostility there, only some kind of hope. 'I had some sort of breakdown, and I am sorry I don't know who you are.'

'That's all right,' he said. 'We were kids together who just happened to love music. You left home very young to try to make it in the big time. After a lot of teething troubles, we did make it, to become one of the first Australians to top the charts in America. We were doing well until you decided to quit. We could not understand why you decided to walk away. It left us stranded without a lead singer. We tried to work with other female singers, but they weren't you and the group folded up. Mike now works in advertising and Ken is out of work. I thought you owed us an explanation of why you did this because, in a way, it ruined all our lives.'

'I'm so sorry, I wish I knew. I wish there was some way I could make up for something that I appeared to have done wrong by you.'

'In fact, there is. I have been planning a reunion special on the TV. I think it would get a lot of air time and could get us started again.'

'I am getting married soon so that is not possible and besides, I don't remember the songs that I used to sing. When I lost my memory, I lost my music for a while as well. I have regained it and writing *Seabird* brought a lot back. I don't know how to do what you want. I'm not even sure if people can go backwards to another time.'

He was persistent and tried to press harder to get her to change her mind. 'It would not take much of your time. Just come down for a week at the most. I'm sure you will be able to relearn the songs. For us, it could be a turning point. I am not asking you to restart with the band I am only asking for a week of your time. Surely you owe us that much.'

She looked helplessly at George who stood up as if to go. 'All right, if it is only one week. I don't remember anything about Australia, but I do have an Australian passport. Maybe this is a good time to get away for a while.'

He beamed at her. 'I'll make all the arrangements, and all you have to do is turn up. You won't be sorry, and it will be fun to get together.' She wrote down her e-mail address and said for him to let her know the 'when and where'.

'That went well,' George commented when they were out of the hotel. 'You really stood firm and let him know who the boss is. By the way, what do you think the boss is going to say when you tell him?'

That night, she told them of the plan to go to Australia for a week. Jacinda was frustrated at her lack of interest in the organisation of the marriage. She tried to reassure her that it was in a way better than her getting in the way. Riccardo thought it was a good idea because it is something she needed to get out of her system. One week is not going to make all that much difference as the wedding planner seemed to be able to get things ready all by himself. The old man did not approve. What if she got pulled into that kind of lifestyle she may not want to come back? However, she could not really see that it would be a life-changing event, just a short diversion.

The next day, she went with Jacinda to see the designer for their dresses. She knew that this would be a rough day because they were so different in their ideas of what a bride should wear. Jacinda wanted to know what she wanted her to wear. And she told her to choose anything she wanted, but of course, that would not be easy because Jacinda wanted them to match in some kind of way. Darius, the fashion designer, was a big man with an enormous sense of self-importance and he wanted to showcase something that would be remembered. He had a bald head and shining grey eyes. He knew he had a flair for making women of all shapes look good, and a way for him to get what he wanted was to make them feel good about themselves. Thus, he was a little taken back when he found Marion had ideas of her own. They sat down at a table with a sketch pad and patches of different fabrics. She said she did not want to wear white or a long dress. She was thinking of something along the '40s style, something with a tight bodice and full skirt. He drew out a style, but that was not it. She took a pencil and drew a picture of a dress with a sweetheart neckline short sleeves coming into a waistline and them flowing out to mid-calf length. He thought he could work with that. Then they looked at fabrics. She wanted something soft but would be full at the bottom. That would require an underskirt of two layers of something stiff. She found fabric in the most delicate lemon, and he thought they could enhance it with pearls on the bodice. Jacinda thought if she had something in a soft apricot colour, it would match. In the end, even she was pleased with the idea. They could not decide what sort of veil and evidentially decided on a headpiece with flowers the same colour as the dresses set in tulle, more like a flash hat than a wedding veil. By ordering the flowers in the mixed colours, it would look quite nice. That was the hardest part of the job done. Jacinda said that she would tell the wedding planner to use these colours in all the table settings.

When she came back to the house, Marion found out that the boys were taking leave. She was a bit unhappy about this because she had come to rely on them being there. After they had explained that it was in their contracts that they could go at any time, she got the idea it was on one of their secret trips, and no amount of persuasion would make them change their minds. They assured her they would be back in time for the wedding.

She could feel something different in them, something like steel. It was as if they had already left and changed into something else. She had to just say, 'See you,' and go before she started to cry.

Rick knew she would not be happy about the day's events and but he took her out to dinner that night. She told him about her trip with Jacinda to see Darius. 'He is well known for dressing a lot of famous people. I am sure he will make something pulchritudinous.'

Sitting across him at the restaurant, she gave voice to all the fears that were unsettling her.

'I thought getting married would be easy, I had not considered the way things are done here. Jacinda has told me that it is imperative to include all your extended family. She thinks three months is rushing it a bit and wonders if people will question why the hurry. The first thing they will think is that I am having a baby and am marrying you to make it legitimate. And there are longstanding business people who will expect to be invited as well. She said it is anticipated for you to have a big affair. Otherwise, people will think you cannot afford it, and that could affect your stocks. I have not taken any of this into account. She said she will arrange an engagement party as soon as she can. Then there is a wedding shower where the women of the family all will want to give me advice. Then she said that only having one bridesmaid will again also be considered different. She is not happy with me going away for a week. It could look as if we are having trouble.'

Riccardo tried to understand her concerns. He had not given much thought about arrangements as it was usually left to the woman's family.

Traditionally, men kept out of what was considered a woman's concern. Most males just went along with whatever their womenfolk decided. Their primary job was to turn up on the day as sober as possible. Marion was completely vulnerable in this situation, not even being able to speak the language. He made a mental note to make sure she had an interpreter present.

'I am confident you will manage,' he told her. 'There is one thing we should discuss, and that is how to handle the press. I have been thinking about this, and the best idea is to give an exclusive to one magazine like *Vouge* or *Vanity Fair*. They have their own way of dealing with the competition, and it stops a free-for-all. What do you think?'

'I don't know. Maybe we should ask Jacinda, I'm sure she had all the ideas on whom to choose. I thought it was up to security to make sure that unwelcome people don't come.'

'That is true, but they have ways of getting pictures, even if it is by air or by using a satellite. You are right; it is another thing to discuss with the wedding planner and Jacinda.'

'I am glad to be away for a week; At least I will not have to deal with it all for a while.'

'That is another thing we have to talk about. Now that the boys have taken leave, you will need another minder. We have an ex-cop in Scotland who we call Big George. He is very efficient in crowd control. I thought he would be the best to go with you to Australia. He is a nice person although he can be a bit autocratic at times. Would you be happy to work with him or would you rather one of the guards from home?'

'I don't really care. It is just another thing I want to get over with. I can't imagine how this show will go if everyone thinks I'm dead. I just hope I can get some answers as to why they believe that. And I do want to see some sights because they may bring back some memories. Will you miss me?'

'You know I will, but we can talk every day, or you could Skype me. Father is worried you will go over to the dark side and decide not to come back. I told him not think that way because you love me. Let's go home so you can show me how much you will miss me?'

Marion's next appointment with the doctor was disadvantageous for her. She had gone down with Abrax who was to wait for her. She felt serene and had talked to him about her car. As she did not use it much, she had told him he could drive it if he wished to give it a run, making it sound as if he was doing her a favour. She asked about his children, and he told her that Celine, the eldest child, was top of her class and they had high hopes for future, hoping she would be able to go to university.

She thought she had made some decisions on her own without consulting Riccardo and the good doctor would approve. When he showed her into his room, she suddenly felt unhappy. He looked at her and put the tape on his desk on, and then said. 'I have heard about your plans for a trip to Australia, you have created a situation that has the potential to harm you. I would like you to rethink this action.'

'I realise that it sounds a bit busy, but getting away from the house and all the excitement must be better.'

'I don't think you have thought it through. Given past experiences, you need to be constantly aware of the potential for danger that you create in the situations you get yourself into. For example, are you sure that marrying

Riccardo is the best thing?'

'I must admit that I had not thought it would be so involved. Rick has always been there for me. He saved my life. We have agreed that we are good together. He puts up with me, and I put up with him. And we are both changing. He is trying to see things from my point of view, particularly when I point it out to him. I know he loves me more than he has loved anything else and that is good for me because it makes me feel cared for and safe. I want to marry him. The worst part is the thought of a big wedding. I was hoping you could help me find a way to get through the day.'

'What is your motive for going to Australia?' It is fraught with danger for you. I would have thought you would have had enough at the awards.'

'Carl came all the way over to ask me to help them get back together as a group. All he asked was one week of my time. He told me it was my fault that the group broke up in the first place and the least I could do is to help. That sounded reasonable to me. I have to know what happened. Rick wants me to change my citizenship status. I am not sure because I can't remember anything about Australia. I am to take a new minder who is a specialist in crowd control to keep me safe. I am to travel with a commercial airline, but I think I will have headphones on and that will help.'

'How have you been feeling otherwise? Are there still times when you feel overwhelmed?'

'I wish I did not have to do the wedding thing. My usual minders are on leave, but they will be back for the wedding, and they are now my honorary brothers, my family. When we are together, I feel like I have a family and Riccardo seems so relaxed now with them. I believe he no longer sees them as just servants. I can feel that they act as equals when nobody is around, and I realised that he has had no real friends to speak of. I think they have a significant role to play in our lives.'

'When are you leaving for this show?'

'I think in about a week. Carl had promised to make all the arrangements and e-mail me. He wants it to work bad enough to do all the work. He seemed genuine when I talked to him, and I did not feel any hidden agendas in him. As you can see, I use my feelings more than ever, and now I can find no reason to shut them off except when they get too strong. What will happen if I use headphones and keep my eyes down, will that help?'

He looked at her sadly, trying to find a way through the maze of her mind to keep her on an even path. 'The trouble with that idea is first you can't keep headphones on all the time, and two its still does not solve the problem of overload. I think that when there is high emotion in your immediate area, you will feel it as a shock wave unless you try to desensitise your feelings and to do that you have to work with me, which you are not always prepared to do.'

'Are you trying to tell me I should not do things?' she stormed at him.

'I am only trying to tell you to be careful and don't jump into the deep end before you can swim.'

'Don't spoil my plans. You said I should think for myself and that is what I'm doing. I know I need your help, but be happy for me when things are right.'

'I will be here for you, and you can always call me. I sincerely wish you luck. I'm just not sure you have thought it through enough. If you have doubts or fears, don't be afraid to come to me. I will always help. I would like to see you when you come back.'

As she left the office, all serenity had gone, and he had sown the seeds of doubt in her mind. What if she could not do it? What if she was deluding herself and there would be nobody to catch her this time? Could she call it off and stay safe? She would no longer call him the good doctor because of his lack of trust in her ability to go to another country and perform. She decided to call him her shrink from now on because he was trying to shrink her world into a smaller space. She thought about why she had left the group so suddenly; there must have been a reason. Rick believed in her ability to do this, or he would not have recommended her to go. 'Well,' she thought, 'I'll show them all and do it well and not fall apart.'

William McKlean sat down to write in the case file. He reached for folder with the file with the number: 786245 Marion

He listened again to the tape. He wrote,

1. Marion was unaware or unwilling to face up to the consequences that could result from impulsive actions.

2. A driving force is a deep need for her to create a family.

3. Her empathic skills seem to be growing stronger. This could suggest that these skills may have developed after a major event in her life rather than an inherent ability from birth.

4. There is another possibility that; they have been dormant and never utilised until there was a need; this is not a probable scenario.

5. Avoidant personality disorder (APD). She continues to have low self-esteem. She covers her shyness by finding ways to opt out of situations and states she prefers to be alone. That way she does not have to connect too much with those around her. She still feels extremely sensitive to what others think of her.

6. She expressed her desire to 'fit in' when she is in large groups. She uses empathic skills as she is hyper-vigilant in appraising movements and expressions of those with whom she comes in contact.

7. Tends to idealise the relationship she is in. I have advised her not to consider marriage at this point.

8. What part does depression play in her decision to stay?

9. Is there still other uncovered factors?

She is impulsive and refuses to accept the notion that she needs to think things through before acting. That places the importance of ongoing counselling high in her treatment. Her kind heart feels for the suffering of others. Thus she is easily swayed towards other points of view. The trip to Australia is ill-advised especially as it seems to be a quick decision.

Two weeks later she was back in his office to tell him about the TV show. She told him about the time in the air and stopovers at Singapore that cost her two and a half days. Three of the days they spent five hours a day in rehearsal. She had listened to the album but decided she learned better reading the sheet music. When she arrived, they were there to meet her and hugged and kissed her; it was so strange because she did not know them. She was invited to stay at Carl's house, which was huge and looking over Sydney Harbour. Big George did his job and kept everyone away who was not necessary. She was disappointed that nobody was prepared to talk about what had happened to her. In fact, they maintained a stoic silence as if they had decided not to mention the past at all.

The show was performed live in front of a studio audience. Marion was doing all right until the night of the show. Then the anxiety of the people around her got the better of her, and she ended up throwing up in the toilet just before they were due to go on. Once on the stage, she went into auto-pilot and just did what they had rehearsed. One point nine million people watched the show, which was sponsored by Nissan and Choosy. That is a big number for Australia and helped the TV station towards the top of a rating war that was going on. She found it curious that a lot of people thought she was dead. Because of the rush, she did not have time to explore this further, and she cried on the way home out of frustration. She dived into her bag and gave her shrink a CD of the show. 'I did not see what I wanted. However, getting back home became more important.

'I talked to Rick every day, and he continued to encourage me. He told me that no matter what happens there, the sun will always rise in the Mediterranean. I can't understand why they wanted me because they all have a lot of talent and can do it on their own. I got them to sing some songs where I was just a background voice. And it sounded excellent to me. I also encouraged them to record their own songs and release that to the public. And as you can see, I survived without falling apart.'

He looked pleased, but she felt that he did not like being proven wrong. 'What is next on the agenda?'

'I have to survive this wedding shower. Rick has asked a cousin who is good with language to stay near me and act as an interpreter. I have been advised that it is a big and noisy affair. I can't wear headphones as that would be rude. Do you have another suggestion?'

'That depends on how important it is to you. I know you

hate taking drugs, but this time, taking something that calms you down might work. It is a little more potent than alcohol. But the effect may be similar. I would try it out first to see what your reaction is. Would you like me to write a script?' 'Thank You,' she said.

When Marion was alone with Rick, she showed him the script, 'I have to try it first to find out what reaction I get.' He laughed and told her he wanted to be around when she tried it. 'I want to get in on the fun.'

'I don't think it's funny,' she said. 'I could end up like you do when you have too much to drink.'

'I'm counting on it,' he laughed. 'Did I tell you I have asked Brian to be my best man? I have to admit my reasoning is that at least he is another person you know.'

'Have you heard from the boys?' she asked. 'Nothing, but I know they will get here if they can.'

The wedding shower was about as bad as one can get. Marion was kissed and hugged so many times, she started to feel bruised. That tablet she had taken acted like a barrier and made everything seem surreal and distant. She just smiled all the time and nodded her head if someone addressed her. People were handing her bits of paper or an envelope, and she held on to these thinking they were recipes. Everyone wanted her to try their own cooking as the women were proud of the way they prepared meals. After a while, she could not fit another bite in, and she sensed the ladies were disappointed. She tried to make up for this by giving them extra hugs.

Finally, the ordeal was over, and Jacinda gushed that it had been a great success. She told Jacinda that these people were the kindest people she had ever met. She felt overwhelmed by their generosity and their acceptance of her. It was only later she looked at the papers in her hand. It was money and a lot of it. Each person had put their name and address with the notes so she could thank them. Jacinda explained they traditionally used to pin it to the wedding dress, but now they gave it first in case the bride would want to get something for the wedding. 'They like it if you can say what you bought.' The worst was over and even when she knew she should not drink, she poured herself and Jacinda champagne. 'You have been a treasure to me. I can't thank you enough for your help. 'Jacinda's reply was, 'don't go all soft on me, I still think you are a witch.' The drink went straight to her head, and she nearly fell on the floor. As luck would have it, Rick came in and saw the state she was in. He just picked her up and carried her to their bedroom. He was tempted to have his way with her but changed his mind and thought it would be better when she slept it off a bit.

As the day of the wedding drew near, she was worried that George and Flynn would not make it. She knew it was wrong, but she tried to find out where they were. After calming herself down, she concentrated on Flynn.

She imagined his face she thought about his body, and when she had him fixed in her mind, she looked around him. In her thoughts, she saw him driving a car along a dusty road. His mind was concentrating on following a car in the front of them. She looked at him and saw he had army clothes on. She wanted to tell him to come home but did not want to break his concentration. She felt his awareness of her presence, and she quickly withdrew, breaking the connection. How much did he feel, she wondered, and would he be cross? Anyway, it was a reminder for them to finish what they were doing and come home. She decided not to tell anyone about this new skill.

Brian arrived a week before the wedding. She was happy to see him. His laidback casual style was good for everybody. She played the CD of the concert in Australia. 'I knew you had done this before,' he said. 'What are your plans now?'

'I don't have any I just want to be a wife, that's it. Maybe when I'm old and grey, I'll teach music. I am teaching one of my minders, and I found out he had this amazing voice, but I really want to get married but without the fuss.'

'Have you planned a honeymoon yet?'

'Rick told me I could go anywhere in the world. I'm thinking of thinking a trip around Britton in a car and just stop off where ever we find ourselves. He should see the other side of life. It would be a real getaway as nobody will know where we are.'

Two days later, George and Flynn arrived back; both looked worn and bruised. As soon as she found out they were at the gatehouse, she went down to see them. She told them of her adventure in Australia and of the plans for the wedding that was now in full swing. She could not stay for long as there were things she must do, but she just had to tell them how happy she was now they were back. Flynn said he would walk her back to the house. As soon as they were alone, he told her how cross he felt at her for 'fucking' with his head. He asked her how she had done this. And she told him all she did was to think about him. 'I saw you in a car with uniforms on but no badges. You were chasing someone, and as soon as I realised what I had done, I stopped.'

'Well, you did fuck with my concentration. But worse than that is you should not have done it in the first place.'

'I am so sorry, I missed you, and I just wanted you to come home and be here for my wedding. I did not know I could do this and I did not know you would notice. I hope you did not tell anyone, not even George because now I feel ashamed of even trying. I won't do it again.'

'In a way, it is flattering, Marion, that you should care so much that you would try to get in touch with me, even if it is by an unconventional method. It can be our secret if that is what you want. But I would have thought it would be something you could do to the boss, not to me.'

It was the day before the wedding; there were people everywhere. Some were family guests, and some were people putting up a large marquee across the back lawn, others putting lights and an army placing tables and chairs covered with soft yellow fabric. They were turning the backyard into a fairyland. There seemed to be a lot of 'suits' around; everyone entering the grounds were checked. For Marion, there was no escape.

The first thing they were required was to go to the domed basilica Metropolitan Cathedral of the Annunciation for a rehearsal. Marion had attended a couple services at the church and at least knew a bit about it. Jacinda and Brian came too, and they made a nice-looking couple, but the Patriarch was surprised by the lack of assistants. Usually, there were at least six maids of honour. The Patariarch took them through the whole process and explained the sacrament of marriage as a ritual and its symbolism. It has remained unchanged since the start of the Eastern Orthodox Church. First was the blessing of the rings and the exchange of them. He took a ring and slipped on her right hand then back to his hand, making a cross on his forehead and then on to her finger. She did the same with Riccardo's ring. There was the lighting of candles signifying as Christ was a light to the world, they would also be a light to the world. The crowning was also steeped in symbolism. On a silver tray were two small crowns that were to be placed on their heads. Then there was reading from the Bible concerning the state of marriage. After that, another ritual was the drinking of wine from a common cup signifying they were to do things together as one. The last section was a ceremonial walk as husband and wife. When that was finished, they could kiss and stand before the congregation as husband and wife.

Back at the house, she retreated to the farthest corner of the pool area. George and Flynn were there, and so were Brian and Rick. Flynn and Brian seemed to have the same sense of humour and bounced jokes off each other, keeping the mood light. Rick sat close to Marion, hoping to keep her mind off events that were happening around her. That night, Brian had organised a boys' night out, but Marion had decided to go to bed early. But first, she wanted Brian to listen to George sing and asked him to get his guitar, and she would get hers. Brian said he never travelled without one so they could 'jam' together. When they again sat down, she asked George to sing a couple of songs she had written for him. She sang softly in the background and harmonised through the choirs. Brian was impressed as she knew he would be. Flynn said he had never even sung in the shower before. Marion explained she had found out George could sing by accident, but since then had been training his voice as well as teaching him music. Brian asked if he was interested in changing jobs, as he was sure he could mentor him into the industry. But he only said he liked what he was doing now and did not want to change anything. They looked for some songs they all knew and sang together. Brian also had a good voice, and they found they could harmonise well together. It was not long before other people came out to listen to them. Jacinda was still getting to know Brian who would be her partner for the day. She had liked him instantly and was impressed that he was good at what he did. She had made up her mind that she would have a lot of fun with him, and who knows where that would lead.

As good as it was, Marion found she could not take much more and decided to retire to her room. Rick followed her and asked if everything was all right. 'I'm just getting the jitters, it's nothing.' Somehow she knew she should be the life of the party or at least be gracious to everyone. She felt she was not being fair to Jacinda, who was doing everything, but the noise was becoming too much for her to cope with and she was afraid she would go into meltdown. She tried to remember how to meditate and put her mind in a better place. All this was not a good idea; she should have known better; it was not going to happen.

Finally, she rang her shrink. After explaining to him her fears, he helped to calm her down by breaking things into small steps. The next thing was to attend the evening meal with the women staying. Most of the men would be out for the evening and were not expected home until the morning if lucky.

There was much-excited talk around the table about

the roles each would take in the preparations. Marion asked what she was supposed to do and was told as it was her day; she was not expected to do anything. The stylist would arrive in the morning, and they would start by doing her nails, hair, and makeup. That would take nearly all day. The service was due to start at 5.30 p.m. The car would arrive at four thirty. The photographer would come at 2.00 p.m. and take some pictures before putting on the wedding dress. Other than that, she could just relax and enjoy. She could not see any joy in the whole day. She hoped when the formalities were over, she could at least be with Rick and she hoped he could keep her calm.

Surprisingly, the old man came to her rescue. He invited her into his office. He explained he knew about the sensory overload. He told her it is not unusual for the woman to have second thoughts at this time. He reminded her it was him taking her down the aisle. 'I just want you to think of the many walks we do together. I want to say to you that I am pleased that you will become a member of our family, I am quite fond of you and I see the changes you have made in Riccardo. I never thought I would say this to anyone, but he has become more of a man now because he feels responsible for you. You have even made peace with Jacinda. It was a good idea to let her take charge of the preparations. She likes to be needed and now she owns the wedding, she had stopped complaining about the extra things she had to do. You have created a place in this home that has been left vacant since my wife died. I want you to know how much that means to me. I have something I hope you will wear for your wedding.' He brought out a red velvet case and gave it to her. When she opened it up there was a diamond necklace inside; it was beautiful. 'My wife wore it on our wedding day,' he said. 'I would like you to wear it on yours.'

'It is such a lovely thing to do for me, thank you,' she said. 'I will take care of it. She felt the tears sting her eyes. 'That is the nicest thing anybody has done for me.' She got up and went to the desk and gave him a hug. She looked into his eyes and saw they were glistening. To her, it was a very emotional moment, He was not a man given to emotion, and thus it was special.

She went to bed in the nanny room because the small space seemed to be good. She fell asleep for a couple of hours and them dreamed of a volcano on an island. It had been blowing smoke, and the ground started to shake. Some locals refused to leave. There was one small penguin that wanted to stay close to her. She put it into the water but it kept running after her, and then she had no option but to take it with her. She looked over at the volcano; it was glowing red. She noticed the tall, dark man in the corner of her mind again. She pulled out her dream diary and wrote it down. Two things stood out was the fact she had not panicked. She thought that meant it was not going to happen shortly. And she had not felt the urgency to it.

The next day started off quiet enough. The usual breakfast: several cups of tea. Then things began to go a bit crazy. The girls came into her room and painted her nails. The hairdresser arrived, and she had not decided what to do about a style. Jacinda came into the chamber and she showed her the necklace. It changed the way she would do her hair to show if off to the best advantage. Jacinda thought she should have it up in a French twist. And then there was the way she should place the headpiece so the crowns would fit. A makeup lady came in to do their faces. Then the photographer wanted to take before-and-after pictures. It seemed to take hours. The dresses were faultless; the colours blended into a soft hue, making them look like a watercolour painting. It was time to go, Jacinda gave her a hug for luck and the ladies standing in the hall all gushed at how cute they looked. The old man, who was standing at the bottom of the stairs, felt a surge of pride because they looked as if they were sisters.

The ceremony was long and tedious, and they were glad when they could escape the church. More photos and back to the house for the reception. Marion felt exhausted long before it finished and kept trying to stay focused. It struck her funny whenever someone said Marion Rodregious. She liked to watch the men dance together; it seemed natural and energetic. Even Brian, George, and Flynn who had never done this kind of dance before joined in, and it incorporated then into the family. After that, the ladies also joined in, and everyone seemed to be happy. The band played a mixture of Greek music and modern tunes. So people were able to mingle and dance. She had a dance with all the men in her life, even dancing with the old man. Finally, people started to go home. She kicked off her shoes and sang with the band 'There will never another you.' The photographer, standing near the reporter, wanted to take more pictures, but the boys came over to them, standing in front of them and said that was enough; this was a family thing now, and it was time for them to leave.

They went back to the house for the night, leaving early the next day for a two-week holiday in the British Islands. She fell on the bed so tired she could hardly move. Rick came over and helped her off with the dress, and she took off the rest and pulled the covers over her, and she was asleep in minutes.

Chapter 17
A GILDED DREAM

Their honeymoon was to be the best time they would have together. It would be the first time that they would have two weeks continually alone with no outside influences unless they wanted it. Rick had said she could choose any place she wanted to go. The plan was to have no exact idea, just to drive around Britain. The first night was spent at the Old Vines, an eighteenth-century inn, in Winchester. It was the ancient capital city of England. They parked the car and checked in. There was still plenty of time to explore the City Museum across the road and the cathedral opposite. The bar area was lively and gave them a great start to their honeymoon. Their room was quaint and snug. The next day, they travelled through new forests to the ancient stone circle, the mystical Stonehenge. Here she could feel the age and the reverence that had passed down through the ages. There seemed a presence that was not quite tangible but there nevertheless.

From there they went to Bath. It is where the only hot springs in England are situated. Marion thought it was romantic because it had been the location in many books. It has a Roman-built bathhouse and is a world heritage–listed city. They stayed at Macdonald Bath and Spa. Their rooms were elegant and had their own private spa. Outside there was a beautiful garden area, just the thing for a romantic walk. The evening walk felt as if she had been transported to a fairyland where the two of them were the only people on the earth. She felt free for what seemed like the first time in her life and totally relaxed. The next day, they spent some time exploring the town and the many unique shops. It felt odd that she did not feel any background noise.

From there they went to Cardiff. It seemed to be such a contrast to their trip so far. This was a modern city and the hotel Cardiff Central Sleeperz was just about as modern as one could get, with bright colours and an upmarket look. The best part of the stop off was a trip to Dr Who's theme complex. Here, one could be a child again and walk through the various sets and visit the TARDIS. They visited Cardiff Castle, which was purported to have resident ghosts. However, there were no ghosts. She told Rick that if there were any ghosts, she would feel them. By this time, Rick was getting a bit sick of castles and longed to head for the open road.

Stratford-upon-Avon though was a must-see because it was the birthplace of William Shakespeare. The morning was spent looking around all the places that Marion thought of interest. Marion liked to gather up brochures and read the history of every place they went. A short drive to the village of Honiley in Warwickshire where they stayed at Brook Honiley Court Hotel. This beautiful place was a sixteenth-century farmhouse.

Up until now, she had not had any dreams. However, that night she dreamed she was facing the wall of fire. Marion tried to get through to the other side because there was something important she had to see, but the heat was too intense. She woke up to find it was only 3.30 a.m. but she knew sleep was over for her. She crept out of bed, trying not to disturb Rick. Then went outside and watched to dawn break into a beautiful day. Marion loved the countryside because the greens were as bright as she had seen.

They had lunch at another quaint Inn and then headed north, taking in the drive through the Snowdonia National Park, stopping off at a village by the strange name of 'Betws-y-coed'. There were a lot of artworks displayed showing the natural wonders of the area. Back on the open road, they went to Caernarfon. There was a castle built by Edward the 1st. It is the place where Charles was proclaimed Prince of Wales in 1969. They did not stay there long as Rick was getting bored with castles. They took a scenic drive to the Victorian town of Llandudno and spent the night at Bodygallen Hall and Spa. Rick could not get over the strange names of the places they passed, and Marion tried to keep up on the maps and brochures. It was just lovely except it was cold. There were some fabulous gardens to be explored. It was the kind of place Marion would have liked to have spent a week in. The short jumps meant they had all day to explore. They would get up sometimes quite early and set out to another place so as to get the most views of each area. The drive across the north coast of Wales was exciting as there seemed to be new scenes at each turn.

They stopped at Colwyn Bay for brunch. They had a strange encounter with a lady called Maggie. They were sitting in the window seat of a café when this strange woman walked by. She was a small old person with wizard hair, brown clothes that seemed to encompass several layers. She had a shopping trolley, and as she walked by, she stared at them. Marion gave a small kind of wave. Then she walked back again and stared at them. Then she walked back again. It was starting to look like a John Cleese movie, and both of them began to laugh. Suddenly, she walked in the café and pointed her finger at Marion. 'You are one of them,' she stated. 'I never thought to see the likes of you in my life.' With that, she marched out. Rick felt annoyed at her intrusion and jumped up and chased after her and asked what she meant. 'She's fey' she said. He asked what the hell did that mean; she answered. 'She has the third eye and can see things.' He walked back to the café, puzzled. Marion told him not to take notice. 'It's the green eyes, they get you every time.' She laughed. 'We will look it up later.' They decided to avoid the city of Manchester and travel directly to the Lake District.

The Lake District in the north east of England was a surprise. It comprised quite a large national forest and lakes that afforded many activities. They stayed at the Derwentwater Hotel in Keswick, which looked like a big country house. They could walk down a tree-lined path to the lake. They decided to stay two nights there so they could have leisure time and do some short drives out to scenic spots. There was a sunroom that covered the back part of the building. The walls were cream, and the furnishings were a dark rose colour. After dinner, Marion retrieved her guitar from the car, and they went into the sunroom. She sat on one of the chairs and played and sang some old English songs she could remember. Other people came in and joined in singing, and she learned a few new folk songs. Rick was happy to sit back and watch his wife.

Being together was a way for them to learn and appreciate the best qualities of each other. Rick learned to relax more and to be less uptight. He laughed a lot because of the different way she saw the world. She saw beauty in every turn and made him stop and look at things so he learned to see the wonders of nature that he may have passed by if she had not been there. He discovered that when Marion was tired, a slight dark shadow appeared under her eyes. Often she refused to give in to this and would go until she dropped. She had an adventurer's nature and often would do something first and think later. She learned to rely on his steadiness and thoughtful nature. He was her rock that kept her from doing dangerous things. She felt she could trust him to always be there for her.

However, there were times when she enticed him into doing things he would have never tried if she had not been there. On one of their drives, they came to a small spot on the lake where there was nobody around. 'Let's go for a swim,' she said. He was dismayed because it was cold and the water would be more chilled. 'Come on, just a quick dip, just to see what it's like.' Against his better judgement, they took off all their clothes and jumped into the water. It was freezing, but they managed to swim out a little way, kicking and splashing each other, playing in the water and then back again. They were shaking as they put their clothes back on, but laughing at the same time. When they climbed back into the car, they hugged together to get warm. 'You are mad,' he said. 'It was fun, though, wasn't it?'

On the way to Edinburgh, they stopped off at Gretna Green. This was a place where couples in days gone by could elope and say their vows over an anvil, in the old blacksmith shop. Today, it is still a place where marriages are held. The Gretna Hall Hotel is set in a lovely landscape. The hall was built in 1710 and reflects a way of life that was gentler than today. One could not help falling in love with the romance of the place. Their rooms looked like something out of a movie set, and they could not help but fall under its spell. They decided to stay an extra day here just because they could spend the whole day in bed. They only came out for meals, which were delicious. It was here that Marion felt that some kind of weight had been lifted off her shoulders. She could not explain what it was, but it afforded her freedom she had not had before. She made love with more intensity, the colours seemed brighter, and she felt lighter even though her weight had not changed. She had always loved to sing, but now it became a pure pleasure and not just a way to keep the demons away. The depression that had plagued her for so long was gone, and they were happy.

The next stop was Aberdeen. Rick explained that he had a security company based here and he would have to incorporate some time with the manager and staff while they were here. Even though it had been a great trip, Marion was excited to be able to meet some of the people who worked for her husband. She had felt excluded from his business interests, and this might be a start to becoming more familiar with what he did. They were booked to stay in Rox Hotel in Market Street as it was close to where the security office was. It was a bustling area, not far from the docks and it had the look of many city areas. Dotted around were small speciality shops that invited one to explore and try their wares. Musa was a food hall and arts centre that was one place where Marion thought she had gone to whisky heaven as there seemed so many different ones to try.

After settling into their rooms, they went to the security offices. The building had a plain front built in stone and a small plaque stating Aberdeen Security Company. Riccardo introduced his wife Marion to Roy McInns who was the manager of the security firm. He was a pleasant man of about forty years. He had brown pants, a cream shirt left open at the top, and a tweed jacket. His face was weather-beaten brown, had a nice smile and blue eyes. He seemed to be a man determined not to be hurried. He invited them home for dinner that night and said he would go over the books with Riccardo tomorrow. Roy turned to Marion and said, 'I believe you already know one of our people, George.'

'Yes,' she said. 'He came with me to Australia. He is excellent at crowd control.'

'I thought you would find him a bit too bossy.' He smiled at her.

'How many are on your staff?' she asked.

'It changes, but there are usually somewhere about thirty. We do a lot of public functions and shows, and employees change offices if necessary.' She would like to have quizzed him more, but a look from Rick was enough for her to let it go.

The next morning, he told her he would be at the office most of the day and would she mind looking after herself.

'I will get one of the boys to act as a guide for you.'

She looked at him and said, 'I promise it is not necessary. I can stay out of trouble for one day. I like being by myself and will not go too far from here. Please.' He relented but only if she would refrain from doing anything different, like trying whisky by herself. She laughed and agreed. They met up for dinner, and she told him all about the wonderful shops. 'I usually hate shopping, but I bought a beautiful coat because I am always cold here. It was a soft white woven wool coat, and she matched it with a cap.' That night, she was able to try some different types of whisky, some very old. Rick took out a notepad and wrote down the names she liked the best and said he would have some sent over to them. She felt a little sad to be leaving Aberdeen as she realised she had only touched the surface of a city that had so much to offer.

They drove down to Edinburgh and stayed at Le Monde Hotel. It was a pure contemporary luxury and full of surprises. Rick liked the bar area because it was full of bright lights. They spent a delightful evening there with another couple from America. The room also had that something extra with a fish tank above the bed. The next day, Rick had a surprise. He had booked a day tour in a small luxury bus. Rather than drive around, they only had to sit back and watch the highlands, Glencoe and Loch Ness. It was fun being tourists for the day, and they were not too tired to stay up most of the night.

They drove to the Yorkshire moors as Marion wanted

to see a place she had read about. They drove up a winding track and got out to walk for a while. Suddenly, she called to Rick in a small voice for him to come here. She had fallen into a bog and was up to her knees. 'Look for a stick and pull me out, don't come too close or you might get trapped too.' He looked around and found a relatively long stick and pushed the end over to her. He pulled and pulled very hard until she started to move. When she was out and covered with what looked like smelly tea leaves, he started to laugh. 'You are a magnet for trouble.'

'Yuck! I wonder if there are any people down there who could not get out.'

'There must be a need or there would not be long sticks lying about.' He could only see the funny side and teased her about the smell.

The next stop was to be Harrogate in the north county. As navigator, Marion was to make sure they were on the right road. About halfway towards the town, the car broke down. Stranded in a country lane not knowing how to fix a car, they waited for a while to see if someone would come along. The afternoon was coming to an end, and they did not know what to do. Then they spotted some sheep wandering along. 'That's it,' she said. 'All we have to do is follow them, and they are bound to be going home.' They tried to follow them, but the sheep seemed to be running away from them rather than going anyplace. Now they were lost in fields of grass and away from the car. The idea of sleeping in the grass with sheep poo was very unappealing. A short time later, they heard a low whistle and a dog bark. This was a promising sign as dogs do go home. They jumped up and down, making funny noises hoping to attract the owner's attention, but the dog appeared. He barked and growled at them. Then the dog ran off. They tried to follow but lost him in the grass. But soon, the dog returned this time with a man. They had some difficulty explaining about the car because his accent was hard for them to comprehend. One would question if this was even English. When the man asked where the car was, they could not remember as they had been walking around a lot. He got them to follow him, and they came to a barn where he produced an old tractor. Clinging to the sides, they sailed down the lane until they found the car. He hitched the tractor to the car, and Rick sat in the car to steer while Marion held on to the side. When they got back to the barn, he looked at the engine and, with a couple pieces of wire tied, something together, and the car ran. They could not thank him enough. He just told them to 'be-gone.'

They arrived at the White Hart Hotel, happy to be somewhere that was clean. The next day, they took the car to a garage in town and when the serviceman saw the repair, he laughed out loud and told them they must have run into Ted, who could fix anything with a bit of wire. They had to stay an extra day for the car to be fixed. They could not complain because the hotel was lovely and the food was great. The country around this area had some spectacular scenery. The winding roads afforded sights of the mores as well as green pastures as lovely as any picture. The small villages clustered together were quaint and different from anything they had seen before.

They left early the next day. Rick wanted to take her to Cambridge where he had spent his higher education. Cambridge University is sixty miles from London. Marion was not prepared for the size of the university, as it was a city in its own right. It had many imposing buildings set out in neat grounds. As they drove through on their way to their hotel, she wondered how anyone would ever be able to find their way around. The De Vere Hotel, University Arms, was situated in the centre of the city. While they were settling in, she read brochures about Cambridge. It was founded in the twelfth century. The oldest building was St. John College. Women could not get a degree from the college until 1998, even though they had been studying there for 100 years before that. Students needed to pass exams in Latin until about thirty years ago. Also, she found out that it is one of the wealthiest institutions in England, deriving its wealth from the land around it. The next day they spent a lot of time looking at the elegant buildings. Rick was happy to show her the Judge Business School in Trumping Street. The entrance was through iron gates with the name of the school on top. The building was vast, and she was impressed by the architecture. Inside it was quite modern with splashes of red and blue through the halls. They went to see the King's College Chapel which was stunning. She learned that Rick played rugby, a game which she thought quite brutal. They went for a forty-five-minute river tour in a chauffeured punt. It was another way of viewing Kings College Chapel from the water, the Bridge of Sighs, the Mathematical Bridge, and the Wren Library. They drove around some of the colleges, which left a lasting impression on Marion. 'If I get to live another lifetime, I would like to study here,' she said.

All too soon, their holiday was over, and they were on their way home. It carried with it a mixture of sadness and delight. They were aware they could not live in the bubble they had created for themselves forever, but they wished time had not gone so fast. On the other hand, they were looking forward to getting back to the people they had left behind. The newfound bond between them would be there forever, and they had their whole lives to explore each other's personalities.

Chapter 18
RIPPLES OF LIFE

Three months later, it seemed as if they had never been away. The household continued its usual routine. Jacinda continued to be pleasant but distant. The old man was happy to have her back, and they continued to go for walks together when possible. They had slipped into a comfortable relationship; she valued his insights into life's questions mainly because she perceived he had no other agenda other than to be her friend. Rick went back to work, but he seemed more at peace and become agitated less often. George continued his music lessons when he was available. Flynn appeared to be a little more distant; she could sense something was troubling him but could not work out what it was. She thought it better not to ask.

Her visits to her shrink were back to once a month. This time, Flynn drove her in her car and waited outside until she was ready to go home. She had tried to explain to the shrink what had changed.

'I think I have grown stronger now, maybe it is because I feel safe. I noticed that my world had become brighter and

I believe that this is because I am no longer depressed. I have come to terms with this way of life. The old man said that it is because I am no longer living in sin. He thinks that it bothered me because I am quite religious. I try to stay away from situations where people crowd me with negative thoughts. I have noticed that I get drained and try to push through this and so when I go to bed, I can sleep better. I still get dark dreams, but the one about fire has changed. I see a wall of fire, and I need to get to the other side, I have tried to get through, but the heat is too strong. I find this unsettling, but I am not panicked like I used to be. I think what is on the other side is my old life. As far as I am concerned, I have been alive for four years, and the past life is just that, another lifetime.'

'I am glad for you that everything has turned out just as you wanted,' he said. 'I would like to think that this is the end of your troubles. I am concerned that any break in your carefully planned life could send you spiralling back to where you were before. I now wonder if it is necessary to pursue hypnosis at this point. That may depend on how much you want to know what happened to you. The wall of fire is there for a reason, and only you know how important it is to break through. Are you still reading people to understand how to react to them?'

'Yes, I do it all the time. It seems normal to me. While we were away, we met a woman who said I'm fey; I looked it up but could not understand why she would say that. I may have Celtic blood because of my eyes and skin, but I just don't know. Anyway, I am not a fairy or a witch. My understanding of the third eye is that they can foretell the future, and sometimes I can do this, but it happens only sometimes, and I cannot turn it on or off. I'm sure you don't believe in that stuff. And I only half believe in it myself.'

'It may be that I have a scientific explanation for the superstitions of a past age. Whatever the reason, there have always been people who have extraordinary skills. How they interplay within the community seems unclear. You have those skills, but how you use them can and does affect your life. I personally don't think you can be truly happy until you understand how these skills drive your life because of the danger of getting caught up again in situations where you have little control. I would like you to continue writing in your journal because that is still the key.'

On the way home, she tried to find out what was going on between her and Flynn. 'I think there is something not quite right between us. Have I done anything to upset you? I can feel something is there, but I am not a mind reader, please tell me if I have done anything?'

'No Marion it's nothing you have done. I am just trying to do my job. You know I care for you maybe more than I should, but you are the boss's wife. I don't want anything to change, so I just have to suck it up.'

The next week, Rick announced that he had business in Hong Kong. He planned to be away for three days. He would take Marion, George, and Flynn. At first, she was happy about the trip. She liked it when they travelled in the jet as it required not a lot of preparation. She talked to Rick about getting some clothes made there. However, the next day, she felt anxious about the trip. Something was not quite right. She thought her imagination was working overtime; nothing was wrong. The feeling persisted and became stronger until she was forced to tell Rick that they should not go at this inauspicious time. He was incredulous, making light of her feeling. She went to talk to George about it. Sitting in a big lounge chair, it did sound a bit farfetched. But the feeling would not go away. He suggested that maybe it was she who should not go. But she knew it was not her. She decided to not say anything more about it and hope she was wrong.

The trip there was uneventful, and everybody had something to do. She started to sing tunes in her head as a way of distracting herself.

Rick owned an apartment in a big circular building, and the boys stayed at a hotel not far away. The first day she was there, Flynn took her to a tailor shop where clothes were made to order. She liked it that they could choose colours together.

In the evening, they had dinner together, and they dropped her off at the apartment before going on to an appointment. She changed into some pretty lingerie, made a drink, and settled down to read for the night. It was very late when Rick came back. He was ruffled and angry. She followed him into the bedroom to find out what was wrong. She tried to get him to say what was wrong. Instead of talking, he grabbed her and threw her face down and forced very rough sex on her. Shock stopped her from making any sound, at first. Then she was crying for him to stop. He ignored her and when he had finished, she just climbed into the bed. He did the same. She wondered what had happened. About a half an hour later, there was a knock on the door. She got up and pulled a robe on and went to answer it. It was two policemen. They pushed their way into the room and demanded to know where her husband was. She told them he was in bed and had been there all night. Rick came out of the room but did not say anything. The police continued to question her about what they had done that night. She told them they had gone out for dinner with their bodyguards and then had come back to the apartment. 'We are just married,' she said. 'You must understand that.'

'Where are your employees?' they asked Rick.

'I don't know.'

'Then you know nothing about what went down at the docks tonight, right?''

That's right,' he said. They closed their books and left.

Marion turned on him and said,

'What have you been up to?'

'It's none of your business.' he growled.

'Don't lie to me, I am your wife, and have just been abused by you, and then I lied for you. So don't tell me it's none of my business. Where are the boys and are they in any danger?' He looked at her as if he was seeing a stranger. 'They can take care of themselves, and as soon as it is safe, they will get back to me.' Riccardo poured them a drink and sat down, looking somewhat confused. Marion went to have a shower and found that she was bleeding, she hoped she would be alright and not get sick from the rape. After a while, he collected his thoughts and told her that the meeting was, in fact, a setup. They had been caught in the crossfire, and George had thrown himself in front of him and had taken a bullet meant for him. He had just got away just in time and had come back to the apartment. The place would be crawling with police by now, and he had to depend on the skills of the boys to avoid capture. 'They get paid big bucks for this.'

'No amount of money is worth dying for. I did try to warn you; you did not listen. I will be very upset if my minder is dead.'

'You're a tough little cookie, aren't you? Don't worry; we will all get home safe. Go to bed, and I will let you know as soon as I hear something.'

The next day, Rick booked a commercial flight for them to go home, leaving the jet for the boys to use as soon as they could. It took another two days before he could tell her that George was in a French hospital. The bullet had been removed, and George was now out of danger. He did not know where Flynn was. 'I must see him; I need to be sure he is okay.' Rick agreed to take her the next day after work. He would make arrangements for them to take a commercial flight and then they could bring the jet back. She could feel herself spiralling down some hole and tried to keep an even grip on her emotions. She had always known he could be devious and sometimes had little concern for what others felt. But she had thought that part of her life was over; now she was not so sure. She had promised Flynn she would not use head games with him, but now she was worried he was left to fend for himself. Sitting in her bedroom, she thought about him. She did not mean to try to find him, but somehow it happened, and she realised he was in France. She stopped as soon as she could, but the damage was done.

They took an evening flight to France and went to see George. He was asleep; he looked ashen as he had lost a lot of blood. Rick put a chair near the bed for her to sit on and she started to cry. He woke up and rubbed her head, tried to smile, and told her he was okay. He looked over at Rick and tried to reassure him too. 'I'll be back before you know it,' he said. Rick replied for him to take all the time he needed. 'There always will be a place for you to stay even if you can't do anything for a while.' Marion got up and kissed him on the cheek and told him she loved him and would be devastated if anything happened to him.

As soon as George was released from the hospital he and Flynn came back home. Marion was glad they were back. She did not ask what had happened as she did not want to know. She wanted to forget about it and try to keep her life as quiet as she could. She was afraid she would not be content with the answers they would give and then she would feel she had to do something about it. Flynn never mentioned about her intrusion into his mind. She was learning there were things she should keep out of.

Carl from Australia had been trying to get in touch with her, and she had not answered either his phone calls or e-mails. On a whim, she thought she should call him to find out what he wanted. He told her that as the TV special had gone so well, he would like to put together a reunion tour. He wanted to do just one show in each city. She told him she did not think it was a good idea. He said he would make all the arrangements, and all she had to do was turn up. He suggested that the TV special was not that bad and he could not see any reason that the tour would be any different. He said he was hoping she would see more of the country and that had to be a plus. She said she would think about it and let him know in about a week's time. After the call, she wondered how strong she really was. The Hong Kong incident had shaken her much more than she cared to admit. It would take time to trust Rick again. She realised that she was outraged with him. The only reason she would consider this proposal at all was to give them time apart for her to get over what she thought of as his betrayal of their relationship. He had hurt her in a way he promised he would not do again.

She told him about Carl's idea for a tour, and he seemed happy for her to go. Maybe he also wanted time out. He suggested that she take Big George again with her as he appeared to do a good job before. Suddenly, she found herself agreeing to something that in hindsight would not be a good thing. She called Carl and told him he could arrange the concerts if he did not put her in the middle as she was not good in crowds.

She missed her next appointment with the doctor as she knew what he would say about it and she did not want to hear anything detrimental about her life choices.

The old man was not happy for her to go. He did not know what had happened in Hong Kong, but he was aware there was some tension between them. She just laughed it off, saying it was just the usual settling in time.

Big George had arrived the day before she was due to leave. Abrax was to take them to the airport in the evening as they were going to start the longest part of their journey through the night, Marion was hoping that she would sleep most of the way and then arrive refreshed. Rick was going to see them off. He felt a bit worried that she would be able to cope and he wanted to make sure she had a good book to read as well as the laptop to keep her entertained. She told him that she was the eternal optimist and expected everything to be good. She promised that she would call him every day and inform him of all that was going on. She was full of hope that everything was going to be as it was before and there would be nothing to worry about.

When they arrived at the airport, she was surprised to find that a lot of people had come to see her arrive. Carl was there to welcome her, and he told her that they had a big following in Australia. There was also a contingent of reporters wanting to take photos and ask how she felt to be home. She felt the panic surge up from somewhere deep inside and tried to look for a way out of the building. This is where Big George was at his best and moved people aside so she could get out of the terminal building. Through waves of nausea and fear, she somehow managed to get to the car. Once in the car, she told Carl that she could not do this. He managed to calm her down and assured her that everything would be managed better. He told her that they underestimated the popularity of the group. All the tickets had sold out, and he had heard people had travelled from as far as New Zealand to see them play. This did not help allay her fears, and she wished she could just go back home.

'I think this is why I left the group in the first place,' she said. 'I did not know why myself at the time, but I am sure now. I will not talk to the press. You are going to be the voice of the group.'

When they arrived at his house, he gave her a strong drink of whisky and sat her down and said he would do everything possible to make sure she was not mobbed again.

'I know once you are on stage, you forget nerves and do just great.'

The next couple of days, Big George became a problem. He was doing his best to keep everyone away from her, but he was also keeping people who she should talk to away as well. She told Rick George was making life harder for her. He agreed to send Flynn, and she should send Big George back. It was hard to say to him that he had to go. And she tried to make light of it by saying Rick need him back there. When Flynn arrived, she felt relieved because he knew how to blend in and still keep an eye on things. He looked the part at his scruffy best. The concerts went off as planned and Carl kept his word by doing most of the talking. He told her that this had improved his status at the TV station. It still was a nightmare for her to get through, each day saying she could not go on and then trying to keep going. She had an obligation to stay after the concerts to talk to people but, usually left as soon as possible. The second last night, Flynn met Pam who had travelled from New

Zealand and was a big fan. He worked his magic and got her to meet Marion. And when they left to go back to the hotel, she came with them. They stopped off for a drink on the way, and Flynn asked if Marion minded if he disappeared for the night. She laughed at him and said, of course, it was okay. 'Just be back by sometime in the morning.'

Perth was the last concert and Marion felt relieved. She told Carl not to call her again.

She said, 'not that it hasn't been fun some of the time, but I just can't take the crowds.'

They left as soon as they could and stopped for another drink before going back to the hotel.

'I can't believe I made it, I must be stronger than I thought.' Flynn's laugh was infectious. He had a cheeky way about him that made you trust him. 'You cannot imagine how I feel just now. Knowing you were there has helped me a lot. I don't think I could have done it without you,' she said.

Back at her room, he opened the door and went in to look around as he usually did. She stayed by the door, and as he was about to leave, he kissed her. Not on the cheek, but on her lips. It was a soft kiss, just brushing her lips and staying there. She felt the pull of his personality and the kiss got a little deeper and deeper. She wanted to kiss him all the way. He leant over and closed the door. She felt the press of his body against hers and a deep longing for him came over her. She did not understand it as an empath thing; that the feelings she was having may have been his feelings transferring to her. She only knew the tenderness was a mutual inclination. Their lovemaking was not fast and furious but rather tender and gentle. Not like anything she had experienced before. She felt delighted at his touch and saw the smile in his eyes. She felt such comfort in his arms and was at peace.

The next morning when she woke up, she saw he was already awake and was just looking at her. She felt a disquieting feeling in the pit of her stomach. 'What have we done?' she said. 'I'm not sure how this happened, I'm not sorry because it was very nice, but I'm afraid of the consequences.' He leant over and kissed her and said, 'It was nice wasn't it?' Her mind was working overtime trying to rationalise the whole experience. Was it because of the relief she felt at ending the tour? Or was it because she drank more than she could hold? Was it something she had wanted to do for a while? At the same time, she was trying to think of what to do about it.

'We have to talk about this, let's get ready and have breakfast and then work out what we are going to do.'

At breakfast, he told her that he had expressed to the boss his feelings for her, and the boss had told him that if he laid one a finger on his wife, he'd kill him.

'You have known for some time how I feel, only I did not know how you felt except for getting into my head.'

'I love my husband,' she said. 'This can never happen again. I never lie to him and am not going to start now, so I am going to tell him the truth, and he is going to be furious. I am frightened for you because he is unpredictable and just might carry out his threat. I know he is capable of doing this, maybe not by his own hand but he could take out a contract on you. I don't think it is a good idea for you to come back just yet. Last night, I assumed you were going over to be with Pam.' He nodded and said, 'Something got in the way.'

'Are you sorry?' she asked.

'What do you think? Of course, I'm not sorry. As I see it, we have two choices, one we run away together and I don't think that is going to happen and another option is we simply don't say anything. That way I get to keep my job, and we can have time to work this thing out.'

'I can't do that. I don't think we should be left alone together again because I will be tempted to do it again and you will be too. I think you should go and stay with Pam, She is a sweet lady, and she is head over heels in love with you. I will try to talk the boss around. He can't stay mad with me forever. I know you have other obligations, but I will talk to George, and between you, there must be a way to absorb this into your life for the moment.' He did not respond, just looked resigned to the way things were. She was aware she had hurt him in some way, but she could not see any other way out.

They went back to the room to get their things together. She felt very distressed at having to leave things the way they were. She saw him coming towards her and thought he was going to kiss her. Panic set in, and she held out her hand for him to stop. Instead, the force of her will sent him flying across the room landing him on his bottom against the far wall. She put her hand to her mouth and stared at him in horror. 'Fuck!' he yelled. 'Why the hell do you need self-defense lessons?'

'I'm so sorry' was all she could get out. She grabbed her case and ran out of the room.

On the plane home, she felt so frightened that she wished herself into a small ball, which would become so small it would disappear. The trip was one of constant turmoil. The noises of the people around her could not compare to the anguish that was going on in her head. The question of why had she given in to him. She knew what he was like and should have been warier. She thought her attraction to him may have started as early as the night he said he would help with her journal. She had felt he wanted to kiss her, thought better of it, and told her to go back to bed. What if she had stayed? Then there were the two sides of him. He was a trained killer who had no compunction in dispatching people from this earth. And there was the tender man who could understand her better than anyone. Could one love two people? She knew she was in love with Rick; he was her hero and saved her on several occasions. He loved only her and wanted to give her anything she wanted. She wanted only to make him proud of her and be happy. So how could she have slept with Flynn? Flynn's famous saying was 'It just happened.' Nobody really believed this. But for her, that is exactly what happened. It just started with a small kiss. Then there was the way she had pushed him. She did not know how this happened.

By the time the plane landed in Greece, she was a total wreck. Her world was spinning out of control, and she could scarcely stand. The hostess was concerned and asked her to stay back until all other passengers were off. They would get a staff medic to assess her and decide if she should go to the hospital. She was unaware that Rick had come himself to welcome her home. When she did not come out with the other passengers, he went to ask about his wife. He was told she was unwell and was being assessed. He insisted that he be taken to her straight away. They had taken her off the plane and put her in a restroom. As soon as she saw him, she put her arms around him and cried into his shoulder. He told the staff that they need not worry about her as he knew how to look after her. They agreed to let the limo come to the side entrance so he could get her into the car.

She sat quietly for a while as they drove along. Riccardo waited for her to say what was wrong. Eventually, she asked him to stop off somewhere as she needed to talk to him. He found a small bar and they ordered a drink. She found it hard to tell him about her transgressions. In the end, she blurted it all out. 'I slept with Flynn.' He was dumbfounded. He asked her to tell him everything about it. She was as brutally honest as she could; she even told him all the things that had been going over in her mind on the way home. He understood now why she was such a mess. He felt angry and hurt, but another feeling was overriding all, and that was the concern for her fragile mental health. She kept telling him that she loved him and could not understand how she could betray him. He thought the best thing was for her to see her shrink and maybe he could make sense of this. 'I am not going to punish you,' he said. 'It seems you can do that all by yourself.' He forced a laugh and said,

'You are just a magnet for trouble. Where is Flynn now?'

'I'm not going to tell you because you said you will kill him.' He did not answer her because at that moment, that is exactly what he planned to do. He rang the Institute and asked for Dr McKlean. He was busy, but Helen said he would call tonight. He took her home and made her stay in bed until she felt better. He would just tell the family she was jetlagged.

Doctor McKlean called her in the late afternoon, and she told him about what had happened. He could understand her confusion and distress from the jumbled way she tried to describe how she felt. He told her to rest in bed for a couple of days and would set up an appointment as soon as he could. He then rang Riccardo and asked him if it was possible for him to come and see him this evening. He agreed to come later in the evening.

Riccardo then went to talk to George and find out what he knew. George told him he had been in touch with Flynn and said he was an idiot to get involved. He stated that he was staying with a girlfriend for the moment and was considering his future. Riccardo wanted to know if this was just another fling or did Flynn have real feelings for her. He had told him he had, but Riccardo did not believe he would do anything that would put his job in jeopardy. George said that sometimes, Flynn just couldn't help himself; however, he had told him that he thought he was in love with her. George would not say where Flynn was, but he did say he thought they had some kind of special bond. Riccardo explained that his immediate concern was for Marion's health and he would deal with Flynn another time.

That evening, he went to see her shrink, hoping he would shed some light on the whole affair. The doctor met him in an objective way. He told him that she failed to attend the last appointment and he guessed that was because she was determined to do the tour which he would have said was not a good idea. He explained that she was unwilling to accept the limitations of her condition and then made rash decisions that put her into situations that would cause her conflict. She is an 'empath', and that means she can feel others' feelings as her own. She picks up on the energy that they give off and then cannot distinguish the difference from her own feelings. You remember when she sang to your father a song that his wife used to sing? She picked up on his longing to hear that song and made it as if it was her own. This is the same kind of thing. I believe when Flynn kissed her she picked up on his longing to have a deeper relationship with her and she made it her own. When she realised what had transpired, she tried to use logic to rationalise it out, but she does not have the skills to do this. That is why she nearly had another breakdown. I would venture to say that Flynn is as confused as she is. He would see it as mixed messages. He had told both of you that he had feelings for her that were not appropriate and tried to keep his distance. She told me she was getting stronger and I think this must be true, or she could not have come through these concerts as well as she did. I am glad she has told Carl not to get in touch with her again, that shows some strength. I know this must be hard for you to and I am wondering if you are able to keep going with her.'

Riccardo told him he loved her; he understood that she was a bit different, but that is what made her special. More than anything, he wanted to make her happy and could deny her nothing. Riccardo did not tell the shrink about the Hong Kong affair. Could this be the reason she went to Australia in the first place? He wondered if things would ever change or would she have to be careful all her life. The doctor said that she needed to continue with counselling and she could have a good life if she kept away from the things that were likely to cause her confusion. When her life is predictable, and there is no conflict around her she can and will get stronger. She may need help to sort out her feelings for Flynn, It is possible that her desire to create a family is confusing familiar love with the love she has for you. So any pressure to hurt Flynn could be counterproductive. I think she knows they must not be left alone together again. However, I believe that this is just an episode and will die in due course. I cannot speak for him, though. I understand he is a bit of a wanderer.'

Riccardo felt relieved by the doctor's explanation. He thought there had to be some explanation other than the obvious because she had this internal code that she would see as a sin. This left the way open for him to deal with his other feelings such as his anger at Flynn, whom he trusted.

By the time he got back home, he had resolved in his mind how to handle her. He went up to bed and to talk to her. She seemed much better. 'When we got married, you said you would overlook my mistakes, and I should do the same. That is what I intend to do. Look at me now and tell me what you think you see.'

'I feel you care about me and want me to feel safe again. I don't see any anger in you directed at me although I deserve it. I feel that you want to make love to me. I don't think you are really going to hurt Flynn.'

'Then trust those feelings, and we will get over this. I love you and want you by my side always, no matter what. Now show me how much you love me.'

The next day, he again spoke to George. 'I am going to give Flynn his job back, but not here. I am going to send him to our Aberdeen office. If he wishes, I will pay for his girlfriend to transfer there too. Will you make arrangements for this? I have been thinking about Marion, and I believe it is the time we moved into a house of our own. It will give her something to focus on and keep her out of trouble. I am relying on you to help her through. She must also attend appointments with her shrink. I am sure she will be back to her old self in a couple of days.'

A couple of days later, Marion came down to the gatehouse with a paper in her hands and told George that they were going to get a house of their own. 'Will you help me?' she asked.

'Of course, that is my job.'

'It's not just that, I value your opinion. You are right about so many things, and I should listen to you. I have done a stupid thing, but I did not mean to, it just happened, and the trouble is I am not really sorry because it was nice. Are you mad at me? I know I've been a bit off lately and I could have got Flynn in a lot of trouble. The boss and I are okay now, but I miss not having Flynn around. I've had no time to talk to you. Have you spoken to Flynn and is he okay?'

'He is fine. You can't hold a person like him down for long. So now we are going house hunting.'

Two days later, George said he had to take some leave, and he did not know when he would be back. Marion said she would wait until he was back before they looked at more houses. She asked him if Flynn would be going with him and he did not answer her; he just nodded his head. 'Please be careful, you know I worry when you go off the radar for any length of time.' She put her arms around him and hugged him then said, 'See ya!'

Abrax took her to Doctor McKlean's appointment. She felt quite apprehensive about seeing him knowing that he knew all there was to know about her recent activities. She expected him to be aggravated with her. Instead, he was kind and thoughtful. He switched on the tape recorder on the desk and asked her to tell him her story from the last time she had seen him until now. She was more coherent now and could put together the whole story including the Hong Kong incident and why she had chosen to do the tour. Her feelings for Flynn were less clear. It meant that she had to admit to him that she had used her mind to get in touch with him. She explained she did not know what she was doing and as soon as she realised what she had done, she stopped. She told him that Flynn had felt her presence and had told her off. But once the connection was made, it was easier to do it again.

'I know it was wrong and I was messing with his head.'

She explained that she had done this twice and each time, he had known. He had told her he cared for her more than he should and had tried to keep a distance between them. She told the shrink that she was attracted to Flynn but had no intention of taking it further. Until that night, she thought she understood the empath thing, but she felt it was more than that because she had not seen him for a while now and still felt strongly about him. She said how much she loved her husband and did not want to hurt him. Then she told him about how she had pushed Flynn across the room without even touching him. She was scared to even think about this.

'You should have heard the language he said. I ran out of the room, and I have not seen him since. I think I have hurt him in some way.'

'What is troubling you the most now?' he asked her.

'I think I am back where I started, except more things are happening that I have no control over. I did not mean to get in touch with Flynn. I just sat on my bed and thought of him and wondered where he was. I imagined seeing his face and body, and there I was. I could see all around where he was. I was aware he was concentrating on something. I stopped straight away, but the damage was done. He felt it, and although he did not tell anyone, he told me to stay out of his head. And I said I would. Then after Hong Kong, I did not know what had happened to him, and I did not even have to try hard, and I found out where he was. This is not the empath thing, is it?'

'You know already you have created a bond that is hard to break. I think it is a part of the empath experience. When we first tested you here, we noted that you could keep a connection over a distance. I think you are still evolving in this skill. It seems that you can do it only with someone that you are very close to. The word telepathy is another expression of communication, which can be seen as the transmission of information from one person to another using only the mind. The term was first used in 1882, and although a popular idea, it has no grounds in science. There have been some experiments that are said to prove its existence. However, it is more likely only just a theory. People who claim to receive messages from another source are seen as delusional or have some kind of psychosis. Then some psychics claim to find answers for people in other countries. It has not been proved scientifically. It would be hard to verify that you are using telepathy, but it is not out of the realm of possibility.'

'When I pushed him, I did not know what I was doing. I did not mean it, I just wanted to stop him from coming closer because I thought he was going to kiss me and I would want to kiss him back. Again we have not told anyone about this. But it has to stop.'

'I think as you become stronger mentally, then your skills are growing more active too. With time I thought they would fade out a bit, but that does not appear to be the case with you. Usually, when people learn to reconnect with the world they don't use hyper-vigilance as much, you, on the other hand, seem to rely more on these skills rather than using your ordinary senses. One would ask why it is so. I can only speculate that it may be because you refuse to acknowledge that it is what you are doing. Rather than gaining control over it, you are letting it control you. Saying you want it to stop is not enough to make it stop. Is there a reason you can't divulge the things you believe about others?'

She shook her head but realised that she had many things she thought about what the men in her life were up to, and could not out of loyalty tell anyone. She knew she would not change that part of her thought process because of an idea she could help them. She had used edited versions of the truth since the beginning and had not been able to embrace the notion of total change. At least now she knew why. 'You have given me a lot to think about, and at our next meeting, I will be more prepared to look at ways I can deal with things.'

Two weeks later, George came back. He seemed to be in good spirits and said he was up to looking at houses again. They started music lessons again, and he was still trying to teach Marion self-defence. He was pleased to see she was back to her old self and the boss seemed happy too.

Marion had been sleeping better and with fewer dreams.

The wall of fire seemed to be more pressing now, and she knew that it had to be addressed. She awoke one night full of dread the dream she had was one about Flynn being captured by some group, tortured until he was beyond recognition. She was shaking and crying. Rick woke up as he herd her cry out.

'Are you having another one of those dreams?' He had learned that usually if the dream was very detailed, it was more likely to be true. 'Tell me what is up?'

She was unsure if it was something he should know, so she decided just to let it ride for now. 'Go back to sleep.' She said, 'I will go and get some hot milk and then come back to bed.'

The next night, she dreamed the same dream but in more detail. Again, she woke up crying; she felt as if she had been hit in the face and it was numb. All her joints were hurting. She knew she had to warn Flynn but did not how to go about it. She thought about the dream and could not see George. The attackers were Middle Eastern, but she did not know what country. She tried to write it down but not in her journal. She thought he had been betrayed by a friend or a person he knew. It was a suicide job that had little chance of success. For the first time, she saw him talking to the people who pulled his strings. There was a lot of sophisticated equipment around. She was sure it was not the regular army but some sort of covert section. Not officially sanctioned, but paid for by the English Department of Defence. She went back to bed and waited for Rick to wake up. Then she told him that Flynn was in trouble and she needs to talk to him, she explained to Rick she believed Flynn was going to hurt himself in some way.

He felt angry at her insistence she could help. 'Do you know how ridiculous this sounds? You want me to let you go to a past lover and talk to him. Why would I do that? If he wants to kill himself, that's his business.'

'I know he is in trouble and if I do nothing in some way I will be responsible. I know he does not want to talk to me right now. Please let me help.'

'All right, against my better judgement you can. I have to go to Scotland for business soon anyway. I may as well bring it forward. This is crazy; I must be out of my mind. You can meet him in a quiet place, get your problems out in the air, and then leave. I'll organise a room at the Rox Hotel for you to meet him. Promise you will try to behave.'

She had an appointment with Flynn at 9.30 a.m. in room 106. She was nervous about meeting him again. She went over in her head what she would do. She would be kind but firm. She had come because she promised not to mess with his head. He must find a way out of this job. At the appointed time, she went down to the room. She knocked on the door but received no answer. She tried the handle and found the door open, so she just walked in, calling out his name. It was then that she saw him. There was some girl on the dressing table, and he was having sex with her. What she saw was the way his naked back part of his body was working. She said his name again, and he turned his head towards her, Marion did not wait she just ran out of the room and back to her room. He knocked on her door about half an hour later; she answered the door but as soon as she saw him, she told him to go away. 'I can explain,' he said. But she just slammed the door shut. Rick had promised to take her out for lunch, and when he came in, he saw she was upset.

'It did not go well then?' He enquired. She told him what she had seen. And he started to laugh.

'It's not funny,' she said, 'I have never seen a man's backside like that before.'

The story made him laugh more.

'Would you like me to get a mirror so you can see us doing it? Only you could find the odd thing in this story. Why you would find a man's backside, so disturbing is anybody's guess. Don't worry, I'll tell you what to do. We will get him to come to lunch with us, and you can talk to him then.'

At lunch, she could not even look at him without blushing. She was aware that Rick thought it was funny. They ordered fish and chips, and Rick made pleasant conversation then went to the bar to get some drinks.

'How are you now?' she asked. 'Are you still mad at me? I'm sorry I still can't work out how I feel about you. I miss you so much, and I wish there was a way for us to be together as friends.'

After a while, their meal came and some drinks, but no Rick. Flynn went to find out where he was and was told he had left. He returned to the table shaking his head. She tried to eat, but it was more important to tell him what she knew.

'I promised not to get into your head, so I had to come and see you. I know you are mad at me and probably do not want to talk to me. I care about you so very much I could not bear it if you were hurt.' She told him about the dream and asked him to please not go.

'I am going to do this regardless of what you say,' he said. 'Then I will tell you that there is someone who is going to betray you, don't trust anybody.' She pulled out the piece of paper; she had written down of all she could remember of the dream. 'This is not in my dream book,' she assured him.

He looked over at her and put his hand on hers. 'I want you so much it hurts. Do you really think that anything matters to me more than that?'

'Then what was this morning?' she asked. 'It just happened, and I forgot the time, I'm sorry.'

'You are incorrigible,' she said.

'That is part of my charm, you like bad boys.' He gave her a cheeky smile, enough to melt her heart.

'Back to the point,' she said. 'I have not told George because I did not see him in the dream. What am I supposed to do?'

'It is a one-man job, leave him out of it. It is just in and out, the less noise, the better. I have already agreed to go tomorrow, and that is that. Thank you for coming all the way to warn me, but I will be fine. I have told you before; you should think more about your husband than me.' He saw the tears in her eyes and found it hard not to respond.

'By the way,' she said, 'where is the boss and why has he left us together?'

Flynn looked about 'I think he has planted a shadow.' He ran his hand under the table to see if there was listening device. They looked around the room to see if there was anybody who might be a shadow. Flynn suggested that a sure way to find out was for her to kiss him. He said that the boss would not be able to resist saying something and then she would know.

'I am afraid to kiss you. I might not want to stop."

'I'll make sure you stop.' He smiled at her. 'I can control myself, you know.'

'The problem for me is I still feel the same way about you even though I am happily married. Do you think that someone can love two people at the same time?'

'I don't think it would work for us,' he said. 'Just kiss me goodbye and go.'

Back in their room, Rick had finished for the day and was waiting for her. He told her they could go out for dinner later if she were okay. She said she was a little despondent as it appeared that Flynn would not listen to her or take her seriously.

He gave her a penetrating look. 'Even a kiss would not change his mind? Then you have done all you could do.'

She felt the rage coming up from deep inside. 'So you did have a shadow on me then.' She ran at him intending to hit him as hard as she could, but he grabbed her arm before she could land a blow. 'I hate you,' she said. 'Flynn told me you would have someone watching me and we kissed to see if it was true, that was all. I should give you some of your own medicine.' She threw her body weight on him and pushing him back on the bed. She threw herself on top of him and tore his shirt off breaking all the buttons. Sitting on top of him she tried to be as rough with him as he could be with her. It was easy for him to pull his arm away from her grasp and pull her down. At a hint of a smile, she slapped him across the face. Her wild passion was no match for him, though, and in the end, she was just exhausted. She just collapsed on top of him and cried. He tried not to laugh and said mildly 'You can get mad at me anytime. Little

Miss Fire and Ice.' In the end, they did not bother about getting a meal; they just stayed in bed, and he held her until she calmed down and fell asleep. He realised that the day had been stressful for her as she tried to deal with conflicting emotions. He did not feel the need to explain himself to her; she would just have to deal with it. She had done all she could, and that would be the end of it, and he did not want to hear about it again.

Life went back to more or less normal. Marion went for as many walks with the old man as she could. She looked to him as a stabilising influence in her life, even if there were things she could never discuss with him. Whereas other people seemed to be afraid of him and jumped when he told them to, she would take his advice not out of fear but rather because she loved him. She became aware that Rick was in fact almost a carbon copy of the old man in so many ways. She hoped to soften his ideas and make him more conscious of the other world around him away from power and money. She wanted Rick to see the beauty of the world around him.

She continued to look for a house for them. There seemed so much to consider. She wanted something that was not too far away. Not too big and secure. Most of the houses they looked at appeared to be either too imposing or too small. Also, she wanted enough land around it to have a nice garden. A lot of the houses were built close to other houses; they were comfortable inside but as far as she was concerned to close to neighbours.

Marion knew she would recognise the house when she saw it. George was the epitome of patience. He would just drive her around to the various places and told her at least they saw the countryside. 'It is really a lovely country, isn't it,' she said.

They saw a house at Nea Makri. It is a little seaside town about thirty minutes from Athens. It had a marvelous driveway that went past an overgrown garden. The house was run-down and in need of a renovation. But she saw what it could look like after some careful work. George could not believe she thought it appealing. 'It's a dump,' he said. She insisted it was just right. She called Rick on her cell and when he answered, she sent him some photos. She loved it, she explained, and there was no hurry so they could fix it up. He agreed to look at it on the weekend. The next Saturday, she took him over to the house, showing him it was not that far. She showed the harbour area and suggested they could bring *Yolanda* over there and thus would get more use out of it. Inside the house would need as much work as outside, but she insisted she could do it by herself and she would create a haven for them. He could not say no to her about anything, and so he agreed. In the back of his mind was the thought that this project would keep her out of trouble for some time. They wandered around the house and took as many pictures as they could as she planned to do a book of before and after.

That night, they told the family what they were going to

do. She asked Jacinda if she would come on Monday to look at the house. 'I know you will think it junk, but you have such good taste you could suggest some colours. I believe that we may have to get a horticultural expert to find out what the original plants were so we can restore the garden.'

Rick laughed at her enthusiasm because they had not even put in a bid for it yet. 'We had better buy it first.'

On Monday, they went over to the house and walked through the rooms. 'It's quite small,' Jacinda pointed out. 'We don't need much,' Marion said. They walked into a room that looked as if it had been a library. 'This could be Rick's study,' she thought. She walked over to some books left on the shelves and dusted them. Something moved, and a small door opened to reveal a small room. There were some boxes in there, and they carried them out. One of the boxes had pictures of how the house had looked before it had run down and some family photos. She suggested to Jacinda that they should keep the room a secret and it could be a surprise for Riccardo. She made up her mind that she would pay for the renovations herself and she would hire only people who lived close. Thus the first room to renovate should be the kitchen, and then she could provide a midday meal and allow the workers to have a two-hour break in the middle of the day. That way she could put some of her ideas of social justice into practice.

The next afternoon, Rick came home with a big smile on

this face, 'I thought I should show you this before I put it in the safe.' It was the title deed to the house in her name. 'Now you will forever have a place to call home,' he said.

She kissed him and thanked him but reminded him it was to be their home, not just hers.

'I have never known what it would be like to be homeless. You have, and that is why I want you to have it in your name, so no matter what happens, you will always have a home. It is a freedom gift, and you can do whatever you want with it.'

She felt overwhelmed with the feeling of gratitude at the security that he was giving her. It was as if he understood all the things she had feared since she had met him. She thought that she was making a change in him after all.

Her next visit to her shrink was full of the new house. A new optimism had energised her. She was full of hope that she could make a home that would be perfect for them but also would help the surrounding area struggling under financial depression. Her infectious personality buoyed the doctor up as well, and he thought that maybe she was getting on top of things. 'You must not become complacent about your skills as they still have the power to overtake you. I can understand that right now you are on top of the world. However, it is a fragile world. There are issues that you must deal with, and I know you are going to say not now. You must make time in your head for dealing with things. If we say in two weeks, will you consider working on these issues?' She agreed and decided to look at which area was the most important to deal with.

In his case notes, Dr McKlean noted her reluctance to engage in any contentious areas of her life. He noted that she always seemed to find some way of avoiding dealing with her issues by constantly creating other projects that took up time and energy.

Her contentment was again short-lived. Her nightmares had become more frequent, and the tall, foreboding figure was present in most of her dreams. She had a feeling of being smashed against a wall or rocks; she could have been dumped by a big wave on rocks, and she found it hard to breathe. She was held captive and unable to flee from the constant pain that racked her body and when she awoke, she again felt sore all over. She tried working so hard that she was exhausted and sometimes that helped to allay the dreams. Rick was becoming mildly concerned as she was losing weight and looking tired a lot of the time. He asked George what she was doing over at the house. He told him she had scrubbed out the kitchen area ready to replace the stove and other furnishings. 'Why is she doing this when she should be paying someone else to do it? She has to stop.' Rick was at a loss in understanding her motivation in driving herself so hard. It was only when he thought about it, he realised she had not been sleeping well either. He asked her what was going on; she could not tell him because she did not want to know herself.

It was only two days later that they saw in the newspaper, that a British spy had been captured in Pakistan. There was a grained printed photo of a man who looked as if he had been severely beaten. The old man was sitting in his study looking at the paper before breakfast and called Riccardo in and asked if that was one of his people. It was hard to imagine that the person in the photo was Flynn. His father asked him what one of his security people doing over there. He said he did not know anything about it. As Marion came down, they called her in the study and showed her the paper. She was appalled at the photo. The old man asked her if she knew anything about this.

A sick feeling washed over her 'I am not sure of anything, maybe it's a mistake,' she offered.

Riccardo got her a chair and sat her down. The old man told her she was to have nothing to do with this. 'I do not want anything from this incident ending up on my doorstep. Do you understand me?'

'I understand you perfectly,' she said.

She got up and ran upstairs and sat on the bed. She did not know what to do. She went to her laptop to see if there was anything else about this breaking story. So far she could not see anything. Rick came up and asked if she was all right. She managed to get out a jumbled story about dreams and the tall, dark person that stood off on one side of her mind.

'I have to go,' he said. 'But if you need me call and I will come home.'

After a while, she walked down to the gatehouse. George was in the kitchen, a cup of tea in his hand and concentrating on the paper. She sat down and looked at him for some kind of explanation that would help her. 'How much do you know about this?' he asked.

'I don't know anything. I thought Flynn was going to do something silly and went to see him. I asked him to listen to me, but he would not. I did not get you involved because he asked me not to. I have had a bad feeling for the last week. I am afraid he is going to die there.'

George gave her one of his inscrutable looks that said nothing and said a lot. 'I will be taking leave starting this afternoon. You can say my mother is ill if you want.' She could not help but ask what he intended to do.

'I am going to see a man about a dog.' He said. 'Ask no questions, and you will be told no lies.'

She told George that the old man had told her not to get involved. 'If you think of some way I could be of use without getting me into trouble, please ask.'

She put her arms around him and said, 'Please be careful, I need you here safe.'

As she walked back to the house, she thought of all things that were left unsaid because she did not have the words to define her feelings. All she had to ascertain from George was a kind of steel approach to whatever he was thinking. All her energy had gone, and she could not face going over to her house. She rang Riccardo and told him that George's mother had become ill and he had to go to her.

Don't leave the house today,' he advised her, 'I'll get you another bodyguard as soon as I can. I do know how hard this is for you and I wish I could make it better but you have to remember, you tried your best, and that is all you could do.'

She went up to her room and looked again at the news; still no comment. She thought about her dreams and wondered if they had anything to do with Flynn. She sat down on the bed and thought about him, what he might be going through. Her mind slipped into a darkish room; Flynn was on the floor. 'I am here, I can feel your pain, I want to help, but there is no way for me to do this. Please stay strong. I think help is coming. I love you so don't die. I hope you can hear me I just want to help.' She felt a searing pain through her head, breaking her concentration and she fell back on the bed and cried. There was no one who she could tell the truth to without breaking confidence and no one who would understand what she was going through and she felt as alone as he did. She hoped she had reached him. She could not tell as there she felt no response. She hoped in some way she had given him comfort.

The next day, Riccardo introduced her to David, an Australian ex-cop from New South Wales. He was another 'suit'; late thirties, good-looking, and fit. David had short sandy hair, fashionable stubble, hazel eyes, and looked as if he could be a model. He had been in the tactical response team (TRG) but then resigned and thought to establish a new life in another country.

They made arrangements to go out for dinner as Riccardo had to go back to work. Marion took him down the gatehouse and told him where he could sleep and stow his gear. He told her he had applied for a job in France but had been sent directly here. He did not know much about what he was supposed to do. 'I think you must be tired. Are you sure you don't want to rest first? I bet your feet have not stopped running since you left Australia.' He said he would like to know a bit about the job first. She took him into the sunroom and offered him a drink. 'I bet you like beer. You are not on duty now, so it's okay. After getting him a beer, she launched onto his job. 'First Riccardo Rodregious part owns the security company you work for, when he is not around, we call him the boss. Your job is mainly to babysit me. I hope you don't like wearing suits because I would rather you did not when we are together. I am refurbishing a house now and so most of the time you will be over there. I know a little about the NSW police force, and so I will not ask why you decided it was better for your health to leave the country.'

'Do you have any questions you want to know?'

He had an appealing smile, and she thought she would like having him around. 'Yes, what happened to your other bodyguard?' She laughed and said, 'I drove them mad, and they had to take leave. They will come back in due course, I hope. That will not affect you because when we move we will need extra people anyway. You are the man on the spot, and so you can help me design a house for our security people. I'm sure you will get the hang of it, and other staff can fill you in. Now I am convinced you need to rest. People stay up here late into the night so get the rest while you can.'

When Rick came home, he was not happy. 'It seems as half of my French staff have sick mothers. This is impossible for us. We have functions to attend to, and now we may be obliged to hire extra staff. Do you know anything about this?'

'Why should I know any more than you?' she asked. 'I really would like to know more, but I promised your father not to get involved. I can find out nothing from the news and the only way I may be able to find out more would be to look at their local papers. I am trying to keep my mind off it as much as I can.'

They went out for dinner together with David. Riccardo was at his urbane best. He gave her an affectionate hug and explained that his wife had unusual ideas about how things are done. 'You could say she is a high-maintenance client. We try to keep her out of trouble. I like to keep her happy, and so she is overseeing the renovations of our new house. Try to stop her from doing too much, and you will get on fine.'

When they were alone, Rick wanted to know what she thought of David. 'He is admirable and uncomplicated, he does not have any hidden agendas, and he is so straight that I doubt he ever even goes over the speed limit,' she said. 'I think he is quite tough and straight talking if he has to be, but not the kind of person you would take with you on 'doggy' meetings.' Rick laughed at her saying how did she get all that out of one short meeting. 'You know, I read people,' she said.

She searched every site she could think of to see if she could find out anything. Then through chance, she looked up Amnesty International to see if he was listed. He was not but there was an Irishman named Edward Kelly listed as a political prisoner. She laughed; of course, he would not use his own name and what better than Ned Kelly, an infamous Irish/Australian bushranger. She then looked up what charges were being put forward. He had been marked as a terrorist. That was not a good thing because they need not have a trial and could kill him anytime. Further, she found out that enquiries into his activities suggested that the British government said he was not one of theirs; they had disowned him. His only hope would be if George did something. She was full of fear at the thought she could lose both of them. Not to mention a storm they left behind.

She forced herself to work at her house most days and tried to get Rick involved in choosing colours and styles. She used people from around the area as much as she could, even by asking them if they had relatives that could do special tasks. Marion paid above-average wages and made sure they had food and two hours off at mid-day. They all thought she was wonderful. When David said, he was impressed, she just told him that is the way to get the best job done.

Working her way through the news, she found a small story about a riot in northern Pakistan. It was said to have been started by a group of foreign mercenaries. Two British journalists were among the dead. Her heart skipped a beat. What if it was them? Who were the British people killed? Why was there nothing in the British press? She looked but could find nothing more. About one week later, Faustus called her to say a black man wanted to talk to her. She told him to put him in the sunroom. When she came down, he introduced himself as James Williamson; he showed her some ID, and she asked him to sit down. David was in the corner, reading, and appeared to take no notice. 'I have come from your charity. They are seriously short of funds and as you had said if you could help them, you would, I am asking for your help.' Relief flooded over her; it was hard to keep a straight face. 'If you wait here I will organise for you to pick up a money order.' She was gone for about five minutes and came back with written instructions. 'I have arranged for you to go here and pick up 10,000 US dollars. Will that be okay? They know you are coming. You are only to speak to the manager. I've written down instructions and if you follow this exactly using the words I have written. I don't think you will have a problem. If they want confirmation, tell them to call my cell. Tell my charity that this is my Christmas present.'

When he left, David asked if she usually gave out money to strangers.

'No. I only have one charity. "Medicine Sans Frontiers" I believe in giving silently and without fuss. I never speak about it. Otherwise, it has no value other than to make you look good.'

He looked thoughtfully, wondering if this was a hint not to talk about it. She smiled at him telling him it's okay as it is her own money.

'I have an ongoing supply for the moment. I get royalties from the sales of my songs.'

Things got better when a few days later, Marion received an e-mail from Thailand saying the children were safe and well and thank you for the Christmas present. She knew they must be on the move or they would never have sent the e-mail. She wondered where they would go and if Flynn was really okay. She did not think so as he was nearly dead the last time she thought about him. She knew she should not go there but could not help herself. She closed her eyes and tried to picture him. At first, it was hard as there seemed to be a fog in the way. Something was blocking her. She tried again, and this time she got through, and she could see him and where he was. He was in a lot of pain; having been moved around had not helped. She moved closer and tried to inspect what was wrong, her mind searched him to find out what was the most important. There seemed to be so much she doubted if he could be fixed. 'Stay strong,' she whispered in his mind, 'I'll get you help.' She let her mind come back to the present. And she thought about what to do now. She had promised not to interfere, and she felt bad for doing something she was told not to, but she was sure it would not rebound on her. She sent an e-mail to her real charity, giving them George's mobile number and asking them for real help. There was nothing she could do now except wait.

Chapter 19
HER STORY

Relieved from the worry for the safety of the boys, she attended her shrink's clinic. He chided her for not attending the last two sessions that she was booked into. She told him that she had been preoccupied with getting the house working. He noted she had lost weight and thought she may be working too hard.

'I thought about the last visit and I realise I have to deal with the wall of fire and the dark figure I see in the corner of my mind. I am terrified of what I will find if anything, but I can't put it off any longer.'

The doctor assured her that he would control things at all times and if he thought it was too much, he would stop. 'I believe that this wall of fire is not just symbolism. There may have been some real fire. There will be no mistakes, and as always, you are safe here. She lay back in the recliner, and he put the blanket over her. He gave her the injection and held her hand for a while, telling her she was safe. Then he set the video recorder on and started to take her through the process of complete relaxation.

'Now I want you to go back to the beginning of the day of the fire. Tell me what you are doing. Remember, this is just a story of your life, and nothing can hurt you now. Start by telling me where you are and why.'

'I am in Sydney with my husband and two children. I have to go to court. I am being sued about a song I wrote and then sold it to another band. There was a train accident, and people were killed. I wrote a song putting the story in another setting. But the family members say that my song is offensive because it implies that the driver was at fault. I know he was; only nothing was done about it because he was dead. I have pleaded not guilty, stating that it is only coincidence that the families think this is about them. If I lose the case, I will lose everything and may have to declare bankruptcy.'

'Tell me about your husband and children.'

'John is a social commentator, singer, and songwriter. When he was younger, he was just another protest singer. As he got older, he became more serious about how our country is run. I agree with him because our country is one of the few countries that have never known a civil war. It is a country where the whole nation stops work for the running of a horse race. The second weekend in September, the entire nation goes mad about football. Our people are hard workers, but they do not take enough notice in the way our nation is run. John and I are soul mates. We both believe in the notion of social justice and equality. We have a farm in the Blue

Mountains. We have some horses, cows, sheep, and we grow fruit trees and vegetables. The children go to a small local primary school nearby.'

'You had your own band, why did you leave it?'

'We got on fine until we added a new manager. His name was Sydney James. We signed contracts with him without reading all the fine print. He received 10 percent of all we earned, so it was in his best interest to keep us working hard. We never took breaks, and it became so hard for me to deal with the crowds and people all of the time. I think the word may be burnout. Anyway, I just quit.'

'Did you lose the court case? How much would you actually lose?'

'We have separate bank accounts just for this reason. The farm is in a family trust and cannot be sold. This means that I will lose everything I have, but they cannot touch any of the family's money. We will survive, but I will not be able to earn any money for five years.

'It is towards the end of the day, what are you going to do now?'

'We are going to pick up a new cook and drive home.'

What happened on the way home?'

'It was very dark, the road is winding and in some places, there are sharp turns. The children and the cook are in the back seat. The kids are tired and fighting. I take my seatbelt off and turn around to tell them off. Something happens and the car is travelling through mid-air. I look at John, and he looks at me, we know. Suddenly, I am thrown through the front window, and the car rolls two more times. It then bursts into flames. I try to get to them, but the heat is driving me away. Everytime I try to get close the fire drives me back. All I can do is watch as my family turn into black ridged figures. I stay there until the flames die down, and then I walk away. My last memory is seing John as a dark figure in the early morning sun shaded by parts of the car.

I just walk and walk. I can't feel anything.'

'What do you do next?'

'I go back to the farm, put some thing's in a bag and walk away, I have John's card, and I take all the money out and put it in the bag.

I walked away from everything. I just keep walking. I see a paper that said we are all dead in a terrible accident. I know they think the cook is me. I don't go to the funeral, I can't see the point. I spent a long time on the road. While on the road I started having strange dreams about a tall dark figure. He had a long cloke with a hood. He seemed to be watching me. Somehow I end up in Cairns. I decide to go away to another place, and so I book a trip. I get some luggage and clothes and get on a plane. I end up in Greece and lose my entire luggage and my identity. I just start to walk again. I still don't feel anything. I don't ever want feel again I just can't stand the pain. That is when I decide to end it for good. In my mind, I see John standing there. He is waiting for me. I swim out until I think I will drown, but I am picked up, taken to a house, and raped. I hate it because it makes me feel. I want to die, I want it to stop and the only way to end it is in my head.'

'Do you think the tall, dark figure you see is John?'

'I have never thought about it, but yes, I believe he is trying to look after me by warning me when something is wrong.'

As a child do you remember any time when you had any extra-sensory perceptions or flashes of intuition?'

'I don't think I am any different from other people, sometimes I think something is going to happen and it does, but that is not often. I get spooked when I am in some places where people have died. I can feel their energy. When I was little, I used to be afraid at night because I felt there was someone there in my bedroom. I could feel them, and I would call out to my father to cheek. He did, but he could not see anyone there.' anyone there.'

You are feeling relaxed, and at ease, you are going to wake up soon, and you will not remember anything of the story you have told me. You will remember the next time you see the dark figure in your mind that he is there to help you and not hurt you. I am going to count backwards, and you will wake up. How are you feeling now?'

She sat up and thought about how she felt. 'I feel good. Somehow I don't feel as afraid as I usually am. I feel something has changed, will you tell me what it is?'

'Marion, I am not sure the time is right just yet. I know you feel impatient, but I would like to put all the pieces together before I present them to you.'

'And I think you are stalling,' she retorted.

'Please come back next week, and we will talk about it.'

Clinical notes: Marion File no. 786254

Dr McKlean looked at the video of the last session. It provided answers to the questions he had posed himself in the first meeting.

1. The cause of memory loss seems to be a Corollary accumulation of incidents occurring one after another. Starting with the court case and followed by the death of her family. She suffered post-traumatic stress disorder followed by exposure while walking. The process caused loss of self through unresolved grief. A suicide attempt and rape were the last contributing factors that caused a complete mental breakdown.

2. Depression caused her to become subjective to

suggestion. Loss of identity instigated a belief there were no options open to her.

3. There may have been some latent extra-sensory perception in early years. These were pushed to the background by the belief that it was not real or possible for one to have such skills. This must have caused some cognitive dissonance. After breakdown when there was no way to decide who to trust or how to proceed, these skills were utilised. Thus, it is apparent that the development of these skills was due directly to the trauma she sustained. There seems to be evidence that she continues to develop these skills to a much higher standard than one would expect. Questions arise about what level she is willing to divulge information on her use of these skills.

4. Further testing may indicate she has a higher IQ than before. It has become evident that although the past has been erased, her learning ability may suggest an excellent memory.

5. Given her still fragile mental state, one would question whether she would be better off if she knew her story. How would she respond if she knew that the reason for her breakdown was caused by her husband? And what would she do if she was aware that the dark figure in her dreams was, in fact, her soul mate? Is this in her best interest? What value would it serve?

Chapter 20
TIME LINES

Marion became more settled after the last visit to the shrink's office. She could concentrate more on the house. She tried to get Rick more involved in deciding what style they would like to live with. His usual response was, 'Do what you think is best.'

'We have to decide. The original house was used as a country house. The furnishings should reflect a casual wood look. However, you may prefer we could go for a more classic look like here. I can't make this decision on my own. You have to tell me what you like so I can incorporate it into a look that covers the whole house.' He just looked at her and said. 'Why don't you get an interior decorator to do it?'

'I don't need one, and I want to get as much work through the local people as I can. You must come over and see what we have done so far.' He gave her a second look and realised that she had changed. She looked better than he had seen her for a while; he realised that she had not had nightmares for quite a while. Working on the house had given her another creative outlet, and it suited her. He thought he had actually been preoccupied that he had not taken notice of her like he should. 'You are right; I need to take more interest. I will come over after work. We can look at the house and then go out for dinner.' She smiled at him and said she would let Faustus know.

When he arrived at the house, he was surprised at the work that had been done. The front yard was cleared of weeds, and the garden had been restored. Inside her house, the kitchen had sandstone tops and pale grey tiled floor; every appliance was silver, giving a clean and modern appearance. All the servants' quarters were done mostly in cream and bright curtains and matching bedspreads. Along the back wall was the security house. It was built on lines not dissimilar to the gatehouse, except she had added a large gym that had its own entrance.

'I can see we are quite close to moving in,' he said. 'I'm impressed, I had not realised how far you have got.'

'So now you can see why we need to decide the kind of lifestyle we want.' She took him into the study and showed him the secret room that had a lever in the bookcase. 'Nobody knows about this except your sister and we should keep it that way.' In the room was safe but she told him she could not open it. 'This is where I found the pictures of the house when it was used as a country house. I know you like your house. Do you want the décor to be similar or would you rather a more informal style?' He looked at her and said, 'What do you want?'

'No, you don't, I asked first.'

'All right then, as I will probably inherit the big house anyway. I don't need another large residence. But at the same time, I want the house to reflect your style. I think you seem to prefer an informal way of life. I am so sure you will make it a pleasant place to live in no matter what style you do it in.' She shook her head in frustration. 'It's your house too, don't you want to have a say? And I don't know what your favourite colours are.' He hugged her and said he could live in a shack with her and be happy. 'I like what you have done with the kitchen, and I trust in your sense of colour. I'm sorry, I am no help. I would just call a decorator and get them to do it.'

'I think it will be ready in about two weeks. Could we spend next weekend and get the boat and bring it around here?'

'That will be a good idea,' he said. They picked up David and went out for dinner. Riccardo took them to an Italian restaurant that had not been open long, simply by going there, he lent the place some prestige, and so their host was doing everything to make it a good night. They stayed until quite late, and Riccardo wondered again about what she had said about David. How straight was he? Riccardo told them he had contracted an American called Mason to come over and he would be there in about a week. He had been a navy seal and had a pilot's licence. Marion asked Riccardo if he had heard of their wandering staff and was surprised to find that most had returned to work. He expressed his discontent that those people should all choose to leave at the same time. 'At one time,' he stated 'I would ordinarily dismissed them, now I am becoming soft in my old age.'

A week later, they started to move things into the house. Marion had been busy working in the lounge when she had a feeling something was not right. She walked through and found a man going through the drawers in the sideboard. He seemed to be looking for something. As she knew everybody who worked at the house, she knew he was a stranger. 'What are you doing?' She yelled. Then she thought she would do like George said. Using the element of surprise, she ran at him, but it was like hitting a brick wall, and then he hit her, all the lights went out. By the time she woke up, everyone was making a fuss. David was there; he had called Riccardo, who came charging over like a 'wounded bull'. Her face was swollen, and he insisted she go to the hospital for an x-ray. He was yelling at David, but she could not understand what he was saying and she doubted if David could too as most of it was in Greek. He insisted the place was to be closed until security was properly in place. There would be no more coming and, going and everybody was to have name tags made and checked against their jobs for the day.

Her immediate concern was what this man was looking for. He had been in the study and had gone through the papers in the desk. She knew he was not here to steal; it had to be something else.

In the midst of this, George came back. One of the other security guards said her boyfriend was back. As soon as she heard he was there, she ran down to the gatehouse and hugged him and kissed him on the cheek.

'Get off me, woman, you are like an overgrown puppy.' He said this with a smile on his face. He was aware that David was standing there and was surprised by her reaction. 'So you've met David, he has been my minder.'

'What happened to your face?'

'It's a long story. I'll just say your self-defence did not work. The intruder was built like a rugby player and hitting him was like running into a brick wall. The boss is acting like an overprotective bully.'

George could not hide his mirth at the same time, saying to David.

'Didn't he tell you to keep her out of trouble?'

David nodded. 'I was not that far away.'

She became serious and told George she wanted to talk to him at another time when he felt like it. She suggested could he meet by the pool later in the day after he had a rest. And please, could he bring his guitar. He nodded, and she left.

George turned to David and said, 'What do you think of our girl?'

'She is nice, but a bit of a nutcase,' David responded.

Marion went upstairs and rang Rick and told him about George. She was upset because it seemed as if he had aged twenty years. 'I think he must have been through a very rough time. Can you come early and maybe have a drink with us?'

Rick came home about 5.00 p.m. and found them sitting by the pool. As soon as George saw him, he stood up and Rick went to him and kissed him on both cheeks.

'I am glad to see you that you are safe and well.'

He too was shocked at his appearance; he definitely looked as if he had carried the 'weight of the world on his shoulders'. He asked David what he drank, and David said, 'usually only one beer.' Rick poured out two whiskies and got a beer for David and red wine for Marion. They all said thank you. Rick raised his glass and said,

'Here's to absent friends.'

They settled down to listen to Marion play and sing. Then she encouraged

George to sing with her. 'I can see you are a little rusty, we should fix that.'

She said.

Riccardo thought it had been a while since he had heard his wife sing.

He wondered why he never even missed the music until now.

When they were in their room, he asked her if she had found out anything.

'I was going to quiz him, but I thought I had better let him get settled for now. I don't think he is in any real state to answer my questions yet. Did you notice how the years seemed to roll off him as soon as we started to relax and make music? I'm going to have to be patient and wait until he gets better. I know this means putting off moving for another couple of weeks. I have an idea I would like to put to you. Now that we have extra staff, it is going to get harder for you to organise everyone. Would you consider making George in charge of the Greek contingent?'

'Why would I do this when he keeps going AWOL all the time?'

'It's because he is the most stable and mature of the crew. And you know he does not do anything without reason. And have you forgotten he took a bullet for you and has never mentioned it? But the most compelling reason I can think of is that he knows how to keep me in line.' Rick laughed at her.'

'You are a bright thing, aren't you? But I think you are right. As usual, you seem to be able to assess situations so well.'

She waited a couple of days before talking to George. It was an awkward conversation, one he knew was coming; nevertheless, he would have preferred if she would leave things alone. He would tell her only what she needed to know and try not to let it get out of hand. He explained to her that while they were travelling, Flynn was in a lot of pain and said things to him he typically would not have said. He told him how she had been getting in his head. Flynn had told George that she said she loved him. At first he did not want to believe it but realised that it must be true; otherwise, how could she have provided so much help when she was not supposed to get involved? It had taken thirteen different operations to put him back together. And he had more physiotherapy to do. And there was Abdula; how did he know how to reach her?

'I don't suppose you will tell me what he was doing there in the first place. Do your people always do what they are told even if it means that you may get killed?' George looked down and did not answer her. 'What could be so important that you would agree to go into another country and try to extract other people who had been caught? It is a bit like the spider saying to the fly come into my house. I am aware that I am not supposed to use my skills on Flynn. He has already told me not to. I just can't seem to help myself. The problem is the more

I do it, the easier it gets. I saw him on the floor, in prison and he was dying, I had to try to give him hope. I did not know that time if I reached him as he made no response. I guess you know how he feels about me, but what you don't know is how I feel about him. I know it's impossible to love two men but I think I do, for different reasons. I am not about to change my marriage status, but I feel that I need Flynn around as well. I need your help to bring him back here so we can look after him.'

George looked dangerous and said, 'Don't you think you have done enough to him? I don't know what he wants to do now.'

'You may think I am selfish, but I really just want to help him get better. No matter what you say, he is still safer here than anywhere else. I think he needs us both.'

'I'll think about it. Flynn is still not fit to travel yet and when he is, and if he asks me, I will find out what he wants. If I were him, I'd run a mile.'

'He tried that, and it did not work. I know I have to be careful around you both, because I think of you like family, and even the boss thinks this way now. I'm not going to quiz you anymore as I can tell you are having trouble with it. I'll let it go and see how it plays out. By the way, I have put you up for promotion. I hope you don't mind.'

Mason arrived late one night. He rang on the gate and David, who had been reading, went to get him. He introduced himself and was showed where he was to stay. David told him that he would inform Faustus in the morning. And he would set up an appointment with Marion. Meanwhile, he was just to settle in and make himself at home. Mason was forty-three years old, tall, lean with golden skin, blue eyes, and close-cut hair that was almost bald. He stood straight and had the look of a Marine or just out of the army. David said there were some beers in the fridge and some food if he felt like cooking.

Mason wanted to know as much as he could about the people he would be working for. What were they like and what did they expect him to do. David explained that he had not been working long for the family. He said that Mr and Mrs Rodregious would be moving to a new house in a couple of weeks and then his job would be more defined. David told him that Mr Rodregious had a temper and was very protective of his wife. She, on the other hand, was a bit different; he did not explain why as he thought it was better that Mason finds out for himself. Mason wanted to know all about what business he was in and what he did. David said he was not involved in that part of the operation.

'Who is involved in that part of service?'

David said that probably George, but he was asleep.

'So he is the person I should be talking to then?'

Again, David said he was not sure, and he would have

to ask George. Mason looked around the gatehouse and observed that the house was watched 24/7.

He wondered why this was necessary. Is this usual in this country or were there underworld connections? He would have to resign himself to waiting until tomorrow to find out more.

He was up early and went for a jog around the property and noticed other security guards seeming to be standing around. They wore grey suits, and he thought this was what he should wear for the interview. He went over and introduced himself; they shook hands but other than that were not very communicative. He was beginning to get the impression it was going to be harder than he thought to get in with this family. After his jog, he showered and changed into a suit and got himself some breakfast. David was up, but George was not. He wondered if they were allowed to choose their times of work. A call came down for him to go up to the house at 10.00 a.m. Marion met him at the door and showed him into the sunroom. She said she liked this room the best because it was less formal. He waited for her to sit down before he sat down. 'How long have you been out of the army?' she asked.

'I was in the Navy; I am a SEAL.'

'Okay then, how long have you been out of the navy?' He hesitated and said six months.

'And what have you been doing since then?'

'Mostly I have been looking for a job.'

'I would have thought they would retrain you given your experience.' He was starting to feel uncomfortable; he was wondering where she was going with the questions and tried to second-guess her by saying that it was hard to fit back into civilian life. 'Being a security guard is a big step down, don't you think?' she said.

'I thought it would offer me opportunities to use my skills in a different way.'

'I'm sorry to tell you that it is not that interesting. Have you met David?'

'Yes, he let me in last night.'

'His job is mostly babysitting me.' She noted the look of disappointment on his face and thought she should let him off the hook. 'Maybe David mentioned that I am a bit different. That is because first, I don't like our staff to wear suits unless they are on an actual assignment. The men in the yard are Mr Rodregious senior's team, not ours. We will be moving soon, and that is why we require staff to cover our new place. Right now, there is not a lot to do except get your bearings. Go look around the city and find the best places to eat. You are not expected to have everything at your fingertips just yet. Find out from the others how things are run. There is enough gossip in this place to keep you occupied or a while. You have to work out what is true and what is not.' She stood up and said she hoped his stay would be pleasant and held out her hand to shake. As he was walking back to the gatehouse, he mulled over what she had said. Was she deliberately elusive or was she just thick?

By the time he was back to the gatehouse, George was up. He shook hands and introduced himself. 'You have just had the royal treatment by Marion.' He smiled. Mason wanted to know what he meant by that.

'She has this unique skill; she can read people. You don't know it, but by now, she knows everything about you.'

This information came as a bit of a shock to Mason because he thought the interview seemed vague. 'What does she do with the information she thinks she gets?' he asked.

'Usually, she passes it on to her husband unless it's personal and that is rarely. He takes an interest in what she has to say as she is usually right.'

'So she is really the boss.' George looked at him for a while and said he did not think that is so but it may inform his decisions.

Riccardo called George and asked him to come into his office that morning. This was a time when he would use a suit. He had just bought a new SUV and was looking for a chance to drive it. In the office, Riccardo told him that his wife thought it would be a good idea if he were put in charge of the staff in Greece. He hoped he would take the job as he could foresee problems arising due to lack of coordination of services and rosters for both houses.

'It may mean you have less time to be out on the field, but I am prepared to give you overall say in the running of the show.' George said he was flattered that they thought enough of him to offer him the job if it did not interfere with his contract.

'You will need to make sure that you have rosters done ahead of time.'

'I guess it also means that I just can't take off whenever I like without checking with you first.'

Marion has brought up some interesting observations on our newest member. She thinks his story does not fit with the credentials he provided. She thinks he is a 'yes' man, but she is not sure who he is saying yes to. She also told me that he seems more interested in my business affairs than would be considered normal. She suggested that I get you to consider his motives and watch him for a while. She is very perceptive and picks up on things I may well miss. Are you able to do this?'

'Yes, no trouble, she also voiced concerns to me. I'm not sure how far she thinks I can go, but I'll try. One other thing is Flynn. Now he is ready for discharge, she wants him back with us. I'm not sure it is a good idea, but I know this will make her happy.'

'How bad is he really? Is he likely to be able to work

again?'

'He may be well enough to work, but I have told her, that he may not want to come back. And we should consider what he wants to do. She thinks we could start him on light duties such as watching the monitors. She seems to have it worked out in her mind. She wanted me to sway you to the idea.'

'Do you think she is in love with him or is it just she feels responsible for him?'

'I know that she is in love with you and you should not doubt that. Flynn falls in and out of love so many times it is hard to say what he thinks. I can guarantee he would do his job to the best of his ability. I feel some responsibility for him and would like to help him if I could. We have been mates for a long time.'

'All right, that is good enough for me. I think I understand this whole affair and most of it has to do with Marion being an empath. I am willing to give Flynn the benefit of the doubt this time. I also like Flynn, and I am reluctant to fire him. But I can only take so much, and if he mucks up again, I probably will kill him. She does not say much about him, but I am sure that you keep in touch with him.'

George stood up and shook hands with Riccardo and left the office. It went well, and Riccardo was more pleasant than he had known him to be before. Maybe she was right, and he had changed his mode of looking at people.

Anyway, it was still up to Flynn. Flynn had never even thought there was a way for him to come back. He wondered where this would lead. His thoughts went back to Mason. What was he up to and what did he want with the boss? He could do some checking under the table and see what came up. What if she was right? They would have a problem that they would get must get rid of.

Up until now, George and Flynn had agreed to keep her out of their other job, but what if she endangered them or what they were doing. The problem was she had told Flynn she could find out more but had chosen not to, but she was unpredictable and the fact he now knew the truth, that she could get into Flynn's head meant that she could extract information if she tried. But then would she? He had not told the boss that she thought she loved Flynn as this would complicate things. He was confident he could reason with her to behave. He would ring the hospital where Flynn was staying and find out his thoughts.

On the weekend, Rick and Marion flew down and picked up the boat to bring it back to its new mooring. They were excited at spending time alone at sea for the first time. It was not that far but the time it took to reach their goal could vary, depending on the weather. He expected it to take a couple of days. He had told Pantos that they were moving the boat and wanted him to get enough provisions for a couple of days. He was sorry for Pantos as he knew he liked his job, but he would make sure he had enough money to soften the blow. Marion had also bought him a thank-you gift, a jumper of his favourite football club. Rick thought that only she would know which club he followed.

The trip was easy, and they took turns at the helm. They stayed out to sea but kept the coastline in sight as well. When darkness fell, they dropped anchor and stayed for the night. It was fun sleeping in the bunk bed, which folded down to make a double bed. Cooking was a challenge as Marion had to make do with what was in store; however, if there was enough wine, it did not seem to matter. Rick was relaxed and easy going; the boat was his favourite toy. The sea always had a calming effect on him. Now, he had someone who enjoyed it as much as he did. 'You are much better now than before. I have noticed you don't have many nightmares and you are also managing crowds better as well. What has changed?'

'I don't know, I think that somehow my life is calmer and I don't feel afraid. I know I am safe at last, the past is behind me, you are just right for me, and I love you. When I see the dark shadow in my dreams, I am no longer afraid, and I think of it as a guardian angel rather than something to push away. I can't wait to get into our own home and then we can live just as we want to.'

'Are you happy about George being back? And what do you think about Flynn?'

'They complete my family. I know it seems a bit crazy. Somewhere, I lost my family, and I know you understand the need to have a family. Maybe we could have one of our own? Have you thought about that?'

'One day, we'll see.'

George rang the hospital Flynn was in and asked to speak to him. It was another thing he did not want to do; he felt is if he was interfering. Flynn came on the line and the first thing he asked was how things were going for him. 'I'm back at the big house for the moment. We will be moving into the house that Marion has restored soon. We have new security staff on now, and I have been placed in charge. How are you?'

'I am as well as can be expected. I've nearly got this walking thing off. I am feeling a bit exposed here on my own. I hate to say this, but I miss you, man.'

'There is a place here for you if you want it, you could do light duties like watch the monitors. I do not need to say this, but Marion would like to have you here. She seems to have this curious idea that only she can fix you. The boss appears to have gone soft in the head and now says she can have anything she wants. If it were me, I'd run a mile. I have told them it is up to you to decide what you want to do.'

'There is no real decision to make. I definitely want to come back. I just thought it was not possible. I still care about Marion, and that won't change. I've discovered I would rather be near her than not. She knows that I'd be safer there than anywhere else.'

'Okay, man, you're on, just come back when you can. I could use your input as I think we might have a situation on our hands. Maybe the three of us can resolve this head thing as well. I try to keep her in line. Anyway, I'll see you soon, okay?'

Monday early morning, Marion appeared at the gatehouse. George was making breakfast, and the others were sitting around the table. She looked fresh and ready to go. 'I see the sea air agrees with you.' George smiled. 'Want anything?'

'No, I've had breakfast, thank you. Now you are the other boss, what am I supposed to call you, boss number 2?'

'Very funny,' he quipped. 'What do you want?'

'I want to get into my house as soon as I can. I want you to approve. I thought Mason could go out and get what gym equipment you need and any equipment you think I could actually use. I consider you might have to work it out for yourselves. The boss will need to be assured that it is secure. So I was conteplating the notion of doing a safety report to satisfy him. David helped in the design of the security building, so if you don't like it, blame him. I am happy to have David as my minder for the most part, and Mason can do the parameters. What do you think?'

'I'm having breakfast, and you put all this to me in the morning?'

'Oh, George, I am sorry, I should have thought first. It's just that I have more energy today. I know it's going to be a great day. Just give me a yell when you are all ready to go over to the house. Mason can drive me in my car, and David can go with you.'

They set out for Nea Makri at 9.00 a.m. She told Mason, 'It takes little more than thirty minutes to get there. It is a small seaside town in East Attica.' She directed him to drive along Leof Poseidon's to the beach where he could view the coast and the mountains in the background. She showed him where the boat was moored. It was a charming place, and he now could see what the attraction was for her to choose this area. The road wound around and came to their property. There was now a long stone wall with a big iron gate complete with a grate installed to press a button for entry. She used a key button to open it. He was impressed by the house. The gardens were nicely set out. The outside was not yet finished, but he could see that it all has been recently cleaned.

'We are going to render it with a limestone colour, and of course, the security house will be the same,'

Then they all got out and walked around to inspect it. David had been there for the most part of the process, but it was the first time for Mason, and George had not seen it for a long time. She opened the front door, and

George was surprised again at how much had been accomplished. It had a nice feel to it, comfortable but lacking the formality of the 'big house.' She had used earth colours throughout the interior, blending them so when walking from one room to the next, one could hardly notice the change of colour. There was some built-in furniture and some odd pieces, but she explained the rest would be coming as soon as they could have someone there to receive it. They walked out the back to look at the security house. Again, she pointed that it would be rendered. There were also gardens in the back. George commented there was no place for the cars.

She looked alarmed 'I haven't thought of that. Where will we build a garage? In the pictures, there was no place for cars. Maybe they did not have them. It means we will have to take space from the front or back garden. We could put it over in the front corner.'

George told her she could not do that from a security point of view because it would make it easier for someone to jump the fence. 'I suggest you place it on the right side of the house. You could create a walkway between the two. It would screen out the security block, but that makes it safer.

'Won't it look out of place?' she asked.

'I don't think so because you have the land and all it means is the house will look a bit wider.'

Watching the security house, she asked if there was anything else that needed to be done on the inside. They agreed that apart from hooking up monitors with cameras and getting the gym things, they should be comfortable.

'Whatever you need, just write a list and I will get it. I decided to get bigger beds as you are all taller than the average. I wanted you to feel like home as much as you can. So I don't care if you put up pictures or anything else to make it more homely. This is not a barracks. I am hoping a couple of you can move in directly so we can get the staff back to finish the work stopped by the boss. Anyway, that is up to George now.'

On the way home, George told her how impressed he was that she had changed the dump into a reasonable house.

'I feel once we move, it will be better still, and I know Rick will feel free to do as he pleases rather than conform all the time. I think we will still spend a lot of time over at the big house because I promised the old man I would still go for walks with him. If we have our own gym, maybe we could talk the boss into doing some exercise too.'

George told her about the imminent return of Flynn. 'I know you will be happy about this, but you must behave appropriately with him. If you try to kill him with kindness, it will only make him feel worse.'

'I know he just wants to do his job. I will respect that. It is going to be a bit awkward for us at first. I understand that I should not have used my mind on him. He told me he would not tell. It just happened. Now I must make it stop. I just don't know how.'

It was decided to move Mason and David over into the new house. Their job would mostly consist of keeping records of who came and went and what work was done. George had written out a security report naming positions for cameras and sensor lights to be installed. It was hoped they all could move in, there in two weeks.

In those two weeks, Marion and Rick made use of their time trying to sort out what they needed to get. When she told Rick they did not have a garage and needed to put one in, he was surprised that it had not been thought of. She said that it was because it's a 'bloke' thing, and George had pointed it out because he's into new cars. He has just acquired a new gold SUV and would not like it to be left out. She told him that George had placed the garage in the most secure location and not where she would have chosen. Rick noticed that she seemed tired and wondered if she was again working too hard to bring about an early entry.

It was during this time that Flynn came back. He looked well and tanned. He seemed to have developed extra muscle particularly on the top part of his body. He had been working out, and it showed. One would not notice any change in him if they did not know him before. To Marion he seemed to be more serious and less self-assured than before. Marion was glad she had a chance to talk to him alone before anyone came home. She felt awkward around him, wondering what to say to him, whether it was okay to kiss him on the cheek as she usually would. He had dumped his gear at the door of the gatehouse and walked straight up to the house. He was surprised by how frail she looked. She looked tired, and she had lost weight. They stood looking at each other, wondering what to say first. She was not usually lost for words and struggled to find the right thing to say. Finally, she asked him to come out to the pool area and have a drink. She did not ask, she just poured two whiskies and handed him one. Finally, she said, 'Welcome home.' He nodded and drank his drink down. She got him another and said,

'I am sorry I have caused you so much conflict. You know how I feel and sometimes I just can't help myself.'

'You did not do anything, I managed to do it all by myself. You tried to warn me, but I was not in a mood to hear you. I heard you when I was in prison, and it did give me the strength to go on. But I felt very uncomfortable when you wanted to find out what my injuries were. I would rather you had not seen me like that. I am grateful for the doctors that fixed me up. Without them, I would not have made it, and I would not have liked to live my life as a cripple. In fact, I decided I would end it if I could not walk or even if my face could not be fixed.'

'George said you would not come back here, he said if

it were him, he would run a mile from me. I am different now, I am stronger, and I can stand up for myself most of the time. I am not depressed anymore. The boss and I seem to manage to get along most of the time. George thinks he has gone soft on me. He does not really know how I feel about you. Well, I'm not sure how I feel either. I only know you are important in my life and I am so grateful you decided to come back. We have two new staff members, and George is now in charge of our operations in Greece. He will not tell you this, but he needs your support.'

'Are you sure you are not saying this to make me feel better? I still feel the same way about you even if you are a pain in the neck some of the time.'

'You should know I speak my mind and I would not just say so. I think we have a problem with one of our new staff. I have asked George if he could do some kind of check on him using the fancy equipment that your puppet masters have. I will tell you once, I could have checked up about your other job more, but I chose not to because I was told by the old man not to interfere, and I won't, but I am not going to pretend I don't know what is going on with you and George.'

She got up and poured out another drink for them both. Flynn smiled for the first time. 'What are you doing, woman, do you want us to get drunk?'

'I just thought that our first meeting was going to be a bit hard, so why not make it easier and have some fun if we can?'

He looked at her again and commented that maybe she had not changed that much after all. He thought it would be him that felt strange and had not realised that she may feel the same.

'As long as it is all good and we don't have anything that we are afraid to say, then I think we will be okay. I want things to go back to where they were before, and I assume that is what you want too, right?' He nodded and smiled again.

'I will go and settle in, and then I may have to go again. If you need information, there are people I should talk to.' She stood up and this time kissed him on the cheek and hugged him.

When George came back, he was delighted to see Flynn. 'How are you? Man, you are looking as good as new. Have you seen Marion yet? Did it go well? I missed having your ugly face around.'

'I'm fine, yes, I have spoken to Marion, she knows the way to a man's heart, and she gave me a few whiskies. I think we are on the same page, so don't worry about that. She told me that you may have a problem that needs attention. I must report to the powers that be anyway, so she thought you may need some help with something.'

'We have acquired two new staff, and she has

reservations about both. One is a US Navy SEAL with a pilot's licence, which would come in handy. She had an interview with him, and he thought she is a bit vague or not too bright. She thinks his story does not hold up. He is very keen and wants to please, but she thinks he is a 'yes' man and wonders who he is saying 'yes' to. She told me that when she said his job maybe babysitting her, he did not seem happy and wanted to work with the boss. So she thinks he is interested in the the bosses affairs for some reason. And she has asked if we could do a check on him, quietly. The other one is an Australian police officer formally with the TRG. She told me she knows what is happening over there and believes his story. She said he is so straight he probably would not even go over the speed limit.'

'How much do you think she knows about the boss?' Flynn asked.

'It is hard to say. I think that she knows more than she lets on. But I get the idea if she really knows, then she will have to do something about it, and I don't think she wants to do that because then the shit will really hit the fan. She has made her feelings about guns well known and after Hong Kong where she lied through her teeth to get him out of a sticky situation. I'm pretty sure she has a good idea that all is not as it seems. We still can't prove he is directly involved in anything. And we are close to him. He appears to slip out of everything, making sure the dirt does not stick to him.'

'When I saw her, I noticed she looks a bit frail,' Flynn said. 'She has lost weight and seemed a bit tired. Have you seen any change?'

'Not really, but I see her every day. Mentally, I think she is much stronger. She seems to be less afraid now and more confident. She has put this house together without much input from the boss. Everything was going well until she found a stranger in the house looking for something going through some papers. She tried to tackle him, and he knocked her out, which wouldn't be hard to do. It's a bit of a coincidence that Mason turned up after that. Anyway, the boss closed everything down until security was put in and it has only just started up again. We will all be moving over there in a week or so. I should have a closer look at her and what she is doing.'

'Just tell me when you want me to leave, and I'll do it. I don't think I am fully operational just yet. So what are you going to do with me? I don't want to be just dead wood.'

'Flynn, if I think it is time to put you out to pasture, I'll have the guts to tell you to your face. Take a day or two and then go, okay? Spend some time with Marion. If you think she is not well, we should tell the boss.'

That evening, they spent some time out by the pool, playing music, drinking and telling stories. It was fun, and they quickly slipped into the casual camaraderie they had before. Flynn commented George's music had become better as new songs were added to his repertoire. Rick was happy to sit back and watch his wife sing. He felt at ease and could relax without feeling he had to do anything. This was the life he liked best and he felt that in the new house, this is what he could look forward to for a long time. He could imagine them, growing old together and going for walks along the beach.

George told Riccardo that Flynn had some business that would take him away for a couple of days, but then he will be back for the foreseeable future.

'Just don't make it six months like the last time,' Riccardo replied.

George ignored that and went on to say that they would put Flynn on light duties for a while and gradually increase his workload. Riccardo stated that he was glad that George had the headache of sorting out staff now and it was one thing he did not have to worry about, so George should just do what he thought best and did not have to seek his permission unless it was serious.

Up in the bedroom, Rick asked Marion if she was happy now. 'Yes, and I know you are too. Our little family is back together, and you can't pretend to me that you don't like it too. You don't have to worry about me because George has already read me the riot act about how I should behave.'

He laughed, 'Good on George, but I'm not worried because you are stronger now and less likely to get hooked into others feelings than you used to be. I am pleased that Flynn looks so good, given that he received such extensive injuries.' She fell into bed and sighed; once again, Rick noted how tired she looked.

The next morning, Marion was up and in an anticipative mood; she had a good night and no dreams. It seemed as if she had energy to spare. She told Rick she was hoping George would teach her some more self-defense moves.

'I don't see why you keep trying. You are never going to be good at it.' He said.

She looked happy and said, 'I might learn enough to keep you in line, and then what will you do?'

He laughed again and said, 'I'll just kill you with kindness.' He wanted to pull her back into bed, but she slipped out of his arms and ran out the door.

At the gatehouse, George had just finished breakfast and Flynn was reading the paper. 'I thought you could teach me some more self-defence,' she announced. 'All right but just for a half an hour that's all,' said George. He pulled the mat out onto the lawn and reminded her that this was self-defence, not offence. He showed her how to get away from someone who was trying to grab her by dropping down as a dead weight then moving out of the way fast. They tried it a couple of times and then he applied some pressure. It worked and seemed so natural. 'That is enough for now.' It was only later in the day he noticed big bruises on her arms. He had not held her that tightly that it could cause an injury. He was sure the boss would become concerned if he saw them and wondered if he should call him. Flynn suggested they leave it for a while and see what happened. She had noticed her arms and made sure they were covered up with a shirt.

The next day, she had a migraine and could not get up. She refused any medication and said she would prefer to just stay in a dark room until it stopped. Faustus was on instruction to call Riccardo if it did not get better by the middle of the day and to let George know she would not be coming over to the house today. Flynn was due to fly out that evening; he was unhappy to leave if she was not well. He waited until everyone had left and went to see her. He sat down on her bed and held her hand. 'Are you okay?' he asked.

'I just get these headaches from time to time, it's nothing.'

'I don't think it is nothing. I think something is wrong. I've noticed bruising on your legs and arms. You are often tired. I will always care about you, and I am worried you are not looking after yourself. You should see a doctor and get a proper check-up.'

'Thank you for caring, but I'm all right.' He leant over and kissed her on the cheek; he longed for it to be more but knew he had to accept that was all he could do. 'I'll see you when I get back.'

Two days before the big move, she woke up full of energy; she jumped on top of Rick hugging and kissing him. He woke up with a start. He was going to growl at her then thought better of it and decided to just enjoy the moment and let her have it her way. 'You are so happy right now I'm glad I please you.'

'It's two days before we will be in our own home. Tonight, will be our last sleep in this bed unless we are here for a visit. Today, all the rest of the furniture is arriving, and our new help will also be starting. I have so much to do. I do so want you to be happy with everything. Tonight, I must take extra care of your father during our walk because he feels as if he is losing us. I keep telling him we will be here often and of course, he can visit us. It is not that far away.'

It was when she had no clothes on he noticed the bruises on her arm. 'What is this?'

'It is nothing, just me being uncoordinated when George is trying to teach me self-defense.' He sat up in bed and pulled the sheet off and looked at her. There were several bruises on her hip and legs. And he noticed her loss of weight. 'You have not been looking after yourself.'

'I am fine, don't stress, it is just the excitement, once we are in the house, I will regain the weight.' He felt a twinge of concern and said, 'I will tell George that you are not to do any of the work yourself, just let others do for you, which is what they are there for.' She pulled the sheet back over them cuddled up close to him and closed her eyes and tried to pretend that they could be like that all day.

By early afternoon, she felt tired and asked George if he would take her back to the big house. She did not feel sorry about this as she had achieved most of what she had set out to do. Also, she was mindful of the night ahead and wanted to get through it okay.

George dropped her off and then went to the airport to pick up Flynn. In the car, Flynn told him about what he encountered when going into work.

'I am on extended sick leave, and then I can come back after a psychological evaluation. You are not in the good books either. I was told that because the operation was considered a success, there would be no repercussions. However, if you pull a stunt like that again, you could face charges. Like Marion said, I wonder who these journalists were as there was nothing in the papers. I was told they were innocent bystanders taken a hostage, but because they failed to say anything at work, I really wonder who they were. On the other matter, I checked up, and it seems as if Marion was right again. He is working for CIA, so what does he want with the boss? How do we deal with this? Should we tell her or do you think she may go running to her husband?' George considered the options open to them.

'I believe we will have to talk with her or she will keep

on trying to find out for herself anyway. We can ask her not to say anything and get her cooperation. Maybe she may have a creative idea on how to get rid of Mason without his cover being blown.'

Back at the house, George rang Faustus and asked if they could meet Marion at 5.00 p.m. by the pool. He told them she was asleep but would wake her in time for the meeting.

She came out to the pool; she looked refreshed, but Flynn noticed she had makeup on. They told her about Mason and asked her not to divulge anything to the boss just yet. She asked them if they would like some wine and then poured out three glasses. She sat down looking thoughtful, trying to put together a scenario of Rick that would interest the CIA. 'The only thing that I can come up with is Hong Kong. Do you know what that meeting was about?'

Flynn said that he did not recall what the meeting was about. 'But that is because when I go to these meetings, I just stand there and zone out on the conversation. When we arrived at the meeting in Hong Kong, shit started happening just about as soon as we got there. It was a setup. I think someone who he had upset wanted to teach him a lesson.'

At five thirty, she told them she was going out to walk with the old man and would be back around six thirty. She said to make themselves comfortable. The boss comes back at about 6.00 p.m., and she would see them later. And turning to George, she told him to have his guitar so they could play. She went to get the old man, and he grumbled about having to go out, but she just smiled at him and told him it was good for him. They walked around a park not far from the house. She told him how excited she was to be moving into the house of their own.

'It is not that I haven't enjoyed my stay here, but there comes a time when the chicks have to fly the nest. I will not forget your kindness to me, and we will see you often. You see Riccardo nearly every day anyway, so I don't think you will miss us that much. And I hope you will come over and see us as well.'

He linked his arm in hers and told her that she seemed to be much happier now and he had seen the change in Riccardo.

'You seem to have rubbed the hard edges of him, and he is content. That makes me happy to see my son settled at last. There was a time when he went out with all sorts of women and never even liked them. I wondered if he would ever find the right girl to marry. I misjudged you at the beginning. I thought you were just like the others. I am glad you proved me wrong.'

'We had a rough start, and I did not know I would fall in love with him. I always knew we got along, but we were so different and having amnesia did not help. It took a long time for me to put aside the idea of going back to some other life. Once I accepted that it was not likely to happen and I had not done anything to cause that loss of memory, I knew we would be okay. I think that together we can work out anything, and I look forward to a long and healthy life together. You never know, we may even have children.'

Riccardo came home at six, and the boys were sitting by the pool, still chatting. He got himself a drink on the way out and sat with them. They told him his wife was out with his father. Flynn broached the subject they had been talking about, and that was Marion's health. 'Because I have not seen her for a while, I noticed that she seems a bit frail and she tires easily.'

Riccardo felt a bit defensive as if he did not know how his wife was doing. 'I noticed the bruises on her arms, and I was going to tell you, George, to be a bit more careful with her.' Flynn butted in. 'I think it is more than that. I think she may be sick. I told her she should get a check-up with a doctor.' Riccardo conceded that he would make her see someone as soon as they moved.

Marion came back out to the pool area; Jacinda also appeared from the house. She did not approve with mixing with the help, but they seemed to be having fun, so she stayed. Marion picked up her guitar and sang another of her sad songs that sounded lovely. Then she sang with George some old tunes from the '60s era. Between them, they made it feel like a party, and everybody was enthralled until the evening meal was about to be served. Socialising with the help was one thing but eating with them was not even contemplated. So they parted company. After dinner, Marion played Chopin on the piano for the old man. She played for a half an hour and then said she was tired and needed sleep. Rick came up with her. Now it had been pointed out to him, he felt concerned for her health. With no makeup on, he could see the lines of exhaustion under her eyes. 'When we settle in, I want you to find a local doctor and have him look at you to make sure you are okay,' he said. 'I told you this morning I'm fine. But if you insist I will be a good wife and do what I am told.' She fell asleep almost as soon as her head hit the pillow because she really was drained.

The next morning, she was full of life again, and they were having their last breakfast together. Jacinda was very nice and seemed genuinely sorry to see them go. She looked at Marion and said,

'At least with you around, life was never dull. I can't imagine how you are going to run that house by yourself.'

'Oh I have hired enough staff to help, I think I can manage that.' She smiled. Rick jumped up and kissed her on the cheek said, 'I will see you at home then.'

The day was exciting. She had hired as many of the locals as she could. She had furnished the servants quarters but gave them a choice of staying there or going home. Alexis was the cook; she was young and eager to do well. She had dark short curly hair, brown eyes, and olive skin. She was short and a bit on the plump side. Marion had to get her a small step ladder to reach the top shelves. She had always liked cooking, and most of the dishes she produced were pure country Greek. Marion said she would teach her more dishes as time went on. She said she preferred to live in so she could sleep in more in the morning. She also said that she loved her room and it was much better than the one she had at home. Sanya was the housekeeper; as this was not a big house, she could manage the work by herself. She was middle-aged, slim with slightly greying hair which she tied into a bun. She had been employed for most of her life until the last couple of years when there was no work to be had. She had never married and was considered unfortunate not to have caught a husband. She did not care; she just did what she liked. She was used to caring for others and on her days off, she would go into the town and shop for fun things which she brought home and sometimes placed around the house. The garden was taken care of by Roberto. He often used his family members to help, thus sometimes there would be four or five people in the backyard. It was a bit confusing because they all had to be issued with a pass. They were told not to swap, but they did, so written on each card was family of Roberto. Roberto was also a handyman who could turn his hand to just about anything, and so if anyone had a problem that needed fixing, he could do it. Now that the inside was done, there were also various trade people coming and going working on the outside. The four security guards made up the complement of staff. Marion introduced a two and half hour break at midday, as much for herself as for anybody else. She paid above-average wages and provided a midday meal. The staff all considered her a saint because she was concerned about each person and their families.

Their first meal felt strange; just the two of them. 'I hope you like the plates and table wear,' she said. 'I bought most of it online rather than go to shops which I hate. Do you know if I wanted to I could do all our shopping online and never leave the house?' He replied that he liked all the house colours. 'You have chosen well, I wonder where you got the idea of using colour as you have.'

'It is easy for me as I have a natural eye for things like colour. I think it has something to do with the empath thing I seem to remember the shrink saying that empaths are also affected by colour.'

'Talking about doctors, I want you to find one near our new house and go and see him or her. Some good news is that I may have to make another trip in the next couple of weeks and we could take the boys with us. How are you getting along with the staff? Are there any problems?'

'I'm not as bad as your sister implies. We now have a staff of seven, and that is not too much to handle. There may be settling issues, but nothing has come up. George is very efficient in dealing with the security staff for both houses, and although Flynn is champing at the bit to do more work, he is still on the monitors. I told Mason that everyone has to do boot camp at least once a year and the aim is to beat Flynn's score. He doesn't believe me.'

'He is a bit of a hotshot and really wants to work with me. What do you think of that?'

'I think it has only been six months since he came out of service and he is finding being in security a bit annoying. He thinks he is better than that. Maybe he should calm down, or maybe it is simply not for him. I wonder what would be exciting about working with you. Is there something you are not telling me?'

'I think he may want to get his hands on the jet.'

'I'm not sure Neil would like that, and we would not want to lose Neil because he does the maintenance as well.'

As they finished their meal, Rick suggested that they play a game of chess before bed. She laughed at him saying, 'Are sure you want to lose again?'

'If I lose this game, I know how to win the next game. So it's a challenge to see which game you want to win.'

That night, she had another bad dream; the tall, dark figure was standing over her seeming to challenge her in some way. She could hear a lot of noise in the background. He did not appear friendly. She sat up with a shiver, wondering what he was after. She tried to sleep, but she was afraid. She had to get up and get a hot drink and try not to let it get to her. Every time she would fall asleep, he would be there.

The next morning, they woke up realising that they did not have to go to breakfast at exactly 7.00 a.m. It did not matter what time they turned up. It afforded them a luxury they only knew when they were in the beach house. They snuggled together for a while, but by the force of habit, they got up. Marion had promised to find a local doctor; she asked Rick if he would come with her, but he said that he was busy. In the end, she had to ask George to come and act as interpreter for her. She told him she felt funny asking him to do something so personal, but as Rick did not want to, so would he? He said, of course, he did not mind. As she had to have a minder with her anyway, it might as well be him.

At the doctor's, she was told she was run-down due to the move, and she had anaemia. He wrote a script for an iron tonic and told to get another test done. He said that for that test she would be in a hospital for a day and he would need her to fast from the midnight before. He said an appointment would be sent out. He told her that one of his partners spoke English and came to this clinic once a fortnight and maybe she should see her; he would be happy to pass on information to that doctor. She agreed to see Dr Pavlov next time.

Back in the car, she talked to George about her concern

for Mason. 'I have a plan, but it is complicated. You remember Phil Ford, one of Rick's business associates, the guy with a different blond on his arm every time you see him whom he introduces as his niece. He is the man that has the big boat he uses mostly to hold parties on. He made a pass at me one time. I told him to come back in five years when the honeymoon is over. He has an ego as big as this country. He likes to win at any cost. He thinks he is better than Rick because his boat is larger. The next time I see him, I could convince him he has not arrived until he has his own jet. And then say we have the best pilot who also happens to be a Navy Seal. I think he would offer any amount to acquire something that Rick has. Mason has already expressed his ambition and would have to accept the job or explain why.' George looked at her and liked her plan because it required her to do something nobody would believe; unless they knew her, she could read his responses and make changes to her plan if necessary. 'It might work. I'll have to think about it.'

At home that evening, she told Rick there was nothing to worry about her health. 'I am a bit anaemic and have to take some iron tonic. I have one more test to do, but I'm sure it's okay.' She asked when they would be going overseas. He said he thought it would be in about two weeks. 'There are some loose ends to tie up before we go so that the trip will run smoothly. I don't want to waste my time waiting around for people to fit me into their appointments. We will be stopping off at Hong Kong for a break, and you could have some more clothes made if you want.'

'I like coming with you,' she said, 'because it gives me a break from routine and I feel like it's a holiday even if it's not one for you.'

'By the way, Phil Ford has asked us to one of his evenings on the boat. He heard about your singing with George and wondered if you could sing for them.'

'I would like to know how he heard about that. I'm not that fond of him, and it is a strange coincidence I was just thinking of him the other day. You should tell him to bring his wife. I don't mind coming and singing, but I can't say for George. It's up to him. You will have to talk to him. I don't know how he would feel doing something we just do for fun, in front of others.'

George agreed to come more to protect Marion than for any other reason. When he had a chance to talk to her, he asked if she intended to put her plan into action. 'I am going to try unless you can come up with a better idea.'

The mail that day had the time and place for her to go for the test. There was a leaflet describing the procedure. The doctors will take some fluid from the bone marrow to test, and they also may take a tiny bit of the bone itself. It may take a few days to have an answer sent to her doctor. Marion told George that it was a good idea to sing on the boat as it would take her mind off the subsequent test. 'You know, I am really a coward when it comes to needles,' she said.

They practised their music each day for a while to make sure they had it right. Mason requested to go with them as another guard. Rick saw this as his way of showing he was willing to work extra to get ahead. Marion told George that it would be a good way to talk up his skills.

That night, she dressed with extra care, thinking she might be able to engage Phil in conversation. The boys looked the part in dark suits. Rick was not concerned about dress; however, he always looked good in evening attire. They asked Abrax to bring over the big car. And all piled in together. The boat looked festive; it was lit up with strings of lights from the front to back.

Marion commented that it looked like a small ship afraid of being boarded by pirates. It was a lovely balmy night and the drinks flowed freely for those who chose to partake. Phil was as gregarious as ever, meeting everyone with a hug and a kiss. Most of the people there were business people who had their own agendas to attend to. It was on these occasions that deals were struck with a handshake until the lawyers looked over the proposals. Thus a good impression was important. Rick held Marion's hand, hoping that she would not 'freak out' at the noise. She struggled to keep the energy of others from overcoming what she saw as her prime target. Phil fussed over her, making sure she had a drink and at the same time trying to get her away from Rick. At one point, she whispered to Rick she needed some air. He nodded at her and sent eye contact to Mason to follow her as she walked to the front of the boat. After trying to calm herself down, she saw that Phil followed her. He did not notice Mason; he had her alone, and that is what he wanted. He slipped his arm over her shoulder and pulled her towards him. 'I have been hoping you have been thinking about my proposal,' he purred. She looked around and saw Mason standing there. 'May I introduce you to Mason? He is our newest acquisition. He is a US Navy Seal and a pilot as well. We like to have our jet ready for any occasion and having such an experienced person on our staff is such a blessing.' They shook hands and Phil appraised him as a possible employee as she knew he would. She continued to say that boats were great, but there was nothing better than having one's own jet plane as it takes the pain out of travelling. 'It seems that everyone is doing it these days, maybe because it's safer and it makes a big impression on clients.' By this time, she was wondering if she had overdone it a bit and thought she had better stop. 'I believe we are going to sing for you and George is here to help. I think we are lucky to have such a talented team.' She walked back to the other end of the boat and asked Mason to get the guitars out of the limo. They set up at the end of the vessel, and Phil made a big point of introducing them. He had a microphone set up, and although they did not really need it, she placed it in front of them. Then sang three songs, had a break and sang three more. They received a rousing applause. The right people were impressed, and that was what mattered. She felt her job was done and found Rick and asked if it was too early to go home. He whispered to her to wait another half an hour and then they could go. She looked for the least congested part of the boat and sat down. George came over to see if she was okay. 'I'm not really. I am just holding it together.'

'Is there anything I can do to help?'

'I don't think so. I just have to wait a little more.' She tried to fight down the feeling of sliding down into some pit. It was taking every bit of her energy not to be taken over by the feelings of others. George took it upon himself to go to Rick and say his wife needed out now. Rick immediately came over to her and stated that they could go. She needed some help to stand up, but once on her feet, she put her head high and smiled at everyone and said goodbye. Once in the car, she said, 'Thank God that is over.' Rick looked surprised. 'I thought you were having fun.'

'I'm having fun now,' she said. Abrax dropped them off at home and went back to the big house. Marion sat out the back and smoked and had another glass of wine. Only George would know the price she had paid to get rid of Mason. Now they would have to wait to see if he took the bait.

The night before the test, she asked Rick to come with her. He refused, telling her he had too much work to do.

Hiding her disappointment was hard. In the morning, she talked to George about her fear of the test. 'Remember when you told me how you just stopped being afraid? I wish I was like that. I seem apprehensive so many times.' George asked her what part of the test she was afraid of. Is it the test itself or what they might find? 'I think it is a bit of both. Call it a premonition if you want.'

'I will send Flynn with you. He needs to get out more.' She reminded him that they should not be alone together.

George told her he thought they were past that. 'Not really, it is just we have been trying to be just friends.'

'It's my decision, Marion, and I think this best for you both.'

Flynn went with her. He opened the back door of George's car for her, but she jumped in the front seat. She told him of her fear and asked him if it would be too weird for him to come in with her.

'I'd do anything for you, Marion.'

Flynn said he would come in with her and had to put on a white coat. It was painful. They put a needle in her hip area and drew out some bone marrow. They also did another test in her lower spine to get a piece of bone tissue. Even though they gave her a needle first to numb the area, it still was painful. She held on to Flynn's hand, and after the second test, he was told to apply pressure to the area to stop bleeding. She tried to relax but found it hard and she was drawing strength from Flynn to get by. Finally, she relaxed and was in a half sleep. He told her he was going to get a coffee and would be back. The clinician said that she would be there a couple of hours to make sure the bleeding had stopped before she went home. He also said it would take a couple of days before the test results were known. He was speaking to Flynn as if he was her husband. When Flynn realised his mistake, he told him he was her minder. The clinician then said she was lucky to have a minder who loved her. Flynn wondered if it was that obvious.

On the way home, she got him to stop off at the beach for a while. 'I wanted to say thank you for helping me. You gave me your strength when I felt it was too much.' He did not know how to answer her, so he leant over and kissed her; it brought on the usual feeling of longing. He was aware she would feel this; she shook her head and said they had better go home.

A couple of days later, Marion received a call from Dr Pavlov to come into the office that day. She said that they were going away and could they make an appointment later. The doctor wanted to see Marion and Riccardo immediately. She rang Rick at work and asked him to come to the appointment with her. He grumbled about his work but relented and said he would pick her up. When they arrived at the clinic, they were ushered straight into the doctor's office. She stood up and introduced herself. 'I am taking over your case because

I speak English.' She was a middle-aged woman who had an abrupt manner about her. She was plain with mousey type of hair tied back in a ponytail; she had clear-rimmed glasses and no makeup on her olive skin. 'I have some bad news for you. The test results coupled with what little we know about your history indicate you have Acute Myeloid Leukaemia (AML). This is a type of blood cancer. It starts in the bone marrow, the soft tissue inside the bone. Inside your bones is where the blood cells are made. You have red cells that carry oxygen to all parts of the body, white cells that fight off infection, and platelets which help your blood to clot. Leukaemia is when the body starts making abnormal white cells. And they start crowding out the healthy cells. They grow faster than other cells and can spread through the whole body and into the organs. When I say acute, I mean that it is spreading faster than other types of Leukaemia. I understand this may come as a bit of a shock to you and you need time to process this information.

However, we need to start treatment as soon as we can if we are to have a positive outcome.' Rick asked what was considered a positive result, and she said, 'It may buy you more time, that is all.'

Marion said they were going away for a week and would consider what to do when they come back. Rick felt too stunned to say anything for the moment. She handed them her card and said she would be happy to talk to them anytime.

Rick called the office and said he would take the rest of the day off. He went into his study and started making calls to find a specialist in New York for another opinion. He thought it was a mistake because she was not that sick. He called his father, telling of his fear of losing her. His father told him not to give up hope and try to find the best place for her to go.

Marion walked down to the security house; all the boys were there, and she told them she had Acute Myeloid Leukaemia. Flynn asked what that meant, and she told them it was a death sentence. 'As you can imagine the boss is not taking this very well. I have an idea he is going to drag me around to see if he can get another opinion. What I want is a holiday. Anyway if you hear us yelling, don't take any notice.'

He came out of his office and said that he had set up an appointment with a specialist in New York. He put his arms around her and said that all he wanted was to make sure she had the best treatment possible. 'Have you thought that I may not want treatment?'

'Of course, you must have it, there is not another way.'

'Yes, there is, I could live out what time I have left happy and not being sick from chemotherapy.'

'But there is still a chance you might beat it, and then we could have a long life together.' She looked at him and felt his pain and confusion; she wanted to console him, but she wondered who had their head in the sand. She found it hard to stand up to him and say, 'It's my body,' when she could feel he was like a lost child. 'Can we have this trip together happy and worry about it tomorrow?'

'Only if you promise to see this other doctor, and then I will leave it alone for now.'

Chapter 21

LIFE'S BATTLES

The trip to New York was uneventful. They arrived in the early hours of the morning and by the time they got to the apartment; the sky was beginning to pale. New York is a city that never closes and is always busy. Marion just wanted to fall into bed, but Rick was already planning the day's appointments.

'If I go to sleep now, I will feel groggy when I have to wake up. Anyway, I did have some rest on the plane.'

She could not entice him to come to bed anyway, so she kissed him and said, 'Good night.' She slept for about sixteen hours and woke up refreshed. She showered and changed into fresh clothes and did her hair up. She felt free from the burden of trying to be someone else. She was determined to have a great time. She walked out onto the little balcony to view the scene below. It took her breath away in all its splendour. All the lights were glittering and twinkling. The real world seemed a long way off. There was little sound carrying up to the penthouse except for noise of the wind. She went to get a drink when she noticed a note Rick had put for her, it said, 'I called in, you were still asleep, and I did not want to disturb you. Please ring me when you get this.' She called his number, and he answered. There was a lot of noise in the background and he had trouble hearing her.

'We are at a bar not far from you. I'll come and get you.'

She hung up and thought about the time. She had slept the day away. What a shame to lose even a day of her break. Rick opened the door and grinned at her. 'You look lovely.'

She laughed and said, 'You look like you have been drinking too much.'

'Come on then, you will have to catch up.' He held her hand and pulled her out of the building as he had a taxi waiting and they didn't wait for long. Back at the bar, she could see the boys also had been drinking as well.

'I think you need some food or you are going to fall over.' She said.

George looked serious and said she was right; they should eat. They went outside and caught another taxi and Rick told him to take them to the best restaurant in town. The driver looked doubtful and said he was not sure they would get in. Rick said asked him to call them and say he would pay double for a table and give seriously big tips. The driver called through and arranged it. When they arrived, there was a queue. The driver doubled parked and got out and took them to the front of the line and spoke to the doorman. He smiled at them, and Rick gave him a large note. They were shown a table and found the menu was in French. The boy's all spoke fluent French and knew what food was the best to get from the dazzling array offered. The wine list was presented, and Rick picked a light red for Marion, and they said they would drink beer. The food was excellent; the waiters were impressed knowing he had promised a big tip.

'I did not realise how hungry I was until now,' she said. Riccardo commented that's what happens when one sleeps a whole day away. They enjoyed their meal, taking the time with each course. However, they were not inclined to stay out all night as the boy's had had little sleep.

The next day at Dr Carl Ruben's office, one of quiet opulence. He was a man in his early fifties. He was of medium build and clean-shaven. The first thing Marion noticed was his hands. They had tapered long fingers and with manicured nails. He spoke with a soft even voice. People paid a high price for his service, and he made sure each patient was treated with a holistic approach. 'You have come to me for a second opinion from Greece.'

'My husband heard you are the best in the field. He is Greek, but I am Australian.'

'What do you like to do?' he asked.

'I have just finished renovating a country house for us to live in.'

He told her to go behind the curtain and change into a gown provided.

He looked at Rick and said, 'How long have you been married?'

'Two and a half years.'

She came out behind the curtain, and he started to examine her. He obtained a blood sample from her and called a girl to get it and check the blood count. He checked under her arm and got her to place her finger in a spot. 'Do you feel that lump? That should not be there. How is your sex life?' Marion looked at Rick. It seemed that he was not going to answer, so she said that he had called it fire and ice.

'Is that because you have felt tired?' She shrugged.

He looked directly at Rick and asked if he had noticed the lump under her arm, as it is often the husband who notices these things first. Rick said he had not seen it.

'How long would you say you have been feeling tired?'

She said, 'I don't remember maybe twelve months.'

'What about the bruising?' Again, she said about twelve months. 'Who first noticed your loss of weight?' She looked at Rick. 'One of my minders had been away for six months. He noticed it straight away. He said I had lost two dress sizes.'

Carl Rubin asked about her minder. He must care for you to notice the weight loss. A lady came in with the result of the blood test. He offered them a drink, saying, 'At these meetings people often feel their mouth go dry.' Marion stated she would like a cup of tea and Rick said a cup of coffee. He asked her to get on a bench to look at her again. And while he was examining her, he asked, 'what do you like to do?'

'I sing, and I write music. I like to read, and sometimes I like to paint.'

'You must be a very creative lady. Are you a brave one as well?'

'No, I am scared a lot of the time.'

'Who around you apart from your husband do you lean on?'

'I have two minders that are like brothers to me, and I have a psychiatrist and my father-in-law.'

'You are going to need the support of all these people,' he said. 'People often come to me hoping their diagnosis is a mistake. In your case, it is not. If you are to have any chance at all, you must get treatment straight away. If money is no object, I would suggest you attend the clinic in Genève. They are doing the most research at the moment. I would be happy to call for you and see if they have a place.' She asked what would happen if she did not have the treatment. 'Then you have three months or at the very most six.'

'And what would happen if I get the treatment?'

'Some people can beat it. This depends on your age, general health if you have had other cancers if you smoke or have been exposed to any toxic chemicals. For you, the best is it may go into remission, and you could have five years.'

He looked at Rick and suggested that he find a support group in his area and join.

'Will I call the clinic and see if they have a place?'

Rick said, 'Yes, of course, she must go there.' He picked up the phone and said, 'This is Carl Rubin's. I have a lady here with Acute Myeloid Leukaemia stage 2. Are you able to accept her? Marion Rodregious—Australian—a bit shell shocked I would say. In a week if that is all right? Thank you.' He put down the phone and told them it is all arranged. He handed them a card and said he would send the information on.

'Do you have any questions for me?'

They shook their heads. Doctor Rubin got up from his desk and walked around to her and placed his hands on her shoulders. 'Try to stay positive, for example, new treatments are coming out all the time, and you will be in the right place to try them. Try to be brave and keep talking to your psychiatrist. Use your friends for support as you cannot do this on your own. I wish you well.'

Back in their apartment, Rick pulled her to him and held on to her. He kissed the top of her hair, hoping she could not see the numbing grief he felt. 'I am so sorry,' she said. She was aware of the pain that had taken over him.

'You agreed, we would forget it for the rest of the trip,' she said.

He seemed to pull himself up and said he had an appointment at 2.00 p.m. and should go.

About a half an hour later, there was a knock on the door. It was George. He came in and said the boss had given him the afternoon off. 'I thought you could use some company.'

She opened a bottle of wine, handed him a glass, and sat quietly for a while.

'I don't think the boss is going to handle my illness very well. He is very like his father, less his experience. I feel he sees me as diseased. I hope he changes his mind because it is going to be hard enough for me.'

She outlined the doctor's interview. 'I really don't want to have to go through the treatment. I would rather spend the next three months having fun. But I know he won't let me. I think I am going have to learn to be brave and keep in mind he loves me in his way. I wish I could be more like you and just accept life as it is. I have heard it said the worst fear is fear itself. I really want this trip to be happy and not worry about tomorrow, is that hard to understand?'

'Marion, you know we will give you all the support we can. I care for you a lot, but I'm a typical man and don't know what it is you need so you will just have to tell me. Let's start now and get out of this place and do something you would never do.'

'Like what?' she asked.

'Let's go shopping. You hate it and then you will be thinking about that and not about being sick. We could spend an extravagant amount of money, just because we can.' The idea appealed to her because she would have to deal with something else rather than what the doctor said.

They created a fun afternoon trying on hats and coats she would never wear. She had her face made up by a beautician. She thought it made her look like a china doll, George thought it was cute. She looked at high-heeled shoes but could not walk in them. She settled for a wedge sandal instead. They walked past a jewellery shop, and she thought she would get some cufflinks for Rick. There was a pair of gold cufflinks with diamonds in the corner of the square. 'What do you think?'

'I reckon they are very flash, but they are very expensive even for Rick.'

'Then I will buy them.' The cell rang, and she picked it up. It was Rick.

'Where are you?'

'I am out shopping with George.'

'Well, come home now, okay?' She laughed and said, 'Yes, sir,' and hung up. 'It's just as well we have to go home now as we have our hands full of parcels.'

Before they went inside, she said thank you to George for being there with her. 'You are so kind and thoughtful, and I really appreciate the time you have spent with me.'

They went from New York to San Francisco where they were booked in an opulent hotel. Rick said he had only one meeting and would spend the rest of the day with them. He was going to take George with him and leave Flynn to look after her. She complained that she did not need watching 24/7 and could care for herself, but Riccardo insisted.

She found it hard to put on a brave face for Flynn. She did not really want to do anything and thought she may be feeling a bit depressed. There was nothing she could think of to lighten her mood. Flynn was kind and took his cue from her and waited for her to want to talk to him.'

'I guess you have talked to George about me,' she finally said. 'You know I am not that brave, and I feel scared more about the treatment than anything. Rick told me that he is my husband and I have to do what he says. I am not afraid of being dead, but I am scared of the act of dying. I am trying to push it away so it does not spoil our break, but it is always there.'

'Marion, you are possibly the bravest person I know. You have been through so much, and you always find a positive spin on things. I can't imagine what you are going through right now. I remember when I was in prison, and I could hear you saying be strong, don't die, and help is coming, it gave me the strength to keep on fighting and not to give up. I wish there was a way I could do the same for you.'

'Will you be there for me? It is going to be hard given how we feel. I know you just want to be a professional and do your job. I have been trying to respect that. But if they keep throwing us together, I'm not sure how that goes. I thought that while you were away, my feelings for you would change, but they haven't. So you see that although they said that I just felt what you were feeling, I don't believe them. I think you are the only one who understands me. Maybe it is because you believe in the idea of a fey person, or you are just able to accept people where they are. Sometimes I think there are two of you. One is the person who works for the Ministry of the Defence and the other person who is still that boy who could be easily hurt. I have sometimes noticed when you and George are about to go off on one of your trips, you seem to become something like steel, and nothing can break through. And when you come back, you become just like everyone else, only better.'

'What if I tried to kiss you now, will you throw me against the wall?' he asked.

'Of course not, then I was confused and overwrought. Anyway, I had no control over what happened. It has only happened to me a couple of times. I don't even know where it comes from. I'm not advocating we do kiss, but if it happens, I think I would like it.'

'Don't worry, I'm not about to take advantage of you unless it feels right.'

'I'm worried about Rick. I don't think he is prepared to deal with my illness. I have tried to get him to think of people as the same as him and not just commodities to be used for his own purposes. I think in a way he has changed and respects people more now than before. Then there are times when I think he just doesn't get it. I always hoped to find out what he is up to and put a stop to it before he gets caught out doing something he should not do. You have not been sent to spy on him, have you?'

'Marion, I am not a spy. But if we could prove he was doing something that would endanger our country or the people from it, we would have to say something. He is very careful in his business, he covers all his tracks. Even if we thought there was something wrong, we would have to prove it. This is not our job to look into his affairs. If anything, we should watch you because you know more than is good for you.'

'Why then would the CIA want to be involved?'

'They could be looking into something entirely different, and his name came up. It could be as simple as one person who he is involved with through the course of his business, or it could be something to do with shipping. Who knows? I would not worry about Mason. We have his number, and we will ensure he is neutralised, and then he won't stay for long. At this point, nobody knows anything about him except us, and we can keep it that way. Anyway, he is not as good as he thinks he is. This may well be his first assignment, which would suggest that the boss is not high on the list.'

'He looked at his watch and said. 'You should eat something, do you want to go out and see what we will find?'

'I don't think I can eat, I feel 'gutted'. I just need to be quiet for a while, do you mind?'

'Okay, I have a good idea, what about we order an ice cream sundae with the lot on top? It's bound to give you a lift.'

'I think you are right, it is a great idea and very decadent.' He went to the phone and ordered two of the biggest ones they had. As she watched him, she thought about her feelings for him; she would not be able to live without him. Again, she pushed this idea aside because she was married and it would be wrong. But she knew if they were left together for any amount of time, it would be inevitable.

Rick and George came back in the early evening. She was asleep but jumped up when they came in; she woke up feeling restless and edgy. She thought they could take the guitar to the park in the next street and play for a while, as she said to keep the demons away. They were sitting in a park in the centre of town singing. She had left her case open, people who walked by doped coins in. She thought that was funny.

'Maybe we can get enough for the evening meal. Let's see what happens.'

A strange boy came over with a drum and asked if he could join in. Then another person with a banjo came over. Rick was not used to sitting on the grass and found it a bit of an adventure that only she could create; she was in her element. In the middle of all the noise, he received a call from his father. He wanted to know how things went at the doctor's. 'Not good,' Riccardo said. Sarvis asked to speak to Marion, and Rick called her over. 'How are you?' he asked.

'I'm okay now, I'm just singing in the park. We thought it would be fun to see if we get enough money for our evening meal. I am sorry to tell you may not be coming home, maybe not forever. Riccardo has made up his mind that I go for treatment, but it may not work. I am his wife and must do as I am told. If something happens to me, please make sure he finds another partner. I don't want him to grieve too much. I'm sorry this has happened, but that is life. You can always pray for me.' He promised he would and said goodbye. She went back to the group, but reality had hit her in the face again. She sang two of her favourites and then decided to pack up. They thanked the boys for coming over. 'You guys are cool,' one of them said. Back at the apartment, they counted the money out and found they had enough for McDonald's.

The next day they flew to Hong Kong. They arrived in the middle of the day and went directly to their apartment. Marion thought Hong Kong had a smell all its own. It was a hot and sticky day with little wind. She was glad of the air-conditioned rooms. Even though she had slept on the plane, she was tired. Rick told her he would be busy for the rest of the day. He would need both the boys. She assured him she was not going to go anywhere and would have her hair and nails done. 'Are you going down to the dock area?'

'Yes, I have unfinished business to attend to. Don't worry about us, we will be fine.'

She looked at him and said, 'famous last words'! I hope you are right. Please be careful.'

When they came back, he told her that everything had gone to plan, in fact, better than he expected and there were no problems. He told her she looked delightful and they were going to have a great night. He had booked them into a great restaurant that had many traditional dishes to try. He showered and changed, they headed off. The city was one of the busiest cities Marion had ever encountered. There were people everywhere and even in the cab, she found it stifling. However, once in a private room in the restaurant, she felt better. They had some Chinese rice wine with dinner; it tasted sweet but had a punch if you have too much. She was careful not to overindulge. They had a table full of different dishes to try, and the idea was to take a small amount on your plate at a time. Chopsticks were expected, and she was glad she knew how to use them as the boys had no trouble eating with them. They were relaxed, and conversation flowed easily. This was her idea of happiness, she was with the people she loved, and there was no tomorrow. She wished she could stay here forever.

When they had finished their meal, they went to a karaoke bar. They were lucky to find a booth that was a bit farther from the main group. The idea was the entrants put in so much money into a pot. Each had a turn; they had a box that determined the sound in the room. The ones who had the lowest sound were eliminated until the last man standing took home all the money. She begged George to enter with her, and he could not say no. There were several lists you could choose from in different languages. He brought the list of songs back to the table, and they pored over them, trying to decide what to choose. There were several that they knew, but the background could be different. They were given a number that was third last in the order of entries. This was good because they could see what their competition was like. They decided on three different songs. One of them was one that Marion had written. 'I feel a bit naked standing up there with no guitar,' she said. 'I wonder if they have any outback.' She got George to come with her to translate for her, and she asked if there was any rule that they had to sing with the box. 'No, most people just do it that way.'

'Do you have any guitars here?' She asked.

He took them out the back and showed them several and said they could choose any if they wanted. They spent some time finding ones that she could tune. And they brought them back to the table. The first two songs they sang the applause was about in the middle of the group. That is when she decided they should switch to their own songs. They were told that one couple of men won all the time and they did not stand a chance. This was just what she needed a challenge. When it was their next turn, she told the crowd that George had never sung in public before and he was going to sing an original song. He sang the song, and she just harmonised in the background. The crowd loved it and shouted for more. This was a good sign. The two men sent a bottle of champagne over to their table and raised their glasses to them. They wanted them to drink more so they could not sing. The number of contestants was getting smaller. Then there were only the two groups left.

Marion got up and sang one of her sad songs by herself, unaccompanied by music. The crowd went mad for this, and the box scored the highest ever. Flynn and Rick were laughing and crying at the same time. How could one be so alive on the stage and be dying at the same time? The men conceded to the sound box, and the winner was announced. The men came over to the table and introduced themselves. They questioned George to see if he had an agent.

'You should record those songs because they are admirable.'

Marion wanted to know how they could do this and found out that one of the men, in fact, owned a recording studio. 'We should while we have the chance,' she said to George. They arranged a time and place for the next day. Then she said to George, 'What are you going to do with the money?' He did not know; anyway, half was hers.

'Let's go and buy you a real guitar. Something with great sound, I have an ear for this, and if we choose right, it will gain in value as you go along.'

By the time they got back to the apartment, she was exhausted but happy. 'Rick, I have had the best time. Thank you for making it so enjoyable.' He grinned at her.

He felt happy too, whether it was the drink or seeing her doing what she does the best, he did not know; he just wanted to enjoy sex with her, to complete the night, and she would not let him down.

The next morning, it was hard to get up in time for the recording session, which was at 10.00 a.m. Marion felt a little weak but would not let the boy's know. They sang the songs they knew without making any changes and received a disk for them to keep. This was an expensive exercise, but it was worth it.

It seemed no time, and they were on the plane again. Marion was tired and went down the back of the plane to sleep. Riccardo checked her a couple of times and then decided to change course for Genève. When she woke up, she was furious. She stormed at Riccardo.

'You promised that we would decide what to do when we got back home.'

'You are my wife and I will decide what is best for you. You are sick and need treatment now. You will do as you are told and behave yourself. Flynn has agreed to stay with you, I am not going to change my mind.'

Marion wanted to talk to George about what was to happen. It was back to reality again. She had asked Rick to stay with her, but he said he had too much work to do. He intended to get her settled in and then leave. He told her that George needed to come back with him as there were things he had to do.

'This is not fair to Flynn. We agreed we should not spend too much time alone. I don't think you understand he is suffering from post-traumatic stress disorder, and this is putting another burden on him he could do without.' George's reply was that if he asked Flynn, he would want to be there.

'Marion, what do you want me to do then?'

'I think you should rotate him with David. And I was thinking you should send Flynn to boot camp. Because it's a bit like riding a horse if you fall off and don't get on it again, you end up by thinking you can't. I think it might just switch him on again. I know a little of how he feels because I was there with him.'

The clinic was just like most clinics around the world: a nice garden out front, a big lobby area for different things, such as signs and outpatient enquiries. A lady came and gave Rick a lot of forms to fill out. Marion felt as she was being pushed around: height, weight, blood pressure, temperature, and gown then up to a room.

'I hope I can wear my own clothes,' she said. And she was told it would be allowed after a while. The room was plain white with little furniture with a TV mounted on the wall. She was told the doctors would be around in the morning. Rick stood around, looking like a fish out of water. It was obvious that he did not like being in hospitals and was looking for a quick getaway. She thought this was no good; if only half his attention was there, he may as well not be three. So, she gave him an out.

'You don't need to stay; I'll be all right. I'm sure I will be well looked after.'

She could feel his relief. He learned over and kissed her. 'I'll make sure you get your things and you can Skype me, okay?'

She nodded and he left. She turned her head to the pillow and cried and cried. She could feel she was losing him. There are many men that cannot stand by and watch their wives during an illness. They usually find some excuse to avoid the situation. She knew this but had hoped he would love her enough to see it through.

Flynn was in early the next morning. He brought a bunch of flowers, her laptop, and guitar. She was happy to see him after a disturbed night.

'The flowers are the one bright spot in this plain room. How are you?'

He put on his sad face. 'It's a bit lonely as the one and only person in this big old house.'

'Did the boss leave as soon as he could?'

'Yes, after dropping me off at the house, they just left. I was surprised, I thought he would stay. I've hired a car to use when I'm here because I don't get cars much. How was your sleep?'

'I did not have a good night. I had lots of bad dreams and kept waking up. The tall dark figure is there and he seemed closer to me. I thought for a while he was not malevolent. Now he seems menacing again. He stands over me and looks at me although I can't see his face. I think it means something, but I don't know what.'

'Have you been keeping your dream journal?'

'Not for the last couple of weeks.'

'Maybe you should call your shrink and talk to him. It can't hurt you, and he may even help.'

'I feel bereft about the boss not staying. I thought he would put his work aside and be here for me. I understand his need to continue his job. I knew what he was thinking last night. He could not wait to get away. So I told him to go.'

The doctor in charge of the clinic came in and asked Flynn to wait outside.

Marion said she wanted him there as he was family.

'The tests show you have acute myeloid Leukaemia stage 2. Stage 2 is where it leaves the original area and travels through the bloodstream to other sectors. You will have chemotherapy three days a week. At first, we want you to stay in the clinic for the treatment to make sure you are able to take it. Then you will be allowed to go home for the other days. You will need a nurse, and if you don't have one, we will organise one for you.

Don't look so anxious. It is not as bad as it seems. We have drugs that will take away the most nausea. A new drug we are trialling reduces the instance of hair loss. You still might have to cut your hair short as it will thin out a bit. While on the treatment, you will need to keep away from crowded places because the biggest killer is an infection. The chemotherapy kills off the cancer cells but it also reduces the good cells as well, so you are more likely to get an infection than anything else. Is there anything want to ask?'

They both shook their heads. The doctor told them if they had anything they were not sure of, please call him. No sooner had he left than a woman appeared and said she was a nutritionist and was there to discuss diet. 'One of the side effects is inflammation in the stomach area, and so it is important that you follow these guidelines.' She handed her a piece of paper and some brochures of where to get different things. 'Get one of your friends to get it for you.' Marion realised that up here she had no one other than Flynn. She could not tell anyone she had no friends.

The week passed, and the days after the treatment, she felt sick. Flynn reminded her about the time when he was in the cell, and he heard her voice in his head telling him to be strong. It gave him the strength to keep on fighting. She talked about that time. She had the same dream for several nights. She said she felt like she was being smashed against a wall or dumped under a big wave on a pile of rocks and she could not breathe. She knew what she was dreaming was happening to him in some way. 'Always in the corner of my mind is this tall, dark person who watches me. And when I woke up in the morning, I would be stiff and sore. I knew it was you. I wanted to help so much, but there was nothing I could do.'

'Did you tell anyone about your dreams?' he asked.

'No one would believe it anyway. You're not going to be happy, but I told George he should rotate you and David as I am worried you might get burned out. I know you care but you have to look after you, or you will not be there when I need you.' He was not happy with this but had to agree it would be better if he did not burn out. She told him David was okay; it's just he sticks to some rule book in his head. 'I don't think we would ever be friends.'

Rick came up on the weekend with George and David. Marion felt good that day as she had time to recover from the treatment. However, the first thing Rick said was, 'What have you done to your hair?' She just walked away for a while trying to get hold of her emotions. She thought, 'What did he expect from chemotherapy? Usually, it falls out,' and the new medication had saved her from that at least. The boys sat around talking; he did not even notice she was gone. When she came back, she saw the enquiring look on Flynn's face. She smiled at him. The big topic was that Mason had been persuaded to take a job with Phil Ford as a pilot. Rick was angry because he expected loyalty from employees and that Phil had offered him a second salary to do the job. Marion asked if he had gone to boot camp, and she was told he had. 'But was he as good as he thought he was?'

'He did not reach Flynn's top score if that is what you mean.' This at least gave her a sense of satisfaction.

George took her aside and asked how she was really going and if she still thought it was a good idea to rotate David with Flynn. 'I won't lie to you, it is hard going and I know Flynn wants to look after me all the time. It is simply is not right for him. Get him to do boot camp, and then we will have an idea of where he is. I think he needs a counsellor, but he will not have it.' George approached the subject of the boss. 'What is going on?'

'He simply can't deal with a sick person, so he hides behind his work.'

'Is there anything I can do to help?'

'Only, if it's possible for you to come up for a couple of weeks. You must know I am going to die and nothing is going to change that.'

Later that night, she tried to talk to Rick about what is happening to their relationship. She tried to be direct and as unemotional as she could. 'I know you are avoiding me, I think you don't want even to have sex with me. You know I can read you, so don't make excuses, just try to tell me what is happening to you, so I can understand.'

'I love you, and it hurts me to see you sick. I am scared to have sex with you not because you are less appealing, I'm afraid I might break you.'

'I don't believe you. You never worried about that before, even when you did hurt me. Now you leave as soon as you can and don't even call.'

'All right,' he said. 'I just cannot handle it at the moment. I keep thinking about all the things we were going to do, and now there is nothing.'

'Rick,' she said, 'I am not dead yet. There is still a chance I might beat it, shouldn't you be thinking about the better things we could do between now and then? I have not changed that much. It doesn't matter about my hair. When my treatment is over, I will be coming back home, unless you would prefer me not to be there. What are you going to do then?'

He felt trapped and angry; he wanted to lash out at her for letting herself become sick. This is not an issue he had ever faced before. His mother's death had lasted a couple of days in the hospital. She never regained consciousness, and never came home. It brought back the memories of the days he spent by her bedside all to no avail; she had died anyway. 'You are going to have to give me time to adjust to this.'

'And now, are you planning to ignore me?'

'Of course not, I really care for you; it's just that I'm finding it a bit hard.'

She glared at him. 'And I am not? What would it take to make you change and see me as before?'

The anger he felt was not far from the surface. This confrontation was not one he could run from; he had to do something, he did not know what. As if reading his mind, she said, 'You could try making love to me.'

'I hate it that you are an empath and can understand my feelings.'

'So now you want to pick a fight with me, and that would give you a reason to leave. Well, 'my husband', it is now or never, so now is the time to make up your mind.'

He stood still, full of indecision; he was aware that she was not about to let it go. He thought he loved her, what was the problem? He thought of the way her body had felt before she had lost weight. He thought of the times when all he wanted was to conquer her completely, and now she was offering herself to him. Then he thought of Scotland when she had got so mad at him she tore off his clothes. That was fun for him. The fight was over Flynn. 'I know what is up with you.' He said slowly, hoping the words would sink in. 'You have been having it off with Flynn.'

Now she was angry 'How dare you? Flynn and I have kept a professional distance and have done the right thing. Sometimes I could kill you with my bare hands.'

'Come on just try, you can't get near me.' She jumped at him, grabbing his arm and twisting it around the back until it hurt. He dropped back on the bed and tried to roll away. She grabbed his other arm and tried to push it back. He looked at her face, and he could see she was angry; she always looked good when she was angry. He tried to get one hand free, which was not that hard, and then he rolled over until he was on top of her. He kissed her, but she was still mad. She used all her strength to roll over again.

'Now I really am going to kill you.'

She let go of the one arm that was causing him to hesitate, and that was all he needed to get her in a position of control. He leant down and again kissed her hard. She continued to fight him 'Get off me, you brute.' But there was no way he was going to let her go. His anger turned into a passion and the fire that had been dimmed exploded and even if she had said no, he would not have stopped. She found that the release she had been looking for was fully answered. When all their passion was spent, it was she who felt like the fish without water, gasping and trying to catch her breath. He rolled over and laughed.

'What are you laughing at?'

'That is one hell of a way to get rid of anger, better than a punching bag I would say. I told you in Scotland you could get mad at me anytime you liked.' He pulled her near him and kissed her gently. 'Now I know we will be okay.'

During the two weeks with David, life developed a sense of order. He worked out a routine and followed it. He made sure she followed her diet just as planned. Encouraged her to do gentle exercises and introduced her to tai chi.

Marion thought he was a nice man, but he just was not Flynn. The staff at the clinic were surprised that she had another minder. It was a bit harder to communicate with them as David only spoke a little French.

Marion rang Dr McKean's office and asked if they could Skype a session. She was given time when to call. When she called the shrink, she told him all about what was happening with her. He listened attentively to the long saga and her current status. He told her he was sad to hear about AML and that it and reached stage 2. As a medical doctor, he understood the implications of this. He said he was happy to hear Flynn was better but reminded her that they should not spend a lot of time together alone. She stated that they had told people this, but no one thought it a problem. Maybe they thought their feelings would dissipate since she was ill. She told him how devastated she felt by what she called Riccardo's rejection of her. It seems as if he can't stand hospitals. And there is some part of him that thinks of me as diseased, and that revolts him.

'This is a problem for me as I can read the feelings coming from him. I feel hurt, and I act accordingly. I feel concerned that the dark figure in my dreams is becoming stronger. I had started to think he was there to care for me and warn me of danger. I am not so sure now. Sometimes, he has even come closer and one time I dreamed he was learning to me. I saw the shadow but no face. I don't know what it is about. I think he may want something from me.'

Her shrink told her not to be afraid of the figure. I am sure he is there to help. 'You know even in your sleep, you can ask him what he wants. How are you dealing with your probable death?'

'I don't know. It seems to be a bit surreal, and I am more afraid of the chemotherapy and its effect on my mood. I feel all over the place. When I am sick, I hate it and then for a day I feel better only to have it start again. Riccardo is making me feel sub-human as if I am the sickness. I don't want to be this way. I thought he would stand by me and be there for me and he is not. I know this is a little harsh, but he just cannot deal with me. On the one hand, he tells me he loves me and on the other he shows by his actions he does not. Someone is here, and I have to go now. I will talk to you again.'

She was relieved when Flynn came back. She thanked David and said she would remember all he had taught her. She could not wait to get Flynn alone and find out how he had been. He told her that to his disgust, he had to do boot camp. 'How did you go?'

'I was surprised that I did pretty as much as usual. The only part that was not as good was the obstacle course, and then I was about one minute slower. I think it means that I should do more running.'

'How did that make you feel?' She asked. He gave her one of his cheeky grins and said, 'That there is life in the old dog yet. The rest of the time I just trailed George around. He is doing a good job at keeping the security staff on track. I think the paperwork suits him.'

'Is he practising?'

'Not as much as he used to.'

'How is the boss?'

'He spends most of his waking hours at work. Nobody knows what he does there. It seems the only place he is comfortable. I feel sorry for him. He really does not know what to do. Marion, he talked to me and asked me to make sure you are happy. He told me he did not care how that happened and he did not want to know. He knows I love you and he knows we should not be left together. I think he does not care as long as he feels you are being looked after. I am not going to change with David again. I am here for as long as you need me.'

She moved up on the settee and put her head on his shoulder. 'I'm glad you are here.' It was not hard to put his arms around her and hold her. It even felt natural when he kissed her. She could sense his desire to take it further and his hesitation. She could not decide what she wanted. But because they both hesitated, each waiting for a cue from the other, it seemed as if a decision had to be made. She said,

'I told you I love you, and it's strange to love two different men, but that is the way it is. And right now, I want you as much as you want me.' Every amount of restraint went out the door. He just bent down and let the kiss take them away to another place where all that mattered were the feelings of peace and enjoyment.

In the morning, he wondered if she would regret her actions. He knew there had to be a catch, and somehow he would again come off second best. But she made no mention of it and said she wanted to cook him breakfast and had sent the cook-off for the day. She showed him tai chi and was surprised he knew all about it. He said he would teach her more as it was the best thing for her. They watched movies on the TV and made love again. He ordered pizza and a bottle of red wine. And he really felt at peace. He thought he had never been in love before and everything else paled into insignificance against this day. That night, he slept in her bed.

The next time she was due for treatment, the nurse said she was concerned that she had a temperature. She called the doctor, and they called off the chemotherapy for that day. Even though it seemed slight, it was serious. They said she should stay in the clinic for the day to be sure. They questioned Flynn to see of any of the people she was with had a cold or a sore throat. He called George and asked if he or the boss had any sickness. George thought that nobody had any kind of infection. By mid-afternoon, they moved her to intensive care and put a monitor on her. Her temperature continued to climb. She lost consciousness. The nurses brought some ice packs and placed them around her body. When the doctor came in, Flynn tackled him about what was happening. He was told that her immune system had broken down and she had little reserves to fight with. 'Should I call her husband? He is about two hours away.'

'Yes, it is important he is here because he may give her the strength to fight.'

Flynn called Riccardo's office and was told he was busy and to call back. He used some colourful language and hung up. He then called George and told him that the boss should be here that his wife may be dying. He pulled up a chair and held her hand. If only he could use this mind thing on her, but it only went one way. Every few minutes, someone was in there checking the equipment. There was no change. About 6.30 p.m., the boss decided to show up. Flynn found it hard to keep the contempt out of his voice as he explained what was happening. Rick went to look for the doctors and ask about his wife's chances of pulling out of this. The doctor took him into a small room and described the gravity of the situation. 'It is really up to her in a way. I have seen people pull out of worse things than this, but they have to want to live, or they can just slip away. Her minder is good, but he is not her husband. You need to talk to her. The hearing is one of the last senses we lose and even though you think she cannot hear you, she might.' Riccardo went back to the room she was in. He looked around at the equipment and thought he would rather die than be like this. He felt silly talking to someone who may not even be able to hear him. He remembered talking to his mother and telling her to wake up, but she died. He walked up to the bed. She was pale and still. The only sound was the monitor and the oxygen flow. 'Marion, I need you, come back to me. Marion, don't die. Come back to me, Marion, wake up. I need you, please get better. Marion, I cannot go on without you, come back.' He kept repeating these words as if they were some kind of mantra. Then she turned her head slightly towards him. Flynn ran to get a doctor to see if there was any change. They found her temperature had dropped a little and her blood pressure had come up a little. The doctor told them to keep doing whatever they were doing as it seemed to be working.

Gradually, she appeared to get better regaining consciousness for a while and then slipping back. As she became aware of Rick standing there, he kept calling to her; she tried to respond but was not able. She looked for Flynn and at first could not see him and then saw him standing at the end of the bed. She looked into his eyes and saw hopelessness there. She tried to smile, but something was on her face. She tried to pull it off, but Rick took her hand down. She tried to hold a thought but found just a jumble of pictures flickers across her mind. The most compelling thing was Rick saying he could not live without her and she had to come back. She heard Rick tell Flynn to go home, that he could look after her for now. Sometime in the early hours of the morning, she fell asleep. Her dreams were mixed up with her feelings for Rick and Flynn. They kept changing places. Then the dark figure came and stood between them. Then he held out his hand for her to come with him. There was something she was supposed to say, but she could not remember. Her dream changed, and she found herself encased in a box made up of machines. She tried to get up but was held down by Rick until she was covered up all over. She woke up gasping for air. Rick was sitting back in a chair half asleep, and he got up and replaced the oxygen mask over her face that had slipped off. 'How long have you been here?' She asked. He said, 'Since yesterday afternoon.' She dropped her head back on the pillow and rested for a while. 'I think I am dying,' she said. 'You are not going to die because I will not let you, okay? I am going to find the chief doctor and find out when you can come home.' He sounded so confident that she almost believed him. But what if she did not want to go home? If she went home, she would lose Flynn. It was too hard to think about; she just drifted off, not thinking of anything in particular.

Rick found the doctor and went into his office to discuss

his wife's condition. What was the next plan? 'She is a very sick lady. She will remain in intensive care for a couple of days. I don't think her body can deal with any more chemotherapy in the direct form at the moment. I will advocate she have some radiation therapy and put her name forward for stem-cell treatment. There is also a new medication we are trialling. I will talk to the committee to see if she fits the criteria for it. Changing minders may not have been a good idea because she must have picked up the infection from somewhere. I will check Flynn out to make sure it was not him that brought it in even though it could have been any of you. You don't need symptoms to pass on an infection.'

'When can she come home?' Rick asked. 'That depends on how stable we can get her. I can't say at the moment. I had hoped the treatment would put it into remission, but it may not. I have to say at this very moment her chances are not good. She needs you here with her as she seems to have no one to lean on and she needs support.' Rick felt defensive about the doctor's comments and said he would be with her as often as he could get away from work.

He went back to her and tried to tell her she could come home as soon as they got her settled on tablets. She looked at him and said, 'Do you have any idea of how many tablets I am taking now? I hate drugs of any kind I think they mess with your system and with your head.' He told her that the doctor thought she had caught an infection from when they changed minders last time. He told her he intended to give Flynn a medical check to make sure he did not have anything that may have caused the flare-up. A guilty thought passed through her head. What if... ? In that case, she did not care. She remained in intensive care for another two days and then Rick said he had to go. He promised to see her soon and call often.

She felt flat and just lay there trying not to let herself get upset. Flynn came back in the afternoon. He seemed as if he felt awkward not knowing where he would stand in this situation. She put out her arm and drew him near her so she could kiss him.

'I think we should talk about what is going on between us. I don't really want to, but I am aware that you feel caught between my husband and me. I know it is not fair, but I have no idea how to resolve it. Before, I believed in honesty and trust, and I thought so did he. I was naïve, to say the least, to think he would change that much. Now as far as I am concerned, I just want to be with you, and I am going to take your first advice and not tell anyone. While I am here, I am going to live in the moment, and if or when we go back to Greece, then things will have to go on as they did before. What do you think?'

He took her hand and kissed her fingers.

'I'll take what I can get if it means I don't have to be sent away. The boss is a fool if he can't see what is before his eyes.'

She was still not sure she was doing the right thing for him. She wanted him to be happy, but she knew there were no happy endings in this story. She wanted to answer his questions, and she knew there are no answers for some things and things don't come in tidy boxes.

'Is this going to be enough for you or is it going to tear you up?'

'I have been through worse things than a broken heart. It will mend, and I will have happy memories, and that is better than nothing. Don't worry yourself about me. I am a survivor.'

'Then I am content, and we will try to make each moment count. I know it seems silly to me in intensive care. But you are here beside me now, and I love you for it.'

He had to laugh because it is not that they could do anything with someone coming in and out all the time. She saw the humour in it as well and laughed. It took some of the sting out of the words she had just spoken.

'I just can't wait to get back to our house and have you to myself. Did you see the doctor? I think they want to make sure you are not carrying an infection like a sore throat or something.' She smiled and said, 'Too late if you did.'

She was moved from intensive care in the evening to a smaller room. The way the room was designed meant that if someone was sitting on one side of the bed, they could not be seen from outside. Thus it afforded them some privacy. 'Do you play chess?' she asked. 'I am a great chess player,' he boasted. 'Can you get a set then we can play with it?'

'I can do that. Are you sure you can't cheat?'

'You understand that I can only read feelings or energy, I can't read your mind. I would know if you are concentrating or if you are just letting me win.

Other than that, I would not know what you are doing. It's just enough to keep you on your toes.'

After two days, she was allowed to go back to the house. She would have to stay for another four weeks. She was to have radiation therapy. After that, they would do a blood count to see if it remained the same. If it was considered satisfactory, she could go home. She was to take the tablets for two weeks and then have two weeks off. After that, she would have another blood count and providing she could maintain the same level, she would be all right.

The two weeks on the tablets were hard as she never felt very well, but they were together, and that helped. There were days that she felt so ill she could barely move. On those days, Flynn would prop himself up on the bed holding her with one arm and read a book so she could rest. He used a damp cloth to wipe her face. The closeness they felt in those times could not be replicated. Their naked bodies seemed to become as one. Marion enjoyed the feel of his body, the soft hair on his chest, she loved the smell of him. Unlike Riccardo he just used soap and had a natural musk smell. She would gently run her hand down his chest to indicate how she felt about him. Ther were times when she felt a bit more adventurous and let her hand travel down his body until it found it's target and holding it tight she would rub up and down. He would lose interest in the book and closed hie eyes and enjoyed the moment.

She tried to stick to the diet that the cook prepared for her. It was bland with no salt or pepper, but every once in a while she would break out and have something she liked.

There were times when she felt the weight of her illness pressing her mood down into places where she would rather not go. She knew she was dying and nothing was going to change that. She wanted to have everything done to ease the pain for the people she loved. There were so many things she knew she could not achieve that might have been achieved if she lived longer. She knew Rick had hoped they would have at least five years. She could not tell him that it was not going to happen. There was not going to be any remission. When she spoke to him on the phone, he was excited that she was coming home. She knew he took it that she was getting better.

She felt confused about Flynn. On the one hand, she wanted him to stop the other job he was doing, but on the contrary, she knew in a sense that was what defined him. He had once told her that sitting on a knife's edge and winning was an adrenalin rush that was better than sex. What would he do with his life? He was young and extremely bright, she could not see him taking a mild job. She remembered the time she had seen him fighting with George; he liked to fight maybe because he knew he was good at it. He lived hard and played hard, and she could not imagine him changing. She was afraid of the danger. He lived in it. He had said he would not want to live if he was in a wheelchair or even if his face could not have been repaired, and she knew he would not hesitate to initiate his own demise just as he would do to others if the need were there. George was so different from Flynn. He was cool under pressure, considered his actions carefully, but he also would not hesitate to kill if the need were there. George had very specific notions about what he was doing and why. He would always put his country before anything else. And then there was the George who was a sensitive man, who loved music and cared about the people around him. He proved he would break the rules to save a friend. But of the three men in her life, she thought George was the only one who could come out of life unscathed.

During the four weeks she had with Flynn, she tried to brush aside the numbing exhaustion she often felt. She suggested they go for drives to see the country. Outside the city area, the country was stunningly beautiful. She appreciated it more because she thought she would not see it again. In a way, it seemed that Flynn had not spent the time to really look at the world around him. Even the flowers beside the road were lovely if one took the time to look at them. They bought a camera to record the two weeks and took pictures of scenes and flowers and of course each other. He started to see the world through her eyes. In the evenings when she was unable to even converse with him properly, he would hold her until she fell asleep. She woke up sometimes times during the night as bad dreams plagued her. She explained this is what Rick had to put up with as well. The tall, dark figure featured in many of her dreams. She remembered to ask him who he was, but he did not answer. He held out his hand for her to follow him, but she was too afraid to do it. A couple of her dreams featured on the news some days later. Flynn was astonished how accurate she was when she described them to him and then he would see it on the news. She hated this because what was the point of it if she could not do anything about it? She talked to Flynn about after death; she was not sure what life would be like if there was life after death. She told him she wanted to go to a church. She asked him if he could find a church in English for her to go to. She said that she had been to the Eastern Church in Athens and had talked to the Patriarch there, and she was, of course, married there.

While she was receiving treatment, Flynn looked for an English speaking church she could attend. He found a small church that held services mostly for tourists. The one he found was a Catholic church, and he took note of the times of the services. Marion said she would be happy to attend. She could not tell him why she wanted to go; only she thought as she was going to die, maybe she should get her mind above her navel once in a while. When they arrived at the church, Flynn said he was not sure he wanted to go. She told him he could wait in the car if he wished. Then on second thought, he said he would go. They sat near the back, both feeling strange and out of place; however, when they started singing, Marion realised that she knew the music. Looking at the song book provided, she sang along with the rest of the church. It came as a bit of a shock to her. She remembered the old man saying he thought she was religious and did not like the idea of living in sin.

When they came out, Flynn said, 'Well, That was an experience. I felt like time had gone backwoods and I was a kid again.' Marion said she thought she might have been a Catholic because she knew the music, but she could not remember going to church. 'I must have at one time, or I would not know the music.'

After the first two weeks, she went to the clinic to have a check-up and blood samples done. The senior medical doctor asked her into his office by herself. He started by saying her blood count had remained the same; this meant for her that she would not have to take this medication for another two weeks. He told her that she would start to feel better and be tempted to do more.

'You must stick to the diet and do gentle exercise.' She told him that at home, she had a cook and housekeeper and did not have to do much. 'I know this is none of my business, but I can't help but notice that you are closer to your minder than to your husband. He never seems to be around, and I see the look you share with Flynn. Is this going to be a problem when you go home?'

'I don't think so. Flynn knows where he stands with me. I know that Riccardo thinks I am in remission. He has a problem with the idea of me being diseased. I realise that there is no use in upsetting him. I just have to deal with it myself, and as you know, I have Flynn's and George's support. I think I would prefer it if you did not speak to him about me, just tell me and that is enough.'

The next two weeks, she felt better, and they could do more. She had an idea that this indicated how she would manage at home. They went to the church again and ate lunch out; eating all the things she was supposed to stay away from. This caused her stomach to become painful, and another tablet was added to reduce the inflammation in her stomach.

The last night with Flynn was the hardest ever; they knew that they may not be as close again for some time if ever. She wanted him to know that whatever happened, she would always feel the same about him. He wanted to share all the love he could give her and accept it if this was all there was. It was made harder considering he viewed her as a vibrant and exciting woman who could match him mentally as well as passionately.

Neil came up to get them. They drove the car back to the hire place and proceeded to the airport by taxi. Marion could not help but notice that she seemed to have acquired a lot of baggage and was relieved they did not have a weight quota. Abrax and Rick were waiting at their hangar as the jet taxied in they had the big car to pick them up. Rick had a posy of flowers for her and embraced her warmly.

Riccardo shook hands with Flynn. 'Glad to see you back and now you can do some real work,' he quipped.

He told them that he had reserved a place in the best restaurant for dinner and George would come along too. They drove home, and Marion asked if they could stop off at the beach on the way. She took her shoes off and ran down to the water to paddle her feet. 'Come on, what's the matter with you? It feels great.' The boys took off their shoes and walked down to the water, being careful they did not get their pants wet. Rick thought, 'This is what I missed most, the sheer fun of doing the mundane.' They climbed back into the car, leaving a trail of sand for Abrax to clean. At home, the staff put away her things and Rick told her he was aware that she got tired, and so he was going to make sure one of the staff made her rest every day. George came over to say hello and gave her a hug. Rick told her he was not going back to work that day and he personally was going to make sure she slept.

He could not keep the exhilaration out of his voice. He knew all along he was right. He acted as if the last three months did not happen.

In their room, she explained about the medication. 'Two weeks, I may not feel great, but the other two weeks, I should be okay. This is my first week without this drugs, so by next week, I should be good. One of the first things I want to do is to invite ourselves to dinner at your father's house. I miss the old man, and I want to go for a walk with him.'

'That is an excellent idea because he is always asking about you.'

'Then I want to go fishing.' He was so happy he said he would take some time off work and show her some of the islands.

He told her something so startling that she thought it would be impossible. Jacinda and David seem to have hit it off. He has taken her out a couple of times. 'How could that happen? Given her notion of the divide between servants and her?' she asked. 'I'm at a loss to explain it, and so is our father. Maybe it is a fatal attraction.' She thought of all she knew about David and said that Jacinda could do a lot worse. He was so straight he would not lead her on. He is extremely good-looking and smart. 'Has it changed her?'

'Not that much as she tries to show that it is not that important to her, but when he is around, she can't take her eyes off him. And he seems to find reasons to go over to the big house as much as he can, and she has been looking after me, even though I am not home that much.'

'The night we were singing by the pool and she came out to listen, it must have been then she noticed him.' Marion said.

'You can't get by the fact that he's drop-dead gorgeous.'

'Is he?' Rick said. 'I've never noticed.'

That evening, having dinner with the boys was something she thought she would never do again. It was special because of the way they interacted with one another. It was a bond that she hoped would never be broken as they needed each other in different ways and it allowed them to be grounded through the hard days to come. She hardly noticed the flashy restaurant or the good food. As far as she was concerned, they could be eating on the beach and the fellowship would have been same. Flynn had a funny way of putting his experiences with the clinic into almost a comic routine. And they laughed until tears were in their eyes. Then there was the new love interest for David.

'It is the quiet ones you have to watch,' George said.

Marion thought that was funny as she always considered George to be the quiet one. 'I guess it takes one to know one.'

'I hear you are becoming a wiz at paperwork,' she told George. 'You are definitely management material.'

He looked seriously at her and said he liked things as they are. 'You are right, and I think the wine is going to my head, I'm not used to drinking as much these days. Someone is going to have to catch me if I fall over.' Flynn offered, 'it's okay, Marion, we will carry you out if necessary.'

Marion and Riccardo spent the next weekend at the big house. They took David along and left George and Flynn to care for their home. The old man was delighted to see them. He welcomed them as if they were distinguished guests rather than just family. Marion told him she was going to take him for walks as she had perceived he had not been doing them. Jacinda disappeared down to the gatehouse. They went out for a walk early as they wanted the time to talk. She slipped her arm through his. He told her that Jacinda wanted David to come to dinner. He had said no, but he wondered what she thought. 'David is a good man, and she could do a lot worse,' she said. 'We have come to a time in our lives when we must take the line of least resistance. You may find that he is the right person for her, give him a chance. He looked after me for two weeks, and I found him to be very straight, honest, and considerate.' The old man told her he was happy that she was getting well.

'That is not exactly correct. Riccardo thinks I am in remission and have at least five years. The treatment has bought me some time, but that is all. I don't wish to upset you, but I don't have that much time left. I am so worried about him. I don't want him to mourn too much. He needs to find another partner to love. I want him to remember me just like a book he once read.'

They walked on in silence for a while, and the old man said,

'And what about you, how are you coping? Are you afraid of dying?'

'Not that much. I was at the beginning, but I have come to understand that there is a time for everything. In my mind, I have been alive for only six and a half years, and in that time, I have achieved many things that some people never complete in a lifetime. Every day is special to me as it could be my last, so every sunset is magical. I sometimes feel more alive because I notice the things that are important. That is why I am here with you because you are special to me, I love you like a father, and I respect you. I don't want you to feel sad for me, just be happy for what I have had.'

By the time they got back to the big house, she was so tired she could barely walk. Riccardo noticed her and picked her up in his arms and took her upstairs to rest. He told her he would come back when it was time to get ready for dinner. The exhaustion she felt was total, and she could not keep her eyes open. It was not Riccardo who came to wake her up, it was Jacinda. She came into the bedroom and sat on the bed and shook her awake.

'I just came to say thank you for talking Father into letting David stay for dinner.'

Marion looked at her and considered the best thing to say was.

'As you may know, David spent two weeks looking after me when I was in Genève. He is not only nice to look at; he is a very nice man. He is very straight, does not drink much, or uses drugs. I found him to be kind and considerate. He is not the sort of person who would use you up and then walk out on you. I think you could not do better than him. If you think of him as just a servant, then you are not looking at him right. He was at the top of his field when he decided to come over here. He has a s brilliant mind and would be an asset to you. So, don't lead him on unless you really care for him.'

Jacinda looked offended. 'That is just it, I honestly care for him, I want him to be part of my family, and that is why I asked Father if he could stay for dinner.'

'Then I am glad for you, I don't think your father will put up much resistance. I hope you both will be happy.'

After dinner, Marion played the piano, using some old classics and singing some new songs. They made sure the overhead light was on, and they had a special night. She did not stay up late as she was becoming tired again. In the bedroom, she remarked,

'It seems that I have broken down a few social barriers in this house.'

He smiled at her. 'That is some achievement. Before you came into the scene, it was a big no-no to bring one's love life into the house unless you intended to marry them.'

On the way, back to their house, Rick broached the subject of getting another person to replace Mason.

'I thought of Abdula as you already know him.' She said, 'I understand Abdula only wanted to work alone. The boys know him and like him. He also had a sick mother recently, that might suggest he could develop connections working in a team which he has been unable to do so far. I know him to be an honourable man. Because of the safety in our house, we might benefit from having him.'

'I will give him a call then.'

Flynn went with Marion on her next visit to the shrink after she had come back home. She told him she may be a bit longer; he could take off and come back to pick her up in about one and a half hours if he liked rather than sit around waiting. Dr McKlean was happy to see her again but refrained from talking about how she was looking. She told him he may like to video this session for his records. She said she would use the reclining chair because she felt bit tired. After he had set it up, she told him why she had asked him to do so.

'This will be my last visit to see you, and the first thing I want to say is to thank you for everything you have tried to do to help me. I know I have only weeks left and I want to do the right thing by people who I care for. I am not in remission and have never been. Every time I go to the doctors to get a blood test, my red cell count is getting lower, and the damaged white cells have invaded my organs, and things are not working properly. I am getting more exhausted with each day. All my joints are inflamed, and I am in a fair amount of pain. I don't want to take drugs for pain as they mess with my head. So, in a way, it will be a relief when I'm finished.

'My big worry is for my boys. I don't know why I call them boys when they are, all of them, alpha males. I love them all in different ways, and I worry that I can't help them more. I believe I have given each one a gift that I hope will carry them through their lives. Riccardo is my husband. I love him, but he was spoiled and did not care for people around him. And yet to me he is my hero, he saved my life, gave me a home, and made sure I was looked after. I feel I gave him so little in return. He thought his money would solve anything, and now he knows it does not. It is so sad because he did not know who his true friends were. My gift to him is to look at people around him differently and judge them by their actions. Also, he had never actually looked at the beauty all around him. I wanted him to take the time to smell the roses, admire the sunsets. This is a stunning country. I would like him to enjoy it. But most of all, I want him to find another person to love, one that does not give him so much trouble.'

'I gave to George my gift of music, my great passion. It is the only thing that crossed the divide of my lives. I would have liked to teach him more. I hope he uses it to chase away any demons he may have, to sing in the shower and entertain his friends. I love him. He is so strong and thoughtful. I would trust him with my life. Every time I needed advice, I would turn to him. Any courage I have, I gained from him, and he taught me how to overcome some of my fear. He is my best friend. He has a lot of talent and could write his own songs one day.

'To Flynn, I gave the gift of love. I don't think he was ever in love before. I hope he now knows the difference between sex and love. I could not help loving him, and as far as I am concerned, I will love him forever. He did not have a very fair deal from me because of my marriage commitment. I hope he forgives me. The trouble for us is we are the same kind of people, we laugh at the same things, and we are both impulsive and tend to rush into things without a lot of thought. I hurt him without understanding that he is prideful and my intrusion only made life harder for him. I never planned to break into his life. I never expected to find myself loving two men. One I made a commitment to and the other just by chance. I could never choose between them because they both mean so much to me.

'I am afraid for them. I don't want to cast a shadow

on where I have been. I want them to grieve for me because that is a part of healing, but I want them to get on with their lives. I need to get George and Flynn out of the house for the next week, so I can spend time with Riccardo as I should.'

'How are you going to send them away?'

'I'm not sure yet, I am going have to find a legitimate job for them to do. I have some ideas about how to get them to go away, and I will work it out.

'I have a lawyer, and I have arranged my funeral, so Riccardo will be spared the trouble of having to decide what to do with me. By the time the boys come back, it will be over, and then I hope they will be able to help him. I chose them as my brothers and want them to continue to be close.'

'You sound like you have taken a lot of trouble to organise things just as you want. Have you thought they may have liked to be more involved?'

'I wish that it could be so, but given the way Riccardo did not cope with my illness, I worried that he would not cope with my death that well. I don't know what else I could do to make it easier for them. I tried to talk to the old man about it, but he did not want to listen. I wanted to tell Riccardo that time was short but I was afraid it would only upset him. Then I thought it was better to try and let him have peace rather than worry every time I was tired. There is so much about my life before I wanted to know, but now it seems irrelevant. I have this strange idea that one should not be put into a grave until three days after death. I found that this is an idea in many cultures. Even Jesus was in the tomb for three days. What do you think?'

'I believe that it is up to each person to decide what they think. I feel sad for you because you did not reach your full potential as the gifted psychic that I think you may have become. Also, I will miss our meetings, which have not been without their challenges. I am finding it hard to reconcile the notion that you will die so soon. I can't imagine how you feel about this. Despite your fears, you are adamant to hold it all together simply out of love for those around you. There is just one thing I want to show you.' the tape ended.

When she had finished, she found Flynn waiting in the car, eating an ice cream. He had not been there long. 'I'll pick one up for you if you like,' he said. They drove for a while in silence until they found a small shop selling ice creams and he went and got her one. As he was handing it back to her, he leant over and kissed her; it was a special kiss that lasted for some time, and the old longing came back again. She took the ice cream from him and said. 'Flynn, I can't.' They sat in silence again, and she ate her ice cream, and he smoked a cigarette. 'If not now, then when?' He said. She looked at him and felt something that was not there before; he was feeling the loss of her already. There was nothing she could do to take that feeling away. She thought that she would have to find some contact in the Ministry of Defence whom she could hack into and find them a job. She needed to do this soon as it was getting harder for her to resist the temptation of falling into his arms; she needed the comfort from him too. She planned to set something up that afternoon while everyone thought she was taking a nap.

That night in her dream, she saw the dark shadow moving towards her and then he stopped as if he had been hit a force field. She remembered that even if it is in a dream, she could speak to him. 'Who are you?' She asked. The shadow did not answer he just waved his hand, beckoning her to come with him. 'No,' she said, 'I am not ready, I have things to do.' He turned to her, and all she could see was black skull where a face should be. She could see brown teeth that seemed to smile at her. She was filled with horror and screamed. Rick was holding her and telling her it was just a dream. 'He wants me dead,' she said. Rick told her again it was just a dream; it was not real. She did not say anything more and went downstairs to get a drink. She went back up the stairs and found Rick had gone back to sleep. She crept out the room and went over to the security block, wondering how she could sneak past whoever was on the monitors. It was Flynn; she beckoned him outside and told him of her dream. He put his arms around her; she was freezing and shaking. He told her to wait and went in and got his bedding and brought it outside. They lay down together, and she said the dark shadow had come to get her. 'That is silly. People don't come back from the dead to make someone die.'

'But he is there all the time. Either in the corner of my mind or one time he came right up close.' Flynn pulled the blankets close around them to get her warm. What happened next was unavoidable. They made love spending the time to enjoy each other in a bittersweet moment. He gave her the comfort she needed. It drove away from the dread of the night and gave her strength to go on. She cared about what she had done, but at the same time, she was grateful. He was there and philosophical about the outcome. They stayed together until the sky was beginning to get a little lighter and she had to go.

The next day, the boys said they had to go away for a couple of days, a week at the most. Rick was angry at the lack of notice and said he was glad he had Abdula and could pull in others if needed. Marion walked up to the security house and saw they were getting ready to go. Abdula was on the monitors and David was doing the perimeters. Flynn was in the hall when she came in. She leant up against him and kissed him until George told them to stop. She whispered in his ear goodbye. Then she went over to George and gave him a chaste kiss on the lips and said goodbye and left. George looked at Flynn. 'That was some kiss, probably the closest thing to sex without doing it.' Flynn just stuck his finger up and walked away.

George and Flynn were sitting in a car, waiting for a target to appear with a parcel they were supposed to get. It was boring; they have seen the target go into a small shop empty-handed. Flynn had to ask the question of why they were here. Anyone could have done this. It was not a hard task. It suddenly dawned on Flynn that she had said goodbye; she never said that. After some minutes of atrocious language, he told George that he suspected that she had set them up. She wanted them out of the way. A cold feeling settled in the pit of his stomach. He jumped out of the car and said, 'I am going to get that fuckin parcel, and we are going to get out of here.' Just then the target appeared with the parcel and Flynn pounced on him and grabbed the package as George started the car and drove forward so Flynn could jump straight in. There were some shouts of anger and some shots fired, but they were well away before any harm could come to them. When they reported back, they were told the phone in George's box had not stopped ringing. 'I know we have to go. I will inform you what happened later.'

Chapter 22
LIFE AFTER DEATH

George and Flynn got to the house as quick as they could. They did not wait but ran straight in. The boss was sitting in the lounge with his head in his hands. He looked up as they came in. 'She is dead.' Flynn sat down, and George questioned him about what had happened.

Riccardo had woken up at the usual time, and as soon as he moved, he was aware she was awake and looking at him. He jumped up to get ready. She had half sat up and then dropped her head down on the pillow and said she was going to have a lazy day and stay in bed. She smiled at him, and he went into to shower and change. When he came out, he looked at her and noticed she was white and her lips were blue. He had screamed for help. They called the doctor who pronounced her dead at 7.00 a.m. It seemed as if she had some kind of internal carcinoma. She is now at the morgue, and they could see her at 2.00 p.m. He told them about an hour after she was pronounced dead, a lawyer had come to the house and showed him a paper signed by her declaring him executor of her will. He had told Riccardo that everything had already been arranged.

There was no need to do anything. 'Marion must have known.'

Riccardo had sent David and Abdula to Dr McKlean's office with instructions to get every bit of paper, tapes, and files about her from the institute and not to come back without them; they could use force if needed.

He just wanted them. They had not come back yet, which suggested they might be having a hard time getting them. George offered to go there, but Riccardo said he was sure they could handle one man. The boys stated that they would go shower and change and come back again.

Walking over to the security house, George commented that he was sure she did know and had set everything up. Even that bloody kiss. 'If she wasn't dead, I think I would kill her for this. I wanted to be near her when she died. I figured we had time or I would have never left.' Of course, the big worry is how did she arrange it? She hacked into what exactly and who knows? 'How are we going to find out without getting caught? The only way is to get hold of her laptop and see if we can get in.' Flynn pointed out the difficulty with the laptop; she had told him that she had placed a virus in it and would self-destruct if someone tried to hack into it.

They went back to the house and went to see her at the morgue. She looked as if she had just fallen asleep.

There seemed to be a hint of a smile on her lips. Her lemon wedding dress made her look lovely, and it seemed hard to believe she was not sleeping and would not wake up soon. They stood there each encased in their own thoughts. George pulled out his phone and took a couple of photos. They found it hard to walk away, but someone came and said other people were waiting to see their loved ones and they had to go. There was nothing to do, just leave her there. They went to the local drinking hole and sat there drinking whisky shots. She would have liked that. Riccardo said that someone should say something at the funeral, but he did not think he could. George offered to speak, but he thought Riccardo still had to say something. George suggested that Riccardo write out a short talk, thanking people for coming and saying a little about what he thought were her good points. He remembered when he first met her, and she had spoken of the KISS principle.

When they got back, they found his father and sister were there. By the look on Sarvas's face, one could tell he was taking the news of her death very hard. Riccardo had greeted them warmly but could not do anything and sat in the lounge room not even able to focus. Jacinda, on the other hand, was practical and arranged for the evening meal. She told Riccardo that she and her father would stay for a couple of days to make sure he was all right. She offered to help her brother write out something to say. George said he would also speak and wrote down some ideas. Abdula and David came back with two boxes of material they had collected from the institute. And they placed them on the floor near Riccardo. They refrained from saying how they obtained them.

The day of the funeral was overcast and black. There was to be a church service at St. Paul's, Kifissia, followed by the graveside service. To Riccardo's surprise, the ladies of the town had come early in the morning, bringing plates of food and drinks, which they set up on the back patio. Riccardo told George to leave the gates open and not to bother checking who came. He said he wanted them near him because that is what she would have wanted. 'You were nominated as her brothers at our wedding, and so you will be at her funeral. I don't think I can do this without you.'

The cars came as they walked out the sky looked as if there was to be a big storm. Jacinda commented that she hoped it held off until later in the day. He could not believe it, but it seemed as if the whole town had come. There were some reporters but not so many as to make a nuisance of themselves.

Somehow they got through the day. The people of the town, especially the individuals who had worked on the house, all descended on the house to eat and drink. Each, in turn, came up to him and told him how sorry they were for him. Many expressed the notion that she was a saint who cared for the people in the town and helped many who were in danger of falling into complete poverty. The priest form St. Paul's church had told him how she had saved the local school from closing down. She had never spoken of any of this or even mentioned that she knew the priest. Flynn, who mostly stood behind Riccardo, could only think of the last time they were together; even then she was planning for him not to be there when she died.

Jacinda and David worked together to make sure that everything ran smoothly, keeping cups of coffee coming to the other members of the family. David told her he was impressed at how organised she was. She told him how she hated Marion at first and how rude she was to her, and then tried to get rid of her. Then slowly she came to respect her because she was inherently kind and stood up for herself.

'She would also stand up to Father and tell him just what she thought, and she was never afraid of him. After all, I did to her, she had talked Father into the idea that we should be together. Now I am going to miss her, and I wish I had not done all those bad things I did at the start. She came into our lives and had changed each one of us in some way.' That evening, they had dinner and sat down and watched the *Seabird* movie again. David had never seen the movie and was surprised at how beautifully it portrayed her love of the sea; he thought how incredibly gifted she was. The movie had just finished when the sky opened up with a huge flash of light and thunder that shook the house. All the lights went out, and there was nothing to do except go to bed.

The storm raged all night; it seemed as if even the sky was angry.

The next day was clear and it was as if everything had been washed clean. Riccardo woke up from a disturbed night, feeling angry with everything but especially with Marion. He thought he had plenty of time, and she would get better somehow, and she died on him, just like his mother. He came down the stairs and into the lounge room, and she was sitting there. She was dressed in a white dress. She smiled at him and looked at the box beside the chair. His eyes followed hers and looked at the box. When he looked back, she was gone. Did he imagine it or was he dreaming? She looked so real. He went to the box, and sitting on top was the last tape she made. He put it in the machine and watched it. How carefully she had laid out the reason for her not telling him. The dreams she had for him and her love of both him and Flynn. She had done all this, understanding he would go after the material from the doctor's office. He would do this just as he had done to close the office in Syria. He searched the box and found the other tapes and played them. They answered many questions he had about her. When he heard her description of that first night, he cried for what he had done. He knew that what he had obtained was material that must never see the light of day. He took the boxes into the secret room and went to get her laptop and placed it in there as well. He kept the last tape out to show George and Flynn. He rang up and asked them to come down when they were ready. When they arrived, he told them that he had seen her. They, of course, did not believe him, thinking it was grief. He then told them to sit down and played the tape. They all found it hard to fight back emotion, and he got them all a drink of whisky. 'I think she even planned this, knowing what I am like, she would know I would go after the tape,' Riccardo said.

It was going to be a messy day and a long one. Each felt the need of the company to help them deal with this event. They told stories about her that came to mind, indicating the kind of person she was. Flynn said he thought she was a devious little brat who knew how to manoeuvre people about to suit her needs. George came to her defence saying she had tried to do what she thought was the best for everybody, and that was what the tape was about.

Riccardo felt as if he did not really know her. She had not spoken about so many things to him. But one thing he was certain of was that she did love him and was truthful about their relationship. She had been honest about Flynn, even though she could have lied and got away with it. She was different, and that was her appeal to him. He had been somewhat unaware of the fear she carried each day until he looked at her files. He looked up at the boys and spoke about her skill at understanding people with empathy.

'If we were to tell anybody about these skills, they would think we are insane,' Riccardo said. 'There is no such thing as life after death. I must have been dreaming or wishing it to be. I don't think I will stay here, to me her presence is everywhere even if I had not seen her. I will probably move back home and close up this house.'

George pointed out that would mean sacking the staff. And would they go back to France? Riccardo became agitated. He could not lose them, and sending David back would cause a family disturbance. He wondered if they could find another job for David may be in the company. He would send Abdula back. As for the staff, she had just given them a generous amount of money from her will; they should not complain.

'I would keep the housekeeper on in a small way and the gardener.'

George asked when he planned to do this, and he thought next week.

'I have to go through her things and give some of them away. I hate the thought of doing this.'

'Both Flynn and I are willing to help you sort out what you want to do.'

It was mid-afternoon, and they were tired from the lack of sleep through the storm last night and the amount of alcohol they had consumed this morning. Riccardo's eyes were beginning to close, and George suggested he have a rest for a while. He agreed, and they helped him upstairs as he was not steady on his feet. He collapsed on the bed in a drunken sleep and passed out for several hours.

George came down the stairs first while Flynn was taking Riccardo's shoes off. She was standing by the piano. She was dressed in a white dress. She had her hair pushed behind her ears. She looked solid and not like one would expect a ghost to look like. She was gazing at the piano seat where she sometimes put music she was working on. George stood where he was for what seemed to him quite a while. She walked to the seat and looked at it again, and he followed her look. When he looked up, she was gone. He went to the seat and opened it. Sitting on the top was a new song and a tape. He then looked at the papers under and saw that there seemed to be some lessons she had planned to give him. He took them out and sat on the stool and tried to process what had happened. He was not that drunk that he was delusional. The music was intended for him.

Flynn came down the stairs while George was sitting on the piano seat.

'What's up?' he said.

'She was here just now. I saw her, and she pointed to the piano seat, and when I looked at it, she disappeared. I have found music lessons she had intended to give me.'

Flynn was more inclined to believe George perhaps because, in his culture, apparitions were more likely to be accepted. 'What did she look like?' She looked just like us. She had a white dress on. She did not speak to me. Flynn knew George to be accurate in his assessments of people; his job required quick thought.

'If you say you saw her then you did. The boss also described a white dress, but I know she does not have one. I wonder what that means.'

George said, 'Up to now I did not believe in ghosts. However, she seemed so real and substantial.'

'Do you think this house is haunted because it is her house?' George shrugged. 'I think it is one of the things about her we will never know.' Two nights later, Flynn was still feeling the pain of grief. He had cried out in his mind for her, wishing he could see her again; finally, he fell asleep. He awoke when he felt someone was in his room. He opened his eyes carefully, already preparing to fight if necessary. Marion was standing by his bed. She was dressed in a white dress. She had a look of compassion in her eyes.

'Move over, I'm cold,' she said. He moved over and she jumped into bed with him. She felt warm and soft.

He told her. 'This is doing my head in, am I in bed with a ghost?'

'Do I feel like a ghost?' She kissed him and her lips tasted like red wine. 'You called out for me to come. I love you, so here I am. You are having a dream. I can feel you have so many questions running through your head. I don't have the answers. It might have something to do with the bond I established with you that has never been broken.'

He held her in his arms. 'Where are you, what is it like?'

'I don't really know where I am. It is somewhere between time and space. I am not in a heaven, but I am not in hell either. It is someplace else. It is sort of dark. I know there are others here. I can feel them, and sometimes I think I can hear whispers.'

'Are you watching over us?'

'No, I can't see you except when I am allowed to come for some reason. I have a purpose for being in this place I am in. I now can remember my whole life, I need to make some kind of sense of it, to understand what I have done wrong and be sorry for it. In order to have done wrong, you have to have knowingly and willingly done wrong. We have been shaped by our parents and the culture we grew up in. So what seems wrong for me maybe not wrong for a person from another culture. We have been given gifts that we are supposed to use for helping others. I was afraid of my gifts and tried not to use them most of the time. Also, there are inbuilt laws we should follow, like not trying to kill yourself. I think that it is going to take a long time for me to understand. I can't stay long now, I have to go. I heard you call. I felt I had to come. I love you. I know you will get through this time. I just want to help.'

She disappeared; he felt the weight on his arm lighten. He got up and went for a drink and smoke. When he went back to bed, he felt where she had been lying. The bed there was warm. How then could this be a dream? He had felt and tasted her; she was not any kind of ghost he had heard of. He thought about the white dress and he realised maybe it was not a dress but the gown she had on when she was in intensive care. He remembered that she had almost died then and the only reason she came back was that the boss had called her, saying he needed her. She had told him that the dark figure in her mind had wanted her to come with him then. Maybe she was supposed to go with him and refused because she felt she had more to do while still alive. Then maybe it was truly only a dream, and if he told anyone, they would think he had lost the plot, and send him for psychiatric review. He eventually fell back asleep for a couple of hours and woke up feeling angry with everything.

They had promised to help pack up her things, Flynn was still undecided whether to tell George or not. He drank a lot of coffee and showered and changed, but his thoughts were on the night's event. It occurred to him that this must be what she felt after one of her bad dreams. He just could not shake it.

They went up to the house to find Riccardo still looking under the weather. He had a pair of jeans on, no top, his hair was not done, and he had not shaved. He had a sick look on his face. They had never seen him look this and that was cause for concern about his mental state. They thought the first thing to do was to get him to drink some coffee and eat something. They joined him having some more coffee. Then they went to find some boxes. There were some left in what she called her art studio. While they were there, they noticed a picture covered up and took the cover off it. It was a portrait of Riccardo. It captured him well showing him on the boat. Flynn wondered if he even knew it was here. They left it there for now and took the boxes down to the nanny room. The three of them stood there wondering where to start. Riccardo took a big box from the top of the cupboard and put the stained glass dress in it.

'I cannot give this away as I don't want anyone else to wear it.'

He took the award and a picture from the paper that was under it and placed them carefully in the big box and moved the box outside the door. Then they looked at her clothes. Riccardo said he intended to give them to the charity shop. As they took each article of clothing down, they remembered when she wore them. With each thing they folded and put in the box, it felt that they were throwing away a part of her. Riccardo wondered why he had not taken more notice of her. She was so precious to him, but he took for granted that they would always be together. Often he did not notice what she was wearing unless she made a point of it. He sat down on the bed and looked at Flynn. 'Why did she have to go?'

Flynn could not answer; he was struggling with these questions himself. George saw that they were becoming morose over the clothes and suggested they leave it for a while and come back later.

Outside, the day was fresh and clear. George decided it would do them good to go for a walk down to the beach. Riccardo picked a top that was lying on the floor and put it on. And they left some of the pain behind as they set out at a brisk pace. Riccardo had to concede that being physical was a good thing. They ended up by jogging along the beach. The movement cleared his head for a while, and he wanted to push his body until some of the pain of the last couple of days eased. They sat for a while remembering the day she came back home and ran down to the water. On a whim, Flynn stripped off his clothes to his underwear and ran into the water. He swam out a bit and called to the others to join him, which they did. Splashing around and jumping on each other renewed the feeling of the joys of life. They jogged back home invigorated and more able to face the rest of the packing. George offered to put the boxes in his SUV and take them to the charity shop in the morning. Riccardo announced he was going over to his father's for the evening and was not sure if he would come back for the night or not.

Left alone, George and Flynn decided to search the house for the laptop.

They agreed they also needed to find out what she had

said to the shrink.

They went through every room. Because they had the time they were careful not to disturb anything too much so their search would not be detected. After a fruitless search, they considered what could be done. Flynn reviewed what they had done so far. 'It must be here because he has had no time to dispose of them. And he probably would not do it anyway. He is somewhat ordered so there would be some logic behind where he would put them. After the break-in, we assumed that the perpetrator was looking for something and we could not work out what it could be. This would make him more careful. I think we are looking for a safe of some kind. His study is the logical choice.' They went back into the study looking for a safe or hidden place. It was not immediately apparent. There was nothing on the walls.

'I want a drink I think it is going to be a long night,' Flynn said.

When they came back, she was standing there looking at the bookshelf.

Flynn's first reaction was to rush and hold her, but George stopped him.

Within seconds she was gone.

'Why did you stop me?'

'Because you might as well try to catch the air, she was telling us where to look.'

They both went over to where she was standing and looked at the books. They tried to take them out to see if there was a safe behind them and that is when they saw the leaver. They pulled it, and it opened up to a small room. 'Amazing!' exclaimed Flynn. They saw the two boxes and the laptop in the middle of the chamber. They took the tapes into the lounge, got another drink, and watched them. It felt like an intrusion into the deepest part of her mind. They had seen the last tape only, and now they watched the others they saw a different picture of who she was. George was only half looking at the tapes and was reading the clinical files. He came to realise how fragile she had really been. Through the laughter and some tears was a lady who had seen more pain than anybody should have to bear. Her treatment from Riccardo was despicable. He had indeed used her as if she was a toy. And he bullied her if she tried to stand up for herself. She continued to think he was her hero until she died. Nowhere had she mentioned anything about their actions; it seemed that she kept her word not to compromise them in any way. She had told him of her love for Flynn and how she had got into his head without saying what he was up to. He handed the files to Flynn and told him he should read them. Flynn felt disgusted at the whole process and just wanted to put them back. 'What about the laptop?' He asked. George said, for now, it was safe and if they needed to get at it, they could now they knew where it was.

Walking back to their rooms, they talked about what

they would do. George thought there was nothing they could do right at the moment. 'I remember when she talked about natural justice and said that people paid for their misdeeds in one way or another. If he has read the files, I think he may be already paying. She wanted us to know, I think there must be a reason for her to show us where it was.'

It had been a very long day fraught with exhausting emotion. Flynn fell into bed and tried to sleep. He wanted to close out everything for a while and rest. It was hard as his mind was in turmoil; as events of the day came back to him, he understood less about everything. This was not a natural state for him. He had the ability to compartmentalise things into what needed to be done, doing it, and then thinking about what needed to be done next. He seldom dreamed and could function on several levels. Yet now he felt the boss's words of why did she have to go. How could she just appear and disappear? Why did she let them find the notes? As if answering his question, she was there again sitting on his bed.

'I'm sorry you have had such a bad day,' she said. Again, she looked at him with compassion in her green eyes. 'I should not be here, but I came because you need to find answers. I showed you where to find the files to let you know that I had not compromised you. I was very conscious of your need for ambiguity, and I told you I would respect that. The laptop will be no help to you. I told you I had seen your puppet masters. All I needed was one name, and the rest was done through internal memos. If you go searching, you will find that it goes round in a circle. This will cause more trouble for everyone.'

'How do I know this and how could you do it?'

'It's a bit like money laundering. By the time it passes through many hands, nobody knows where it originated. Finding that one name will only cause you grief. You will just have to trust me when I say the truth of how you got that job will never come to light. As you saw on the tape, I had to send you away. I did it to protect you and me from causing further harm. I am truly sorry that I have hurt you and George. I believed that I should spend my final days with my full attention on my husband and try to make things right.'

'Now you have your full memory back, you must realise what a bad person he is. He did not treat you right. My guess, one reason he kept you near is so you would not talk about how he abused you.'

'Flynn, please don't be so judgemental of him. We are all products of our upbringing and the way we have learned to deal with situations. Of course, I knew his faults, and I could forgive him those, but you have to remember he forgave me mine as well. He forgave you. Those days we had together, he knew something would happen, and he let it because he could not be there for me. He knew I loved you too. I had hoped I would have had time to help him more. He is so like his father, but I think I have had some input for him to change. He needs you and George more than ever. I hope he finds another lady to love. I can see you are so tired and your mind and body need rest. Be at peace, I have to go now.' She leant down and kissed him; he felt her warm body against his and longed for her to stay, but she was gone.

When he woke up, it was late in the day. He could not believe he had slept for so long and that nobody had come to disturb him. George was in the kitchen drinking a cup of tea. 'Well, you do wake up sometime. You looked so peaceful I thought I should leave you there. The boss had not come back, and David has gone over to the big house to see what he could do. Abdula is on the monitors again. I have already taken the boxes to the charity. And we have nothing to do.'

Flynn got a cup of tea and sat down. 'I have something to tell you, I have been wondering if I should say anything or not as I think you will think I'm nuts. Now I have some information that is of concern to you as well as me.' George looked frustrated. 'Spit it out, man, for goodness sake.'

'I have seen Marion for a couple of nights. I have touched her, and I have kissed her. She was not a ghost. She was real.'

'Of course, mate, you know that is not possible, don't you?'

'I am telling you what I saw and felt. And she has told me things that I could not know any other way. She told me why she got us out of the house and how she did it.'

'Now you have my attention. Are you sure you were not dreaming?'

'How often would you say I dream, practically never? She said she only needed one name to send an e-mail to. The rest was done through an internal memo. She said it is the same process as money laundering. The paper trail goes round in a circle until nobody knows where it originates and if we tried, it would cause a big commotion and heads might roll. There is no point in trying to get into the laptop as everything was deleted right down to DOS.'

'Well, what else did she say?'

'Most of it is personal, but she did say we should not be so hard on the boss because she forgave him his mistakes and he forgave her and me. She said he knew that we were having an affair while she was at the clinic and did not do anything about it because he could not be there and he knew she loved me.'

'Flynn, I don't know what to say. Are you off your head or is there something else going on? I'm sorry. I can't believe that she can come back from the dead. I know we saw some kind of spirit in the study, but it could have been just our intense concentration that brought it to pass. Maybe you should go and see her shrink?'

'Maybe I will.'

That night, Flynn left it until late and then decided he would run himself until he was sure he would fall asleep. He did a workout in the gym and went for a long run. By the time he got back, he was exhausted. And he slept through the night and woke up bright and early the next day. The boss came back and said they were going to close down the house. He was unhappy about sending Abdula back to the French office. George said he had to go away for a couple of days and would be back to the gatehouse as soon as he could. Flynn and David agreed to close the house and lock down.

While they were in the process of closing down, David told Flynn about his new job offer, working in the export part of the company.

'Are you sure you want to do this?'

David explained he would do anything to stay near Jacinda and was afraid they may send him to the French office. 'I am thinking of asking her to marry me,' he said.

Flynn laughed and said in a way that it would in a way make them brothers-in-law, because Marion had adopted them as brothers. They gave a final look at the house and moved back to the gatehouse.

Flynn decided to visit Dr McKlean. He took Marion's car; he wanted some explanation for what was happening. There was no use making an appointment as he knew the doctor would not want to see him. He arrived and was let in by a student and went straight to his office. He listened at the door to make sure he had nobody else in the office, and then he turned the handle and walked in. The doctor was at his desk and, seeing Flynn, became angry. 'I thought you people had done enough, what do you want now?'

'I don't know what happened. I was away at the time, as you already know. I am sorry if you were treated poorly, but you must have known that Riccardo would do something to protect his name, in case the material would be used against him.'

'They started by asking and when I told them that it was privileged material, they held a gun to my head and gave me a choice my life or the material.'

'That sounds about right. It would be the most conducive way to fix things.'

Flynn sat down in the chair. 'I have not come to argue with you. I have come to see you about myself. We have all seen fleeting images of Marion in the house. She has shown us where things are. But I have had a deeper experience. I have not only seen her, but I have also felt her and kissed her, and she told me things that I could not know any other way. I loved her so much and wanted her to be near, but I never expected it to happen. If I tell anybody else, they are going to think I am delusional. She feels real, and she is wearing a white dress or the gown that she had on in the ICU. I want to see her so much, and then, on the other hand, I am concerned that I may be going mad. I am hoping you can give me an explanation as to why this is happening to me.'

'Flynn, I am a scientist, my first reaction would be that there is no quantifiable evidence for life after death. New studies I am aware of are Virginia's Department of Psychiatric Medicine researching into the possibility of survival of consciousness after bodily death, and the University of Arizona is conducting investigations into mediums. There are many different explanations for these things. It is not an area I am concerned with.

'We can look into dreams. There are lucid dreams which seem as if you are waking up, even to the point of going for a cigarette or having a drink. Then there are waking dreams that occur in the twilight between wakefulness and deep sleep. These can be seen as hallucinations and are called hypnagogic. They seem real, and one is left with a sense of having contact with the dead person. In sleep paralysis, the person is in a wakeful state but feels the presence of the dead person. Lastly, there are apparitions where the dead person is seen for a moment in time but quickly disappears.

'There is little scientific evidence for these. However, there is a great deal of anecdotal stories from quite reputable sources of people seeing people who are dead. I have heard little about where they can touch or even kiss so I can't comment on this.'

Flynn looked disappointed. He had hoped the doctor would believe him that this was different. 'She had these unique skills and could get into my head. She could find me even from a long way away. I thought she was still using this skill to come to me. She told me she was in a place somewhere between time and space and she is not sure exactly what she is supposed to do there, except to view her life and see where she made mistakes and be sorry for them.'

'I agree she had special skills, way beyond my understanding, and instead of diminishing, they seemed to be growing stronger. I understand your frustration that I cannot give you the answers that you are looking for. I suggest that you ask her if she comes again. Then you will have to decide where you stand. I understand you are a very aware person. Maybe there is some truth in what you say. However, if you say it out loud, people will only perceive you as being unstable. I will be happy to see you again if this continues.'

Flynn thanked him for his time and left. Dr McKlean turned off the recorder under his desk that he had switched on unnoticed, pulled out a new case file folder, and marked it, *Flynn. No. 786255.*

About the Author

M. Kelly was born and lives in Western Australia. Although she has written many academic papers, this is her first novel. She developed the story based on her interest in paranormal psychology and the story, although fiction, is based on facts. She has a strong belief in social justice for all peoples of the world.

She is a proud grandmother of seven. She shares her life with one of her grandchildren and a crazy cat named Whiskers.

Her primary interests are keeping up with the latest technology, painting abstract art and travelling.

www.ingramcontent.com/pod-product-compliance
Lightning Source LLC
Chambersburg PA
CBHW070150120726
47909CB00001B/52